Pra

# *The Mrs. Murphy Series*

## THE TAIL OF THE TIP-OFF

"You don't have to be a cat lover to enjoy Brown's eleventh Mrs. Murphy novel.... Brown writes so compellingly... [she] breathes believability into every aspect of this smart and sassy novel." —*Publishers Weekly* (starred review)

"Rita Mae Brown's series remains one of the best cat mysteries.... Brown keeps the series fresh."
—*The Post & Courier* (Charleston, SC)

"The animals' droll commentary provides comic relief and clues helpful in solving the crime."
—*The Washington Post*

"A tightly woven mystery, peopled with the delightful characters of small-town Virginia... a real three-point play: an intriguing mystery, great characters, and an engaging sense of humor." —*I Love a Mystery*

"A fast-paced plot and enough animated feline personalities to keep readers entertained."
—*Daily News* (New York)

"A not-to-be-missed exciting cozy."
—*The Midwest Book Review*

"Nobody can put words in the mouths of animals better than Rita Mae Brown... fast-paced action... Harry and her menagerie are simply great."
—*Abilene Reporter-News*

involved with plots, plans, and emotional entanglements. *Pawing Through the Past* is no exception."
—*I Love a Mystery*

## CAT ON THE SCENT

"Rita and Sneaky Pie know how to grab a reader. This fun-loving and delightful mystery is a must even if you're not a cat lover." —*The Pilot* (Southern Pines, NC)

"These provocative mysteries just glow."
—*Mystery Lovers Bookshop News*

"Features all the traits of purebred fun.... The antics of the animals, Brown's witty observations, the history-revering Virginians, and the Blue Ridge setting make this a pleasurable read for lovers of this popular genre."
—*BookPage*

"Animal antics and criminal capers combine captivatingly in *Cat on the Scent*."
—*The San Diego Union-Tribune*

"A charming and keen-eyed take on human misdeeds and animal shenanigans... Told with spunk and plenty of whimsy, this is another delightful entry in a very popular series." —*Publishers Weekly*

"A fine murder mystery... For fans of Mrs. Murphy and her pals, both two- and four-legged, *Cat on the Scent* smells like a winner." —*The Virginian-Pilot*

"Charming." —*People*

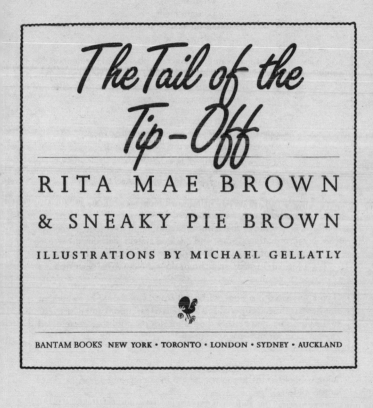

# The Tail of the Tip-Off

## RITA MAE BROWN
## & SNEAKY PIE BROWN

### ILLUSTRATIONS BY MICHAEL GELLATLY

BANTAM BOOKS NEW YORK · TORONTO · LONDON · SYDNEY · AUCKLAND

THE TAIL OF THE TIP-OFF
A Bantam Book

PUBLISHING HISTORY
Bantam hardcover edition published March 2003
Bantam mass market edition / April 2004

Published by
Bantam Dell
A Division of Random House, Inc.
New York, New York

This is a work of fiction. Names, characters, places, and incidents either
are the product of the author's imagination or are used fictitiously. Any
resemblance to actual persons, living or dead, events, or locales
is entirely coincidental.

Library of Congress Catalog Card Number: 2002074792

ISBN 0-553-58285-2

Manufactured in the United States of America
Published simultaneously in Canada

OPM   10 9 8 7 6 5 4 3 2 1

# Cast of Characters

*Mary Minor Haristeen (Harry)* The young postmistress of Crozet.

*Mrs. Murphy* Harry's inquisitive and intelligent gray tiger cat.

*Tee Tucker* Harry's faithful Welsh corgi.

*Pewter* Harry's shamelessly fat gray cat.

*Susan Tucker* Harry's best friend.

*Fair Haristeen* An equine veterinarian, and Harry's ex-husband.

*BoomBoom Craycroft* A tall, beautiful blonde who has always irritated Harry.

*Miranda Hogendobber* A virtuous and kindly widow who works with Harry at the post office.

*Tracy Raz* Miranda's former high-school sweetheart who reunited with her at their fiftieth reunion. Also a referee at UVA women's basketball games.

*Reverend Herbert C. Jones* The beloved pastor of St. Luke's Lutheran Church.

*Cazenovia* and *Elocution* Reverend Jones's two cats, whom he dotes on.

*Big Marilyn (Big Mim) Sanburne* The undisputed queen of Crozet society.

*Little Mim Sanburne* Big Mim's daughter who is still struggling for her own identity.

*Tally Urquhart* Older than dirt, she says what she thinks when she thinks it, even to her niece, Big Mim.

*Coach Debbie Ryan* The motivated leader of the UVA women's basketball team.

*Andrew Argenbright* Coach Ryan's assistant coach with the women's team.

*Rick Shaw* The overworked and understaffed Sheriff who prefers to play it by the book.

*Cynthia Cooper* The sheriff's deputy and Harry's good friend.

*Tazio Chappars* A young, brilliant architect, and a recent addition to the community. She's on the Parish Guild with Harry and BoomBoom at St. Luke's.

*Brinkley* A half-starved yellow lab who loves Tazio.

*Matthew Crickenberger* A powerful but generous businessman and contractor who also sits on the Parish Guild.

*Fred Forrest* The cantankerous and combative county building code inspector with a reputation for scrupulous, if sour, integrity.

*Mychelle Burns* Fred's assistant. She models her behavior, unfortunately, on Fred's.

*H. H. Donaldson* A fiercely competitive local contractor. Hot-tempered but good-hearted, yet he has a wandering eye.

*Anne Donaldson* H.H.'s long-suffering wife. Though wary, an intelligent woman and a good mother.

A gray sleety drizzle rattled against the handblown window-panes in the rectory at St. Luke's Lutheran Church. As if in counterpoint, a fire crackled in the large but simple fire-place, the mantel adorned by a strip of dentil carving. The hands of that carver had turned to dust in 1797.

The members of the Parish Guild were seated in a semi-circle around the fireplace, at a graceful coffee table in the middle. As anyone knows, serving on a board or a commit-tee is a dubious honor. Most people recognize their duty in time to avoid it. However, the work must be done and some good folks bow their heads to the yoke.

Mary Minor Haristeen had succumbed to the thrill of being elected, of being considered responsible, by the con-gregation. This thrill thinned as the tangle of tasks presented themselves in meeting after meeting. She liked the physical problems better than the people problems. Fixing a fallen drainspout was within her compass of expertise. Fixing a broken heart, offering succor to the ill, well, she was learning.

The good pastor of St. Luke's, the Reverend Herbert C. Jones, excelled at both the people problems and teaching. He gladly gave of himself to any board member, any parishioner. As he'd baptized Mrs. Haristeen, nicknamed Harry, he felt a special affection for the good-looking woman in her late thirties. It was an affection bounteously returned, for Harry loved the Rev, as she called him, with all her heart.

Although the guild was bickering at this exact moment, it'd be fair to say that every member loved the Reverend Jones. It would be also fair to say that most of them liked— if not loved—Harry. The one exception being BoomBoom Craycroft who sort of liked her and sort of didn't. The feeling was mutual.

Like large white confetti, papers rested on the coffee table along with mugs. The aroma of coffee and hot chocolate somewhat dissipated the tension.

"We just can't go off half-cocked here and authorize an expenditure of twelve thousand dollars." Tazio Chappars crossed her arms over her chest. She was an architect and a young, attractive woman of color, with an Italian mother and an African-American father.

"Well, we have to do something," Herb said in his resonant, hypnotic voice.

"Why?" Tazio, combative, shifted in her seat.

"Because the place looks like hell," Harry blurted out. "Sorry, Rev."

"Quite all right. It does." Herb laughed.

Hayden McIntyre, the town's general practitioner, was a fleshy man with an air of command if not a touch of arrogance. He slipped his pencil out from behind his ear and began scribbling on the budget papers, which had been handed out at the beginning of the meeting. "Let's try this. I am not arguing replacing the carpet in the rectory. We've put this off for four years now. I remember hearing arguments pro and con when I first came on board. This is one of the loveliest, most graceful churches in the Piedmont and it should reflect that." An appreciative murmur accompanied this statement. "I've broken this down into three areas of immediate need. First the sacristy: must be done." He held up his hand as Tazio opened her mouth. "It must. I know what you're going to say."

"No you don't." Her hazel eyes brightened. "Well, okay, maybe you do. Pick up the carpet and sand the floors."

"Tazio, we've been over that. We can't do that because the floorboards are so thin they can't take it." Matthew Crickenberger, head of Charlottesville's largest construction firm, clapped his hands together softly for emphasis. "Those floorboards are chestnut. They've been doing their job since 1797 and frankly they're tired and we can't really replace them. If you think the bill for new carpeting is high, wait until you see the bill for chestnut flooring even if we could find it. Mountain Lumber up there off Route 29 might be able to scare some up and give us a preacher's price, but we're still talking about thousands and thousands of dollars. Chestnut is as rare as hen's teeth and we'd need a great deal of it." He glanced down at his notes. "Six thousand square feet if we were to replace everything now under carpet and this doesn't factor in the other areas currently in use but not quite ready for recarpeting."

Tazio exhaled, flopping back in her chair. She wanted everything just so but she didn't have to foot the bill. Still, it rankled to have a vision amputated because of a small pocketbook. Such was an architect's fate.

"Hayden, you had a plan?" Herb pushed the meeting

along. No one wanted to be late to the basketball game and this discussion was eating up time.

"Yes," he smiled, "what people see first is the sacristy. If we can't come to an arrangement among us, can we at least agree to go ahead with that? The cost would be about four thousand."

"If we are going to have the place ripped up, then let's just get it over with. We know we have to do this." BoomBoom, gorgeous as always, shimmered in her teal suede dress.

"I agree. We'll find the money someplace."

"We'd better find the money first or we'll have to answer to the congregation in the church, in the supermarket, and"—Matthew winked at Harry—"in the post office."

Harry, the postmistress, sheepishly smiled. "And you know my partner in crime, Miranda, is a member of the Church of the Holy Light, so she won't bail me out."

The little gathering laughed. Miranda Hogendobber, who was a good thirty years older than Harry, quoted Scriptures with more ease than the Reverend Jones and while she tolerated other faiths she felt the charismatic church to which she belonged truly had the best path to Jesus.

As the humans batted around the cost, the need, and the choice of color for the carpeting, Harry's three dear friends lurked in the hallway outside the large room.

Mrs. Murphy, a most intelligent tiger cat, listened to the intensifying sleet. Her sidekick, a large round gray cat named Pewter, was getting fidgety waiting for the meeting to end. Tucker, the corgi, patient and steady as only a good dog can be, was happy to be inside and not outside.

The Christ cats—as Herb's two cats were called by the other animals—had escorted Murphy, Pewter, and Tucker around. They'd gossiped about every animal in the small Virginia town of Crozet, but as the meeting was entering its second hour, they'd finally exhausted that topic.

Cazenovia, the elder of the two cats, nestled down, her fluffy tail around her nose. A large calico, she had aged gracefully. The young foundling that Herb had taken in a few years ago, Elocution, had grown into a sleek pretty cat. A touch of Siamese in her, she never stopped talking.

"—*tuna breath!*" Elocution uttered this insult. "*How can you stand it?*"

"*She doesn't.*" Mrs. Murphy giggled.

They'd been discussing the blue jay who tormented Pewter. He also tormented Mrs. Murphy but with less enthusiasm, probably because he couldn't get a rise out of the tiger.

"*Oh, I will snap his neck like a toothpick someday. You take my word for it,*" Pewter promised.

"*How thrilling,*" Cazenovia purred.

"*And un-Christian,*" Tucker chuckled.

"*Well, we are cats,*" Pewter sniffed.

"*That's right. Our job is to rid the world of vermin,*" Elocution agreed. "*Blue jays are beyond vermin. They're avian criminals. Picking up stones and dropping them on neighbors' eggs. Dropping you-know-what on freshly waxed cars. Do it on purpose. They'll sit in a tree and wait until the job is finished and then swoosh.*" Elocution glanced up at the rat-a-tat on the window. "*Not today.*"

"*Why don't blue jays go south in the winter?*" Pewter mused. "*Robins do.*"

"*Life in our barn is too good, that's why. Harry puts out birdhouses and gourds and then she plants South American maize for the ground birds, cowpeas, and bipolar lespedeza.*

*The winter might be cold but she serves up all kinds of seeds for those dumb birds."*

*"Birds are descended from flying reptiles,"* Elocution announced with vigor. *"That alone should warn us off."*

*"What in the world is going on in there?"* Tucker listened as Matthew Crickenberger raised his voice about labor costs.

*"Say, have I shown you how I can open the closet where Herb stores the communion wafers?"* Elocution puffed out her chest.

*"Elo, don't do that,"* Cazenovia warned.

*"I'm just going to prove that I can do it."*

*"They'll believe you. They don't need a demonstration."*

*"I wouldn't mind,"* Pewter laconically replied.

*"Thanks, Pewter."* Cazenovia cast her a cold golden eye.

*"Come on."* Elocution, tail held high, bounded down the hall.

The others followed, Cazenovia bringing up the rear. *"I know I'll get in trouble for this,"* the old girl grumbled.

Elocution skidded at the turn in the hall where it intersected with another hall traversing the width of the rectory, itself an old building constructed in 1834.

Pewter whispered to Mrs. Murphy, *"I'm hungry."*

*"You're always hungry."*

*"I know, but you'd think the Rev would put a bowl of crunchies out somewhere. And I don't smell anything edible."*

*"Me neither,"* the mighty but small dog whispered, *"and I have the best nose."*

*"Here"* Elocution stopped in front of a closet under the stairwell that ascended to the second story. *"You all stay here."*

*"Elocution, this really isn't necessary,"* Cazenovia sighed.

Ignoring her, the shiny cat hopped up the stairs then slipped halfway through the banisters. Lying on her side she could reach the old-fashioned long key that protruded from the keyhole. She batted at it, then grabbed it with both paws, expertly turning the key until the lock popped.

"*Oh, that is impressive.*" Pewter's eyes widened.

"*The best part is, Herbie will flay Charlotte for leaving it unlocked.*" Elocution laughed.

Charlotte was Herb's secretary, second in command.

As the lock opened, Elocution gave a tug and Pewter, quick to assist, pulled at the bottom of the door with her paw. The door swung open revealing bottles of red wine and a shelf full of communion wafers in cracker boxes with cellophane wrappers. Elocution knocked one on the floor then squeezed her slender body all the way through the banisters, dropping to the floor. Within a second she'd sliced the cellophane off the box, and using one extended claw, she opened the tucked-in end.

The odor of wafers, not unlike water crackers, enticed Pewter.

"*Elocution, I knew you were going to do this,*" Cazenovia fretted.

"*Well, the box is open. We can't let it go to waste.*" The bad kitty grabbed a wafer and gobbled it down.

Temptation. Temptation. Pewter gave in.

Cazenovia suffered a moment. "*They're ruined now. The humans can't eat them.*" She, too, flicked out wafers.

Tucker, being a canine after all, rarely worried about the propriety of eating anything. Her nose was already in the wafer box.

Mrs. Murphy allowed herself the luxury of a nibble. "*Kind of tasteless.*"

"*If you eat enough of them you get a bready taste, but they are bland.*" Cazenovia's statement revealed she'd been in the communion wafers more than once.

*"Does this mean we're communicants?"* Pewter paused.

*"Yes,"* Mrs. Murphy answered. *"We're communicats."*

*"What if I'm not a Lutheran? What if I'm a Muslim cat?"*

*"If you were a Muslim cat you wouldn't be living in Crozet."* Tucker laughed.

*"You don't know. This is America. We have everything,"* Pewter rejoined.

*"Not in Crozet."* Cazenovia wiped her mouth with her paw. *"You've got Episcopalians, Lutherans, and Catholics. More or less the same thing and I know Herb would have a fit, a total fit, if he knew I'd said that, but fortunately he doesn't know what I or any other cat in this universe has to say."* She took a deep breath. *"Then you've got the Baptists busily fighting among themselves these days and then the charismatic churches and that's it."*

*"Let's open a Buddhist shrine. Shake 'em up a little."* Elocution hiccuped. She'd eaten too many wafers too quickly.

*"No. We build a huge statue of a cat with earrings like in ancient Egypt. Oh, I can hear the squeals now about paganism."* Mrs. Murphy laughed as the others laughed with her.

Tucker swiveled her ears. *"Hey, gang, meeting's breaking up. Let's get out of here."*

*"Help me push this back in the closet and close the door,"* Elocution said with urgency.

Cazenovia knocked the box in as though it were a hockey puck. Tucker, larger than the cats, pushed against the door. It closed in an instant. They scrambled out of there. Luckily for them, the doors to the meeting room weren't yet open. They made it back in the nick of time.

"—tomorrow afternoon," Matthew told Tazio.

"I'll be in the office."

"I know you're disappointed about the chestnut flooring but, well." Matthew shrugged.

"I guess I'm a perfectionist. That's what they say back at the office and on the sites, only they say it a lot more directly there." She smiled.

"You've got a lot on your plate, young lady." Hayden McIntyre joined them. "Your design for the new sports complex is just the most ingenious thing. Is that the right word?"

"As long as it's a good word." Tazio picked up her coat hanging in the hall.

"I know H.H. has none for me." Matthew shrugged.

"He'll get his shot." Hayden shrugged right back.

Tazio pointedly did not comment on the animosity between Matthew and H. H. Donaldson, head of a rival construction firm. The bad blood had been made worse when Matthew won the bid to construct Tazio's new stadium. She had hoped H.H. would win the bid because she especially liked him, but she could work just fine with Matthew.

Herb walked out with Harry and BoomBoom. "I sure appreciate you girls coming on over here. You're a welcome addition to the guild."

Both women had just begun their first terms, which lasted three years.

"I'm learning a lot," Harry said.

"Me, too."

"Look at these little angels." Harry knelt down to pet all the cats and Tucker.

*"If she only knew."* Elocution giggled.

*"Don't be so smug,"* Cazenovia chided her. *"Humans don't know what we're talking about but they know smug."*

"I don't know what I'd do without those two." Herb smiled benevolently. "They help write the sermons, they keep an eye on the parishioners, they leave little pawprints on the furniture."

"I'm sure they've left them on the carpets, too." BoomBoom liked cats.

"Well, that they have but I can hardly blame them for wearing those carpets out. Fortunately we are a well-attended church, but it does put wear and tear on the building." Herb checked his watch. "Game's in an hour. You all going?"

"Yes," the two women said in unison.

"Well, I'll see you there. I'd better go through the building and shut some of the doors. On these cold nights it saves on the heat bill. Gotta save it where I can."

As he headed down the hall, Mrs. Murphy urged Harry, *"Come on, Mom, let's get out of here!"*

Cazenovia and Elocution hurried into the meeting room, flopping themselves on the sofa with a great show of non-chalance. Too great a show.

"See you, Rev," Harry called out as she tossed on her coat, opening the door for her pets and BoomBoom.

*"Whew,"* Pewter breathed as she stepped outside into the nasty weather.

## 2

The soon-to-be-replaced basketball stadium loomed out of the sea of asphalt like a giant white clam. That such unparalleled ugliness could be part of the University of Virginia, one of the most beautiful sites in America, was a dismal curiosity. Good thing that Mr. Jefferson was dead, for if he caught sight of the Clam he'd perish on the spot.

Harry had a new wool blanket, which she fluffed up on the seat of her old truck with another older blanket for the cats and dog to snuggle in. The three friends would curl up together, burrowing in the blankets and keeping one another toasty, but not before they complained.

*"I hate this!"* Mrs. Murphy's eyes narrowed as Harry sprinted through the sleet to the stadium.

*"I'd rather be here than there. I can stand the stomping and hollering. It's that buzzer."* Pewter completed two circles then lay down.

Tucker, ears forward, listened as people laughed in the

bad weather, opened umbrellas, slipped in the sleet which was beginning to accumulate. *"It must be hard not to have fur. Think of the money they have to spend on raincoats. Gore-Tex stuff costs a fortune. Barbour coats, too. That's the stuff that really works. But think how awful it must feel to get cold water on naked skin. Poor humans."*

Fred Forrest, the county building code inspector, walked by the truck. His hands were in his coat pockets, his perpetual frown in place.

*"Think Herb found the desecrated communion wafers yet?"* Pewter giggled, a high-pitched little infectious giggle.

*"Can you imagine kneeling at the communion rail and being given a wafer with fang marks in it?"* Mrs. Murphy joined in the giggles.

*"I ate all mine. Did you two really just bite some?"* Tucker snuggled in next to the cats who loved her thick fur.

*"Oh sure. That's half the fun."* Pewter's sides shook.

Tucker laughed, too. *"Gee, I wish I could take communion."*

*"Have to go to catechism first,"* Pewter saucily replied. *"Of course, we have already done cattychism."*

They nearly fell off the bench seat laughing.

*"Know what else?"* Mrs. Murphy, in the spirit, said. *"Have you ever noticed how when they say the Lord's Prayer it sounds like 'Lena shot us into temptation'?"*

*"You're terrible."* The small but powerful dog pretended to be horrified.

*"God gave us a sense of humor. That means we're supposed to use it,"* Pewter resolutely declared.

*"Yeah, Miranda has a sense of humor and she's religious. I mean, she was pretty close to being a religious nut there for a while,"* Tucker thoughtfully said of the older woman whom she dearly loved.

"*She needs it. Working at the post office you'd be loony tunes without a sense of humor,*" Mrs. Murphy said.

"*Why?*"

"*Tucker, it's a federal building. That means it belongs to the American people and anyone can come and go. If you work for the post office you have to deal with whoever walks through that door. It's not like a lawyer's office or doctor's office where they can throw you out if you don't belong,*" the pretty tiger cat explained.

"*They can throw you out if you're a nuisance,*" Tucker rejoined.

"*There go half the people in Crozet.*" Pewter led the others in another giggle fit.

Inside the Giant Clam, whose real name was University Hall, usually referred to as "U-Hall," people settled down to enjoy themselves. Perhaps they wouldn't get giggle fits like Mrs. Murphy, Pewter, and Tucker, but they were primed for a good time.

Just coming in out of the weather produced a feeling of well-being.

Tonight's opponent, Clemson, was in a rebuilding year so the UVA women's basketball team wasn't too stressed. Yet those were the very opponents that Coach Ryan worried about. Never take anyone for granted. Prepare for each and every game.

Harry believed in Coach Ryan and her philosophy, as did many of the season-ticket holders. Harry sat behind the home team's bench about halfway up the first section, a seat she renewed every year. Harry had little in the way of discretionary income and her three horses took up most of that, but her basketball seat meant a great deal to her.

Her ex-husband and friend, Fair Haristeen, DVM, sat next to her in his seasonal seat. Next to him sat Jim

Sanburne, the mayor of Crozet, and his wife, Big Mim, the Queen of Crozet. On Mim's other side sat her aunt Tally, well into her nineties and fanatically determined not to miss a basketball game—or anything else for that matter.

In the row directly behind them sat Matthew Crickenberger and his family, his wife and two boys aged ten and twelve. To the left of Matthew sat the Tuckers: Ned, Susan, and Brooks. Danny, their son, was in his first year at Cornell, so his seat had been taken by Hayden McIntyre's new partner in the practice, Bill Langston. However, Bill was just moving into Crozet, so he wouldn't be at the games until next week. Hayden, a thoughtful man despite his directness which is never seen as thoughtful in the South, had purchased the seat from the Tuckers, hoping it would help ease the young, unmarried doctor into the community. He'd asked Deputy Cynthia Cooper to the game tonight but she had to work the late shift at the Sheriff's Department.

Tracy Raz, Miranda's beau, reffed the game with Josef P. The *P* stood for Pontiakowski—a bit difficult for the inhabitants of such an English place as Charlottesville, so everyone called him "Josef P."

Miranda sat opposite her friends on the other side of the basketball court. She had a very good seat provided by the school for the spouse or friend of the referee. She particularly enjoyed it because she could observe her buddies.

She watched them screaming and hollering because Clemson pulled themselves together and it turned into a tight, fast-paced game. She saw H. H. Donaldson, his wife, Anne, a professor at UVA, and their twelve-year-old daughter, Cameron, who sat in front of Harry, H.H. being one seat to her right, all stand up and clap and stomp in unison to cheer on Virginia. Fred Forrest bellowed the loudest. As he was rows behind Harry and friends, his volume disturbed them little. His assistant at work, Mychelle Burns, a petite, pixieish African-American, was with him. She hollered as much as Fred.

In his late thirties, H.H. was a driven man. Like Fred, H.H. plumbed new depths at sporting events. If Hayden McIntyre was direct, H.H. was plain rude at times. Everyone chalked this up to the fact that he had been born on the wrong side of the tracks and had a chip on his shoulder. Anne and Cameron were lovely, which helped to mitigate H.H.'s mouth.

"Go inside! Go inside!" H.H. yelled at the top of his not inconsiderable lungs.

BoomBoom Craycroft sat two rows behind Harry. She was thrilled the game was close because next to her sat Blair Bainbridge and his date, Little Mim Sanburne. BoomBoom hadn't ever dated Blair, a handsome international model, but she figured she'd get around to it. BoomBoom felt she was entitled to any man whom she found marginally interesting. Since she believed most men were interested in her, and most were, she moved on her own schedule. Now that Blair was dating Little Mim, BoomBoom's nose was out of joint. It wasn't so much that she had to have him, it was just that she hadn't had him. To make matters worse, she didn't have a date for the game because she figured Blair would be there. She hadn't realized his relationship with Little Mim was proceeding. Up until the Clemson game, Big Mim, Little Mim's mother, hadn't paid much attention, either. She was now.

The Clemson center, Jessie Raynor, a six-foot-three-inch girl, was well coordinated—a lot of times those big people aren't. She shot straight up in the air over the head of the girl guarding her, Tammy Girond, and with a flick of the wrist dropped a three-pointer right through the net.

"Oh no!" Harry screamed along with the other Virginia fans.

Tie ball game.

Tracy and Josef, both dripping with sweat, had run as far and as hard as the girls. It had been a clean game up until now, when Tammy, in frustration, pushed Jessie, the Clemson forward, flat on her face.

Josef blew his whistle. He called a personal foul on Tammy Girond. She doubled up her fist in his face and he threw her out of the game. Everyone was on their feet, both benches, all the spectators.

Jessie walked to the foul line and sunk both of her shots.

Tracy Raz tossed the ball to Frizz Barber, so named because of her hair, as she waited behind the end line.

With six seconds left on the clock, the moment was drenched in tension. Frizz quickly passed to her teammate Jenny Ingersoll. The Clemson players, woman-to-woman on defense, bottled up the Virginia players. Jenny, with time leaking out, dribbled two steps to her right, the Clemson player guarding her closely. Then she stopped, spun left and lifted both feet up off the ground, taking her shot. It bounced high off the rim. Jessie Raynor, hands high over her head, jumped up, snagging the ball. The buzzer sounded. End of game.

The Clemson bench emptied, the girls piling on top of one another. What an upset!

The noise from the crowd diminished as though someone had turned down the volume dial on the radio. The Virginia players, crestfallen, crossed the court with Coach Ryan. She shook the hand of the Clemson coach as the girls shook the hands of their now-recovered opponents. Respect reflected on the Virginia players' faces. They'd never take Clemson for granted again. They'd just learned the wisdom of Coach Ryan exhorting them to never, ever underestimate an opponent.

The crowd finally remembered their manners and politely applauded the Clemson team. As the players retired to the locker rooms, quiet fans filed out.

It was mid-season. The teams in the conference were all getting better, together. As the crowd shuffled down the circular halls, they discussed the toughness of Clemson and their thoughts on UVA's next game.

Josef P., still in his ref's striped shirt, sprinted out into the parking lot to his car. He opened the door and pulled out a gym bag and as he turned to run back through the sleet, Fred Forrest stopped him. He was by himself, as Mychelle had hurried to her car on the other side of the lot.

"You cost us the game, asshole!"

Matthew Crickenberger, passing on the way to his car, stopped. "Hey, that's enough of that."

"Don't you tell me what to do. You're the last person who should tell me what to do," Fred sneered.

"What are you going to do, Fred, fine me for being off a quarter of an inch on an access ramp?" Matthew said but with some geniality.

Josef shivered in the sleet as Fred stepped in his path. H.H. came up, having sent his family to the station wagon.

"I'll do whatever I want!" Fred, adrenaline still pumping after the game, shouted. "You'd better remember that." He pointed his finger at H.H. "You, too. Bunch of rich assholes. And you, asshole"—Fred suffered from an attenuated vocabulary—"make a call like that in a playoff and you're dead."

"Go on," Matthew said to Josef as he stepped in front of Fred to block him from taking a swing at Josef. "For Chrissake, Fred, it's only a game."

Josef ran, shivering, back to U-Hall. By now a crowd had gathered around, including Harry, BoomBoom, Fair, Big Mim, Jim, Little Mim, Blair, and others. Aunt Tally sulked in Big Mim's Bentley but her niece refused to allow her to stand in the worsening weather.

The animals, awakened by the slamming of doors, watched. They heard bits and snatches of the fuss, which was a row down from their truck.

Then Fred surveyed his audience. "It's not just a game. Basketball is life." He spit on the ground next to H.H.'s shoe.

"Crude." Blair towered over Fred.

"Drop dead," Fred snarled up at the handsome face.

"It's bad sportsmanship, Fred, and you ought to be ashamed of yourself." H.H. was disgusted.

"Who are you to talk? You crawled over the old Miller and Rhoads building when Matthew wasn't there. Trying to figure out how to run with the big dogs."

H.H., a little raw on the subject of competition with Matthew, swung at Fred, hitting him square in the gut.

Fred doubled over. Fair Haristeen, strong as an ox, quickly grabbed H.H. from behind, and walking him backwards, pulled him to the family station wagon.

Fred, helped to his feet by Matthew, screamed after him, "I will get you! You'd better be perfect because I'm going to make your life miserable!"

"That's enough, Fred." Matthew was disgusted with the wiry middle-aged inspector.

"Asshole," Fred snarled at Matthew then stalked off.

"What a jerk!" Little Mim shook her head, scattering snowflakes. The sleet was turning to snow.

"Don't use slang, dear, it's so common," her mother,

wrapped in mink, her second best coat for winter, said sotto voce.

"Oh, Mother." Little Mim turned her shoulder to her mother, slipped her hand in Blair's. "Let's go to Oxo, shall we?"

Mim glared as her daughter sauntered off. Then she turned to Harry standing next to her. "Think twice before having children."

"I'll be sure to be married first." Harry tried to lighten the moment.

"There is that." Big Mim exhaled, then looked skyward. "We'd better all get home before the sleet that's underneath all this turns to ice."

"Already has, honeybun, already has." Big Jim returned his attention to his wife after watching Fair deposit a resisting H.H. in his car.

"Really, Little Mim shouldn't be out in this. The roads will only get worse."

"Blair took his four-wheel-drive, honeybun. He'll get her home safe and sound."

Big Mim said nothing but headed to the Bentley, her husband in tow. She'd have a word with her daughter tomorrow.

Fair rejoined Harry and BoomBoom, an interesting moment since one was his ex-wife and the other his ex-lover. Life in a small town is filled with such moments and everyone either adjusts to them or gets out. If you got in a huff and declared yourself not on speaking terms, you'd soon wind up with no one to talk to and that would never do. People had to accommodate the messiness of life.

"Ladies, can I take you both out for a drink?"

"No, thanks, I want to get home before the roads get

worse. Mim's right and I know I sound like a wuss, but I hate it when it gets like this." Harry bowed out.

"Me, too," BoomBoom agreed.

Fair, disappointed because he'd wanted to see Harry, said, "Next game. Rain check or rather, sleet check." He laughed.

Harry thought a moment. "Why not?"

BoomBoom replied. "Yes, I think it would be—fun."

BoomBoom's affair with Fair Haristeen had occurred during his separation from Harry, or so she declared. It provoked Harry to file for the divorce. Fair, then in his early thirties, had been going through a crisis. Whether it was midlife, masculinity, or whatever, it was a crisis and it cost him his marriage, something he deeply regretted. BoomBoom, not one to take relationships with men seriously, tired of the tall, blond, handsome vet soon enough. Her conventional beauty and flirtatiousness always brought her another man, or men, which was perhaps why she didn't take relationships seriously. Oh, she always wanted to be on the arm of either a handsome man or a rich one, preferably both, but she never thought of men as much more than a means to an end; that end being comfort, luxury, and hopefully pleasure.

As she matured into her late thirties, she was starting to rethink this position.

Harry, on the other hand, had given her heart and soul to Fair. When the relationship unraveled she was devastated. It took her years to recover, although on the surface she seemed okay. Naturally, Fair's apology and desire to win her back helped this process but she was in no hurry to return to him. She was wondering if maybe BoomBoom didn't have the right attitude about men: use them before they use you. Yet it wasn't really in Harry's nature to be that way about people, and at the bottom of it she didn't differentiate between men and women. People were people and morals didn't come in neatly wrapped gender packages. Living an upright life was difficult for anybody. Once she realized that she did forgive Fair, she wasn't sure she could ever be in love with him again.

She rather hoped she would fall in love again, if not with Fair then with somebody, but somehow it didn't seem so important as it once was. Losing Fair turned out to be one of the best things that had ever happened to her. She was forced to fall back on her own internal resources, to question conventional wisdom.

As each party repaired to their vehicle, Miranda and Tracy Raz emerged from the gym. Tracy, freshly showered after the game, had his arm tightly wrapped around his treasure, Miranda.

Harry waved to them. "See you tomorrow."

Seeing Miranda happy made her happy. She now knew that's what love really was, joy in another person's existence.

She certainly took joy in Mrs. Murphy, Pewter, and Tucker, who greeted her as she opened the door to the 1978 Ford truck.

*"Some game, huh, Mom?"* Tucker wagged her nonexistent tail.

*"We heard the word 'asshole' quite a lot,"* Pewter giggled; she'd had the giggles all day.

*"'Cause Fred Forrest is one."* Mrs. Murphy pronounced judgment. *"Karma."*

*"You ate a communion wafer and you believe in karma?"* Tucker feigned shock as Harry closed the door, started the engine and the heater.

"You all are so talkative. Must have missed me." Harry smiled.

"We're having a religious discussion," Pewter answered. "Can you believe in ideas from different religions?"

"No, that's what Tucker's talking about. Probably suffering a spasm of guilt after eating so many communion wafers. Dogs are such pigs." Mrs. Murphy paused. "I said 'karma' because Fred Forrest will sow what he has reaped."

"She must be a very Holy Dog." Pewter leaned against the corgi.

# 3

The snow fell steadily but roads were passable the next day thanks to the new yellow snowplows the state had purchased. The major arteries had multiple plows continually pushing the snow off into ever-growing banks. Even the smaller roads like Routes 250 and 240, the main roads into Crozet, had at least one major machine keeping them clear.

Then, too, just about everyone out in the country owned a four-wheel-drive vehicle. It was folly not to have one. Those huge gas-guzzling boats so out of place in the city were a godsend in the country.

Rob Collier, delivering the mail sacks from the main post office on Route 29 in Charlottesville, stamped his feet. "Not bad."

Harry glanced up at the big clock, which read seven-thirty.

"Hello!" Miranda breezed in through the back door. "Rob, you're out bright and early."

"I always am. Hey, I hear you all may be getting a new building."

Miranda waved him off. "I've heard that since 1952."

"Might do it this time. You girls are getting cramped in here." He tipped his baseball hat and left.

*"That would be nice, a bigger place to play in,"* Mrs. Murphy thought.

*"Leave well enough alone. Why spend the money?"* Tucker replied.

*"Because the way human government works is they have to spend the money, otherwise they'll squander it somewhere else. Talk about stupid. Every department has its budget and the money has to be spent. Humans are crazy,"* said Pewter.

As if picking up on Pewter's sentiment about humans being crazy, Harry pulled the mailbags back behind the mailboxes. "Did Josef tell Tracy about what happened in the parking lot?"

"Indeed he did. What's the matter with Fred? There's no call for acting like that."

"You should have seen H.H. and Matthew when he threatened to take it out on them. And every other word out of his mouth was 'asshole.' I couldn't believe it." Harry's voice rose.

"Wasn't it a good game, though?"

"Better if we'd won." Harry flipped up the divider in the counter between the public area and the work area. "Look at it come down. I think it's going to be a bigger storm than the weatherman says."

"Have you ever noticed once we get on the other side of New Year's the weather does change? Winter."

"Yeah. Well, the chores have to get done no matter what the weather. God bless the person who invented thermal underwear."

"It's my feet and hands that get cold. I just hate that." Miranda rubbed her hands together.

The main topics of conversation for the morning were the weather and the basketball game.

Big Mim opened the door at eleven. "I'm late. Did I miss anything?"

She usually appeared when the doors opened in the morning.

"No. Weather and b-ball. That's the buzz." Harry leaned over the counter.

Behind her the cats slept on the chair at the small kitchen table. Tucker was curled up on her big beanbag.

"It's just us girls." Mim sounded conspiratorial. "Tell me, what do you think about my daughter dating Blair?"

"Uh," Harry stalled.

"It's wonderful." Miranda came up next to Harry. "Mim, dear, how about a cup of coffee or a hot chocolate?"

"No, thanks. I want to run a few errands while I can get around. If this keeps up, the snow is going to outrun the snowplows."

"It certainly looks like it."

"You really think it's a good pairing?"

"It's not what we think. It's what they think," Miranda replied.

"But he's a model. What kind of prospects does a man like that have now that he's getting older? I know he makes a good living, but, well——"

"He's bright enough. He'll find something to do. He's made some shrewd investments. Remember, he's got Tetotan Partnership."

"Oh, that. All those wells in western Albemarle County. Well, that may pan out for him and that may not. I've heard about the water table until I'm blue in the face and I've heard about the new reservoir being built for thirty years and it's not built yet. Kind of like the rumors about a new post office."

"Oh, you heard that, too?" Harry said.

"These rumors recur like malaria. The one thing I will say for Blair is when he first went into Tetotan he had the brains to have H. Vane Tempest for a partner and H. Vane doesn't make too many mistakes. Of course, Blair made the mistake."

Mim alluded to an affair that Blair had with his former partner's wife about three years ago.

"Nobody's perfect," Harry lightheartedly replied just as Herb burst through the door.

At one time in her life, Harry might have been censorious about an affair but she'd grown up. She realized quite literally that nobody is perfect, including herself.

"Ladies. Oh, Harry, before I forget, quick meeting about the flooring. Won't take long. Tomorrow night, weather permitting."

"Fine."

Pewter opened one eye. *"Wonder if he found the wafers?"*

*"Don't ask. Don't tell."* Mrs. Murphy rolled on her side.

"Wasn't that a contretemps in the parking lot last night?" Herb shook his head. "And Fred *will* get them. Remember when I extended the gardening shed next to the garage? A fourteen-by-ten building and he said it wasn't up to code. He cost me five hundred dollars. He's impossible. I wouldn't give you a nickel for H.H.'s or Matthew's peace of mind until Fred gets over this."

"Or is mollified," Big Mim sarcastically said.

"That's the problem. He can't be mollified. He takes offense at any kindness. Everything is a bribe in his mind. And Matthew's finishing up a big project and about to start another. H.H. is busy, too. There will be hell to pay, forgive the expression." He smiled a lopsided smile.

"There's a game Friday. Let's see what happens then," Miranda said.

"Well, that's the whole thing, isn't it? Intimidation." Herb slipped the key in his brass mailbox. "He's intimidated Josef."

"He won't intimidate Tracy." Miranda winked.

"Fred lives and breathes women's basketball ever since his daughter played for UVA," Harry mentioned. "Guess she's doing pretty good as assistant coach out at University of Missouri."

"He can just move to Columbia." Miranda laughed, mentioning the location of the University of Missouri.

"Say, anyone met Hayden McIntyre's new partner?" Herb asked.

"I think he flies in today." Harry looked out the window. "Then again, he might not be here until tomorrow."

"That's my guess. I bet there are people tied up in airports along the East Coast. The Right Coast." Miranda smiled.

"As opposed to the Left Coast." Harry enjoyed batting ideas and phrases with Miranda.

"Gold Coast. That's Florida." Herb sorted his mail.

Big Mim opened her mailbox. Like Herb she pitched unwanted advertisements and junk mail into the wastebasket.

"Mim, that was a three-pointer." Herb teased her.

As he left, Pewter whispered, *"He hasn't found it. He would have said something."*

*"We're safe. He'll never know it was us."* Mrs. Murphy wished she could be there when he did find the chewed-up wafer box.

*"He might not know but Mom could figure it out."* Tucker had confidence in Harry's deductive abilities.

*"Never. She'd never believe she had pagan pets."* Mrs. Murphy laughed so loud she rolled off the chair and embarrassed herself to the hilarity of the others.

As she was picking herself up off the floor, trying to salvage her dignity, H.H. walked in.

"Ladies."

"Hi, H.H.," they replied.

He opened his box, took out his mail, then came to the counter, propping both elbows on it. "Miranda, I'm on the horns of a dilemma. Just can't make up my mind."

The older woman came over to the other side of the counter, her dark orange sweater casting a warm light on her face. "Well, you could flip a coin."

"Works for me." Harry laughed.

He tilted his head, light streaks of gray already appearing at his temples. "This dilemma is bigger than that. It's not so much right and wrong. I'd hope I'd choose right. It's more like," he paused, "right versus right."

"Ah yes, that is difficult." Miranda rapped her fingertips on the counter. " 'Give thy servant therefore an understanding mind.' " She stopped short. "Have a better one: 'And the spirit of the Lord shall rest upon him, the spirit of wisdom and understanding, the spirit of counsel and might, the spirit of knowledge and of the fear of the Lord,' Isaiah, chapter eleven, verse two."

"I knew you'd dispense your wisdom."

"Not my wisdom. The Good Book's."

Harry folded an empty mail sack. "If there were a TV game show on biblical knowledge, Miranda would win."

"Go on." She waved off Harry.

"I believe she's right." H.H. spoke to Miranda. "I'll reflect on what you've quoted."

"I can quote." Harry grinned.

"This I've got to hear." H.H. squared his mail, tapping it on the counter.

" 'Between two evils I choose the one I haven't tried before.' Mae West."

H.H. laughed as he headed for the door. "I'll tell that to Anne."

"You are awful." Miranda shook her head as the door clicked shut.

"Hey, if you're going to dispense virtue, I'll dispense vice just to keep things equal."

"How about vice versa?" Miranda winked.

"Touché." Harry laughed.

# 4

The darkness troubled Harry far more than the cold. On the winter solstice the sun set behind the mountains at four-fifteen in the afternoon. She took comfort in the fact that sunset had now inched forward to about four thirty-five. Of course, with the driving snow she couldn't see the sun but there was always that moment on a snowy, rainy, or cloudy day when the filtered light failed and the underside of clouds turned wolf gray followed by navy blue.

She'd finished her barn chores as another half inch of snow covered the ground. She hated to be idle; this was the perfect time to pull out everything in the odds-and-ends drawer in the kitchen. She carefully spread a newspaper on the counter, opened the drawer, gazed into the turmoil, and plucked out a tailor's measuring tape. She reached in again. This time a fistful of rubber bands was her reward. It was fun, a real grab bag.

Even the neatest person, and Harry came close to qualifying, had to have a junk drawer. Before she could scoop up all the pencils needing sharpening, the phone rang.

"Hello, Joe's Poolroom. Eightball speaking."

"Harry, that is so corny," Susan replied.

"You call your best friend corny?"

"Someone has to. Now will you shut up? I've got scoop."

Mrs. Murphy and Pewter, lounging on the kitchen counter just behind the newspaper, perked up their ears. It was plenty exciting considering there were rubber bands to steal, pencils to roll onto the floor, but Harry's alertness was promising on this snowy evening.

"Tell."

"H.H. walked out on Anne."

"What?"

"She's over at Little Mim's crying her eyes out. Cameron's with her and being a great support to her mother."

"Who told you?"

"Little Mim. She thought Anne should talk to Ned. Before Ned could get to the phone she told me everything. I could hear Anne crying. It really is awful. What an SOB. He could have waited until spring."

"What's that got to do with it?"

"It's easier to take bad news when the weather's good."

"If that's the case then why did T. S. Eliot write 'April is the cruelest month'?"

"Because he's from St. Louis. I'm sure it is there," Susan puffed into the receiver. "Then he became more English than the English. I knew there was a reason I took all those poetry classes at school. See, you did it again. You got me off the track. I hate that."

"I didn't do anything, Susan. God, apart from being a

good lawyer your husband has to be a saint to put up with you. And is he talking to Anne?"

"On the other line."

"I'm surprised you aren't glued to his side trying to catch anything she might say."

"He'd never let me do that. You know that." Susan's voice registered disappointment.

"Are you smoking?"

"Why do you ask that?" said the woman holding a Churchill cigar in her hand.

"I heard you puffing."

"Oh—well—yes. Harry, I am not going to put on weight this winter. Every damned winter I pack on five pounds and then I turned thirty-five and the next thing I knew it was seven pounds. So I am smoking this big, fat cigar. The little ones are too harsh. Big ones are smoother."

"Can't you take diet pills?"

"All they do is make you go to the bathroom. They don't really work and the ones that do work the FDA took off the market because they damaged something, your liver. Hell, I wouldn't take enough to damage my liver. I just don't want the extra baggage in the winter, which is then so hard to drop in the spring. Maybe that's why April is the cruelest month. A girl starts thinking about how she'll look in her bathing suit."

"Susan Tucker."

"See, I've solved a literary mystery."

"Now back to the real mystery. Why did H.H. leave Anne?"

"That." A long pause followed. "He was having yet another affair."

"Ah, I am sorry to hear that. Did she say who or did Little Mim?"

"No, but I have a feeling it's not one of his usual casual romps."

"Ugh."

As Harry and Susan had been friends since infancy they could speak to one another in shorthand and often they didn't need to speak at all.

"You got that right. Once the tears have wrung you dry, anger sweeps in like the north wind. Let's hope he comes to his senses. Everybody feels temptation. You wouldn't be human, right?"

"Yes," Harry reluctantly agreed.

"Victory means you turn away from it. God, I sound like my father. But it is true. And H.H. has a lovely, sweet twelve-year-old daughter to consider. That's such a great age, too."

"You don't think it could be BoomBoom, do you?"

"Harry, every time someone has an affair in this town it isn't with BoomBoom."

"You're right. Half the town is female."

"Oh pulease. Will you get over it?"

A long silence followed.

Finally Harry muttered, "I am. Almost. I am."

"Good. I love you like beans, Harry, like my second skin, but this has gone on long enough. I don't want my best friend to turn into some embittered woman, and besides, it was a relationship that didn't really go anywhere. He's paid his dues."

"I guess we all have and I know it's snippy to say something like that about BoomBoom but she's so, uh, sultry. Men just eat that up. If I live to be one hundred and ten I will never figure out why they go after women who are so obvious. Is there another word? I'd like to think some of them are attracted to sophistication."

"Some are. They made Grace Kelly a star."

"Women made Grace Kelly a star."

"Harry, you are being argumentative. Very few actors become megastars unless they appeal to both sexes."

"You're right. Okay then, Smart One, Sage of Crozet, who is today's Grace Kelly?" A hint of triumph crept into Harry's pleasant speaking voice, once heard never forgotten.

"Well, how about Gwyneth Paltrow? Cate Blanchett?"

"You know, they are impressive but it's not fair to compare someone to a vanished goddess or even a living one like Sophia Loren."

"And now back to something you just said, that half the town is female. You recall that?"

"Yes."

"How do you know some women aren't lusting after BoomBoom?"

"I don't." Harry laughed. "But she's not lusting back. Oh, I would love it, I mean love it in capital letters if BoomBoom were a lesbian. What a blessed relief." She thought a moment. "Hey, I usually don't think of that, you know, someone being gay, but what if H.H. left Anne for a man? He's always fooling around. Maybe it's a cover-up or a way to run away from his true orientation. You think?"

"Not likely."

"Yeah, but it would be juicy. Heterosexual scandal is a little trite. I mean, there's so much of it."

"You kill me. Anyway, if H.H. were gay, we'd know. You can always tell with men. It's a lot easier than with women. Some women."

"True, but who? Not gay, I mean who is he sleeping with?"

"Who knows? It's not like he doesn't meet a lot of women. Many of his clients are good-looking, often married, since he's usually building houses. 'Course now he's switched to large commercial projects."

"He hopes to switch to large commercial projects. He's not in Matthew Crickenberger's class," Harry commented.

"In time, he could be."

"True. You're saying he meets bank officers and corporate types. I'm sure many of them are good-looking women. Have you ever noticed how many successful people are good-looking?"

"I have. They may not be drop-dead gorgeous but they make the most of what they have. That bespeaks intelligence. You really can't succeed if you don't look good."

"I'm sure there's some animal reason for it."

*"Is she going to say something about us?"* Pewter wondered.

*"Don't know."* Mrs. Murphy listened to the conversation although it was hard to hear Susan.

The animals wished Harry would buy a modern phone system with a speaker switch. Reconstructing the other half of a conversation called for kitty creativity and logic.

Harry felt sorry for Anne. "If there's anything I can do, let me know. I mean, you'll know before I do. It's such a terrible feeling, that moment when you find out."

"The wonder of it is that Anne didn't know before now."

"People don't know what they don't want to know," Harry said.

"Maybe I'm blind." Susan's voice faltered a moment.

"Not Ned. He's true blue." Harry's brightened. "I have some idea what Anne's going through, although it was a little different for me. Fair said he had to 'find' himself. Where do people get these dreadful phrases? Anyway, he found himself BoomBoom. But you know, I think he fooled around before. It's so easy for an equine vet to do it, you know? All those wonderful farm calls. But it's water over the dam." She paused. "Did Anne catch him red-handed?"

"I don't know. If I find out anything more, I will call. Little Mim said that Anne and Cameron would spend the night at her place. It's not a good night to drive anyway. Might not be a good morning to come in to work. Well, Miranda can open the P.O. for you."

"I can get in."

"We'll see, but don't be a hero."

"All right. Thanks for telling me. If I don't see you to-morrow I'll see you at the game Friday night," Harry added. "Wonder if the Donaldsons will be there. That little Cameron loves basketball."

"If all else fails, I'll take Anne and Cameron," Susan said with authority.

"Good idea. 'Bye."

Harry hung up the phone. Through her kitchen window, she saw the big owl that lived in the barn fly in the cupola, a flutter of wings in the snowy darkness, just enough motion to catch her eye.

The phone rang again.

Thinking it was Susan with a callback, Harry picked up. "Yes, boss."

"I like that."

"Herb, sorry, I thought it was Susan."

"Just me."

"Just you is very fine. What can I do for you?"

"Given the weather I've canceled the meeting tomorrow but I managed to contact everyone by phone and get a voice vote."

"Clever."

He paused a moment. "Well?"

"I'm on your team."

"It certainly saves time, doesn't it? You sit there in those meetings and hear who shot John." Herb used the Southern expression that means everyone gives their opinion whether relevant or not. In fact, one person can hold conflicting opinions all by himself—not that that ever stopped anyone from giving them out. "Here it is. Everyone, even Tazio Chappars, has come around to putting down carpet over all the needed areas."

"How did you do that?"

"Matthew Crickenberger said he'd pay for it through his company, using his construction discount, and we could pay it back over two years with no interest. You know, he does a lot for the community. Except for his foreman, I think most of his workers are illiterate. He's giving them good salaries, a chance to learn. I'll say an extra prayer for him."

"I will, too." Harry paused. "This has nothing to do with the carpet but I just heard that H. H. Donaldson left Anne."

Herb didn't immediately reply. "I'd hoped it wouldn't come to that."

"The Donaldsons are Episcopalians." Harry wondered how Herb knew anything concerning their marriage.

"True enough."

"You sure have good resources."

"Reverends have our own pipeline, missy." Herb sighed.

"Guess you do. Maybe H.H. will wake up."

"Yes. Speaking of which, I am very glad to see you and BoomBoom working together. Forgiveness is at the center of Christ's message."

"I don't deserve much credit. I've dragged it out long enough and you're the second person to push me today. Susan was the first."

"She's a true friend. There are people who go through this life without true friends. That must be hell. Real hell."

"Yes."

"All right, that's my sermon for the day." He laughed.

"You forget, I get them on a daily basis from Miranda."

"Oh my, Miranda, now, what a Lutheran she would have made." He chuckled. "She's another friend, and every time I see her with Tracy I have to smile. Life is full of miracles and love finds you when you least expect it. A kind of emotional roulette." Herb lost his wife five years back to a heart attack.

"Funny, isn't it?"

"Life?"

"Yeah."

# 5

On Friday, Harry walked through the lawn at the University of Virginia, the snow covering the undulating quad between the Rotunda and the statue of blind Homer. Footprints crisscrossed the deep snow. Walking directly behind her, since it would be difficult for them to plow ahead, trudged Mrs. Murphy, a crabby Pewter, and a very happy Tucker.

*"I don't need exercise."*

*"Pewter, you need a personal trainer."* Tucker poked her nose at the rotund gray kitty.

*"Whose idea was this?"* Pewter ignored the comment.

*"Mine,"* Mrs. Murphy replied. *"How was I to know she'd want a twilight stroll? I thought she'd just take a little spin, then drive over to the Clam."*

*"What's she care about UVA for? She graduated from Smith."* Pewter's pads tingled from the cold.

"*Beauty. The lawn is one of the most beautiful spaces in North America,*" Tucker rightly surmised.

"*In spring,*" Pewter grumbled.

"*Ah, but the snow's blue, the dome of the Rotunda is changing shades with the dying light. Smoke's curling low from the chimneys. Could be 1840,*" Tucker imagined.

"*A poetic pooch.*" Mrs. Murphy stopped a moment and let the dog walk by her. She rubbed along Tucker's side.

Harry led them back to her truck, parked on the side of the road, never a good idea at the university, but her luck held. "In."

They needed no encouragement, quickly nestling in their blankets.

Snowplows swept away enough of the accumulation so people could drive and park at the Clam. Best to go slow.

Harry, arriving forty-five minutes early, parked close to the main entrance. She'd picked up a *Cavalier Daily*, the student newspaper, on her walk. She cut the lights but kept the motor running for heat. She thought she'd use some of the time to read and to try and organize her errands for the weekend.

She opened the paper and saw a half-page ad from H. H. Donaldson that read, "Trash the Terrapins." Tonight's opponent was Maryland. Two pages later a quarter-page ad showing a turtle, hands up, surrendering to a Cavalier, sword at his throat, had been purchased by Matthew Crickenberger.

Incidentally, or not so incidentally, an article ran in the paper about the bidding war for the sports complex, how and why, according to the writer, Crickenberger won the prize. In one word: experience.

The other firms barely garnered a mention, but

Donaldson versus Crickenberger held the reader's interest. Harry thought she learned more from this article than from the terse report in Charlottesville's *The Daily Progress*.

Although she liked H.H., she had to agree with the writer that Matthew did have more experience with these massive, highly technical projects. Despite H.H.'s competitive bid, his lack of experience at this level would probably have run up the bill. Matthew prided himself on bringing in projects on time and on budget. A project like a new arena would take a year to build and in that year the price of materials could rise. He tried to fold that into the bid as well as weather delays. It didn't hurt, either, that he'd helped to build the Clam originally, back when he was a grunt.

Matthew believed a lowball bid to win the project would only bring misery to all parties if something went wrong. It usually did and time is money. Every delay costs. As a young man working for other people he'd seen men come to blows over escalating costs. He'd seen banks call in loans, ruining people.

H.H., less prudent, relied on a bit of luck. Lady Luck did take a shine to him. This did not always endear him to others.

Harry finished the paper just as Fair rapped on the window. She smiled, folded the paper, fluffed up the blankets for the "kids," then cut the motor.

"Hey." She hugged him as she stepped outside. "I'm surprised so many people showed up."

"UVA b-ball." He smiled as he appreciated the dedicated fans.

As they headed toward the main entrance, tickets in hand, friends and neighbors also streamed toward the glass doors. Miranda, wrapped in a long fuchsia alpaca coat, stood out against the snow. They caught up with her.

Little Mim and Blair waved as did Big Mim and Jim. The Crickenbergers were there in force. Herb was there with Charlotte, the church secretary, her teenage son in tow.

Tracy was waiting at the doors for Miranda. Fred Forrest brushed by him without a word. In fact, he wasn't talking to anyone. He didn't even acknowledge his assistant, Mychelle, out that night with a bunch of girlfriends. He pushed through the crowd making one student bump into the wall fire extinguisher. "In Case of Fire: Break Glass." The student, irritated, pretended to rap the back of Fred's head with the small hammer on a chain. Fred, oblivious, kept pushing people out of his way.

Harry noticed Tazio Chappars with a man she didn't recognize. The architect didn't seem especially interested in women's basketball so Harry wondered why she was here. Perhaps to please the nice-looking fellow with her, or maybe the pressure had become too great and she decided to root for the home team along with everyone else.

What surprised everyone was the sight of H.H. escorting his wife and daughter as though nothing had happened. When everyone took their seats, Little Mim glanced down at Susan as if to say, "I'll tell you later."

Susan, of course, leaned down immediately to relay this to Harry. BoomBoom rushed in late and Harry remembered that Fair said he'd take them both out after the game.

"Oh well," she thought to herself. "Maybe I'll learn something."

The usual array of Virginia baseball caps, pennants, and Styrofoam swords were in evidence along with coolers small enough to fit under the seats. They contained beer and stronger spirits and were certainly not encouraged by the school administration. But most folks didn't bother with a cooler, they just slipped a flask in their pocket.

The businessmen, Matthew in particular, handed out drinks. His cooler was jammed with goodies. People, usually buoyant at these contests, often remembered later. Business could be won through such small gestures.

Fred Forrest, five rows behind Matthew, was out of the mix due to his location. After his behavior, he would have been out anyway.

Tracy and Josef traveled around the Atlantic Coast Conference to officiate. Both men enjoyed just watching a game but also watching other men officiate. Refereeing was a thankless job, but no sport could really operate without unbiased officiating.

The game, unlike the Clemson one, was rather tedious. Virginia dominated Maryland. At one point after a brief discussion with Andrew Argenbright, one of Coach Ryan's assistants, the coach took most of her first-string players off the court and put in underclassmen. Experience gained on the court during battle is worth a great deal to an emerging player.

At one point, sophomore Latitia Hall, sister of senior center Mandy Hall, and hopefully a future star, lobbed one from the middle of the court in a perfect arc which dropped through the rim, barely shaking the net.

The crowd stood up and cheered. People blew their noisemakers, waved their Styrofoam swords, their blue and orange pennants. Harry felt a cold breeze whizz near her left ear. She turned around to see who blew a noisemaker close to her, but everyone behind her was hollering or puffing on noisemakers.

As the game ended and people filed out, Little Mim climbed over a row to reach Susan. Blair joined Harry, Fair, and BoomBoom. Harry waved to Miranda and Tracy on the opposite side of the court. They returned the wave.

By the time the group of friends had reached the parking lot, Susan had the latest on the H.H. drama.

The cats and dog, noses pressed against the driver's side window, couldn't wait for Harry. Herb passed them and rapped his fingers on the window.

*"Guess he still doesn't know."* Pewter put both her paws on the window as a greeting to the pastor.

*"Maybe he's gotten over it,"* Tucker thought out loud.

*"No way."* Pewter smiled big as Herb smiled back and then headed toward his old car, on its fourth set of tires. He'd need new tires soon or a new car.

*"He'll find out before the first Sunday in February. He needs them for communion."*

*"Maybe not, Murphy. Maybe he has an extra stash in the church itself. Bet Elocution and Cazenovia don't get in there very often, because Elo eats the flowers on the altar,"* Pewter said.

*"That's true."* Mrs. Murphy laughed. *"But if those two wanted to get into the church I bet they'd find a way. They're pretty smart."*

Fred stomped by them.

*"What an old grouch,"* Tucker noted.

*"Humans get the lives they deserve."* Pewter then quickly added, because she knew there'd be an uproar, *"Short of war or famine or stuff like that."*

Before the last word was out of her mouth, H.H., shepherding Anne and Cameron, was three vehicles away. He jerked his head up, sweat poured down his face, his eyes rolled back in his head, and his knees collapsed. He dropped down in a heap.

Anne knelt down. Then she screamed for help.

Tucker noticed Fred turn. He saw who it was and hesitated for a moment. With reluctance he walked over to Anne.

"Help me!"

"Daddy, Daddy, wake up!" Cameron was on her knees shaking her father.

Harry, Fair, Susan, and Ned heard the commotion. Susan's daughter, Brooks, was with her friends, behind her parents. Matthew and Sandy, his wife, sprinted toward the fallen man. From the other side of the parked cars, Tracy hurried up.

Fair bent over, took H.H.'s pulse. None.

"Matt, help me get his coat off."

Matthew and Fair stripped the heavy winter coat off H.H., Fair straddled him and pressed hard on his heart. He kept at it, willing H.H.'s heart to beat, but it wouldn't.

Tracy looked gravely at Jim, who'd just reached them. He already had his cell phone out.

"Ambulance to U-Hall. Second row from the main entrance. Hurry!" Jim called the rescue unit closest to the university. As mayor of Crozet, he knew everybody in an official capacity.

The ambulance was there within five minutes.

Fair, sweat rolling off him, kept working on H.H.'s chest. He stood up when the rescue team arrived.

Little Mim had the presence of mind to wrap her arms around Anne because she didn't know exactly what the woman would do. Big Mim held Cameron.

They all watched in complete dismay as John Tabachka, head of the ambulance squad, quietly said, "He's gone."

Herb knelt down, placing his hand on H.H.'s head. "Depart in peace, thou ransomed soul. May God the Father Almighty, Who created thee; and Jesus Christ, the Son of the Living God, Who redeemed thee; and the Holy Ghost, Who sanctified thee, preserve thy going out and thy coming in, from this time forth, even forevermore. Amen."

"Amen." Everyone bowed their heads.

*"Amen,"* the animals said.

6

Fair and Ned Tucker accompanied the corpse to the morgue. Ned, as the family lawyer, wished to spare Anne further distress. Fair thought Ned might need some bolstering.

Little Mim and Susan Tucker took Anne and Cameron to their home in the Ednam subdivision just west of the Clam on Route 250.

Each person, after ascertaining if they could do anything, finally went home.

A subdued Harry flipped on the light in the kitchen. She made a cup of cocoa, feeding her pets treats as she sipped. She felt miserable.

Ned felt miserable, too. He'd never witnessed an autopsy. Fair had. All living creatures fascinated him, how they functioned, how they were put together. He often thought that an autopsy was a way to honor life. How could anyone view a horse's heart or a cat's musculature without marveling at the beauty of it? Any chance he had to learn, he seized. The human animal was complex in some ways and quite simple in others. For instance, humans had simple dentition. Sharks, by contrast, had a mouthful of really complicated teeth.

Tom Yancy, the coroner, had been called by John Tabachka and had everything ready. Anne had insisted on an immediate autopsy. Grief stricken and shocked as she was, she wanted to know exactly how her young husband had died.

Yancy for his part was only too happy to comply. By the time he got to a body it had usually been in the cooler or worse.

Even laid out on the gleaming stainless steel table, H.H. was a handsome man, a man in seemingly good physical condition.

Yancy knew him, of course, but not well. Tom Yancy and Marshall Wells, the assistant coroner, often knew many of the corpses they examined.

"Ned, stand back." Yancy looked up at him as he pulled on his rubber gloves. "If you faint I don't want you falling on the body. Occasionally, organs will, uh, be under pressure. They may somewhat pop out, the brain especially. It sounds grotesque but it really isn't. After all, the inside of the body is experiencing light and air for the first time. If you can't take it, leave the room."

"I will." Ned felt nervous. He didn't want to disgrace himself, but he wasn't sure he would be up to the process.

Yancy's blue eyes met Fair's. "Put on a coat, will you? Just in case I need you."

Fair lifted a doctor's white coat off the peg against the door. He, too, put on thin latex gloves.

"All right, gentlemen, let us closely inspect the outside

before we get to the inside." Yancy measured H.H. "Here." He handed Ned a clipboard, thinking having a task would help the lawyer. "Height, six feet one-half inch. Race, Caucasian. Weight, one hundred and eighty-five pounds. Age, I'd say between thirty-three and thirty-six. Of course, I know he is thirty-six because I knew H.H. and we have his driver's license, but you can still tell age by teeth. Not as well as we once could thanks to advances in dentistry, but they wear down." He opened H.H.'s mouth, pointing to the slight irregularity on the surface of those molars not capped. "Fillings can help us. Silver fillings have a shorter life span than gold."

"Remember Nicky Weems with his gold front tooth?" Fair recalled a man, old when Fair was a teenager, who flashed a gold grin.

"Used a lot before World War Two. Expensive but prized. It's still good stuff. Now, dentists, the advanced ones, use ceramics, and who knows what they'll come up with next? The stuff doesn't even discolor."

All the while he was talking, Yancy carefully felt over the body. "His temperature has dropped a few degrees."

"When does a body go into rigor mortis?" Ned was becoming interested. He was beginning to realize one could read a body like a book.

Of course, it's better to read it while it's still alive.

"Depends. On a blistering hot August day a corpse can go through the stages of death, light death, if you will, to advanced death, in a matter of hours. Putrefaction can begin rapidly especially on battlefields where the temperatures can be over one hundred degrees because of the guns. Gettysburg was a real mess, I can tell you. July." He shook his head. "And the little muscles go into rigor first. But on a temperate day, say sixty degrees to seventy, a corpse exposed to the elements, no rain, will begin to stiffen in two to three hours. Unless"—he held up his hand—"a person has ingested strychnine. By the time they are finished with their convulsions, which are so severe all the ATP in the muscles is depleted, they're in rigor. It's a horrible, horrible way to die. That and rabies. ATP is a molecule that releases energy for muscle contraction. When it's used up, so are you."

Yancy returned to H.H.'s head. He brushed back the nice-looking man's straight hair, cut in the old Princeton style. He checked his eyes, nose, ears.

Then he felt at the base of his neck, running his fingers upward to the ears. Fair, standing just a step to the left of him, squinted for a moment. Yancy, too, stopped.

"What's this?"

Fair bent over. "Looks like a hornet sting without the swelling."

The door opened. Kyle Rogers, the photographer, stepped in. "Sorry. I got here as soon as I could. The roads are okay, but—" He realized Yancy was intent so he shut up.

As Kyle removed his coat, taking his camera out of his trusty carry bag, even Ned was drawn closer to the body.

Ned kept telling himself that this was no longer H.H. H.H.'s soul had gone to its reward. The toned body on the slab before him was a husk. But while H.H. had bid goodbye to that husk, it was hard for his friends to do so.

"Kyle, get a close-up of this right now." A note of urgency crept into Yancy's voice.

Kyle, all of twenty-five, quietly snapped away.

Yancy glanced over at Fair as he reached onto his tray of implements, what he called his "tool kit." He pulled out a calibrated probe so fine it was thinner than a needle. He leaned down and expertly inserted this into what looked like the sting. "Penetration, an inch and a quarter." He pulled out the probe. "No bleeding."

"No discoloration," Fair said in a low voice. "It's as though he were hit with a microdart."

"Yes." Yancy drew out the word.

"I was in the row behind him. If he'd been hit with a dart I would have noticed." Fair thought a moment. "I hope I would have noticed."

"Odd, how every scene is different when you try to reconstruct it in your mind. The most commonplace object takes on new significance." Yancy plucked up his scalpel. "All right." He cut a Y, with the top of the Y looking like a large necklace, the bottom going directly to the pubic bone.

Ned gulped.

"The first cut is the hardest." Fair's voice had a steady reassuring quality.

Kyle worked quietly.

Ned blinked and as Yancy began removing and weighing organs he got ahold of himself. The science of it took over and H.H. as a person began to recede from view.

After weighing the heart, Yancy expertly opened the stilled pump. He pointed to Fair, and Ned even came over to look. "See the scarring?"

"Ah," Ned exclaimed because he could see tiny, tiny scars, tissue different from the striations around it.

"Cocaine. I'll know from the blood tests if he used any within forty-eight hours."

"I think that part of H.H.'s life is long past." Fair defended H.H., who had enjoyed a wild youth.

"That's just it. It's never truly over because everything you do leaves its mark on the body."

"So *The Portrait of Dorian Gray* is the truth?" Ned held the clipboard tightly.

"In a fashion, yes." Yancy intently studied the heart. "Left ventricle contracted. M-m-m, right ventricle normal."

"He died of a heart attack?" Ned was furiously writing on the clipboard.

"Ultimately we all die when our hearts stop beating. No, I wouldn't say he died of a heart attack. It's just that the left ventricle is not relaxed. Something..." Yancy's voice trailed off as he studied the stilled heart, blood seeping through the ventricles. He snipped tissue samples from the heart as well as the other organs. Intent, Yancy was in a world of his own, not conversing again until he was sewing up the body.

As Yancy and Fair washed up, Ned took a last look at H.H., a sheet covering him, as he was rolled into the cooler. H.H.'s body would soon be prepared for its last journey.

"Kyle, get those photographs on Sheriff Shaw's desk as fast as you can."

"Yes, sir." Kyle packed up his gear and left.

The coroner folded his arms across his chest. "Gentlemen, H. H. Donaldson did not die a natural death. The blood work will certainly help me pinpoint what was used to kill him because I can't tell from this exam what poison was used."

"Poisoned?" Ned gasped.

"Absolutely." He hung up his lab coat. "One looks for the classic symptoms, like the odor of bitter almonds for arsenic. Certain types of internal bleeding, the condition of the gums." He paused. "None of those changes are present in H.H.'s body, except the abnormality in his left ventricle. I'm willing to bet you the poison was delivered by whatever pierced his neck but—" He held up his hands.

"My God." Fair shook his head. "I can't believe it."

"Well, I'm sure he had enemies. A man can't go through

life without gathering them, and if a man doesn't have a few enemies, then I really don't trust him. Know what I mean?"

"An enemy is one thing. An enemy who kills you is quite another." Ned's jaw set.

"We'd better go to Anne." Fair dropped his eyes to the floor then looked up at the ceiling. He hated this.

Yancy put his hand on Fair's big forearm. "Simply tell her there are irregularities. Wait until—". He stopped mid-sentence, walked to the phone in the lab, and dialed the Sheriff's Department.

"Coop, is Rick there?"

"No." The young deputy, usually a regular at basketball games, answered. She'd pulled extra duty thanks to the weather.

"Can you come over here a minute?" He explained why.

As the Sheriff's Department wasn't far from the coroner's office, Coop managed to get there despite the snow within twenty minutes.

Yancy rolled H.H. out of the cooler and pulled off the sheet. Wordlessly he pointed to the mark on his neck. "Kyle will have the photos on Rick's desk in an hour or however fast he can work. I'll have my report faxed over within the hour, minus all the lab work, obviously. Deputy, I believe he was murdered."

She exhaled. Cynthia Cooper, a tall, good-looking blonde, could make decisions swiftly. She pulled out her cell phone.

"Sheriff, I'm sorry to disturb you at home. I'm going to seal off the Clam. I need as many people as we can round up."

After speaking to Rick, whom she genuinely admired, she walked back and inspected the mark one more time. "Yancy, how soon before the blood work comes back?"

"I'll put a rush on it, but you never know. Normally it takes three to four weeks. Like I said, I'll beg for promptness."

"I was at the game," Fair said. "I can show you where H.H. sat, where he fell."

"Me, too," Ned volunteered.

"Good." She smiled tightly. "It's going to be a long night."

"I'm used to it," Fair replied.

Ned halted a moment as they opened the door. "What about Anne?"

Cooper turned to Yancy. "Will you call the Donaldson house? I'm sure someone is with her."

"Little Mim and my wife," Ned said.

"Well, one of them will probably answer the phone." Cooper weighed her words. "Just tell Little Mim or Susan that Anne can go ahead with funeral plans. Don't tell them more than that. Not even your wife. Rick will talk to Anne tomorrow."

"If you cordon off the Clam people will know something's not right," Ned sensibly observed.

"That's true, but it's eleven-thirty now. How many people are going to be out tonight? And if they are, they won't know what we're doing. We've got a little window of time. Let's use it."

# 7

The phone felt clammy in Susan's hand as her husband informed her Anne could go ahead with funeral plans. She and Ned had been married nineteen years. She knew Ned inside out. She wasn't getting the whole story or even half the story and she knew it.

She hung up the wall phone in Anne's high-tech kitchen. Anne and Little Mim sat at the table. Cameron had finally gone to bed. The adults were thankful the child could sleep.

"Anne, you can make arrangements." Susan's voice sounded strangled to her.

"Tomorrow." Little Mim, not the warmest person, genuinely wanted to spare Anne further distress.

"Yes." Anne's nostrils flared, she blinked. "It doesn't seem real."

"No, it doesn't," Little Mim agreed.

"Let me fix you some Plantation Mint tea, a big teaspoon

of honey, and a pinch of whiskey. It's very soothing." Susan turned on the stove. "What about you, Marilyn?"

Little Mim nodded. "Yes."

"I guess there are women crying all over the county," Anne quietly said.

Little Mim and Susan looked at each other.

"Tea will be ready in a minute."

"You thought I didn't know." Anne shrugged. "I knew. I just didn't always know who or where. After a while I didn't really care." She grasped the table's edge with both hands. "And that's that."

"This is a terrible shock." Little Mim rose to help Susan with the tea. "Think about the good times."

"I will. Every time I walk into my little greenhouse H.H. built for me, I smile."

Anne was a professor of landscape architecture at the University of Virginia's famous architecture department. Her breadth of knowledge was impressive for she had minored in chemistry. Plants represented whole worlds to her from their carbon chain all the way to their utilization in recreations of eighteenth-century gardens.

The three women drank their tea.

"Honey, do you think you can sleep?" Susan refilled Anne's cup.

"If I drink this second cup, yes." Anne smiled wanly.

"Good. I'll stay here tonight," Little Mim announced.

"I'd feel better if you did." Anne placed the cup in the gold-rimmed saucer.

"Me, too," Susan volunteered. "Tomorrow will be overwhelming as people start to pour in. You rest. Little Mim and I can take care of things."

"But I must arrange the funeral. And Cameron." Anne's lower lip quivered.

"It might be best if Cameron could stay at a friend's house. Someone she could play with and talk to," Susan advised.

"Yes. Once my mother and mother-in-law arrive the drama will intensify." Anne stood up, picked up her cup and saucer, taking them to the sink. "Polly Bance's youngest is Cameron's age."

"I'll call Polly first thing in the morning." Little Mim reached for Susan's cup.

Anne leaned against the sink then turned around. "Guest room on this level. Another upstairs."

"Don't worry about us."

"You're good to do this for me."

"Anne, you'd do it for either of us," Susan replied.

Anne blinked, the tears came and the two friends hugged her, crying themselves.

# 8

"Murder." The word escaped Harry's lips in a cloud of breath. She dropped the flake of hay she was tossing into Tomahawk's stall, bent over to pick it up.

Pewter, warming herself in the tack room, called out to Mrs. Murphy up in the hayloft. *"What did she say?"*

*"Murder. H. H. Donaldson was murdered."* Mrs. Murphy hung her head down over the center aisle. *"Come out here and you'll hear better."*

Tucker, at Harry's heels, walked back to the animal door located at the bottom center of the tack room door, a wooden door with a glass window on top. A screen door, inside that, was open inside the tack room. In summer the process was reversed.

The dog cocked her head, her large ears catching the sounds of Pewter jumping off a folded horse blanket.

Just as the gray cat poked through the animal door, Tucker grabbed her by the back of the neck. *"Gotcha!"*

Pewter rolled over on her back, grasping the dog's face with all four sets of claws. *"You think."*

Susan, who had just walked into the barn a moment ago, stepped over the rolling ball of fur, cat and dog. "It's one nonstop party with those two."

Susan, having left the Donaldson house this morning, Anne securely in the care of her mother and sister, received a phone call from Little Mim at eight this morning. Sheriff Rick Shaw had just paid a visit, and Little Mim called the second he was out her door.

"I came straight over. Actually I would have stayed on with Anne but Marcia Dudley"—she named Anne's mother—"took over. In no uncertain terms. She's a perfect ass. I don't know how Anne can stand her."

"Susan, the phone would have been faster." Harry was digesting the information.

"I wanted to see you. I always feel better if I'm with you." Susan held up her hands helplessly.

"Come on."

"Where?"

"We're going to the Clam."

"Ned and Fair were there until four in the morning along with the entire Sheriff's Department. I haven't even seen Ned. He called on the cell phone. He said he's going to bed. I said I was driving over to you. Poor Fair had a morning call, too." Susan paused. "A vet's life."

"Yes, it's his weekend to be on call." Harry quickly tidied up the barn. She'd fed everyone at the crack of dawn, as was her routine, and her horses—Tomahawk, Gin Fizz, and Poptart, her youngest—were turned out. Although a crisp, cold day, it would probably warm into the low forties. The horses stayed out in the light and would be brought back at sunset.

She liked to have their stalls cleaned, water buckets scrubbed and refilled, their rations of hay in the stalls, crimped oats in their feeders. She fed half their rations in the morning and half in the evening.

Susan had walked in just as Harry finished filling the water buckets.

"We'll never get into the Clam," Susan predicted.

"You have no faith. Come on." Harry flung open the barn doors, the sunlight on the snow, brilliant.

*"Hurry,"* Pewter and Tucker called up to Mrs. Murphy, climbing headfirst down the ladder.

As Harry started to close the door, Mrs. Murphy hit the center aisle. *"Wait for me."*

Harry, hearing her cat, held the door open a crack as the tiger cat scooted through. Then she closed it.

"Your car or my truck?"

"We'll fit better in the station wagon." Susan lifted up the hatch for the three animals to jump in.

Although the temperature was climbing, now up to thirty-eight degrees Fahrenheit, the road remained treacherous because of the patches of black ice, the worst because you couldn't see it. A trip that would normally take twenty minutes on a good day took forty-five minutes today.

Finally they turned into the parking lot. Yellow tape still cordoned off where H.H. had fallen, but no tape barred the doors into the structure.

The sheriff's squad car along with other cars were parked at the back entrance by the large Dumpster.

Once inside the building, they didn't hit more yellow tape until reaching the basketball court. The doors were shut.

"Damn," Susan said.

"Faith." Harry circled around the court, checking every door at the main level. Then she herded everyone up the stairs to the next level for another door check. She found one that wasn't locked. Quietly they slipped inside.

Rick was seated below at the timekeeper's table, alone.

A door closed and Harry caught a glimpse of a uniformed person carrying a small carton.

Boldly, she walked down the steps to the floor. Susan followed. The cats slunk down and Tucker, too, crept close to the steps.

*"When we get to the floor, check every row,"* Mrs. Murphy ordered. *"Check out everything."*

The seats were built along solid rows and unlike a high school football stadium there was no walking under the stands.

*"Where does Mom sit?"* Tucker asked.

*"I don't know but let's start sweeping. She might show us."*

"Harry and Susan, what in the hell are you doing here?" Rick, a study in irritation, looked up from the timetable of events in front of him.

"I thought we could help. H.H. sat in front of me."

"I know that. Fair was here. And your husband, too, as you well know."

"Yes, sir," Susan sheepishly replied.

"You're tired. Want me to get you some coffee?" Harry had that solicitous tone to her voice.

"If I drink any more coffee, you'll peel me off the scoreboard." He rose as the women walked to the table. "Go on, get out of here."

"Well, let me go to my seat. Susan, too. Maybe it will help."

Not awaiting a reply, she bounded up the steps. Susan stayed riveted to the spot.

*"Good."* Mrs. Murphy trotted toward Harry, who sat down.

"H.H. sat right there."

"I know that, goddammit!" He saw Tucker, then spied the cats, all working their way toward Harry but on different rows. "Not them. Thank God, we've already combed this place. You'd pollute the site. Do you know that? You could destroy valuable evidence."

"But I haven't and their senses are sharper than ours. Who knows what they'll find?"

"I can hardly wait to put them on the county payroll." His voice dripped sarcasm, but he didn't blow up. In the past, Harry's two cats and the corgi had sometimes turned up clues or even body parts. It was quite strange.

Susan, in an effort to deflect his wrath, murmured, "You must be very tired. We hoped we might be able to help because at least we got a good night's sleep."

He sat down again, defeated. "All right. Harry, come down here. Since you're here, I might as well make use of you."

Gleefully, she returned to Rick, whose badge reflected the light. "Yes, sir."

"Sit down."

Both Harry and Susan sat in the folding metal chairs at the table.

"Tell me what you saw."

Each woman succinctly described H.H.'s death as they saw it. He was in the parking lot, he stared up at the sky, jerked his head straight up, then dropped.

"Anything unusual during the game?"

They both shook their heads.

"All right." He held up his hand. "Now think. Who disliked H.H.?"

"Fred Forrest. He got ugly after the Clemson game. Yelled at H.H."

"Uh-huh." Rick had had this described to him by Fair. "What about a consistent enemy?"

Both women shrugged.

"You mean like someone who got mad over a building? A disgruntled client?"

"Yeah, or what about someone next to the building? You know when he put in that shopping center up on 29 North they were all screaming and hollering." He rubbed his eyes.

"I don't know any of those people, the ones in the subdivision now next to the shopping center," Harry replied.

"Well, I hate to mention this" Susan's voice was low, conspiratorial—"but he left Anne the day before the game, yet they were back together at the game. Maybe the woman, whom we don't know—"

Harry interrupted, something she rarely did. "Oh, I bet we know her all right, we just don't know her identity at this moment."

"Right. Well, what if she killed him? The girlfriend?" Susan finished her thought.

"Uh-huh." Rick listened noncommittally. "Seems there was a string of girlfriends over the years."

Harry's dark eyebrows shot upward. "Hell hath no fury like a woman scorned. Maybe the girlfriend flew into a rage because he backed out."

Rick put his elbow on the table, resting his forehead on his hand. "Now look, you two, we have swept up every crumb, every piece of paper, every sticky gob of bubble gum. I am tired. I appreciate your help, but—and I mean you, Harry, because you're the worst—spare me your interference." Harry started to protest. He held up his left hand. "If H.H. has been murdered, and I won't commit to that until I have those lab sheets, but if he has been murdered, then whoever did this is walking around out there. Whoever it is is an incredibly intelligent person. This was not a crime of passion although passion may have inspired it. This was methodical, well thought out, ingenious, and committed in front of about six hundred people. And no one saw a goddamned thing."

"Or we saw it and didn't know we saw it," Harry, with no intention of obeying the sheriff, replied. She wasn't going to openly cross him but, after all, H.H. had been smack in front of her, one seat to the right. Her natural curiosity was as aroused as her ego. How dare the murderer? "Will you tell us what killed H.H. when you get the lab report?" Harry pushed her luck.

"Don't put your nose into it. Now will you pick up Mrs. Murphy, Pewter, and Tucker and leave me in peace?" he grumbled, his voice low.

"Yes, sir." Harry whistled.

The three walked toward her from their various places, Mrs. Murphy bounding over the seats.

Rick looked down at the three animals, coats shining, in perfect health. "Keep her out of trouble."

*"We will,"* came the chorus, which made him laugh.

He needed a laugh.

As they walked around the outside corridor, Mrs. Murphy complained, *"Nada."*

*"Old food, old smells."* Tucker had so hoped she'd find something.

"*I didn't find anything except a little trickle of water on the top row. Guess the roof leaks a tiny bit,*" Pewter said.

"*Are you sure it was water?*" Mrs. Murphy's whiskers swept forward.

"*I'm sure. Like I said, I didn't find anything.*"

# 9

"Harry, I am not driving you up there." Susan shut the door to her station wagon with great determination.

"Oh come on, Susan, we're halfway there. If you take me home in a snit, then I've got to drive all the way back up 29." She mentioned Route 29 simply by its number.

"I knew I shouldn't have gone into the Clam with you. Now Sheriff Shaw is half-pissed at me and Ned will hear about it. I don't much feature a lecture from him." She sighed.

Ned Tucker, a good and gentle man, would not be thrilled with the news that his wife was meddling.

The animals, in the back, kept quiet. No reason to further irritate Susan.

"Don't you have any shopping to do?"

"Harry, that is so transparent. It isn't worthy of you."

As Susan drove out of the parking lot, Harry sullenly stared out the window.

"Groceries. You always need groceries. There's that expensive delicatessen up there. Expensive coffees. Fresh rutabaga."

"Rutabaga?"

Harry laughed. "Just wanted to see if you were listening."

Susan turned left onto Route 29. "I hate you, Harry. You get me to do things I would never do."

"That's what friends are for."

"Great, then you come home with me and let Ned tear you a new one."

"What a pretty way to talk." Harry smiled, her spirits restored.

"It's the truth. He doesn't get mad very often but when he does, watch out."

"All the more reason not to go home right now." Harry paused. "Ever notice how when you're wiped out you get these weird energy surges, and then there are times when your mind just goes blank? Zero. Clean slate."

"Mine does that on a daily basis," Susan mused. "Children will do that to you." She considered her statement. "It's not so much the big problems, you know, 'Mom, I wrecked the car.' It's the constant interruptions, although I must say with Dan at Cornell I have only one interrupter who interrupts less as she gets older. I don't remember my mother working as hard as I do teaching children good manners."

"It was good to see Danny over Christmas vacation. College is good for him."

Danny, a smart boy, was excelling at Cornell University, but he found upstate New York a lot colder than Virginia.

"He's a man now, although it's hard for me to see that. I mean intellectually I know it but emotionally I think he's my little boy and I am determined, determined not to be one of those mothers who won't let go."

"You'll be cool."

"If you're going to have children you'd better do it soon."

"It just happens. I'm not planning anything."

"That doesn't sound like you. That sounds almost, almost irresponsible."

"Oh, Susan, you know what I mean. Like you don't want to be one of those mothers who cling, I don't want to be one of those women who start blathering about the clock ticking. If I have a child, I do, and if I don't, I don't. Not to change the subject, but do you have any idea who might have wanted to see H. H. Donaldson dead?"

"Sneak."

"What?"

"You just can't stand to talk about anything personal, can you?"

"I just did." Harry's voice rose. "I told you exactly what I thought about having children but what I didn't tell you is I think you are a wonderful mother and I wouldn't be half as good a mother as you are."

"Why, thank you."

"Susan, who hated H.H.?"

"I told Rick what I thought."

"Kind of. But we don't burden the sheriff with idle gossip or unsubstantiated ideas. However, we can happily burden each other with them. So?" Harry wasn't exactly deluding herself but she wasn't accurate, either. She did discuss half-baked ideas with the sheriff.

Susan shrugged. "I can't think of anyone. Can you?"

"If we retraced his movements over the last few days maybe we'd figure it out."

"I am not spending my Saturday retracing H. H. Donaldson's—Damn, I missed the turn."

"Go up one light and turn left and come around."

"They didn't put in a very good turn lane, did they?" Susan griped.

"Not if you aren't looking for it. I try to avoid coming up 29 so I missed it, too."

Susan finally drove into the shopping center, a very attractive one built as a U, with a supermarket anchoring one end of the U and a big discount store anchoring the other. Smaller specialty shops were in between these large stores.

Businesses were in operation although the discount store was not quite completed. A large sign was in place with a banner underneath counting the days until it would open. Eleven days.

Harry tapped the window of the tailgate. "I won't be very long."

"*Okay.*" The cats settled down for a snooze. Tucker watched Harry's every move.

"I didn't realize how big this was." Susan swept her eyes over the New Gate shopping center, painted muted shades of gray with splashes of red. "H.H. probably could have moved up to a bigger structure like the new stadium."

"This is pretty straightforward stuff. I'd like to think he could but Matthew's been around a long time. Even as a grunt Matthew worked on commercial or state projects like the Clam. He says the trick is not just finding the right subcontractors or whatever, he says it's the bidding. That's where you make it or break it. I'm learning a lot working with him on the Parish Guild."

"I learned a lot on the guild, period. What I learned is that 'consensus' is a magic word. Sounds so good. So hard to get. And why does everyone have to agree anyway?"

"Well, at least we've solved the recarpeting crisis."

"Hallelujah."

"Save that for church." Harry peered in the window of the discount store. "Huge."

"Gargantuan. You don't notice it from the parking lot but it goes straight back."

"I guess they'll stack up a lot of toilet paper." Harry laughed. "I know I can save money shopping at these behemoths, but I can't stand it. I get disoriented. And there's so much to buy I wind up straying off my list. 'Oh, that looks good.' The next thing I know I'm standing in line and the bill is four hundred ninety-nine dollars."

"Not five hundred?"

"Haven't you ever noticed that in the discount stores everything always comes to ninety-nine?"

Susan laughed. "I guess. Well, what are you looking for?"

"I don't know. Wanted to see what H.H. was building. Hey, that's Rob." She saw Rob Collier who delivered mail to the post office on weekdays. She waved.

He saw her, walked over to the front door and unlocked it. "Harry. Hello, Susan. Come on in."

"What are you doing here?"

"Working on Saturdays and Sundays. They're paying time and a half. I figured I'd better make hay while the sun shines." He slipped a screwdriver back into his tool belt. "Well, what do you think?"

"It's so well lit."

"Just putting on the finishing touches. I'm building shelves. This place will open its doors right on schedule despite everything. Poor guy. Keeling over of a heart attack like that. He's two years younger than I am. Makes you think." Rob shook his head.

"Yes, it does," Susan said.

"Rob, was H.H. a good contractor?"

Rob nodded. "No cutting corners. Do it right the first time. No bull. He talked to everyone straight. Kept his cool, too. That creep—if you weren't ladies I'd say something worse—Fred Forrest would come by every single day or he'd send his assistant. Fred's got a hair across his ass." Rob again shook his head, lowered his voice. "In fact she's here now."

"What would they fuss over?"

"Oh, Harry, you wouldn't believe it. That SOB would whip out his ruler, unfold it, and check stupid stuff like the gap between the doorjamb and the door. Anything. Fred lives to find fault and he couldn't find much. That's why H.H. would push everyone, 'Do it right the first time.'"

Raised voices in the background drew their attention.

A young African-American woman, late twenties, wearing a hard hat, armed with a clipboard, strode out the door, Peter Gianakos in hot pursuit. He was soon back in the building.

He focused on Rob before focusing on the two women. "Bitch." He then saw, really saw, Harry and Susan. "I'm sorry, ladies. I'm a little hot under the collar."

"What's the problem?"

"Mychelle Burns has decided that our handicapped access to the men's bathroom is one degree off in grade. First of all, it's not. Secondly, to shave a degree off costs time and money. Do you know what a handicapped access costs us? That one you see out there on the sidewalk is eight thousand dollars." Peter let his arms flop against his sides.

"Why so much?" Susan was curious.

"It could be even more if it were a switchback but this one we could put in right off the curb. It cost so much because you have to taper the sides. You can't have ninety-degree sides. Let me tell you, concrete work ain't cheap. And the guardrails are heavy pipe. The stuff could hold back an elephant."

"I had no idea."

"No one does, ma'am. Not until they have to build something the public will use. It's bad enough just building a house."

"What are you going to do?" Harry felt bad for Peter.

"The first thing I'm going to do is count to ten. Next, I'm bringing in the laser measurer and I am ninety-nine percent sure that grade will be perfect. Code perfect. Then I will call Fred Forrest and ask him to come out and use the laser measurer." His voice was acidic. "If the high-and-mighty Fred doesn't want to come by, I guess I'll let Mychelle use it. Christ, she's a chip off the old block. And since neither one of them can even hammer a nail, I will hold my tongue although even an idiot can use a laser measurer."

"Peter," a man called from the back.

"Sorry to dump on you. Harry, Susan, it's good to see you."

"Give my regards to your wife," Susan said as he left.

Harry waited a beat then whispered to Rob, "Maybe Mychelle wants a payoff?"

Rob frowned. "Well, I'm here on the weekends and at night. I don't think that's going on. I could be wrong. I think Fred's drunk on power. She's a carbon copy."

As Susan and Harry cruised back down 29, Susan said, "Harry, I wouldn't have thought of under-the-table payoffs."

"I know. You're such a straight arrow."

"So was H.H."

"I think he was." Harry noticed that the snow piled on the side of the road was already grungy. "And I do think Fred is drunk on power. Rob's got him pegged. You see that kind of personality in a lot of professions but especially in government jobs. I should know, I have one."

"Maybe you should bring a whip to the post office."

"They'd get an entirely different idea." Harry laughed.

"Pervert." Susan laughed, too.

# 10

Unless inherited, wealth rarely falls into anyone's lap. People who make lots of money work harder, work longer hours, and almost always love what they do.

Matthew Crickenberger was no exception. His office in downtown Charlottesville was a series of three old town houses built in the 1820s. He'd bought them, renovating the insides while keeping the exteriors untouched.

The middle house boasted a lovely walnut door with a graceful fan over the top, the glass panes handblown. Inside, a small lobby where coats and umbrellas could be hung opened onto a larger reception area with a receptionist in the center. All along the right wall behind glass was a temperature-controlled miniature South American rain forest, imitation Colombian artifacts placed among the plants. One, a carved stone, peeped out of a rippling pool.

Matthew, utilizing Anne Donaldson's botanical skills, had paid over one hundred thousand dollars to create this.

Apart from being a shrewd political move, hiring Anne, the wife of his rival, was also economical. Why bring in an expert from Miami University or elsewhere when Anne could do the job?

Brightly colored birds chattered in the thick canopy of plants, a rich green. Little salamanders and all manner of amazing insects lazed about.

At one time, Matthew purchased a pair of monkeys but they made an infernal racket and were donated to the Washington Zoo.

Hopping in and out of the elongated pond were bright little frogs, some yellow, some green with bands. They feasted on the tiny beetles and ants crawling about.

The rain forest wall never failed to dazzle a first-time visitor. Even those with constant access to Matthew admired the flora and fauna.

Not only was this Matthew's pet project, it was his hobby. He adored researching rain forest habitat and gave generously to those environmental groups trying to save these vital ecological areas.

He had visited Colombia once a year until it became too dangerous. He had sailed on the Amazon, too, but he liked the Colombian rain forests best.

People wondered if he went there to buy cocaine but Matthew appeared to have no interest in drugs. He drank at parties but wasn't much of a drinker.

His brother, Lloyd, had fought with Special Forces in Vietnam. He'd tell his big brother, Matthew, about the magic of the rain forest. Lloyd died at thirty-two of a stroke, way too young.

Matthew always said his hobby kept him close to Lloyd.

From the receptionist's desk one hallway headed into the left building, one into the right.

Matthew's office was at the end of the left hall, a hall lined with prints of macaws, toucans, and other aviary exotica.

His office, door always open, boasted a beautiful ebony Louis XVI desk. The walls were painted a lobster bisque, the woodwork a creamy eggshell. Against one wall stood an antique drafting table. Tazio Chappars leaned over the blueprints with him.

"—here." He pressed his index finger on a second-story window. "If we switch these to revolving windows we can entice fresh air into the structure."

"And additional cost."

"I'll get my guys to research that." He smiled. At least she didn't blast his suggestion. His experience with architects was that most were prima donnas.

She checked the large man's wristwatch she wore. "Oh, dear."

He checked his. "Here. Before I forget." He walked to his desk chair, picked up a small carpet sample and returned, handing it to her. "Tell Herb to give this to Charlotte. She can start thinking about fabrics to re-cover her office chair."

"The cost. The Parish Guild will have another long meeting." Tazio grimaced.

"No they won't. What's the most it can cost? Five yards. She's not going to pick embroidered satin." He inhaled. "A hundred dollars a yard if she goes wild. The most it will cost is five hundred dollars." He held up his hand to quell the protest. "I'll pay for it. I'll bet you she goes down to the Second Yard and finds a nice something for twenty dollars a yard. She deserves it." He crossed his arms over his chest. "I'm thinking about time."

"Pardon?" She noticed his countenance.

"Time. As in my life."

"H.H.?"

"Well, yeah. If it happened to H.H. it can happen to any of us. He took great care of himself and poof." He snapped his fingers. "Gone before forty."

"Pretty shocking." She was thirty-five herself.

"H.H. and I got along just fine, for competitors. He was a good builder. A little outspoken. A little hotheaded but a good builder."

A wave of sadness swept over Tazio's attractive face. "Such a waste. To die so young."

"Shame it couldn't have been Fred Forrest." The corner of his lip curled upward.

She hesitated. She loathed Fred but she didn't want to show it. "You know what I think about Fred?"

"No. Tell me."

"He works too hard at being unlikable."

Matthew blinked, his blue eyes focusing on her. "Perceptive."

"He doesn't want us to know who he really is."

"I never thought of that."

"You've known him for a long time."

"Over forty years. We both started out in construction. In fact, he and I worked on the Barracks Road shopping center the summer we were in junior high school. That ought to tell you how long ago." He smiled, citing a shopping center first built in 1957. "And one day the building inspector at the time, Buelleton Landess—there's a name for you—cussed out Fred. Up one side and down the other. And you know, Fred said, 'If you can't beat 'em, join 'em.' So he did, when he graduated from Lane High School. And he missed the biggest building boom Albemarle County ever had. Could have made a fortune. Fool."

"Hindsight."

"No balls, forgive the expression." Matthew smiled again.

"Well, I'd better head out."

"Nice to see you."

"Same here." She slipped her arm into her navy leather coat lined with sheep's wool, dyed to match. "I'll give Charlotte the carpet sample."

Matthew walked her to the door, wishing he were a younger man.

As Tazio drove away she thought that Matthew was easy to work with—which was a good thing. They'd be working closely together in the future on the new university sports complex.

And she also noted that it didn't seem to have occurred to Matthew that Fred Forrest didn't want people to know him. His nastiness was calculated. But then her observations on life taught her that people of color had to look more closely at white people than white people looked at themselves. Simple survival, really.

# 11

Preparing a sermon vexed Herb even though he'd been doing it all of his adult life. He'd jot down a few notes throughout the week and then each Saturday morning he'd settle into his office at the rectory to pull those notes together. Sometimes he'd work in his study at home but he often found his mind would wander. He'd pull a book off the shelf and hours would pass. He'd learn a great deal about Francis I of France or trout fishing but he hadn't written a word of his sermon.

As it was the second Sunday after Epiphany, he wanted to expand on the theme of discovery, of finding that which you have been seeking.

Cazenovia, her fluffy tail languidly swaying, sat on the desk. She closed her eyes and was soon swaying slightly in rhythm with her tail. Was the tail wagging the cat or the cat the tail?

Elocution slept in front of the fireplace, framed by an old mantel with delicate scrollwork carved on it.

Each morning the cats would cross the small quad from the house to the rectory. Bound by a brick wall three feet high, the complex exuded a peacefulness and a purpose of peace.

Not having to pay a mortgage proved a blessing for Herb. He'd saved from his modest salary and was considering buying a cottage as a retreat for himself. Herb was drawn to the Charleston, South Carolina, area, and he thought when the time came, he'd find something there. Escaping the worst of winter's depredations appealed to him, especially this Saturday afternoon, for the sky was a snarling gray, the temperature dropping back from its high in the mid-forties. He rose from his desk to look out the window toward the northwest. The clouds, much darker in that direction, promised another storm.

"Oh well, at least the cold will kill some of the larvae. We'll suffer fewer bugs come summer."

His rich, resonant voice caused Elocution to open one eye. She closed it again.

He opened the dark blue hymnal on his desk. He'd selected his biblical passages, the ones open to him from the church year readings, organized for centuries. Picking just the right mix of hymns appealed to him and he often wished as he hummed to himself that Miranda Hogendobber were a Lutheran. With that angelic voice the choir would surely improve.

"Yes, this is perfect." He reached over to pet Cazenovia as he sung the first stanza of Hymn 47:

> "O Christ, our true and only Light,
>    Illumine those who sit in night;
> Let those afar now hear Thy voice,
>    And in Thy fold with us rejoice."

He cleared his throat. "Cazzie, that was written in 1630 by Johann Heermann, six stanzas. Isn't it glorious how such gifts come down to us?"

*"True, true,"* Cazzie agreed with him but wished Herb could appreciate the gifts of the cats who'd kept Johann Heermann company.

Many times Cazenovia, Elocution, Mrs. Murphy, Pewter, and Tucker discussed the outrageous self-centeredness of human beings. Good as they might be as individuals, they assumed the world revolved around them, blinded by their arrogance to the extraordinary contributions of other creatures to this life.

Herb hummed some more. For all his nervousness about writing his sermon, he cherished his Saturdays in the rectory. He had it all to himself.

The large square carriage clock on the mantelpiece ticked.

"Two-thirty! How did it get to be two-thirty?"

Just then the wind stirred the bare branches of the majestic walnut tree by his office. The tree looked as if it were dancing, its black arms moving against the backdrop of racing clouds.

*"Fast,"* was all that Cazenovia said.

*"Low pressure. That's why I've been sleepy."* Elocution opened her eyes, stretched fore and aft, and walked over to the window, a large one with a deep sill. She jumped up. *"Fifteen minutes before it snows. Want to time it?"*

The older cat checked the clock. *"What do I get if I win?"*

*"My catnip sockie."*

*"That old thing?"* Cazenovia nonetheless added, *"Two thirty-seven on the clock. What do you want of mine?"*

*"Two bites of your special chow."*

Being older, the large calico cat was on a senior diet

and Elocution liked the taste of Cazzie's food better than her own.

"*All right.*"

A rap on the front door drew all their eyes.

"Bother," Herb muttered but he rose, walking to the door, the two cats marching behind him. He opened the door and Mrs. Murphy, Pewter, and Tucker raced in.

"*Did he find it? Did he?*" Pewter's hair was puffed out because it was cold outside.

"*Not yet.*" Cazenovia wanted to hear his shouts but she didn't want to be too close, either.

"*Isn't communion tomorrow?*" Tucker just knew the blowup would occur when they were all there and she, like Cazenovia, didn't want to be too much in evidence because *she* was the evidence.

"*No. We had communion on Epiphany Sunday. We won't have it again until the first Sunday in February.*" Elocution used "we" since she felt she and Cazenovia were part of the service.

"*Rats.*" Pewter was disappointed.

"*Haven't got any.*" Cazenovia followed the humans into the office as did the other animals.

"*You should see Pope Rat, that huge fellow over at the salvage yard.*" Tucker loathed that rat.

"*Yeah, he could start the bubonic plague all by himself.*" Pewter hated him, too.

"*Wrong kind of rat,*" Mrs. Murphy advised them. "*A European type of rat caused the plague. Pope Rat is American.*"

Cazenovia checked the time when they all gathered in the office. It was two forty-five.

The humans sat opposite one another in the two wing chairs flanking the fireplace, a long low coffee table made from an old ship's door between them.

"Rev, I just wanted to drop off the books I borrowed," Harry said.

"I know that, I know that, but I'd like a little company on this gloomy day. Started out sunny enough."

"Finished your sermon?" She knew his routine.

"Half. You'll like it because it's about discovery and I start with the discovery of the New World. Actually it's been discovered successively over the centuries. And by New World, I mean North America, not Iceland or Greenland."

"Can't wait." She placed the books on the table.

An extra one was on the pile. "What's this? *The Voyage of the Narwhal.*"

"You'll love it. Apart from being an incredible story, it's well written."

"Oh yes, she wrote *Ship Fever.* I'm sure I'll like this. Thank you, Harry." His eyes scanned his shelves. He stood up. "While I'm thinking of it, let me give you that book about Byzantium I mentioned the other day at the P.O." If he were blind, he could have found his books, he knew their placement so well. He tapped the spine with his forefinger then slid out the book, returning to his chair and placing it before Harry.

"Fat book."

"You need it for these cold, dark nights." He sighed. "Coffee? Tea?"

*"I win!"* Elocution shouted.

The clock read two fifty-two.

"Elo, control yourself." Herb laughed, not knowing his youngest cat, who was only two, had just won her bet as the first large snowflake twirled by the window.

Cazenovia explained the bet to the other animals while the humans talked.

"When do they start laying the carpets?"

"Wednesday, if all goes well. But hopefully this week no matter what. It should take two full days. We couldn't have done this without Matthew." He rubbed the old carpet with his shoe. "In a way I agree with Tazio, it'd be so handsome to have the floors done and, say, a nice Oriental carpet in here but there's too much traffic."

"Even in your office?"

"If I sand the floors in here the dust will be everywhere so I might as well just rip it up and do the wall-to-wall thing. It will be just fine." He changed the subject. "Called on Anne Donaldson this morning. She's pretty broken up."

The Donaldsons weren't Lutherans but Crozet was a small enough town that everyone knew everyone else and Herb, quite naturally, paid his respects.

"I dropped by, too. I must have just missed you. Susan and I were out running errands and—"

"Where's Susan? I saw your truck but no Susan."

"Oh well, we started out in her car. We went to the Clam and then I wanted to go up to the New Gate shopping center and she ran out of time. She dropped me back home and I realized I hadn't returned your books, so I'm here. Before the storm. The clouds were hanging on the mountains." She looked out the window. "Aha."

Herb looked at Harry, whom he had known for most of her life. Her curiosity was both a good and a bad quality. She had a lively mind, read voraciously and indiscriminately, but she could also get herself into trouble. She wasn't always as smart as she thought she was. If Harry had gone to the Clam and then up to New Gate shopping center, it meant something was up.

Herb decided not to tip his hand. "Forget something at the Clam?"

"No, I just wanted to review events and, my luck, Rick

Shaw was sitting at the timekeeper's table. So much for my sneaking around."

Herb had his answer. "Harry, hear me out."

The tone of his voice made her sit up straight. "Yes, sir."

"I know you. Everyone in this town knows you. Their cats and dogs know you. You are as curious as a cat and you think you're a detective. Because of your curiosity I know H.H.'s demise might be, shall we say, suspicious? There's nothing in the paper. Anne said nothing to me. The sheriff hasn't been by but I know *you.* You took yourself to where he died and then to the shopping center he was building. Am I correct?"

"Well—" She'd promised Rick not to tell.

"I thought so." He crossed his arms over his chest. "Who else knows?"

"Fair and Ned because they went back to the Clam Friday night. They were there all night with Rick and his crew."

"I see." Herb softened somewhat. "They won't tell. What provoked this? I mean, what led Rick to believe H.H. was killed?"

"The autopsy. It was done while the body was still warm, perfect conditions, I guess."

"How?"

"Well, I don't think anyone knows, but there was something odd at the autopsy. I don't know what it was. When the lab tests come back the sheriff will know for certain if it was murder."

"He wasn't shot. He wasn't stabbed. He wasn't run over. That leaves poison." Herb made a steeple out of his fingers, leaning forward. "Who knows you were at the Clam?"

"Rick."

"Pass anyone in the halls?"

"No. It was really quiet."

"The only place you can hide a car is at the service entrance. Did you?"

"No. It was Susan's station wagon."

"Harry." He was upset.

"Well?" She held up her palms in supplication.

"And then you went up to the New Gate shopping center. Who saw you there?"

"The men working to finish the discount store. Rob Collier's moonlighting. Uh, Peter Gianakos is the foreman. I don't know the other guys. Oh, the assistant building code inspector, Mychelle Burns. She and Peter were at it so maybe she noticed me and maybe she didn't. Uh—"

"Harry"—his voice lowered—"the murderer, if there is one, thinks that no one knows yet."

"Not necessarily. Rick had his crew at the Clam. The person might know that."

"But it is not public knowledge at this point and Sheriff Shaw's wily. He could have told people at the auditorium that this was strictly routine. They may or may not have believed him but late Friday night no one is there. The roads did not invite cruising around. By Saturday morning, okay, a few more people might have noticed the squad car and other official vehicles, but still, it's not public knowledge and no one is talking about it because our phones would be off the hook. People are all saying he dropped dead of a heart attack. People in their twenties can drop dead of a heart attack. There hasn't been word one about a questionable death. So—"

*"You were stupid, Mom. I love you but you blew it."* Mrs. Murphy hopped into Harry's lap.

The animals sat, faces upturned to Harry.

"I've got an audience here." She half-laughed.

"My point, but you've got an audience that may be dangerous. The killer may now know that you know."

"Oh, Rev, maybe he's not a local." Harry was hoping against hope.

"Sure, he flew through bad weather, rented a car, went to the basketball game, then killed H.H. in the parking lot." Herb stopped a moment, digesting just how H.H. could get poisoned. "The murderer knows you, Harry."

A chill edged down Harry's spine. "Yeah, yeah, I guess he does."

"And you've dragged Susan into it."

Harry now felt really wretched. "Damn, I am such an ignorant ass." She glanced out the window then back to Herb. "Sorry."

"I say worse when no one's around."

*"That's the truth."* Cazenovia corroborated his admission.

"What can I do?"

"Hope that killing H.H. has settled his score. Whatever that score might be."

"Yeah," Harry agreed, her voice faint.

But the score wasn't settled. The killer had every intention of putting more points on the board.

# 12

Someone else was running ahead of the storm. A yellow Lab, perhaps eight months old, abandoned by its humans, hungry and frightened, was looking for a place to hide. An expensive house under construction, set back on fields west of Beaverdam Road, held promise. He loped up to the rear, checking the doors. He moved around counterclockwise until he reached the garage, where the automatic door had not yet been installed. Shivering, the thin fellow ducked in.

Within a few minutes Tazio Chappars, the architect for this edifice, turned down the drive. She wanted to check it before the storm's battering to make certain every window was double-locked. She'd hurried from Matthew's office.

As she parked her half-ton truck, a forest-green Silverado, she opened the front door with the key. Methodically, she started at the top floor, working her way down. She set the thermostat at sixty degrees Fahrenheit. The foreman had it at forty-eight degrees. Much too low, she thought. Satisfied, she locked the front door from the inside, passed through the mudroom off the kitchen, and opened the door into the garage.

The dog, tired, didn't run. He wagged his bedraggled tail. *"Will you help me? I'm very hungry. I'll be your friend for life. I'll love you and protect you if you'll help me."*

Tazio's mouth dropped open. "You poor guy."

Lowering his head, still wagging his tail, he came to her, sat down and offered his right paw. *"You're very pretty."*

"No collar." She shook her head, for she knew a bit about dogs. Labs weren't wanderers like hounds on scent. "Buddy, I need you like a hole in the head."

*"You do need me. You just don't know it."* He smiled shyly.

Struggling with herself, she reached down to pat the broad head. "I can at least get you to the vet. Come on."

*"Whatever you say, ma'am."* He obediently followed.

She had a folded canvas in the bed of the truck and a couple of old towels behind the seat. She shook out the canvas, placing it on the seat, then she toweled off the dirty, thin dog. "I can count every rib. Goddamn, what's wrong with people?"

*"I got too big. I had too much energy so they put me in the car, drove up from Lynchburg, and dropped me along Route 250. I've been moving for two weeks and the weather's been bad. No one would help me."*

"Come on."

He hopped in, curled up, grateful for the warmth and the attention. *"I won't make a sound."*

She punched in the numbers for information on her cell phone mounted beneath the dash. A small speaker was in the upper left-hand corner of the driver's side so she could keep both hands on the wheel after she dialed. She asked for the number of the vet right outside of Crozet, Dr. Shulman.

A pleasant receptionist, Sharon Cortez, answered. She recognized Taz's voice from the Pilates class they took together.

"Hi, I know a storm is coming, but—"

Hearing the distress in Tazio's voice, Sharon said simply, "Where are you?"

"Ten to fifteen minutes from your door."

"We'll be here."

The Lab went willingly into Dr. Shulman's office although the medicine smells weren't enticing. Humans missed most of the pungency.

"Tazio, what have you here?" The handsome bearded veterinarian bent down to run his hands over the dog's frame.

"I found him in the garage at the Lindsay house. I don't think this fellow has had a meal in a long time."

"Just what he could catch and with this weather that wouldn't be much." Dr. Shulman checked the dog's eyes, ears, opened his mouth. "Not quite a year, I'd say eight or nine months." He took a small stool swab, checked under the microscope. "Okay, no tapeworms, which should come as no surprise. No fleas or ticks thanks to the cold. Tapeworms come from infected fleas, so the cold has been useful. Given what he must have gone through he's in pretty good shape. We'll get some muscle and pounds on him in no time."

As Dr. Shulman quietly gave orders, Sharon gathered up some cans of food, a large bag of dry food, a brush, a collar, a leash, and a dog bed. Then he closed the door and efficiently gave the dog a barrage of shots.

"Dr. Shulman, I—" Tazio stuttered.

"Oh, don't worry. You just pay for the exam and the shots. I've given him his basic shots. Put his rabies tag on the collar. You can buy a commercial dog food, certainly, but given the weather the stores will be crowded so I thought maybe you'd best take some home. This will get you started."

"Oh, that's fine, but—" She picked up the collar.

"You know"—he knelt down to clean out the sweet dog's ears—"Mindy Creighton came in today. She had to say goodbye to Brinkley. He was almost twenty years old." Dr. Shulman fought a little mist in his eyes. "She left his collar, leash, and bed, asking me to give them to someone who might need them. Said she just couldn't bear to bring them back home. So next time you see her, thank her, not me."

"I thought I'd pay to get this boy back on his feet and find a good home for him."

*"No! I want you."* The Lab put his head under her hand.

Dr. Shulman smiled slightly. "Well, you'll need these things until you do and—uh—Tazio, I should tell you that Labrador retrievers are excellent companions. They are used to lead the blind because they're so rock steady."

"I'll put signs up describing him. Someone might be searching for him."

Dr. Shulman looked down at the dog and, when Tazio's head was turned, he winked.

Sharon had already put the rabies tag on the collar, a bright royal blue. She placed it around the dog's neck. "Perfect." Then she tidied the papers at the front desk. "All right now. What shall we call this fellow?"

Tazio, knowing an ambush when she saw one, nevertheless smiled, "Brinkley Two. Seems only right."

"I think so." And she wrote down the name in black ink, block letters.

"Sharon, I guess you heard about H. H. Donaldson?"

"Sure did." Sharon glanced up from her paperwork. "I shed not a tear." A note of sarcasm was inflected in her voice. She looked up again. "I'm one of H.H.'s castoffs." She waved her hand. "Oh, it was years ago but it still stings a little."

"I'm sorry. I had no idea."

"I didn't broadcast it." She handed Tazio the papers with the day written down, the list of shots given, and when the dog would need boosters. "But it's weird—now I don't care."

"Could be the shock."

Sharon shrugged. "Maybe. I feel sorry for his little girl. And Anne. She's a nice lady."

"I guess I put my foot in it." Tazio blushed.

"No you didn't. I just felt like casting a weight off my shoulders. You're still relatively new here, Tazio. This place is full of secrets."

"I guess any small town is."

"Got that right." Sharon smiled, then stood up to pat Brinkley's head. "You're going to love this dog. Trust me."

With a weak little voice, Tazio half-protested. "I work too many hours to have a pet."

*"I will never let you down,"* Brinkley vowed to the architect. *"Not with my last breath."*

On the way home, Taz thought she'd better brave the supermarket. Just in case the storm lasted. The first flakes were falling. She pulled in next to Harry's truck just as Harry put two large bags of groceries into the seat.

"Taz, what have you got there?"

Taz gave her the story.

Mrs. Murphy shouted from the seat, *"Welcome to Crozet, Brinkley. You were named for a good dog, a German shepherd."*

*"Thank you. Do you think she'll feed me soon?"*

*"As soon as you get home, and she lives maybe seven or eight minutes from here. She's very responsible and, oh, make sure*

*you tell her you like her work. She's an architect,"* Tucker helpfully suggested.

*"Don't drool on her blueprints,"* Pewter sassily said.

*"Oh, forgive me. I'm Mrs. Murphy, this is Tucker, and the smart mouth is Pewter. We live out by Yellow Mountain and we work at the post office so I'm sure we'll see you."*

As Harry and Taz talked about H.H.'s death, the shock of it, they moved on quickly, because it was cold, to the next guild meeting and what they both hoped to accomplish.

"Hey, I was surprised to see you at the basketball game. You haven't been a regular."

"I thought I'd give it a try." The cold air tingled in Taz's upturned nose.

"Well, let me know if you need anything for your new best friend."

"Thanks. I'm hoping to find a home for him. I'd better grab some milk and bread and hurry home. Brinkley needs to eat."

*"Yes,"* Brinkley agreed.

When Taz got home, the first thing she did was mix some canned food into the dry food. She watched while the famished animal gulped the food then drank water. When he finished he smiled up at her.

"You know, even though you're skinny, you're a rather handsome dog." She walked over to pet him. "You know, oh, I said that already, didn't I? Well, how about if I put your bed in the bedroom? We don't want it where people can see it."

She picked up the fleece doggie bed, placing it on the floor at the foot of her bed. She thought the dog would curl up and go to sleep for he had to be exhausted but Brinkley was so thrilled to find a person who might love him he followed her everywhere she went until she sat down at her computer. Then he blissfully slept at her feet.

She couldn't help but smile when she glanced down at him.

Harry arrived home before the wind started howling. By the time she left the barn, the doors rattled.

Walking to the house she complained to her animals. "First it's El Niño, then it's La Niña. Okay, that passed and with it the mild winters, but this is ridiculous. Second big blow in as many weeks."

Once in the house she fed her pets, buttered a bagel, pulled out a legal-sized pad, a pencil, and sat at the kitchen table. She diagrammed the inside of the Clam, marking who sat where. She diagrammed the parking lot, noting the spot where H.H. collapsed. Then she wrote down the names of everyone she could remember who either tried to assist or who watched helplessly.

"*Didn't she hear a thing Herb told her?*" Pewter crossly complained.

"*She heard.*" Tucker gazed at Harry, her expressive brown eyes filled with concern.

"*She feels compelled to solve this or to at least shift the focus onto herself and away from Susan,*" the tiger correctly surmised.

"*I think she'll be careful.*" Tucker hoped she would.

"*I'm sure she will but if she's being watched, it's only going to add fuel to the fire.*" Mrs. Murphy knew her human very well.

"*Sooner or later people will know H.H. was murdered,*" Pewter thought out loud. "*Might take some of the onus off her.*"

"*They won't know until the report comes back from the state lab in Richmond,*" Mrs. Murphy replied. "*January isn't the*

*murdering season so those toxicology reports will be back soon
enough, I'll bet. She can get into a lot of trouble in that time.*"

"*Maybe the storm will slow her down.*" Tucker allowed
Pewter to groom her.

"*We can hope.*" Mrs. Murphy jumped onto the kitchen
table.

Harry looked at the cat and back at her drawing of the
parking lot. "Ah, you three were in the truck. I'll add that."
She added their names with a flourish. "Maybe if I can find
out who H.H. was sleeping with I can figure this out."

In a way she was right and in a way she was wrong.

# 13

Although the storm didn't dump a lot of snow on the ground, the winds howled ferociously. Drifts piled up across the roadways, and five feet behind the drifts the asphalt shone as though picked clean. Nor did the winds abate. Shutters rattled, doors vibrated, and the stinging cold seeped through the cracks and fissures in buildings. The storm system stalled out, too, so every now and then a flurry of snow attended the wind.

Harry's three horses, Gin Fizz, Poptart, and Tomahawk, played outside wearing their blankets, each one a different color to please the horse. Unless the ground was glazed with ice, Harry turned her horses out. They needed to move about, burn off energy. She would bring them in at sundown. Often she'd pause during her barn chores to watch them dash around. Poptart, the youngest and lowest on the totem pole, liked to tease the two older horses. She'd sidle up to Gin Fizz, the handsome, flea-bitten gray, then tug his blanket askew. She'd do this until he'd squeal, then she'd torment Tomahawk. Poptart was the baby sister at her teenage siblings' party. Usually Tomahawk and Gin Fizz indulged her. When she'd cross the line they'd flatten their ears, bare their teeth, and snort. If that failed, a well-timed kick, not connecting, usually backed off the naughty horse.

Simon, the possum, snored slightly as he slept in the hayloft. He'd made cozy quarters out of a hay bale. Since Harry knew he was there she'd never pulled out that bale. The owl dozed in the cupola, glad to be out of the wind. The blacksnake, in deep hibernation, was out of it. She wouldn't stir until April at the earliest. Old and huge, she was as big around as Harry's wrist. The mice cavorted behind the walls of the tack room, having burrowed into the feed room. Theirs was a merry life despite the efforts of Mrs. Murphy and Pewter to curtail their nonstop party.

The doors at both ends of the center-aisle barn were shut tight, but they still slapped and banged. The stall doors to the outside Dutch doors were locked, top and bottom, but wind secreted itself between the frames, causing them to shake with each blast.

Inside, Harry's breath spiraled out as she spread a light dusting of lime over the wet spots. She'd clean out the soiled bedding, expose the wet spots and lime them, then let them dry and come back just before sundown to pull bedding over them. Once a week, usually Saturday morning, she'd strip down each stall so it would air out. Then she'd put a generous helping of fresh wood shavings over it. She liked straw because she could make a better compost out of it for her garden, but soiled straw was heavy and strained her back with each successive full pitchfork. Also, straw was getting expensive; more expensive still were peanut hulls. Some people even tried shredded newspapers. The good thing about Crozet, among other fine qualities, was the availability of small sawmills. She could find a suitable grade of wood shavings without any trouble, for a reasonable cost. Toss a little mix of cedar shavings in each stall and the barn smelled wonderful.

She couldn't prove it but Harry believed those cedar shavings helped keep down the parasites, not that she had to worry about parasites in this weather.

Though proud of her barn system, her farm management, Harry wouldn't brag about her accomplishments. She figured the shine on her horses' coats and their happy attitudes spoke to anyone with horse sense. As to the rest of it, if a person drove down the long road to the farm they would behold a tidy, neat, well-loved farm no matter what the season.

Over the years she'd dug two new wells at each end of the farm to accommodate watering troughs. In time she hoped to purchase one of those irrigation systems with pipes interspersed with wheels. The system would roll at a timed rate of speed over the pastures. It was moving sculpture, a beautiful sight to her eyes. Beautiful price, too.

Droughts had begun to visit central Virginia. Not each year, but three years out of ten, say. She needed a good hay crop. An irrigation system could be a blessing.

Harry tried to think ahead, to plan, but no matter how well she planned Mother Nature surprised her. So did people.

She climbed the ladder to the hayloft. Mrs. Murphy followed her. Pewter adamantly remained in the tack room. *Mouse patrol,* she fibbed. Tucker stayed down in the aisle.

Harry tiptoed to Simon's den. Fast asleep on an old white towel, each time he exhaled the small stalks of hay wavered.

She put down a bowl with graham crackers soaked in honey. Simon loved sweets. His water bowl was clean.

Of course, he could drink water out of the horse buckets. The barn stayed warm enough for the water not to freeze over. Sometimes if the mercury dropped into the single digits the buckets would freeze, but if the temperature stayed in the twenties or low thirties outside, the temperature inside usually kept above freezing. The heat coming off those large horse bodies helped, too.

Harry smiled as she peeped over at the possum. She'd even managed last spring to trap him—which he hated—but she took him to the vet where he received every shot possible. He was an extremely healthy possum, no carrier of EPM, a malady affecting first birds, then possums as carriers, and finally horses. Much as she adored Simon, Harry had to see to the health of her horses, hence the shots. He avoided her for weeks after that. No matter how many times the pets told him the traumatic visit had been for his own good, he stayed furious. He finally got over it in June, once again showing himself to Harry, taking small treats from her hand.

By the time Harry climbed back down it was eight-thirty A.M. She'd knocked out her barn chores. She couldn't do anything outside. She felt good about life. Harry loved getting her chores done in a timely and orderly fashion.

The phone rang in the tack room. She picked it up. Tucker sat at her feet.

A muffled male voice hissed. "Curiosity killed the cat. Mind your own business."

Click.

She stood there with the receiver in her hand. "Shit."

*"What a pretty thing to say,"* Pewter sarcastically meowed.

"I've just been warned off," Harry said aloud.

*"I knew it! I knew this would happen,"* Tucker worriedly said.

*"It will only make her more determined."* Mrs. Murphy hopped onto a saddle on a saddle rack.

Harry took off her barn coat. The tack room, toasty, invited one to sit down, inhale the aroma of the stable.

*"Too bad she doesn't have caller ID,"* Pewter, who was interested in technology, said.

*"That's the truth. On a day like today I bet whoever called didn't go to a phone booth."* Tucker swiveled her left ear toward the wall. She could hear the mice whispering.

"That voice was familiar but he must have had a cloth over the phone or something to disguise it. But damn, I know that voice!" She threw her work gloves on the floor. "I am a perfect ass."

*"Don't be too hard on yourself, Mom,"* Tucker sympathized.

The slender woman pulled over the director's chair from the desk. She dropped down into it, lifting her feet up to rest on her tack trunk, a present from her father for her twelfth birthday. He'd built it from glowing cherrywood, carving her initials in a diamond shape on the front.

Harry observed her audience, which included the mice, although she couldn't hear them nor did she know they'd gathered around their semicircular hole partially hidden by that very tack trunk. "Think about it. How can you have an affair in Crozet? You can't even sneeze without someone saying 'Gesundheit.' There are only a few ways I figure a man or a woman for that matter can have an affair. Tucker, you look so interested."

Tucker, her head cocked, was drinking in every word. *"I am. Dogs don't have affairs so the concept alone fascinates me."*

*"What is it that dogs have?"* Pewter sniggered.

*"Sex."*

*"How crude, Tucker."* Pewter, on the saddle rack below Mrs. Murphy—they were in a vertical line—had to laugh.

"Okay, where was I? Oh yeah, so you need to be able to hide in plain sight assuming the affairee is a person living in Albemarle County. If your paramour lives somewhere else that's easier. Too easy. A doctor has plenty of opportunities to get away with it. A private office, hospital rooms, all those nurses. Pretty easy. Anyone in a nine-to-five job, not so easy, but anyone who is self-employed, more chances. H.H. ran a construction firm. I suppose he could enjoy trysts in an unfinished building after the workers left but he'd have to drag a bed in there or a futon. Scratch that. He has an office. A real possibility, although a wife can cruise by and most wives would have a key. Still, that's possible. The other thing is that a lot of construction sites, the bigger ones, have trailers, an on-site office. That would be real easy. Yeah, I can see that. And the last possibility, open to anyone, not just H.H., would be sneaking in and out of the paramour's house or apartment assuming she's unmarried. If she's married, it's got to be the office or the trailer. No way could he take a woman to the club or to a motel. Not in this county."

*"Mother, have you contemplated an affair? You've certainly thought this out."* Mrs. Murphy's long whiskers swept forward then back as she, too, listened to the mice.

"What do you want, pussycat?"

*"For you to behave,"* the tiger replied.

Harry laughed. She liked conversing with her animals although she didn't know what they were saying. "Next issue. What kind of woman? H.H. wasn't attracted to tarts. I've known him all his life. He liked well-groomed women, nice looking. He wasn't the handsomest guy around nor the richest, so he wasn't going to get, say, a BoomBoom but he could certainly attract, m-m-m, a nice-looking secretary. Maybe someone he met socially. He didn't have much free time. What self-employed person does? He liked kayaking." She thought. "No. We'd know. I'm sure. There aren't but so many women on the reservoir."

*"Could be on one of the rivers,"* Tucker said.

As if in response to the dog's thought, Harry added, "But Anne would go with him most times. Not a hobby. Has got to be a woman he met through work or someone at an office where he does business, building supply, another construction company, architects' offices."

*"You forget that he goes to the dentist like everyone else. He would have his annual physical at a doctor's office. That's a possibility."* Mrs. Murphy considered the picking grounds.

"The other issue we have to consider is whoever this was, he nearly left his wife for her. He *did* leave his wife for her if only for one day. So the woman would have to be presentable. H.H. wasn't exactly a snob but he wouldn't risk everything for a woman he didn't think most of his friends would eventually accept."

*"You know, she's smarter than I give her credit for sometimes."* Pewter blinked, the pupils of her eyes changing shape.

# 14

Matthew Crickenberger's rain-forest wall was just wide enough that he could turn around in it. He'd built it four feet deep and to the ceiling.

Outside the office window it was a winter wonderland. Inside his rain forest it was the Colombian jungle.

He could have foisted off cleaning the glassed-in enclosure complete with an expensive air circulation system and humidifier. However, he enjoyed his Sunday-afternoon escapes.

A thorough cleaning, including checking the pond, took three hours. The birds, accustomed to him, opened their wings and their mouths. Matthew always brought treats and not just on Sundays. The neon-colored frogs felt no special affection for the middle-aged man. They hopped for cover. He brought ants and tiny grubs for them, too.

The last chore was washing the inside of the floor-to-ceiling glass. He hummed as he slid the rubber blade to the top of the glass. He could just reach the top. Then he would swiftly bring it straight down. Small droplets fell on his back from the tree canopy overhead. Vines hung like necklaces.

Finished at last, he placed his buckets outside, then stepped out onto a small sisal rug. He shut the door behind him, wiped his feet, and picked up the white towel from the country club draped over a chair. He toweled himself off, making a mental note to tell Hunter at the club that he owed for a towel. Matthew, meticulous about such things, was irritated when people would filch towels, paper, ashtrays. He confronted one of Charlottesville's flush lawyers once, saying, "Never steal anything small." The other men in the locker room laughed. The lawyer, a banty rooster of a man, laughed, too.

The phone rang. Matthew picked it up, assuming the caller was his wife.

"A loaf of bread, a jug of wine," he jovially answered.

"Matthew?"

"Fred." Matthew was surprised.

"The same."

"Are you working on a snowy Sunday? I don't think the county will pay extra." A hint of sarcasm crept into Matthew's voice.

Fred ignored him. "Do you know who will take over Donaldson Construction?"

"Uh—no. Why?"

"Well, I wanted to go through the Lindsay house out by Beaverdam Road and I don't want to disturb Anne."

"Call Tazio."

"She doesn't work for Donaldson Construction."

"No, but she's the architect. You'd have a competent person with you."

"I don't know. I'd like a company representative. It's always better."

"Well, Fred, I don't think this is the time to bother anyone at the company. They're all reeling. Even the site foreman has got to be upset. Make an exception and call Tazio."

"Yeah." Fred's voice faded, he cleared his throat. "I wish I hadn't had that fight with him."

"Guilt is a useless emotion."

"I didn't say I felt guilty." Fred bristled.

"You didn't have to. Now just listen to me. You were not on your best behavior. You really wanted to hit Josef P. but nailed H.H. instead."

"Well—yeah, but if I told you the times I wanted to slug H.H. Arrogant bastard." He inhaled sharply. "Dead. Gone. No more trouble."

"He was either belligerent or a whiner. Let him lose out on a bid and whoever won it was corrupt, paying off. I mean, it couldn't be because someone else could do a better job."

"That someone was usually you," Fred dryly commented.

"In the last few years it was."

A silence followed. "I'll call Tazio."

"Uh, Fred." A light note lifted Matthew's voice. "I assume my helpfulness will only influence you to find fault with my projects."

A rasping laugh followed. "You got that right, Matthew."

# 15

"This time of year gets to me." Susan folded an empty mail-bag. "Spring seems a million years away and the Christmas bills are arriving. Ugh."

Miranda and Harry, having finished the sorting of the mail, had been discussing the merits of painting the small table and chairs in the back.

Harry was happy that no one had called to threaten Susan, because Susan would certainly have told her. So whoever it was had focused on her. Instead of making her fearful, it exhilarated her. Danger got her blood up.

The animals thought she was foolish. She should report the call to the sheriff or Deputy Cooper.

"Red," Miranda declared.

"Yellow," Harry countered.

"Blue." Susan laughed. "Or better yet, paint them yellow with blue and red pinstripes or red with blue and yellow pinstripes or—"

The front door opened, Big Mim burst through. "Why didn't you tell me?"

The three women stared back at her. Mrs. Murphy and Pewter jumped on the dividing counter as Tucker, half-asleep, lifted her head.

"Tell you what?" Harry wondered if Mim had learned that H.H.'s death was suspect. If so, who would have told her but Sheriff Shaw?

"Susan"—Big Mim charged up to the counter—"your husband is going to put together an exploratory committee to consider a campaign for the house seat and you never said a word."

The man who was the state representative in Richmond was retiring that year without endorsing any candidate for the Democratic Party. This was not pique on his part. There were a few good people who might run but no one had declared themselves. Better to wait and see.

Susan blanched. "Mim, it's not my place to make those announcements."

"You knew!" Mim had to know everything.

"Of course I knew. And didn't Ned come and talk to you and Jim?"

"Yes, but you should have called me first." She spun on her heel, opened her mailbox, then slammed it, the metallic thud ringing through the room.

She marched out as resolutely as she had marched in. Outside the day was gray. Inside the clock read eight A.M.

*"Monday morning."* Tucker dropped her head back on her paws.

"I thought we didn't have any secrets between us," Harry said half in jest, for she hadn't known of Ned's decision, either.

"It's not my secret." Susan held to her position.

"It's wonderful." Miranda took the folded mailbag from Susan's hands, placing it on the shelf with the packages.

Susan walked over to the coffeepot, poured herself a cup, and spoke with deliberation. "Ned has this dream that he can change things for the better. He's been quiet about it but this is his chance. I think he'd make a good state representative. He's honest, fair-minded, and not afraid of tough problems."

"All of that is true, but what do you think for yourself?" Harry pressed.

"Oh Harry." Then Susan glanced at Miranda. "I don't want to be a political wife—watching every word, dressing up, attending all those boring events."

"You don't have to do that." Harry waved as Market Shiflett, in big snow boots, passed by the front window. He owned the convenience store next door.

"She can't hide under a rock." Miranda disagreed with Harry. "She has to show her support."

"She can pick and choose her events. I'm not suggesting she..." Harry paused. "Susan, I don't know what I'm suggesting. I really don't know what it takes to get elected to office. Money. After that it kind of looks like a beauty contest to me." She smiled. It faded as Fred Forrest, Mychelle Burns, and Tazio Chappars walked toward the front door. A clean Brinkley followed Tazio.

Neither Fred nor Mychelle lived in Crozet. They were arguing, Fred wasn't paying attention to where he was going, and as Tazio, shaking snow from her boots, stepped into the post office, Fred looked up, his mouth hanging open. He shut it like a bird clamping down on a beetle.

"Hello," Harry, Miranda, and Susan called out.

"Hello," Tazio replied.

Mychelle and Fred merely nodded.

*"How are you feeling today?"* Mrs. Murphy asked Brinkley.

Tucker came around from behind the divider. Harry had installed a doggie door for her because she grew weary of opening and closing the half-door under the flip-up part of the divider. A lot of times she just left that half-door open but every time she closed it, Tucker would claw at it.

*"Much better. Tazio fed me a delicious meal, beef bits over kibble, which she stirred all together. I think she stuck a vitamin pill in there but I don't care. I'll take vitamins if it makes her happy."*

*"She must have given you a bath, too. Your coat looks clean. You know, you'll get some luster once you gain weight."* Tucker liked the Lab.

*"I feel like a new dog."* Brinkley smiled.

*"What's going on with Fred and Mychelle?"* Pewter inquired.

*"Tazio walked out of the bank and Fred was in the parking lot. He said he'd been calling her about the Lindsay house. He's rude. Said he'd read the blueprints for her sports complex design. Design is not his bailiwick but she'd made errors and the construction company would have a hard time building her monstrosity. He used that word. Mychelle nods whenever he speaks. She must be in love with him or something. She agrees with everything he says."*

*"In love with Fred? Ugly."* Pewter wrinkled her nose.

As the three humans began to leave, Tazio winked at Harry.

Mrs. Murphy called out, *"Get Taz to bring you to our farm. We'll give you the tour."*

*"I'll try."* A happy Brinkley wagged his tail and followed Tazio out the door.

"If a fart has human form it's Fred." Harry burst out laughing.

"Harry, that is so crude. Your mother would be horrified if she could hear you speak like that." Miranda shook her head although she did agree with the assessment.

"You'd be cleaning the kitchen floor with boiling water as penance." Susan laughed, remembering Harry's mother. "But he is just awful. Awful!"

"Isn't it something, though, that Tazio got the job, her design was selected and here she is, her office is in Crozet. We all ought to be proud," Miranda said.

"It's a beautiful design, sweeping glass with beautiful curves. Hey, you know what I've always wanted to do?"

The other two women looked at Harry. "What?"

"Put a deep-sea diver on top of the Clam."

"That would be funny," Susan said. "You'd need a crane to get it up there."

"No. They clean that roof. There has to be a way to get on top from the inside." Harry's mind raced forward.

"Sure and you'd slide all the way off." Susan knew that in Harry's mind she was carrying the deep-sea outfit on her back, going through a trapdoor onto the roof.

"Would not."

"Would, too," Susan sassed in good humor.

"You two."

A frazzled Deputy Cynthia Cooper opened the back door, closing it behind her. "What is wrong with everyone this Monday?"

"We're fine," Harry responded.

"That's why I'm here. To escape for fifteen minutes. Oh, orange-glazed cinnamon buns, where are they?" Disappointment shone on her face.

Miranda baked the most delicious cinnamon buns, drenching them with a thick orange-glaze icing.

"Now that you mention it," Miranda checked her watch, tossed on her coat, "they're just about ready."

"Yahoo!" Susan clapped her hands together like a child.

*"Need help?"* Tucker volunteered.

"I'll be right back." Miranda slipped out the door.

"What's going on?" Harry asked the officer.

"Aunt Tally's missing a cow. She was convinced someone stole it. In a snowstorm? Okay, dealt with that. The cow broke through the fence line and was at the next farm. Then a waterpipe burst on Hydraulic Road in front of the Kmart. Naturally the water froze all over the road, which had been slush. We had to redirect traffic at rush hour. That was a lot of fun. It's raw out there today. What a mess. And then some kid sideswipes BoomBoom at the stop sign at Routes 240 and 250. She came to a stop, a full stop, which you have to do even though it's a pain. And this kid gets impatient and pulls alongside her on the right, loses control since the road is slick, and slides all along the right side of her car."

"That's such a pretty car," Susan commiserated.

Miranda reappeared. "Voilà!"

"Miranda, you're a lifesaver." Cooper plucked one off the tray the second Miranda set it on the table.


An Explorer pulled up outside the post office. Two young blonde women disembarked. The driver opened the back door and out popped a medium-sized, reddish, mixed-breed dog, her tail twirling like a windmill. Right behind her, trying to be more dignified, was another dog, wheat-colored, larger.

"Minnesota plates." Miranda noticed. "Why, those girls will feel right at home."

Harry and Cooper laughed as the door opened and the humans and dogs stepped into the cozy post office.

*"Strange dogs,"* Pewter announced as Tucker's ears perked right up and she scratched open the divider door between the working area and the post box area.

*"All dogs are strange,"* Mrs. Murphy teased as she looked down from the counter as the dogs all touched noses.

*"Ignore her. She's grand and airy,"* Tucker advised the two friendly visitors.

*"Excuse me?"* Gina Marie, the red-colored Lab/terrier mix cocked her head, questioning.

Casey Jo, the younger of the two visiting dogs, wagged her tail, her body and then lifted her paw for emphasis but she didn't say anything.

*"Yankee dogs."* Mrs. Murphy glared down at them in mock anger.

*"Is that like a cookie? Yankee?"* Casey Jo vaguely remembered little cellophane-wrapped doodles called, obviously enough, Yankee Doodles.

Tucker, ignoring Madame Supremacy on the counter, said, *"Well, no, it's not a cookie but never you mind. Grand and airy means stuck up. It's a Southern expression and I can tell by your accents that you aren't Southern."*

*"No. But I thought the South was hot,"* Gina Marie said.

*"Not in the winter. And we're right at the foot of the Blue Ridge Mountains so it gets right cold here."*

*"Bet you don't have cats that work in your post office?"* Mrs. Murphy, Pewter now beside her, looked down.

*"No."* Casey Jo, a happy soul, thought the cats amusing.

*"Any dogs working there?"* Tucker inquired.

*"No. St. Paul, where we live is, well, dogs and cats wouldn't be allowed to work in an office or place like this. People pay a lot of attention to rules there and I'm sure it's against the rules*

*or our humans would take us to work.*" Gina Marie thought the rules were dreadful.

"*See, that's what's so great about Virginia.*" Tucker smiled broadly, revealing her white teeth. "*Everyone pretends to obey the rules and then they do what they want. It's all very civilized, of course.*"

"*Well, how can it be civilized if people are breaking the rules?*" Casey Jo innocently asked.

"*Oh dear, they really are Yankees,*" Pewter whispered to Mrs. Murphy, nodding in agreement.

Tucker realized this would become a discussion not just of hours but days and weeks, so she prudently changed the subject. "*It's very nice that your humans brought you along.*"

"*Our humans take us everywhere they can and they are lots of fun. They play ball with us and swim with us and ski with us. They can't keep up with us so we have to slow down, of course, but they don't sit in chairs while we play. They participate.*"

"*Does your human play with you?*" Casey Jo believed humans would be so much happier if they could chase balls all day and chew bones.

Tucker glanced up at Harry, now out from behind the counter to talk to the visiting ladies from St. Paul. "*Yes, but my human works all the time. We farm, you see, so I herd the horses and I guard Mom. The cats are supposed to kill the vermin but*—she lowered her voice—*they are falling down on the job.*"

"*You'll pay for that.*" Mrs. Murphy's tail lashed.

"*Death to dogs!*" Pewter crowed, which made Casey Jo bark.

"*She's so full of it. Pay her no more mind than if she was a goat barking.*" Tucker turned her back on the cats.

"*I beg your pardon?*" Gina Marie's eyebrows raised up.

*"Uh, I don't think I can explain that one but just ignore those cats. How come you're in Crozet?"*

*"Polly Foss,"* Casey Jo indicated one of the women who looked a lot like sisters, *"is here for a management conference so her best friend, Lynae Larson, took off work to come along. They've never seen central Virginia."*

"Come on, girls," Polly called to the chatting dogs.

Casey Jo walked over to Harry and licked her hand before leaving.

Lynae laughed. "She loves everyone."

The two pretty Nordic ladies left carrying orange-glazed buns.

"Now isn't it just the most fun to talk to someone from different parts?" Miranda used the Virginia expression "different parts" which, depending on the intonation of the speaker, could mean a wide variety of things.

"Guess they didn't realize we have real winter here." Harry laughed.

Cooper chimed in. "Yeah, but at least ours only lasts three months. They're stuck with it half the year."

"Poor darlin's." Miranda couldn't imagine that much cold for that long.

As Gina Marie and Casey Jo hopped back in the SUV, they inhaled the delicious aroma of those orange-glazed cinnamon buns and hoped those two girls in the front seat would share.

*"Weren't those cats funny?"* Casey Jo leaned on Gina Marie.

*"Grand and airy,"* Gina Marie said as they both laughed.

Casey Jo replied, *"Animals are nice here but you know, Gina, I can't exactly understand what they're saying."*

Later that Monday when Cooper was back at headquarters, the preliminary lab report came in. H.H. had been killed by a toxin. However, no one in Richmond was familiar with the toxin and they were continuing tests to make a clear identification.

She leaned over Rick Shaw's shoulder, reading the report with him. He put the papers down. She came around to sit on the edge of his desk, facing him.

"If it's got the white coats baffled it must really be weird." He ran his hand over his thinning hair.

"Yeah, well, whatever it was it sure was lethal." Her finger went to her neck. "Wham."

"No dart or shard or anything in the body." He dumped his full ashtray into the trash can. The odor of stale cigarettes wafted upward.

"Isn't it possible that when Fair or whoever loosened the scarf it fell out?" She recalled that Fair mentioned H.H. had had a plaid cashmere scarf around his neck when he collapsed in the parking lot.

"The penetration in the neck was an inch and a half." He drummed his fingers on the desk. "You'd think whatever hit him would have stuck in there. And if it pulled out with the scarf there'd be a tear in the scarf. We combed that parking lot. Not even a sliver on the ground."

"The penetration was deep but thin. You saw the wound."

"I did. That's what worries me. How could the killer hit H.H. and no one see it? He'd have to be close and silent. It's possible the killer could have brushed by him but surely someone would notice a human being jamming something into the neck of another human being. This report disturbs me. These days you don't know what some nutcase is cooking up in a lab."

"Not just here, boss, but all over the world." She sighed.

"You got that right." He frowned.

"Maybe basketball is a trigger in some way?"

"Yeah, I thought of that, too." He drummed harder. "Looks like we need a full-court press on this one."

# 16

The gang rarely missed a basketball game but that Friday night they gathered at Anne Donaldson's for a quiet remembrance since H.H. had loathed funerals. Although Harry and H.H. hadn't been close, they were part of the same community, so she was there to pay her respects.

Friends and neighbors told stories highlighting H.H.'s quick temper, which would evaporate and then he'd forgive and forget.

H.H. had touched a lot of people, including all those who'd worked for him over the years. People fervently wished they had told him how they felt about him while he lived. Nagging guilt nibbled at more than one conscience.

Tazio Chappars fought tears when Matthew recounted how the sports complex job had come down to the wire. How disappointed H.H. had been to lose what would have been his biggest contract ever.

Matthew's pleasant voice filled the room. "He came to

my office to congratulate me personally." His voice cracked for a second. "That's class." Composed again, he continued. "There's no doubt in my mind that H.H. would have won major institutional jobs in the future. It was just a matter of time and who would have thought his time would run out?" He lifted his glass. "To H.H."

Speak no ill of the dead. Matthew made no mention of H.H.'s tendency to whine when things didn't go his way.

The others toasted in unison. As Matthew was the last speaker, people then talked among themselves.

Fred Forrest's and Mychelle Burns's absences were noted. They could have showed, paid their respects if only for fifteen minutes.

Harry scanned the packed rooms. People were wedged together in the hall, the living room, the dining room, the kitchen, the den, the family room, even out in Anne's greenhouse. She wondered if H.H.'s killer was there. If he was, was he enjoying the gathering? Was it triumph or was it relief?

She switched on the truck radio as she drove home that evening. Virginia was defeating Florida State in a lackluster game.

Be a lot of empty seats tonight, she thought to herself.

An oncoming car on the Whitehall Road blinded her with its brights. She cursed loudly, surprising herself. It wasn't until then that she realized how angry she was. Angry at the killer. Angry that she was no help. She felt as if she were driving in the dark with no lights on.

"I'll find out who he was sleeping with! Dammit, it's a start," she said out loud. "She must know something if she isn't the killer herself."

Then it occurred to Harry that if the secret lover did indeed know something, she probably didn't have long to live.

# 17

In one of those spectacular reversals so common in mountain regions, the next day the temperature climbed up to the low fifties. The snow melted, the earth grew soggy, the skies sparkled robin's-egg blue with that crystal clarity only winter brings. Everyone played outside Saturday. After all, Old Man Winter could return in a heartbeat.

Harry, Susan, Big Mim, Little Mim, Fair, and Boom-Boom went fox hunting, returning in the early afternoon. They scattered in various directions dictated by the necessities of daily life.

*The Daily Progress* reported a careful interview with Sheriff Shaw in which he announced that H. H. Donaldson's death was not from natural causes. He said the builder appeared to have been poisoned, and the matter was under investigation.

Harry and Fair, after putting up their horses, met back in

Crozet for a late lunch at the Mountain View Grille restaurant.

"—unusual for you." Fair had just finished telling Harry how happy he was that she wasn't playing detective.

"Rick asked me to butt out." She saw no reason to inform Fair that she was going to get to the bottom of this.

"Since when has that stopped you?" He smiled as she reached over on his plate, snagging a crisp French fry.

"My theory is"—she popped the dark little potato sliver into her mouth—"find the lover and you find the killer." She couldn't resist the French fry any more than she could resist thinking about the murder.

"I see. A woman scorned." He watched as she reached for another one. "Honey, why don't you let me order an extra plate of fries?"

"Because I'll eat every single one and I can pack on five pounds in the winter looking at food. But oh, it's so-o-o good."

"Our bodies have more wisdom than we do. We're supposed to be heavier in the winter. Insulation. Our food supplies ran perilously thin in winter before we knew how to preserve food. We needed every fat cell we had."

"Ever think about the difference between people from warm climates and those from temperate climates? People in the tropics reach up and grab a fruit. There is no tomorrow. But people in temperate climates have to plan ahead because of winter. History of the world right there. If you plan ahead for food, it's not such a big jump to planning ahead to conquer other people."

"Harry, I never know what's whirring around in that brain of yours."

"I read that but it does make sense. And what people drink: warm climates, wine; temperate climates, beer; cold climates, hard liquor. That's what they could make based on what they grew. You with your Swedish blood could drink us all under the table if you were so inclined."

"That's what undergraduate days are about. I'm surprised I'm not dead. Sometimes I think about the stuff I did when I was a kid." He broke into a toothy grin. "First off, why wasn't I killed on the road? Then, why wasn't I shot? Or kicked in the head by a horse? But I came to my senses and began to practice moderation the day I entered vet school. You, on the other hand, were ahead of me there."

"My parents would have skinned me alive. Oh hey, here comes Herbie."

The Reverend Jones walked in, waving to them.

"Come on over." Fair stood up.

"You two are finishing. I can't intrude."

"You are never an intrusion. We were considering dessert. Please join us." Fair pulled out the chair.

Herb sat down, happy to be among friends. "Susan said hunting was wonderful today."

"The earth was a little warmer than the air. It exhaled, so to speak." Fair smiled. He enjoyed studying the mysteries of scent and that's what they remained, mysteries.

"How about that article in the paper today—about H.H.?" Herb cast a swift stern glance at Harry, one unnoticed by Fair.

"We will be overrun with theories." Fair looked up from the dessert menu.

After the waiter took Herb's order and Fair's dessert order, Fair said, "Has anyone thought about the Republican Party? H.H. was county chairman."

"Ah—" Herb pressed the end of the spoon bringing up the bowl of it. "Good at it, too. Young and full of conservative zeal minus the social agenda. I don't know what they'll do, although if they're smart, really smart, they'll draft Tazio Chappars for the job."

"Tazio?" Fair considered this. "That would be brilliant."

"With Ned considering a run for the State House, the Republicans need young leadership to create excitement. Ned will be a strong candidate. Tazio might be able to attract a new, vigorous element into the Republican Party." Herb, keenly political, enjoyed the elections the way some folks enjoy chess.

"Susan mentioned people were very supportive." Harry knew she'd get sucked into all this and she so hated politics.

"Charlotte's down with the flu." Herb brightened when his rib-eye steak sandwich was put before him. "Just what the doctor ordered."

"Better take one to Charlotte then," Harry teased him.

"I tell you what, you don't know how good a secretary she is. These last two days I've answered phones, sorted the mail into must-do, can-wait, and throwaway piles, checked the office supplies. I'm low on everything plus I've had to fiddle around with the rescheduling of the carpets. They swore on a stack of Bibles, and to a pastor, too, that they would be at the church doors at eight A.M. on Tuesday. I think I'd better send Hayden McIntyre over to Charlotte's. I need her!"

"Did you send her flowers?"

"Yes." Herb smiled at Harry as he bit into the delicious sandwich.

"Anything I can do to help? I'm off this weekend. Zack's on call." Fair shared on-call duties over the weekends with other vets. It was a good system, otherwise no equine vet in Virginia would ever have a weekend off. Horses seem to watch the calendar, being careful to injure themselves over the weekend, preferably very late at night.

Tazio Chappars came in. "Hey," she called when seeing them.

"Sit down." Fair stood up.

"No, please sit, Fair. I can't. I've got Brinkley in the truck. I don't want to leave him so I thought I'd pick up a sandwich and go back to the office."

"It's Saturday. A beautiful Saturday," Harry beamed. "You can't go to work; who knows when we'll get another one?"

"I know, I know, but I've got to catch up."

"I'll catch up in 2020." Herb laughed, his deep rumble shaking the table.

"You and Brinkley are becoming best friends." Harry thought maybe she'd better order an extra sandwich to divide among three put-out animals at home.

"I love that dog. How did I live this long without my own dog? I always told myself I was too busy but I have my own office so he comes to work with me, he goes to the construction sites. He's such a good dog, so smart." She glowed.

"Labs are," Fair agreed.

"There's a corgi sitting at home who vehemently disagrees," Harry laughed, "but Labs are incredible creatures."

"He talks to me," Tazio sheepishly admitted, "and I talk back."

"Harry talks to her critters all the time." Herb polished off the rib-eye sandwich.

"Oh, and you don't talk to Elocution and Cazenovia?"

Herb nodded at Harry. "Couldn't write a sermon without them. Just thought I'd throw the spotlight on you."

"Nice to chat with you all. Let me go order a sandwich. What did you have, Herb? It looked good." Tazio inhaled the delicious aroma.

"Rib eye."

"That's what I'll get. And one for Brinkley." She walked over to the counter.

Just then Mychelle Burns entered, looked around nervously, saw Tazio, and sidled up to her.

Tazio, at pains to conceal her dislike, smiled. "What are you doing in Crozet?"

"Nothing," she fibbed. "Saw your truck with the dog in it." Mychelle lowered her voice. "I need to talk to you. Privately."

Tazio's brow furrowed. "Not today."

"Monday? In your office."

"Mychelle, I don't have my Filofax with me. Call me Monday."

"Don't put me off. I will be in your office Monday at nine. You be there. It's important."

"You know, you're becoming like Fred. That's not an attractive prospect." Tazio exhaled through her nostrils. "I need to check my book."

Mychelle lowered her voice almost to a whisper. "Don't fuck with me."

Surprised at the other woman's crude language, Tazio replied, "Mychelle."

"Wait until you hear what I have to say. Here's a preview: Fred, at night, takes debris from construction sites and dumps them at Matthew's site. Here's another preview: H.H. paid under the table for copies of Matthew's job blueprints. You *need* to talk to me."

"All right, Mychelle, all right. Monday at nine." Tazio wondered what was going on.

Without a goodbye, Mychelle turned and left, not even bothering to close the front door behind her. One of the waitresses hurried over to close it.

Harry, along with Fair and Herb, watched the exchange

although they couldn't hear what transpired. Tazio looked back at them and shrugged. She paid for her two sandwiches and left, waving as she did so.

"Mychelle is not winning friends and influencing people," Fair observed.

"She used to be upbeat. Job's affected her. People get upset when something's wrong and it costs money to fix it. I suppose we need these building codes but they seem so, I don't know, too much paperwork, too much interference." Herb ordered Boston cream pie.

The lightbulb switched on in Harry's head. Of course, she thought to herself, how easy, both had access to H.H. Under my nose and I never saw it. One of those women is, was, H.H.'s lover. I'd bet my life on it!

"Harry?" Fair touched her hand.

"What?"

"You didn't hear a word I said."

"Fair, I'm sorry, I just had an idea." She smiled. "I'm listening, really. You have my full attention."

# 18

Coaches ride a roller coaster. While the best of them hope to build students' character, prepare them for life's unpredictables, they still must win and win convincingly. The most successful character builder in America isn't going to get a renewed contract if his or her team doesn't win. And of all coaches, the two most visible to the public are football and basketball, the college sports with the largest following, the lucrative TV contracts.

In the dark ages, no one even knew the women's basketball coach's name. These days they were stars with all the perks and pressures their male counterparts had endured and enjoyed for close to one hundred years—except one. Women's coaches didn't sleep with male students. Male coaches used to cut a swath through the girls, although those days, too, had waned thanks to administrators finally waking up to the abuse inherent in such a relationship even if freely contracted. Then again, the male coaches were usually married, a sticking point.

Married women coaches would pace the sidelines, their husbands and children breathlessly watching. The unmarried women coaches would pace the sidelines, the unmarried men breathlessly watching.

It never occurred to Coach Ryan and her assistant coaches that a murderer was watching. H. H. Donaldson's death, now known to be suspicious, wasn't connected to basketball. At least, no one thought it was.

Since Cameron loved basketball, idolized the players, and worshipped Coach Debbie Ryan, H.H. had purchased a block of ads to run concurrent with the women's basketball season thinking it would make his little girl happy. He'd even bought her a subscription to the University of Virginia newspaper so she could read the fuller accounts of the very games she had witnessed.

Each Monday, Georgina Craycroft, BoomBoom's sister-in-law and head of Virginia Graphics, would design an ad for H.H. based on that week's opponents. The last of H.H.'s ad designs would run out Sunday. Georgina didn't know whether to continue. The staff of *The Cavalier Daily* didn't want to bother Anne Donaldson but H.H. had paid for the season. Still, Georgina didn't wish to create more designs if Anne wasn't interested. She'd refund whatever monies were outstanding. Georgina was a fair-minded person.

Georgina called BoomBoom, who was closer to Anne than she was. BoomBoom was also on good terms with Coach Ryan.

Anne declared the ads were important to Cameron and, no doubt, fun for the team. BoomBoom then relayed this to Georgina who hastened to her office this beautiful Saturday morning. Old Dominion University, always tough, would be an opponent in the coming week, as well as Georgia, reputed to have the best center in women's basketball this year.

BoomBoom, curiosity rekindled by her sister-in-law's call, drove out to Harry's just as Harry pulled into her driveway.

Each disembarked at the barn.

"BoomBoom, what's up?"

Mrs. Murphy and Pewter, noses pressed against the kitchen window over the sink, watched. Tucker barked at the animal door which Harry had secured so the dog wouldn't follow her down the drive when she motored back into town.

"*What's she saying?*" Pewter pawed at the window.

"*I can't read lips,*" Mrs. Murphy replied.

"*We thought you could do everything,*" the dog, also irritated, said.

"*First, she leaves us here to go fox hunting. Then she comes back, unloads Poptart, gets everything organized, gets back in the old truck, and drives to Crozet leaving us again!*" Tucker was beside herself.

"*She did give us a treat before she left,*" Pewter said.

"*They're coming inside. Tucker, go shut the door to the bedroom. Hurry,*" Mrs. Murphy ordered.

"*I didn't shred the socks she left on the bed. You did.*" Tucker stubbornly tossed her head as she moved to the kitchen door.

"*I hate dogs.*" Mrs. Murphy soared off the kitchen counter followed by Pewter, who slid down lest she land with a thump.

The two cats raced for the bedroom. Pewter flopped on her side as Mrs. Murphy pushed the door from behind. When the door was almost closed the tiger cat slunk around it, careful not to open it more than necessary. Then she, too, flopped on her side, claws out to the max. The cats hooked their claws under the door—there was just enough space—pulling it shut. The latch didn't click but it was shut enough that a casual walk down the hall would not reveal their depredations.

"—good of Anne." BoomBoom hung her coat on one of the pegs by the back door.

"She's a strong woman." Harry hung her jacket there as well. "Can I get you something to drink?"

"No. I'll tell you why I dropped by unannounced. Talking to Georgina and then Anne reminded me of that awful night. You have a knack for figuring things out. I bet you have thought about it."

"Well—I don't know anything." Harry motioned for her to sit at the kitchen table.

"Why don't we go down to the Clam and walk it out?" BoomBoom's lovely face became quite animated.

"What do you mean, 'walk it out'?"

"If you and I start from where H.H. was sitting in his seat to where he fell, we'll know how far the killer trailed him."

"How do you know the killer did?" asked Harry.

"I've been reading about poisons."

"But the paper didn't say exactly what kind of poison."

"Exactly." BoomBoom was triumphant. "By the process of elimination I know it wasn't arsenic because it takes too long to kill you and the victim suffers from diarrhea. Wasn't cyanide or his skin would have been red. I think he was given the poison right there at the basketball game. In reviewing what I remember, I wonder if I'm correct. Know what I mean? You now know something, and when you look back, well, maybe today's knowledge clouds yesterday's events. I mean yesterday as in the past. Not literally yesterday. I've thought about who had coolers full of drinks. He could have been handed a poisoned drink. Or popcorn or a candy bar."

BoomBoom folded her hands together. "From my reading, I've learned that poisons and toxins aren't exactly the same thing. A toxin is anything that can kill or upset a living organism. But a poison is a subgroup. Poisons usually enter the body in a single massive dose or they can accumulate into a massive dose over time. Also, poisons are easy to identify."

Alert, a fascinated Harry leaned forward. "I didn't know that."

"Another thing is poisons can usually be nullified with fast treatment. With toxins"—she shook her head—"not so easy."

"What do you mean?"

"Well, toxins can kill you with minute levels. And worse, they can disguise themselves, the symptoms are masked. It takes extremely sensitive analytical instruments to detect low levels of toxins and not all of these dangerous substances have antidotes."

"So technically, you think H.H. wasn't poisoned?"

"No. If he had been, Sheriff Shaw would certainly know by now what had poisoned him. What did kill him was something used in a tiny amount. And it kind of mimicked a heart attack."

"Risky. Fingerprints. And cruel. What if Anne or Cameron had drunk from the same can? Nibbled on the candy bar?"

"*Hi.*" The two cats smiled as they entered the kitchen.

"There you are. I wondered where you all were hiding." Harry reached down to rub Mrs. Murphy's then Pewter's head. She was thinking about BoomBoom's research.

"*You'll sing a different tune when you see what they've done,*" Tucker warned.

"*Shut up, tailless butt.*" Pewter flattened her ears.

"*Lardass.*" The little dog laughed.

"*Carrion breath.*" Mrs. Murphy joined in the fun.

"*Tuna fart.*" Tucker thought she could gross them out.

"*I don't pass gas,*" the cat haughtily replied.

"*You burp a lot, though.*" Pewter giggled.

"*Whose side are you on?*" Murphy crossly questioned the gray cat who prudently stepped close to Harry.

"Hey, kids, we can't hear ourselves talk," Harry reprimanded them.

"*If you only knew.*" Tucker rolled her eyes.

"*That's the great thing about humans. They don't know squat.*" Pewter erupted in a loud laugh, startling the others.

"Perhaps they need to go out." BoomBoom rose and opened the kitchen door. The screen door had another animal door to the side of it which Harry kept unlocked.

The three refused to budge.

"Sit down, BoomBoom. They get like this whenever I leave them home. Now back to your research. The killer must have highly specialized knowledge, like a chemist. If the killer had no conscience, zip, food or drink might be the answer. If the killer does have a conscience, then he or she had to find another way to administer the poison or probably more people would be dead."

"You know." BoomBoom pointed at Harry with her forefinger.

"I do not."

"You're way too calm. You've already figured it out and I bet you've been to the Clam."

"Uh—well, I have been there, yes, but I don't know any more than you do. In fact, you know more than I do."

Harry swung her legs to and fro under her seat. She was getting excited. "Fair was present at the autopsy. He said there was a mark on the left side of H.H.'s neck, a thin penetration wound. And I bugged Coop who confirmed it and said they'd checked his clothes, they'd checked the parking lot. No small dart, not even a tiny needle. Nothing."

"Go back to the Clam with me. Come on."

"I've got chores." Harry wavered.

"All right." BoomBoom stood up. She wanted to check the scene. Would she remember something she had suppressed? She was also hoping spending time with Harry would further repair their relationship.

"It is bizarre"—Harry rose to walk BoomBoom to the door—"that he could be stabbed and we didn't see it. Nor did he yell. It doesn't make a bit of sense."

"If the weapon had been smeared with something like Novocain"—BoomBoom turned to face Harry—"H.H. might not have felt the wound. It's possible."

"It is!" Harry froze in her tracks.

"Come on, let's go." BoomBoom tapped Harry on her shoulder.

They piled into BoomBoom's mammoth Expedition. Her BMW was in the shop after being sideswiped. She had lots of cars and could converse for hours on the merits of a BMW 540i versus a Mercedes AMG 55, or any other models. The animals merrily joined them. Boom loved animals and she didn't care if her seats had pawprints on them.

They parked in the sea of asphalt and hurried to the basketball court where the girls were practicing.

Both Harry and BoomBoom waved as they trotted to their respective seats, the animals with them.

Harry closed her eyes. "I swear I felt something whizz by

the left side of my face. It may not be important... but sitting here, I, yes, I remember a whizz, kind of."

"The whoosh you felt, it could have just been a noisemaker unfurling." Boom turned to Harry from her seat.

"I didn't turn around. My focus was on the game." She threw up her hands. "But then why wasn't there a dart or a metal point in his neck?"

"H.H. pulled it out?"

"That I would have seen. No." Harry shook her head.

"What if the killer jabbed his neck when we were leaving or even in the parking lot then pocketed the knife or needle or whatever?" BoomBoom mimicked a quick jab.

Pewter had returned to the hairline crack in the wall. She sniffed. The trickle of water continued, no doubt from melting snow. Pewter could smell the dampness.

As the humans left she scampered after them. They carefully walked along the circular hall in the direction of the main entrance. Tucker stopped, lifted her nose.

Mrs. Murphy stopped, too. *"Oh."*

*"I smell it, too."* Pewter, eyes large with excitement, followed the dog now in front of a locked door.

Tucker put her nose to the ground. *"Blood. Fresh."*

The two cats inhaled deeply. *"Very, very fresh."*

*"There are other smells. This must be a broom closet."* Tucker processed the information her incredible nose was compiling. *"Disinfectant. Soap, bar soap. I can smell water, not much, but there must be a sink in there. But the blood, yes, quite strong and human. Oh, and perfume."*

The cats crowded at the door, curling their upper lips toward their noses to direct more scent into their nostrils. Yes, a hint of perfume.

*"The janitor could have cut himself."* Pewter lifted her

nose for fresher air. *"Guess it would be a feminine janitor. One who favors floral perfume."*

*"Pewter, there's a great deal of blood. Someone is dying."*

*"Or dead,"* Mrs. Murphy grimly responded.

Tucker cocked her head, swiveling her ear to catch any sound at all. *"Not yet. I can hear the human breathe, ragged."*

*"Mother, someone is hurt. Hurt bad!"* Mrs. Murphy screamed.

*"Help!"* Pewter hollered.

*"Help!"* Tucker added, her bark frantic.

Harry stopped, turning toward them. "Come on."

*"Help!"* they all bellowed.

Harry turned to BoomBoom. "Ever since Tucker took to chasing that rat at O'Bannon's Salvage yard she imagines she is the world's greatest ratter. 'Course, she never caught the rat in the first place."

*"Help!"*

"That's it!" Harry strode back, reached down, picking up a cat in each arm. "I have had about enough of this." She charged out of the building, Mrs. Murphy and Pewter wriggling. BoomBoom hurried in front of them.

She opened the door for Harry to toss the cats in the Expedition. They jumped up and down as though on pogo sticks. Pewter screamed her head off.

BoomBoom, now in the driver's seat, tried to soothe them. "There, there, she'll be right back."

*"Oh, BoomBoom, you have no idea what's wrong,"* Mrs. Murphy cried.

Harry ran back into the building where Tucker was making a fuss. As it was Saturday no one was around to pay attention to the dog. The girls were still at practice.

Seeing Harry, Tucker stood on her hind legs, scratching at the door.

"Get a grip," Harry furiously commanded.

*"You've got to open this door!"*

Harry, as if understanding, placed her hand on the door-knob. Locked. "That's one rat that will live another day."

*"No, no, someone is dying in there. I can hear them breathe. I know that sound! I know the—"*

"Tucker, we are going to have a Come to Jesus meeting right here if you don't behave." She bent down, grabbing Tucker and carrying the twenty-eight-pound whimpering dog to the car.

"They are so upset." BoomBoom worried that they might be sick.

"Spoiled is more like it." Harry shut the door to the passenger side. "I apologize."

Tears welled up in the dog's brown eyes. *"Mrs. Murphy and Pewter, I tried."*

*"You're the best dog, Tucker, the very best dog."* Mrs. Murphy licked Tucker's face as Pewter rubbed against her white chest.

*"I feel so terrible. That person is dying."*

## 19

The day faded. A sliver of white creamy cloud snaked over the Blue Ridge Mountains, with rich, deep gray-blue clouds filling the sky above. When the sun set, the white transformed to scarlet, brilliantly offsetting the mountains. So unusual was the sight that Harry, pitchfork in hand, at the manure pile mostly unfrozen thanks to the sudden thaw, stopped to appreciate the panorama.

The manure pile, contained in a pit housed by three sides of pressure-treated two-by-fours, was step one in Harry's mulch process. Once the manure and shavings cooked for a year, she'd take the front-end loader of the tractor and move it all to the second pit. If the year had had a lot of moisture, the pile would be ready to use and sell. She made a little pin money selling a pickup-truck load for thirty dollars. If it had been a drought year, she waited another year for the mixture to properly cook.

The best fertilizer was goose, duck, or chicken manure if

you could find someone to haul it and spread it. But it was expensive by Harry's standards—sometimes as high as eighteen dollars a ton—so she used it sparingly on the few trouble spots she had in her own garden. Her pastures, lush in all but the worst droughts, displayed the effects of her management.

She'd built two such pits for her neighbor, Blair. He had cattle so his mulch/manure was pretty good, too. She tended it for him since he was on the road quite a bit. Their deal was that she could haul out six pickup loads each year which she then mixed into her own piles.

The steam climbed upward as she turned the pile. The temperature skidded with the sunset. There'd be a hard frost tonight.

Mrs. Murphy, fluffed out against the encroaching cold, sat on the corner of the pit, above it all.

*"You know, the birds pick through here. You don't need to spend money buying special feeds for them."*

"You're a good companion, Mrs. Murphy." Harry observed the scarlet sky deepen to a blood red with mauve tendrils snaking through the color.

*"Thank you. I have other ideas on saving money. Feed Pewter less."* She could say this without an accompanying yowl because Pewter was in the kitchen consoling Tucker, utterly morose because she couldn't help the injured human.

"Beautiful." She scratched the cat behind the ears. "Why would anyone watch television when they can see this? The human race would rather watch something made up than something real. Sometimes I wonder why I'm human. Really, Murphy, I find my own species bizarre."

*" 'Stupid' is closer to the mark."* The cat inhaled the peaty odor of pit mingled with the sharp tang of cooling air. A silent large figure flew out of the barn cupola. The owl be-

gan her first foray of the evening. She circled Harry and Murphy, banked, then headed toward the creek.

"Damn, she is big. She gets bigger every year." Harry respected the predator; her huge claws, balled up, could knock a person off balance. If the claws were unleashed the owl could slice open flesh as easily as a butcher with a knife.

*"And haughty."*

*"Who said that?"* the owl, who had keen hearing, called as she soared away from the barn. *"Who-o-o. You-ou-ou, Mrs. Murphy. Groundling."*

*"I cannot tell a lie. It was I."*

"You two must be talking to one another," said Harry, who half-believed they were. She grew up in the country and knew animals could communicate. She just didn't realize how effectively they did.

*"Come on, Mom, time to close up the barn. Head to the house."*

Harry carried her pitchfork back to the toolshed. She checked the outside water troughs to make sure the heaters, built especially for that purpose, were floating. It was a great luxury not to chop ice in the morning. These small units either dropped to the bottom of the trough or floated, depending on the brand. Plugged into an electrical outlet, they could keep the water temperature above freezing. Horses appreciated that because they didn't want to drink ice-cold water. Less water consumption meant greater chances of colic or impaction. Harry didn't feed pellets which she thought added to winter digestive problems. She only fed lots and lots of high-quality hay—she swore by it and her horses stayed happy and healthy, no gut problems.

She walked back into the barn, closed the big sliding doors, checked everyone's water buckets, and readjusted

Tomahawk's blanket, which he'd managed to push toward the right.

Simon peered over the hayloft. *"Murphy, marshmallows."*

The possum adored marshmallows. His sweet tooth caused him to rummage through the wastebasket searching for candy wrappers. He ate all the grain spilled onto the feed-room floor, too.

*"I'll do my best but she doesn't listen,"* Murphy answered Simon.

Harry checked and double-checked, then cut the lights at the switch housed at the end of the center aisle. She opened the doors enough to slip through, then shut them tight.

Back in the kitchen, she made herself a cup of hot chocolate. Tucker, ears drooping, Pewter at her side, barely lifted her head.

Harry felt the dog's ears. Not hot. She checked her gums. Fine. "Little girl, you look so sad."

*"I am."*

*"She blames herself,"* Pewter explained.

*"If I'd run away from Mom maybe she would have chased me. If I'd kept coming back to the closet door she might have figured it out. I just didn't think fast enough."* Tears formed in the dog's eyes.

*"She's a good human but she's only human."* Mrs. Murphy joined Pewter in consoling the corgi. *"She probably wouldn't have figured it out no matter what you did. There was nothing you could do."*

Tucker was grateful for their kindness but she felt so horrible she closed her eyes. *"Someone has to find whoever is in there."*

She was right. Someone was in for a nasty shock.

# 20

Billy Satterfield, a student, worked as a janitor. He was a sandy-haired, slight boy with clean features, a regular kid who fit in with the rest of the student body when in the jeans and flannel shirts he wore to classes. On the weekends when he wore coveralls, though, students never looked his way. He was invisible, a member of the working class. People's responses to him as a broom pusher taught him a lot. He never wanted to be a negligible person, a grunt. He made good grades if for no other reason than because he was determined to graduate and make money.

A long, loopy key chain hung from his belt, the keys tucked in his right pocket. He walked to the broom closet, pulled out the keys, found the right one, and opened the door.

The sight of a youngish woman, bound and gagged, scared him half to death. Her glassy eyes stared right through him. He wanted to scream, to run down the hall, but he had enough presence of mind to make certain she was truly dead. Gingerly he touched her shoulder. Cold. Stiff.

His knees shaking, his stomach churning, he backed out of the closet, shutting the door. He leaned his head against the door for a minute fighting for his composure. It was seven-thirty in the morning. No other custodial person was on duty. As there was a basketball game tonight, other men would show up later at nine if he was lucky. He breathed deeply.

He pulled out his cell phone, a tiny folding one, and dialed 911. Within seconds he was connected to the Sheriff's Department and grateful.

Coop, working the weekend, spoke to Billy, did her best to soothe him. She was by his side within fifteen minutes, calling Rick on the way.

She heard Rick open the door, the squeaking of his rubber-soled shoes. He wore a dark charcoal suit, as he was on his way to the early service at church.

"What have we got?"

"Knife wound, bled to death internally. Let's just say our killer wasn't skillful. It was a slow death, I would think. Oh sorry, Sheriff Shaw, this is Billy Satterfield. He found the body about thirty minutes ago."

Rick extended his hand. "Sorry, Mr. Satterfield. Do you mind telling me what you saw?"

"Billy, call me Billy." He took a breath and did not look at the corpse. "I usually come in early on Saturdays and Sundays. I got here right at seven-thirty so I opened the door to the closet probably seven thirty-five and that's what I saw. I touched her shoulder—to make sure." He shivered.

Cooper reassured him. "Most people have the same reaction."

"Really?"

"They do."

Rick pulled on thin latex gloves, bent down on one knee, and carefully examined the body. He didn't move it. No sign of struggle. No other cuts. Bruising on the neck. He shook his head. "Is this your rope?"

"No, sir."

"Sorry, I didn't mean yours personally. Was this rope in the closet?"

"No, sir."

"Clothesline." Rick stood up. "I'll call the boys," he said, referring to his crime lab team. "Maybe we'll get lucky and come up with prints or at least fibers or something." He exhaled. "She wasn't winning any popularity contests but this—"

"You know her?" Billy was amazed at their professional detachment.

"Yes. She works for the county. She's a building inspector."

# 21

The wind, out of the west, carried a sharp edge. Tree branches swayed against a still blue sky. Harry walked out of St. Luke's at nine-thirty. She liked to attend the earliest service, matins, which was at eight-thirty on Sunday morning since the eleven o'clock service was packed. Vespers, at seven P.M., also pleased her. The eventide service exuded a cozy, quiet quality, especially in winter.

She didn't know how Herb preached three sermons each Sunday, but he did. He needed an assistant, a young pastor, but so far the diocese couldn't find their way to sending him one, saying there weren't that many to go around. Although overburdened, Reverend Jones thoroughly enjoyed his labors.

Tazio Chappars also liked matins. She hurried along to catch Harry.

"Sorry, Tazio, I didn't know you wanted company."

Harry pulled her cashmere scarf, a present from Miranda, tighter around her neck.

"Isn't it funny how the seasons remind you of people, past events?"

"Yes, it is."

"This time of year makes me think of my mother. She hated winter and complained nonstop from the first frost to the last. But right about the third week of January she'd say, 'A little more light. Definitely.' Then every day after that we'd have to read the newspapers together, myself and my brothers, to find the exact number of daylight hours versus nighttime hours."

"You know, I've never met your brothers. I'd like to."

Tazio quickly put her hand on top of her hat, for the wind kicked up. "Jordan and Naylor, twins. Can you imagine growing up with twin brothers? They were horrid. Anyway, they about died when I moved here. Like a lot of people they have visions of po' black folk being oppressed each and every day. I tell them it's not like that and in many ways it's as sophisticated here as back home in St. Louis, but I'm talking to a brick wall. If I'm going to see them I have to go to them."

"Gee, I'm sorry. If they ever do come, though, let me know."

"I will. It's hard to believe the creeps who put tadpoles in my Kool-Aid are now doctors. Dad's an oncologist, Jordan followed Dad. Naylor specializes in hip replacements. I'm the oddball who didn't go into medicine."

"I couldn't do it." Harry shook her head. "You picked the right career for you." She turned her back on the wind. "Boreas."

"The north wind." Tazio remembered her mythology. "I loved those stories. And the Norse sagas. In college I read the African myths, went on to Native American myths. And you know, all those stories are filled with wisdom. Not that I learned to be wise. I'm afraid that only comes the hard way."

They reached their respective trucks, each one carrying their animals. Brinkley stood up, tail wagging, when he saw Tazio.

"I wish I could take my cats and dog to church," Harry mused. "It would do them a world of good."

"Mrs. Murphy on the organ? Think again, Harry."

"You do have a point, but she is a musical kitty."

"Would you like a cup of coffee? I'll treat. I'm beginning to worry about repairs to the rectory and maybe we could have our own meeting before the meeting." Tazio's lipstick, a shiny burgundy gloss, accentuated her nice teeth when she smiled.

"Sure."

They walked into the coffee shop, quiet on Sunday morning. Harry ordered a cappuccino with mountains of frothy milk. The animals, pleased to be allowed in, actually sat by the table without making a fuss.

*"Brinkley, you're looking better,"* Tucker complimented the young Lab.

*"She's feeding me a high-protein diet because I'm still growing. And last night she put chicken gravy on it. The most delicious thing I've ever tasted."*

*"I killed a live chicken once,"* Pewter boasted. *"A Rhode Island Red and she was huge. Laid huge eggs, too."*

*"Brinkley, don't listen to her. She is such a storyteller."* Mrs. Murphy rubbed against the Lab's light yellow chest.

*"I did so kill a chicken. She walked out in front of the barn. The biggest chicken in the universe and she tried to chase me but I jumped on her back."* The gray cat drew herself up to her full height, becoming more impressive.

"Now for the real story." Tucker chuckled. "She really did jump on the back of the chicken and it was a most plump chicken. But Pewter scared the dumb bird so much she dropped dead of a heart attack. It wasn't exactly a life-and-death struggle."

"That doesn't change the fact that I killed the chicken. Brinkley, they never want to give me credit for anything. They've never killed a chicken."

"No." Tucker clamped her long jaws shut. "Harry would throw me out of the house if I did. And you were lucky she was in the barn watching you or you would really have gotten into trouble. She knew the bird had had a coronary."

"How many chickens do you have?" Brinkley asked.

"Not a single one." Mrs. Murphy laughed.

Brinkley put his nose down to touch Pewter's. "Did you kill them all?"

This went straight to Pewter's head. She puffed out her chest, she swished her tail, she tipped up her chin. It was the Mighty Puss pose. "I did not but I could have if I wanted to."

"Then what happened to the chickens?" The younger fellow was puzzled.

"Well, first you have to understand that our human is the practical sort. But every now and then she gets an idea that doesn't exactly work out. The money-saving venture actually loses and, well, she goes through three pencils doing her sums trying to figure it out. The chickens were one of those kind of things." Tucker smiled.

"At first things were okay." Mrs. Murphy picked up the story. "She bought peepies, put them under an infrared light. Well, Brinkley, you won't get one little egg for six months. But finally the great day arrived and a puny egg appeared. In time more eggs appeared from these twenty hens and the eggs got bigger and bigger as the hens got bigger. Finally, when the chickens *became ever so plump, the red fox down the lane would just yank one out of the chicken coop. Locked doors, screened top, nothing stopped him except that one big Rhode Island Red. He never could kill that chicken until heart disease did her in. Too much corn, I reckon."*

The front door opened and Cynthia Cooper came in and sat down. "Herb told me you all left church together. I checked around and here you are."

Harry knew Cooper fairly well. "What's the matter?"

"Another killing at the Clam." She motioned and the waitress brought her a cup of double latte.

"You're kidding!" Harry sat up straight, as did the animals.

"Mychelle Burns stuffed in the broom closet."

"What?" Tazio's hands shook for a moment.

"If I were the kind of person who jumped to conclusions, I'd say someone was trying to spook the team." Harry slapped her napkin next to her fork.

"At this point no theory seems far-fetched." Cooper took a deep draught of the restorative coffee. "But H.H. and Mychelle?" She turned to Tazio. "Harry told me that Mychelle was unpleasant to you at the Mountain View Grille?"

"She said she wanted to see me. It was important. Usually when she wanted to see me it was about one of my buildings. We never discussed anything but work."

"But wouldn't she give you a hint, something like, 'The copper pipes at the new house are crooked'?" Harry shrugged. "I know I'm not using terminology correctly but you know what I mean. To kind of get you thinking about the problem, real or made-up."

"Made-up is closer to the mark. You know, being a sister, I wanted to like her but I couldn't stand her. Not that I wished her dead. We had nothing in common and I felt she singled me out for particular abuse."

"At lunch the other day when she nabbed you, what did she say?" Harry jumped right in whether she had any business asking these questions or not.

"She was her usual hostile self or maybe 'demanding' is a better word." Tazio stopped herself a moment. "But there was something else."

"Fear?" Harry interjected.

"Well—no, not exactly. She baited me because she knew I didn't want to see her. Apparently, Fred loathes Matthew so much he'll carry garbage from other construction sites and dump it at Matthew's. And she said H.H. would get copies of blueprints on buildings Matthew had done. She admitted she was baiting me and said she had more to tell me so I'd better see her."

Cooper drained her cup, needing the caffeine and sugar. She started to perk up. "Did you ever hear of any improprieties about her? Payoffs? Under-the-table kind of stuff?"

Tazio vigorously shook her head no. "She was honest. She was . . . I guess the word is 'incorruptible.'"

"Can you tell us how she was killed?" Harry wanted details.

"Stabbed to death."

"How awful," Tazio said.

"In the Clam. That's what I don't get. Why there?" Harry's mind raced along.

"Do you have any notes or correspondence from Mychelle?" Cooper waved for another latte.

"Official documents. Nothing personal."

"I'd like to look at them."

"Of course. I can take you over to the office right now when we've finished our coffee."

"Maybe she wasn't a betting woman but her luck sure ran out." Cooper sighed.

*"Maybe she was another chicken the fox got at,"* Mrs. Murphy commented.

*"Some fox."* A note of bitterness crept into Tucker's voice.

# 22

As Cooper and Tazio drove off in their respective vehicles, Harry ordered a coffee to go. She needed the buzz this morning. She also ordered three doughnuts. One for her, one for Susan, and one to be shared among Mrs. Murphy, Pewter, and Tucker.

As she shepherded her small brood into the 1978 Ford half-ton, she considered whether H.H.'s and Mychelle's murders were connected by anything other than location. Both were UVA fans, but their social circles didn't overlap. They shared no hobbies. Their connection through construction must have been rife with tension.

Of course, it was possible that the demise of both people was not connected. Yet both murders occurred within days of each other. It was too suspicious, at least in her mind.

Even though neither H.H. nor Mychelle was close to her, murder comes as a shock. To snatch life from another human violated everything she had been taught. Murder created disorder. Harry loathed disorder.

A morose Tucker, paws on the dashboard, watched the road.

"*Tucker, you did what you could,*" Mrs. Murphy sympathized.

"*It must have been a slow, agonizing death,*" Tucker said.

"*Well, think of all the abandoned animals who die slow, agonizing deaths. Put it in perspective,*" Pewter counseled since she certainly didn't believe human life was more important than animal life.

"*I guess.*" The strong little dog sighed, pushed back from the dash, and landed on Pewter who complained loudly.

"All right, you two." Harry cruised down Susan's driveway, lined with blue spruces. She cut the engine. "Back door. We are wiping paws." She held up the towel she kept in the truck for this purpose. "And we are not begging for food. Do you read me, Pewter?"

"*I do not beg for food. I merely put myself in the vicinity of food.*"

"*Pulease.*" Mrs. Murphy held up her paw as Harry wiped it.

"*Yeah, pulease.*" Tucker drew out "please" even more.

"*Mock me if you must.*" Pewter sniffed.

Harry opened the back door. "It's me."

"Den," Susan called out.

The three animals rushed in, greeting Owen, Susan's corgi and Tucker's brother, followed by Harry.

"Where is everybody?"

"Ned took Brooks to Barnes & Noble after church. He promised her a book if she made an A in her last history test and she did. And once there you know she'll drag him to Old Navy and they'll have to check out the shoe stores and then he'll pop into the clothing store. Ned has more ties than David Letterman, I swear. The shopping will exhaust them. So they'll eat at Hot Cakes or maybe Bodo's. I'll get a loaf of bread from Our Daily Bread. Ain't motherhood grand?"

"Susan, shut up!"

"What?"

"Mychelle Burns has been killed. Her body was found at the Clam. Stabbed."

"What! You waited all this time to tell me?"

"I couldn't get a word in edgewise."

*"Mother can talk,"* Owen laconically said.

*"Can't they all?"* Tucker agreed with her brother.

"I brought you a doughnut. We've got figuring to do."

Harry, knowing Susan's house as well as her own, walked over to the writing desk, picked up a tablet and a pencil.

"If I'm going to eat this doughnut, I'll perish from sugar shock. I'll make us sandwiches, then we can eat the doughnut."

"Susan, later. Come on. Look at this." She rapidly drew a sketch of the Clam, the parking lot, and a cutaway view of the interior of the Clam.

"Harry, you brought coffee but you didn't bring me any?"

"Oh—I'm sorry. I didn't think of that."

"Selfish." Susan walked to the kitchen, returning with a large mug of coffee. She sat next to Harry on the leather chesterfield sofa.

"Okay. Here's where H.H. fell down. X marks the spot. There are broom closets on each floor but if I remember correctly, the first one going in from the main doors is about here." She made another X. "I wonder if the killer works at the Clam."

"Honey, I hate to cast stones at your theory but I don't think where they were found matters. The question is why."

"I know that!" Harry got testy. "But wouldn't you agree that two deaths, murders, right here and here practically back to back are frightening—and probably connected."

"How'd you find out?"

"Coop tracked down Tazio and me after church."

"What's Tazio got to do with it?"

"Nothing except that Mychelle cornered her at the Mountain View Grille"—Harry named the restaurant—"and told her she wanted a meeting with her right then. This was yesterday. Tazio declined nicely and Mychelle became un-nice. Her specialty. Said that Tazio better see her first thing Monday morning. Tazio assumed it had to do with some code violation. I was right there with Fair and Herb. Anyway, we all saw it. Mychelle left, her pout intact."

"Speak no ill of the dead."

"Oh, I just can't be that big of a hypocrite." Harry dismissed the ancient protective phrase.

"I can't resist." Susan reached for the doughnut.

*"Me, me, me,"* Pewter cried piteously.

"That's why I bought this extra doughnut." Harry divided it into four pieces which irritated Pewter who tried to steal Mrs. Murphy's, receiving a box on the ears for her efforts.

Susan savored the delicious glaze. "If Mychelle was the woman behind H.H.'s—"

"Already thought of that. Only one person has a motive under those circumstances. Anne Donaldson."

"I can't believe Anne would kill her husband and then Mychelle."

"People are totally irrational about what we call 'love.' I call it 'mutual psychosis.' "

"Bull."

"I need to trace Anne's activities."

"Like hell you do. That's Rick and Coop's job, and if you've thought of it, you can rest assured they've thought of it. And furthermore, Harry, it's in bad taste snooping around Anne."

"Not if she killed them."

"She didn't."

"Who died and made you God? Since when do you know the unknowable?"

"I know Anne."

"Listen, Susan, she was sitting smack next to him at the game. She could have easily slipped him the toxin, not poison, but toxin, or scratched his neck where the tiny puncture was, is. I suppose it's still there. I mean, he won't decay for some time."

"That is the most gruesome thought." Susan made a face.

"Well, the embalmers load them up depending on the viewing time, the temperature, I guess they factor in stuff like that. And even though he's in the ground he's still intact. That's all I was saying."

"How can you think of stuff like that?"

"I just do. And you do, too. It might take you longer."

"Thank you," Susan dryly replied.

"I don't mean it that way. You're smarter than I am."

"You went to Smith, I didn't."

"That's neither here nor there. Our minds work differently. That's why we're best friends."

"Is that it? I always wondered." Susan's good humor was restored.

"Anyway, she could have so easily done him in and we'd never, ever know. About Mychelle, well, not an elegant murder. Sloppy."

"God, it is ghastly. The murders are so different, in execution, I mean, it's quite possible they were committed by two different people."

Harry replied, "That's logical but I know in my bones that H.H.'s and Mychelle's murders are connected. I've even thought that H.H. might owe money from gambling."

"That's a different kettle of fish and if this is somehow connected to college sports, there will be a lot more dead bodies. Those rings are very well organized. Hundreds of thousands of dollars change hands."

"And the playoffs are right around the corner."

Susan reached in the white bag. "Damn."

"What?"

"I wanted another doughnut."

"I'm sorry. You're always moaning about losing weight. I don't know why. You look just fine."

"You haven't seen me naked lately." Susan laughed.

"No. Should we hit the showers?"

"Hey, golf and tennis season will be here before you know it. Do you want to see me walking through the ladies' locker room, a towel wrapped around me, looking like the great white whale?"

"Susan, you exaggerate."

"A tad." She clasped her hands together. "But now I can't get the thought of another doughnut out of my mind and I have all this correspondence to catch up on." She pointed to a tottering pile on the desk. She thought about sneaking a cigarette to curb her appetite but dismissed that remedy. The doughnut was proving a more powerful temptation.

"Come on. We can pick up more doughnuts. Hey, we could go to Krispy Kreme."

Susan shook her finger at her. "You know how I love those doughnuts. Not fair."

As the humans and animals piled into Susan's station wagon, Mrs. Murphy said, *"The secret of success is to watch the doughnut, not the hole."*

# 23

"What do you mean she's dead? She can't be dead. She's supposed to be in my office tomorrow at eleven!" Fred Forrest shouted at the sheriff.

His wife, Lorraine, hurried back into the living room. She'd left her husband alone with the sheriff and his deputy but hearing his raised voice she thought he might need her. Fred possessed a terrible temper.

"Fred, honey?"

He turned to her. "Mychelle is dead. They say Mychelle is dead." He was standing in front of his chair, having bolted up the minute he got the bad news.

"I'm sorry, Mrs. Forrest." Rick was standing in front of her.

"Sit down, Sheriff. Fred, you should have asked the sheriff and Deputy Cooper to sit down. Please." She motioned to both of them to have a seat. "Now, Fred, you just take a deep breath. Sit down, honey."

He remained on his feet. "I don't believe it."

"I'm afraid it's true." Cooper's voice was steady.

Finally Fred submitted to his wife's tugging and dropped into his chair.

"Would you like me to go, Sheriff?"

"No. Perhaps you'll be able to help us, Mrs. Forrest."

She perched on the edge of the large, cushy chair next to Fred's La-Z-Boy.

"How did she die?" Fred's bottom jaw snapped upward like a turtle's.

"She suffered a stab wound. The coroner's report may reveal more information, though. We try not to jump to conclusions."

"This is terrible. This is the worst thing I've ever heard. A young woman like that. She had everything to live for." His eyes had a wild look.

"You worked closely with her?" Rick asked as Cooper unobtrusively took out her notebook, flipping over the cover.

"I supervised her. She was my best in the field. Soaked it all up. Only had to tell her once." He kept shaking his head. "Who would do a thing like this?"

"That's what we want to know." Rick rubbed his forehead. "Did she have a boyfriend?"

"She didn't say but we didn't talk about personal things, Sheriff. Strictly business. When men and women work together it has to be strictly business."

"I see." Rick avoided glancing at Cooper since they talked about everything and everyone under the sun. "Well, did you ever notice any men meeting her after work?"

"No, sir. That girl did her job, then climbed in her car and drove home. Every single day. Never mixed in pleasure with her job. No, sir."

"Would you characterize Mychelle as a happy person?"

"Well, I guess I would. She didn't complain." This was Fred's version of happiness.

"Did she ever have difficulties with contractors? Architects?"

Fred pinched his lips together. "Any one of them can be a headache on any given day. She was professional. If something was wrong she explained the problem. She knew the county code forwards and backwards. Very professional."

"Did you ever receive complaints about her?"

"Our department gets every whiner in the county. But it wasn't personal, you see. Doesn't matter which building inspector is on the job. Contractor will call back and say, 'Fred Forrest says I don't have proper ingress and egress.' Stuff like that."

"No one ever called and said, 'Mychelle Burns is wrong' or 'She's impolite.' That sort of thing?" Rick queried.

"No."

"What about H. H. Donaldson?"

"No different."

"You didn't like him?"

"No. Man was a pain in the ass. Thought he was an artist. That type. I didn't wish him dead, you understand, but I never liked the guy."

"He never called complaining about Mychelle?"

"No. H.H. just called to complain, period."

"Any other contractor that you would describe as a prima donna?"

"Olin Reid's like that."

"What about a huge operator like Matthew Crickenberger?"

"He's reasonable but, you see, Sheriff, that's pretty much the way it is. The bigger the operator, the better he is. I don't have but so many citations on a Crickenberger job. It's the little guy's trying to pull the wool over my eyes. Do it cheap, you see. Doesn't always have good subcontractors. The best attract the best."

"I see." Rick patted his pack of cigarettes in his chest pocket. He wouldn't light up in Fred's house, but it was reassuring to know his Camels were right there. "Did Mychelle ever come into money?"

Fred's expression was surprised. "Money?"

"An inheritance, perhaps. Maybe she won a lottery ticket, you know, something for a thousand bucks. Anything?"

"No. Never saw her spend much. A sensible girl. Why?"

"Money is often a motive for murder. Perhaps she came into some money. That sort of thing."

Fred shook his head. "No. I would have known. I don't think people can hide money. Even though she didn't bring her personal life to work, I would have noticed new clothes or things."

"Did she gamble?"

Now he was really surprised. "Mychelle?"

"Sure. Gambling's big."

"Only time I ever saw her use the phone was for business. Same with the cell phone. County phone. Gotta have it in the field, you know. No extra calls. No, sir."

Lorraine took advantage of the momentary lull in the conversation to ask Rick and Cooper if they'd like refreshments but they declined.

"Uh, Mr. Forrest—"

"Sheriff, my name is Fred and you know that."

"I do." Rick smiled. "All right, what about sports? Big sports fan?"

"Yes, sir. Loved UVA. Any UVA team. Loved the

Pittsburgh Pirates. Could never understand that." A puzzled expression crossed his face.

"Now, Fred, you're a pretty big sports fan yourself."

"I guess I'd have to agree."

"Well, I agree." Lorraine put in her two cents' worth.

"You ever run into Mychelle at a game?"

"Now, I rarely saw her at football. Stadium's so big, you see. I know she was there but I didn't see her. I'd see her at basketball. Men's and women's. Big fan of women's. Big fan."

"Do you recall if she had dates? Do you remember seeing her with anyone consistently?"

He thought hard. "I'd usually see her with a bunch of girls. All about her age. A couple of times I saw her with a fellow but"—he shook his head—"couldn't tell you who."

"I would guess Mychelle would be good with numbers."

"Sure."

"Fred, I have to chase down any and every idea."

"Guess you do. Guess you do."

"You won't like this question but I have to ask you. Do you think she could have been taking bribes to overlook anything not up to grade?"

Fred vigorously shook his head. "No way, José. No way."

"Do you have any idea why Mychelle might have been killed?"

"I don't, but I sure hope you catch the bastard who did it. She was a good girl, Sheriff. Kept to herself. Not a flashy girl but she did her job and she did a good job. She had a future, she did."

"And someone took it away from her," Lorraine quietly said.

"Mrs. Forrest, do you have any idea why someone might

kill Mychelle Burns?" Rick thought she was relaxed enough to speak up if she had a thought.

"Sheriff, I don't. I don't think she was a happy girl. She was a person finding her way in life but I can't imagine her in some kind of trouble, trouble like this."

"Drugs?"

Fred interjected. "I'd have known. An employee can only hide drugs or booze but so long." Then he turned to his wife. "Why do you say she was unhappy?"

"She did her job just like you said, dear, but I never saw Mychelle animated about anything." Lorraine held up her hand because Fred was going to interrupt her. "Except for UVA sports, like you said. But she never talked about hobbies or her friends or a special friend. My personal opinion is that she was a lonely girl without a lot of social skills. I don't think she was happy."

"You never told me that."

"Dear, you never asked."

# 24

Susan and Harry munched their doughnuts in Susan's station wagon, the cats and dogs in the rear seat, a beach towel on the leather to protect it.

"I am not driving down to the Clam."

"Didn't ask." Harry wrinkled her nose.

"That shows some good judgment for a change," Susan replied in a singsong voice.

"We could go over to Tazio's office. See if she's there."

"Something tells me this has nothing to do with the church guild."

"Coop left with her. Come on, Susan. Just cruise by. You don't have to stop."

As it wasn't far out of the way, Susan drove by Tazio's office. She'd converted the old barbershop just south of the railroad overpass. Tazio's big truck sat in the parking lot.

"She's done a great job on that old building."

THE TAIL OF THE TIP-OFF

Just then Tazio and Brinkley opened the door, turned to shut it.

Harry rolled down her passenger window. "Taz!"

Tazio turned to wave. "Hey."

Susan pulled up next to Tazio's truck since Harry was half hanging out the station wagon window letting in the cold air.

"Tazio, any luck?" Harry asked as Susan parked next to the truck.

"With Coop?"

*"Hi,"* the animals called to Brinkley who responded in turn.

*"This is my brother, Owen."* Tucker introduced the corgi.

As the animals chatted so did the people.

"—empty." Tazio pulled her scarf tighter around her neck as she walked to her truck. "Makes me wonder, though. What if Mychelle told other people she was seeing me Monday? She was whispering about it, as you well know, but being emotionally obvious, if you know what I mean. Someone out there might think I know more than I know—which is nothing."

"If Cooper thought you were in danger, she'd tell you," Susan sensibly reassured the architect.

"I'll cut to the chase." Harry opened the door, got out so she could stand face-to-face with Tazio.

This irritated Susan who now had to twist her neck and lean over even farther.

"What chase?"

"Did you sleep with H.H.?"

"Harry, I can't believe you asked me that!" The pretty woman's voice rose.

"No time to pussyfoot." Harry lamely defended herself.

"I can't believe it, either." Susan agreed with the disgruntled Tazio. "On second thought, I can. She's capable of anything including bad manners—rarely happens but she is capable."

"Come on, you all. Two people are dead. You're fretting over manners?" Harry crossed her arms over her chest.

"No." Tazio folded her arms over her chest, too.

"Then it was Mychelle." Harry leaned back against the station wagon.

"You don't know that." Tazio was again surprised.

"No, but that's my guess. A crime of passion."

"Anne Donaldson might have wanted to kill him but she's not the type." Susan gave up and got out of her car. "I don't believe it."

"Susan, why would anyone else want to kill H.H. and then Mychelle? There is no other motive. They weren't stealing money. We'd have seen it. People can't have money without spending it. Actually, this is America. We don't even need to have money and we spend it. So I can't think that's behind it. Drugs?" She threw up her hands. "What's left? Sexual revenge?"

"You can't jump to conclusions like that and really, Harry, you're usually more thoughtful," Susan chided her. "There could be other reasons. As I've said before, the murders may not even be related."

"What other reasons?" A frosty breath spiraled upward when Tazio spoke.

"I don't know. Someone could have made a bad business deal with H.H. Something we know nothing about, something even his wife knows nothing about. Maybe Mychelle had a boyfriend she crossed. The murders don't have to be related. There really are coincidences in this world." Susan put her hands in her pockets. "What if one of H.H.'s ex-girlfriends flew into a rage when he left Anne for Mychelle? Well, we think it was Mychelle. Why didn't he dump his wife for her, the ex, I mean? People do crazy things."

Harry stubbornly stuck to her guns. "If that's the case, then I am right. The murders are related."

As the humans argued, Brinkley proudly told the little pack in the station wagon, *"I carry Tazio's plans. She doesn't have to get up from her chair. I can carry blueprints without making a tooth mark."*

*"What about slobber?"* an unimpressed Pewter said.

*"I don't slobber,"* Brinkley replied.

*"Tucker does."* Pewter felt like being a pill.

*"I do not."*

*"She does not,"* Owen grumbled. *"Corgis don't slobber."*

*"He's right. They nip your heels. Very big on herding."* Mrs. Murphy wrapped her tail around her. It was growing colder in the vehicle. *"Death from the ankles down."*

Finally, Harry and Susan climbed back in the car.

"I'll see you at the board meeting. And Harry, how could you even think I would sleep with H.H.? I still can't believe you asked me that."

"He wasn't that bad looking."

"Not my type."

"Okay, I'm sorry. I was kind of rude."

"Kind of!" Susan exclaimed.

"Like you haven't done worse." Harry flopped back against the seat. "See you." She waved to Tazio who put Brinkley in the cab of the truck. Then Harry rolled up the window.

"I may have done worse to you but not to an acquaintance."

"I apologized."

"With no enthusiasm. I am taking you back to your

truck. I am not driving you anywhere else. I will not risk more social embarrassment."

"Sure. Get your doughnuts and forget your best friend. I know how you are."

The animals snuggled up to one another, although Mrs. Murphy kept her ears cocked in case the humans said anything of importance.

"My advice to you is to concentrate on other things."

"I told you this was about sexual revenge. I'm going to tell Cooper, too."

"She'll be thrilled."

"You can be so sarcastic."

"Oh, and you are beauty, truth, and light. You're bored, Harry. When you get bored you get into trouble. I have half a mind to call your ex-husband and tell him just what I think."

"Of what?"

"Of you."

"You think I'm terrific." A raffish grin appeared on Harry's lips, glossy with lip protector.

"So modest."

"Don't call Fair."

"Make up your mind."

This was a subject of fruitful contention. Fair wanted his ex-wife back. She had forgiven him at last. They'd been divorced four years. She loved him but she didn't think she was in love with him one day and then the next day she thought she was.

Harry scrunched down in the seat. "Oh Susan, why is life so damned complicated?"

"It just is. Even here in Crozet. But you have to be fair, forgive the pun. If there's someone out there for you, go look. If you want Fair, then just do it. Get it over with. Take him back and make a life again."

"That's what everyone wants me to do."

"I never said I did."

"Actually, you haven't, for which I am grateful."

"Are you confused?"

"No."

"Then let him go if you don't want him. It will be easier than watching him fall in love without you letting him go."

Harry sat upright, her head sharply turning in Susan's direction. "What do you know that I don't?"

"Nothing. I really don't. But people can only wait so long. He's repented. He's been respectful. I don't think he will have another episode like the one that, well, you know. He got it out of his system." Susan held up her right hand for Harry to shut up since her mouth had opened wide. "Listen. I'm telling you what I observe and what I think. I'm not telling you to take him back. But make up your mind. Just damn well do it. Fish or cut bait."

Harry exhaled, blowing the hair on her forehead up. "I hate this."

"Oh, come on, it's not as bad as when your marriage broke up."

"That's true."

"We aren't getting any younger, you know. Forty sure draws closer."

"So what?" Harry replied.

"You're a pretty girl. You need a partner. Life is just better with the right person. I ought to know. I married Ned when I was nineteen, nineteen years ago, and it was one of the smartest things I ever did."

"Ned is pretty wonderful, although he may not be so

wonderful once the campaign starts. Maybe you can paint on a smile."

"I'll manage."

"Guess you will. You usually do. But here's the thing, Susan. I can respond to other men. Remember when Diego from Uruguay visited here? He started my motor. If I can feel that way about another man I don't know if I'm doing the right thing getting tied down again. Maybe this time I'll be the unfaithful one ..."

"Revenge?"

"I've been through the revenge fantasies. I'm over it. I'm even over not trusting him. I'm just"—she shrugged—"stuck."

"Love changes over time. It can't be like when you were first together. The fire burns more steadily. It's better, I think. If you're looking for that falling-in-love high, no, you won't find that with Fair. But what you have is genuine."

"There are advantages to getting back together permanently with Fair. He knows me and I know him. He has his work here and I have mine. I'm not leaving Crozet. I don't care how alluring another man is. I can't imagine not living here."

"Maybe you should take a year off? Rent the farm and live somewhere else. Just to experience it."

"I lived in Northampton, Massachusetts. College was great but I belong here, right here in dowdy Crozet."

"The town's not much," Susan agreed. "Of course, central Virginia is one of the most beautiful places on earth."

"Right, and think about this. Suppose I rented a place in—in—I got one, Montana? I haul my horses out there. I'm not living without my horses. I take the kitties and Tucker. To do what? Think great thoughts? I have no great thoughts. I don't even have medium-sized thoughts."

"I'm glad you have decisively reached that conclusion. Now how about the other one?"

"You're right"—her voice dropped, then rose again—"you are. But you know, I look around and I think I know everyone and they know me and then I remember that we still don't know who Charly Ashcraft's illegitimate child is, nor the mother, and that's a mystery of what, twenty years? I think about that and I think about other things and, well, I can't stand it. I can't stand not knowing things. Poor Fair, I drive him crazy."

Charly Ashcraft, the handsomest boy in Harry's high school class, had fathered two illegitimate children before he graduated from high school. The first one was never identified, nor was the young woman who was the mother. The second one was known to live out of town, but the unknown first child remained one of those mysteries that would every now and then crop up in conversations. Charly himself had been shot a few days before his twentieth high school reunion in a pure revenge killing. Many thought he had it coming.

"Forget Charly's child," Susan firmly said. "It's not possible to know everything about everybody."

"You're right, you know, and that kind of scares me. Do I even know myself? Does anybody?"

"Yes. If you want to learn, time teaches you."

"H-m-m."

Susan pulled into her driveway. "Think about what I've said."

"I will. I always think about what you tell me even if I don't agree."

Susan cut the motor. "And Harry, for God's sake, don't run around and tell people that H.H. and Mychelle were killed because they were lovers."

"I wouldn't do that."

"I guess you wouldn't but you did give me a jolt when you went straight for Tazio like that."

"She can take it."

"Why do you say that?"

"I've gotten to know her a little bit by being on the guild with her. She's tough."

"You know what bothers me?"

"What?"

"I don't think those murders have one thing to do with an illicit romance. I don't know why but I just don't. I'd feel better if they did. But I have this weird sensation that all this is about something else, something way out of our league."

As Susan rarely said things like that, Harry paid attention. She was usually the one with hunches, dragging Susan along.

"Could be."

"And because we can't imagine it, it's dangerous. I think what you don't know *can* hurt you."

"So you do think the murders are related?" Harry couldn't hide the note of triumph in her voice.

"Yes, I do, and once you've killed two people, what's a third?"

# 25

The basketball game that evening was a subdued affair made even more dolorous by a poor performance. UVA lost by seven points.

Mychelle's body had only been found that morning, but the story was already on the television news. Those not watching the news soon heard about it from their neighbors on the bleachers. People, being the curious creatures that they are, walked by the broom closet and stopped to stare. A few were disappointed that blood wasn't smeared on the floor.

Even Matthew Crickenberger, ever ebullient, was quiet. He handed out drinks as always but didn't have the heart to blow his noisemakers. BoomBoom dispiritedly shook her blue and orange pennant a few times but that was about it.

Fred Forrest, too shaken by Mychelle's murder, didn't attend the game.

After the game, Harry sprinted to her truck. She had
talked with Fair on the phone earlier. Both of them decided
this wasn't the night for him to take Harry and BoomBoom
out for a drink.

The lights of the university receded as she rolled down
Route 250 passing Farmington Country Club on the right,
Ednam subdivision on the left. About a mile from Ednam
the old Rinehart estate reposed on the left. Subdivisions like
Flordon and West Leigh were tucked back into the folds of
the land but much of it remained open. A sparkle of light
here or there testified to a cozy home, a plume of smoke
curling up out of the chimneys.

Harry loved leaving Charlottesville, rolling into the quiet
of the countryside. She'd shift her eyes right and left searching for the reflection off a deer's eyes or a raccoon. Seeing
that greenish glare, she'd slow down.

Then she reached the intersection of Route 250, which
curved left toward Waynesboro and then Staunton. She
took the right into Crozet, new subdivisions dotting the
way into town. She passed the old food processing plant,
currently empty and a cause for sadness. She passed the tidy
row of small houses on the north side of the road. A tricky
little curve ahead kept her alert. The supermarket was on
the right and the old, still-intact train station perched on her
left.

When she reached the intersection with the flashy new
gas station she turned left. A blessed absence of traffic allowed her to poke along. She could see the lights on in Tracy
Raz's apartment. He'd renovated the top floor of the old
bank building, which he was buying. Closemouthed, he
wouldn't tell anyone what he planned to do with the building but, knowing Tracy, it would be interesting. He hadn't

even told Miranda, whose curiosity was reaching a fever pitch.

When she finally pulled into the long driveway to the farm she felt oddly happy. She loved her little part of the world and most of the people in it. She knew people's grandparents and parents, she knew their children, she knew their kith and kin including the ones not worth knowing. She knew their pets and their peculiarities—both the pets' and the people's. She knew who had the oldest walnut tree, the best apple orchard, who put up the best Christmas decorations, who was generous, who was not. She knew who liked the color red and who liked blue, who had money, who didn't, and who lied about what they did have. She knew who could ride and who couldn't, who could shoot and who couldn't. She knew the frailties of ego and body. She'd seen the ambitious rise, the lazy fall, and drink and drugs claim their fair share of souls. She'd watched the ebb and flow of gossip about any one person and had been a victim of it herself, divorce being a spectator sport. She'd seen undeserving people prosper occasionally and the deserving brought low through no fault of their own. She knew chaos was like a chigger. You couldn't see the little blighter but the next thing you knew, there it was under your skin biting the hell out of you.

Murder was chaos. Apart from the immorality of it, it offended her sense of order and decorum. Furthermore, a murder acted like cayenne pepper on her system, it speeded her up. It inflamed her own ego. How dare someone do this? And what really nibbled at her was the fact that whoever did thought they were smarter than other people. She flat-out hated that. She would not be outsmarted.

When she pulled up to the back door, she saw three pairs

of eyes staring out from the kitchen window. She heard Tucker barking a welcome.

She sprinted to the door, walked through the screened-in porch, opened the door to the kitchen and a rapturous welcome.

"My little angels."

*"Mom!"* came the chorus.

"Kids, I'm going to figure out what's going on around here. We'll show 'em."

*"She never learns."* Tucker's ears drooped for a moment.

*"And we do double duty. Her senses are so dull, without us she would have been dead a long time ago,"* Pewter complained.

*"And so would we,"* Mrs. Murphy forcefully said. *"She saved me from a sure death at the SPCA and she took care of you, too, Pewter. She talked Market Shiflett into giving you a home when he found you abandoned under the Dumpster. The fact that you ate him out of his convenience store is another matter. She saved us both. Where she goes, we go."*

Pewter, chagrined, replied, *"You're absolutely right. One for all and all for one."*

Tucker laughed. *"You all are so original."*

As Tucker had been a gift to Harry from Susan Tucker, she didn't feel saved but she still felt lucky. Harry loved her and Tucker loved Harry, devotedly.

"Aren't we chatty tonight?" Harry picked up Murphy, kissing her forehead, and then she picked up Pewter, kissing her, too.

*"Human kisses."* Pewter grimaced.

As Pewter wriggled out of Harry's arms, Murphy kissed the human back, her rough tongue making Harry giggle. Then she put Murphy down and knelt to kiss Tucker. Harry loved her animals and, if truth be told, she probably loved them more than people.

As for her declaration that she would figure out what was going on, she might have been a little less cocky if she had been sitting in on Mychelle Burns's autopsy.

26

Cooper, wearing a lab coat, stood beside the corpse as Tom Yancy worked.

Sheriff Shaw had prowled the corridors of the Clam during the game. He didn't have to say why. She knew her boss. He was a good law officer, his methods were laudable, but he also had a sixth sense. Sometimes if he'd just walk around or sit at a crime scene, he'd get what he called "a notion." Through his example, she'd learned to trust her own instincts. There was no shortcut to hard police work but, still, those instincts could put you on the right track.

"No strangulation. No rape." Yancy talked, his face not two inches from Mychelle's neck. "No bruises."

"No struggle?"

"No. The first wound you saw, the one here right under the thoracic cavity didn't kill her. It was this one, not so easily seen." He pointed to a surprisingly clear stab wound. A few drops of blood discolored the entry point right below her heart. "The weapon nicked her heart but it took some time for it to kill her. She had a strong heart."

"No similarity at all to H.H.?"

"No. Not in method. She faced her killer. He or she stabbed her once, then twice. Close. The killer was very close. He used a stiletto or thin-bladed knife. Delivered with force. The internal bleeding was much more severe than the external. As I recall, you said there was blood but not a mess of it."

"Right."

"She wasn't expecting the blow. There are no fingerprints on the back of her neck. If she had tried to flee, the killer would have reached around and held her by the back of the neck to deliver this wound at this angle. If she'd turned away or he'd grabbed an arm, the wound would be at a different angle, flesh would be torn. My educated guess is this blow was a complete surprise delivered by someone she knew well enough to let him or her get very close."

"Stiletto." Cooper thought to herself that this was an odd choice for a weapon, something for opera, not real life or death.

Yancy half-smiled. "Be a lot easier to knock someone off with a butcher knife but a big knife is harder to conceal."

"Anything else I should know?" Cooper asked.

Yancy shrugged. "She had genital herpes."

"Did H.H.?"

"I saw no external sign."

"Do you have any blood left from that autopsy?"

"Down in Richmond. Yes."

"Better run a test for it. It'll show in the blood, won't it?"

"Oh yeah." Yancy exhaled. "I wish we'd get that toxicology report on H.H. soon."

"Amazing what shows in the blood, isn't it?"

"The human body is amazing, how people abuse it and it

just keeps ticking. I've cut open people whose livers were like tissue paper. I'd lift them out and they'd disintegrate, I mean come apart between my fingers. And that wasn't what killed the corpse. Makes me wonder."

"Apart from the genital herpes, anything else?"

"She was in good health. The knife pierced the left lung, as you can see here"—he held down the chest cavity where he'd opened her up—"then nicked the heart. With each beat of the heart the nick tore a little bit more. The blood seeped out."

"Was it painful?"

"Yes. You can feel your heart."

"Jesus."

"Hope she believed in Him. Maybe it gave her comfort."

"How strong would you have to be to stab her twice like that?"

"Not weightlifter strong but strong enough."

"A slight person could do it with great force?"

"Sure."

"H-m-m, well, the usual. Tests for drugs, alcohol, and I guess poison."

"She wasn't poisoned. The body doesn't lie, Coop. She died by violence."

Cooper noticed Yancy's blue eyes. "More than any of us you see what we do to one another. I see it in a different way but you see it in the tracery of the veins."

"Like you, I try to keep my professional distance and I'd be a liar if I said there weren't people on this slab who didn't deserve it. But a young woman, prime of life, I gotta wonder. Don't take this the wrong way, but if she'd been sexually molested it would make more sense to me. This," he shook his head, "this was about as far away from sex as you can get."

# 27

Wearing a white hard hat, Fred Forrest buttonholed Matthew Crickenberger at the site of the new sports complex. Tazio and Brinkley had just arrived, too. Matthew greeted the wiry man with no affection and none was returned. Tazio said hello to Stuart Tapscott and Travis Critzer who would be in charge of the earthmoving operation. They didn't get a chance to put in another word.

Fred folded his arms across his chest. "Don't think because I'm shorthanded that you can get away with anything."

"Oh, come on, Fred, I'm not trying to get away with any thing. I've always gone by the code, exceeded code." Matthew's voice betrayed a hint of disgust.

"You're all the same," Fred sneered. "I'm hiring someone real soon and I'll have him up to speed in no time. You'd better toe the line. Going to be my special project, right here." He tapped the frozen earth with his foot. "Going to drop by just about every day."

"You can do whatever you want," Matthew, his face florid, replied.

"That's exactly right." Fred, no trace of humor, jutted his chin out. "Think you were damned lucky to get your environmental impact studies passed. UVA." He sniffed, implying the studies were accepted because this was a UVA project.

The truth was the opposite. Any time the university sought to expand or build, the county faced the hue and cry from non-university people that the school, like a giant gilded amoeba, was smothering the county. Any UVA request going before any county board or the county commission itself bore unusual scrutiny. Also, any university project was certain to be reported in the newspaper, radio, and on TV. The public then would respond.

Fred knew that. He wanted to get Matthew's goat. If the opportunity presented itself for Fred to needle Matthew, he took it.

"You've got a copy of the study, Fred. Read it yourself."

"Did. That's why I said you're lucky."

Stuart Tapscott, an older and wiser man, had to walk away. Travis, in his thirties, followed Stuart's prudent example. They didn't want to say something they would later regret.

Tazio stuck by Matthew. Brinkley stuck by Tazio.

"Get that damned dog out of here." Fred pointed a finger at the handsome animal.

"No." Tazio stared Fred straight in the face.

"You'll do what I tell you or I can make life interesting." He practically licked his lips.

"It's not against code for me to have a dog with me on the

job. And you push me, I'll push right back. Go bully someone else."

"You think because you're a woman and black I'll go easy
on you? Think again. You're all the same, you architects, big
construction people. You think you're better than us. Make
more money. We're just clock punchers. I know what you
think. How you think. Get away with whatever you can."

*"Leave Tazio alone, jerk,"* Brinkley warned as he put himself between Fred and Tazio.

"That dog's growling at me. I'll call Animal Control."

"He's clearing his throat." Matthew, feeling unflappable
today, smiled. "Fred, run along. We've got work to do."

"I'll go when I'm goddamned good and ready."

"Suit yourself." He turned his back on Fred, put his hand
under Tazio's elbow, guiding her to a spot ten yards away
where a peg with surveyor's tape was in the ground. Brinkley
remained next to Tazio but looked over his back.

Fred followed them. "Design will never work. Too much
glass. Too expensive to heat."

"It will work. Not only will it work, it will be less expensive to heat and cool than the building currently in use, and
this building is twice the size, thanks to my design"—she
squared her shoulders—"and thanks to modern materials."

"Glass will pop out in the first big storm. Pop out like
what happened to the John Hancock Building in Boston."

"Fred, we haven't even broken ground, why don't you
plague someone else? You can't find fault with dirt."
Matthew winked at Tazio.

*"Yeah, leave my mother alone."* Brinkley seconded the motion.

"I can declare the foundation inadequate. Shifting sub-
strata."

"Go ahead. I've got a geologist and an engineer to prove

you wrong. Go ahead, Fred, get on the wrong side of UVA. You aren't going to find one thing amiss, you're going to delay construction, cost the university money and, buddy, I wouldn't give a nickel for your social life in this town."

"Scares me." He feigned fear then said with malice, "I know how to cover my ass."

"Is that why Mychelle is dead?" Matthew verbally slipped the knife right between his ribs.

"What the hell is that supposed to mean!" The cords stood out on Fred's thin neck.

"That you were banging her, buddy, and it got too hot. You just did her in."

Face contorted with rage, he spat, "You son of a bitch. Liar."

"You were in love with her. I've got eyes." Matthew had the whip hand now.

Tazio and Brinkley watched with lurid fascination. Stuart, Travis, and the other men stopped what they were doing to watch and listen, too, since Fred hit the screaming register.

"Never! Never. I ought to kill you. I ought to tear your tongue outta your head."

"You're awfully emotional for a man who wasn't in love with a woman. Awfully emotional for someone who says he's innocent." Matthew was unfair, but then Fred had been unfair to him.

Fred placed his feet apart, doubled his fists. "Loved that girl like she was a daughter. You'll turn anything slimy, Matthew. Way your mind works."

"Well, I ask myself, why would someone like Mychelle get killed? Sure can't be anything to do with her job. She was an irritant but not a major problem, and there's nothing she can offer any of us, good or bad, to get herself killed. That leaves a few little things, drugs or some kind of sordid affair. I pick the sordid affair and you are the most likely candidate, although why she'd bother with you is beyond me. Then again, I don't claim to understand women."

"Sick. You're sick."

Tazio quietly said, "Fred, you must have an idea who killed her."

The normal color returned to his face. "No. I don't have any ideas. Sick. Makes me sick. You make me sick." He turned his eyes again to Matthew.

"Sex or drugs," Matthew simply said, his voice almost victorious in tone.

"She didn't do drugs. I'd have known. Can't hide that."

"You can for a while, but I agree, Fred, sooner or later it comes out just like alcoholism leaks out."

Tazio noticed the surveyor's tape flutter as a little wind kicked up.

"She was a good girl!" Fred's eyes looked haunted.

"That leaves sex." Matthew shrugged. "Hey, she wasn't my favorite and neither are you, Fred, but I do hope Sheriff Shaw finds her killer. I'm just glad it wasn't you—if you're telling the truth."

"Never forgive you for this," Fred vowed.

"Do I care? You're as likely a candidate as anyone else. You were around her all the time. You're married. She's not. Younger. You're older. Hey, it's not such a far putt."

"I don't cheat on my wife," Fred, angry still but in control, answered. "You do. Matthew, you're a lying sack of shit. Always was. Always will be." He pointed his finger at Tazio. "He'll be on you like a duck on the fly."

"I resent that." Matthew took a step toward the slighter man.

"Maybe you were the one? Huh?" Fred stuck Matthew right back.

"Not my type."

Fred paused a moment. "That's true. For once you told the truth."

"But I'll tell you who was sleeping with Mychelle. H.H.," Matthew said.

"Know that for a fact?" Fred didn't want to believe that since he hadn't liked H.H., either.

"Two and two make four."

"Prove it," Fred immediately responded.

"She could meet him at his construction sites. Nothing untoward about that. Right? She maybe got inconvenient. He dumps her. She kills him. Anne kills her or maybe Anne killed them both. Justice is served."

"You are so full of it." Fred laughed loudly.

"Okay. Your version then."

"I don't have a version. I don't know." Fred looked at Tazio. "Maybe she told you something. Women talk."

"No, Fred, we don't all talk. I knew her from the job and that was it."

"*Yeah,*" Brinkley supported Tazio. He would have agreed with her no matter what.

Fred waited a few moments. "Matthew, you shut your filthy mouth. Remember that."

As he strode away Matthew chuckled to Tazio, "Buffoon."

# 28

The pale sunlight illuminated the thin, low clouds, lining the bottoms with gold. Thicker clouds hovered on the horizon, their majestic curling tops hinting at another change in the weather.

Cooper questioned Sharon Cortez at Dr. Shulman's office, but sensitive to the social currents of country life, the two women went back to the operating room. The stainless steel table, the sink, everything shone. The operating table was the color of the low afternoon clouds.

Dr. Shulman's wife, Barbara, took over the reception duties while Sharon was in the back. Apart from a squad car being parked out front, no one need know what was going on and Barbara was quick to point out that Deputy Cooper was a great friend to animals.

The light, changing fast, threw shadows onto the floor.

"Now, Sharon, I have to ask these questions. Everything

you tell me I'll tell Rick, as you know, but that's as far as it goes."

"What if there's a trial?" Sharon was no fool.

"I'll give you a heads up. Your question tells me you know why I'm here."

"Good police work." Sharon ruefully smiled.

"Some. Want to tell me about your relationship with H.H.?"

Sharon ran her finger along the rounded lip of the operating table. "Started a year and a half ago. Ended at Easter."

"Were you in love with him?"

"Oh." She hesitated, glanced out the window, then said, "I was. I hate to admit it, but I was."

"He must have been special."

"I guess that was it, Coop, he made me feel special. He didn't mind spending money on a girl, you know what I mean? He'd never see me without bringing flowers or earrings, something. He bought me a gorgeous leather coat, three-quarter length so you know that wasn't cheap, and anything I wanted done around my little house, he did it. Of course, he could fix anything. His business, I guess." She shrugged.

"Were you angry when you broke up?"

"Yes. He broke it off. Said his marriage couldn't take the strain and he loved his daughter."

"You were never tempted to wreck it for him? To call Anne? To take your revenge?"

"Sure. All that ran through my mind. Couldn't do it." Sharon curled her fingers inward, then relaxed them. "It wasn't that I didn't want to hurt him, I did. But you know, I couldn't do that to his kid."

"That speaks well of you."

"Thanks, but if I'd had a grain of sense I'd never have gotten involved with a married man. It's a sucker play."

"I'm not sure that sex and love are amenable to logic." Cooper smiled.

"I think they are. I think it's like alcohol if you're an alcoholic. No one puts a gun to your head and says, 'Take that drink.' Same with attraction. You don't have to give in to it." Sharon put her hands in her pockets. "That's what I think. I was stupid. And you know why I was stupid? Not just because he was married but because I knew he played around."

"Did you know any of the other women?"

"Not well. But, sure. And I suppose you've questioned them, too."

"Yes."

"Any of them look like killers to you?" Sharon sarcastically said.

"Looks are deceiving."

"Ain't that the truth." Sharon looked outside the window again. "Front coming in. See it?"

Cooper walked to the window. "Bet the warm weather will march right out with it, too. Jeez, it's been a hell of a winter and there's three months to go."

"We've had the peepers come out in February."

"Sharon, this isn't going to be that kind of year," Cooper remarked. "But I admire your positive attitude. Tell me, can you think of anyone who would like to kill H.H.?"

"Sure. All the women he wined, dined, and ditched. But they didn't. I mean, how often do women kill?"

"I don't know because I think women are much smarter about it than men. I don't think they get caught. But having said that, I think women don't kill as often."

Sharon snorted, "Right. We get some poor sap to do it for us."

Cooper turned from the window. "Mychelle Burns."

Sharon lifted her shoulders. "Nada."

"What about Paula Zeifurt?"

"Oh, Paula. She brings her Yorkie here. Isn't she one of Anne's friends?"

"Uh-huh." Cooper nodded her head.

Sharon whistled. "That's cutting it close. You know, it really pisses me off, excuse my French. I would have liked to have been special. Truly special and not just one more filly passing through the stable."

"You said he made you feel special."

"He did, the bastard!"

"Then you were at the time." Cooper thought for a minute. "Some people deal with stress by drinking or drugging or running away. H.H. needed the excitement of an affair. That was his avocation."

"You're probably right. Maybe it was my avocation, too."

"Well, I'm not a moralist, I'm just a law enforcement officer, but it seems to me we make life awfully hard for people. We expect them to be perfect. I don't know one perfect person on this earth."

"I'm not a candidate." Sharon smiled, her good humor returning somewhat.

"One last question. You must have stuff in here that can kill people. Like the stuff you use to euthanize a dog, for instance?"

"Yes. But for a human you'd need a lot. What I'm saying is you couldn't administer the dose surreptitiously."

"Thanks." Cooper shook her hand and left waving goodbye to Barbara who called after her.

"The Opera Guild is performing Verdi next week. You ought to go."

"Thanks, Barbara. I'll try." And much as Cooper appreciated the offer she thought she'd seen enough tears for the time being.

# 29

The January thaw ended at six on Tuesday evening. Harry got home at five-fifteen, thrilled to be able to blast out of the post office so early. She brought in Tomahawk, Poptart, and Gin Fizz and put on their blankets, leading each to her or his stall.

The barn doors facing the drive were wide open. The chill became persistent. When she walked to the doors she noticed a scattering of low clouds with darker cirrus clouds high above. She smelled the moisture in the air and rolled the barn doors shut.

She swept out the center aisle. Mrs. Murphy and Pewter argued in the tack room over the most efficient way to lure the mice out from behind the walls. Tucker sat in the aisle-way. If her mother would avoid some pet project, like sewing a rip in a blanket, she and the cats could be snug in the house in another twenty minutes. Tucker loved being in the barn but hearing the herbivores munch hay made her long for her bowl of boiled hamburger mixed with crunchies, the hamburger juice poured over the goodies. Harry liked to prepare special dishes for her animals about once a week. The rest of the time she used high-quality commercial foods but she thought the canned cat foods contained too much ash. Once she brought home fresh crabmeat for the cats and Pewter passed out from over-eating. Harry, horrified, paid much more attention to the rotund gray kitty's portions after that.

A blade of wind slipped behind the cracks of the big doors as Harry hadn't shut them tight. She dropped the bolt to secure them.

Harry double-checked each stall, then she hung up her broom.

Simon peeped over the hayloft.

"You'll be happy to know I remembered you." Harry smiled up at the endearing creature.

She walked into the tack room, reaching into a brown paper bag. Out came the marshmallows. She returned to the center aisle, tossing about five up into the loft. Joyfully, Simon scrambled for his special treats.

*"Thank you! Thank you!"*

*"Do shut up,"* the owl grumbled.

The phone jingled in the tack room. Harry stepped back inside, closing the door behind her. The tack room was cozy as it had a long strip of baseboard heat. When the barn was originally built back in 1840, a huge wood-burning stove sat in the center of the tack room on the herringbone-patterned brick floor. Fortunately, no sparks spiraling out of the chimney ever landed back into the hayloft. The efficient potbellied cast-iron stove was ripped out in 1964 and replaced by baseboard heat when Harry's mother and father rewired and replumbed the barn.

Her father, a practical man, had run all the wire through narrow galvanized metal tubes. That way dust wouldn't collect on the wires, creating a potential fire hazard, and the metal tubing also ensured the mice wouldn't gnaw through. Once a month Harry lifted off the baseboard cover to clean the unit, a long string of flat squares placed closely together. She'd kneel down, wipe down everything, wipe down the cover, then pop it back on.

She kept the thermostat at sixty-five degrees. Since she usually wore many layers plus her old red down vest, sixty-five was a toasty temperature.

She lifted the receiver off the back wall phone. "Yes."

Susan launched right in. "The you-know-what has hit the fan big time."

"What are you talking about?"

"Fred Forrest called, his term, mind you, an emergency press conference, at the county office. He says he has to halt construction of the new sports complex until he examines the steel bearing I-beams called for in the blueprints. He says he is not convinced they can bear the load for which they are intended."

"Load of what?"

"The roof."

"What a mess."

"It gets better. While one TV crew, the one from Channel 29, was interviewing Fred, another mobile unit sandbagged Matthew at the site. At the site! He had no idea what was going on. Not a hint of warning. All he could say was the county had raised no objection before. The design and materials had passed all criteria, et cetera. And then, I mean these guys had a wild hair, let me tell you. They got footage of Tazio just as she was leaving her office."

"What did Tazio say?"

Susan chuckled. "She was great. She and Brinkley invited the crew into her office. In they trooped. She unrolled the blueprints. She opened the file cabinet. Pulled out all the paperwork with Fred's or Mychelle's signature on it, right? Close-ups of signatures. Close-ups of the plan's acceptance papers. I don't know what you call that."

"Doesn't matter. I know what you mean."

"She's cool, collected. She asks the interviewer why Fred is questioning plans he, himself, had approved. She says she would comply with any additional studies, nothing could be more important than safety and so forth. Then she brings up the issue of cost and delay, mentioning how important this structure is going to be to the university and really the entire Atlantic Coast Conference as the newest sports complex. Certainly this will spur other institutions to upgrade their facilities. I'm telling you, that woman could be a politician. I hope Little Mim was watching."

Little Mim, a Republican, was vice-mayor of Crozet. Her father, a Democrat, was the mayor. It made for interesting times.

"Did the TV interviewer bring up Mychelle's death?"

"You bet. To both Fred and Tazio. Did they think Mychelle's death was related to the sports complex project."

"Is that how the question was worded?"

"Oh, Harry, I don't remember the exact phrases but watch the eleven o'clock news if you can stay awake."

"Try to remember."

*"What the heck is going on?"* Tucker, like the cats, sat attentive, ears pricked forward.

*"S-h-h,"* the cats said.

Susan hummed a minute, collecting her thoughts. "Not word for word but the question was something like, 'Do you think the murder of your assistant might be related to your new findings?' Not word perfect but close."

"And?"

"Fred said he didn't know."

"Tazio?"

"The question was leading. Uh, 'Isn't your relationship with the county building inspector sometimes adversarial?' 'No,' she said. Then they hit her with Mychelle's death. Could it be related to these new questions about the worthiness of her design? That kind of thing. Again, she was amazingly cool and she said, 'I don't see how it could be.' And someone obviously had pumped those guys because they asked about Mychelle wanting a meeting with Tazio Monday morning. Tazio said that wasn't uncommon and, in fact, she had been looking forward to it and was shocked when she received the dreadful news. I mean the goddamned interviewer all but accused her of having a hand in Mychelle's murder. Sensationalism."

"Jacks up the ratings. They don't care if they ruin careers and lives."

"But you would have been proud of Tazio."

"How do we know she isn't involved?"

"Harry, you have a suspicious mind."

"Well—maybe. Why don't you call Tazio and see if she needs emotional support or anything? You're good at that."

"She doesn't have our network. We should both call her." Susan meant Tazio hadn't grown up with all of them and was a newcomer. "What are you going to do? I know you're up to something." Susan hoped Harry would tell her.

"I'm going to eat macaroni and cheese. Then I am going to call Coop to see if she can pull up on the computer all those buildings Mychelle had inspected in the last two years. Pull up the paperwork."

"Clever girl."

"Actually, I bet Coop's already thought of it."

"Are you really going to make macaroni and cheese?"

"Yes."

"Microwave?"

"No. Never tastes as good. Cold rolled back on us. Have you been outside? I need macaroni and cheese."

"Darn," Susan softly said.

"What's the matter with you?"

"Now I want some."

"Come on over. I'll make enough for both of us."

"Thanks, but that doesn't solve the problem of my extra ten pounds."

"Oh, Susan, you are not fat."

"You haven't seen me naked recently."

"Do I have to?" Harry laughed. "And we had this discussion."

"You know what I'm going to do? Now I'm going to make macaroni and cheese. Ned doesn't really need it, either." She sighed. "Bum."

"Ta-ta," Harry laughed and hung up the phone.

When she walked into her kitchen, the phone was ringing. Miranda told her about the interviews. Then BoomBoom called, which surprised Harry. Fair called. Herb called. By the time she made her macaroni and cheese she was starving but she fed the animals first.

After she ate and cleaned up, she called Cooper who had indeed pulled up everything on the county computers. Nothing seemed amiss.

They batted ideas back and forth, none of them illuminating.

Mrs. Murphy sauntered back into Harry's bedroom

where she caught sight of herself in the full-length mirror on Harry's door.

She stopped. She leapt sideways. She huffed up. She jumped sideways to the mirror. She spun around. She leapt upward, her paws outstretched, her formidable claws exposed. Then she performed a backflip, again attacking her own image.

Tucker ambled in during this fearsome performance. After five minutes of hissing, smacking, and subduing the mirror, the tiger cat hopped onto the bed.

*"Cats are mental."* Tucker giggled.

*"I heard that."* Mrs. Murphy peered over the edge of the bed down at the corgi.

*"So?"*

*"Death to dogs."* Mrs. Murphy dropped down onto her canine pal, pretending to shred her. Then she shot back up on the bed, ran a few circles on it, flew off at the mirror and for good measure smacked her image one more time.

Pewter now entered the room. *"What a mighty puss."*

*"Smoke and mirrors."* Mrs. Murphy swept her whiskers forward, puffing out her chest.

Tucker lifted her head. *"What did you just say, Murphy?"*

*"Smoke and mirrors."*

*"I think that's what's going on. Smoke and mirrors."* Tucker sat up as the two cats stared at her, then looked at one another. Tucker had hit the nail on the head.

# 30

"Where is he?" Matthew Crickenberger stormed into Fred Forrest's office in the county building.

Sugar McCarry, a twenty-one-year-old feisty secretary whose fingernails had half-moons painted on them, simply said, "I don't know."

"You're lying to me, Sugar. I know you're covering up for that sorry son of a bitch!"

"Mr. Crickenberger, I don't know where he is." She stood up, putting her hands on her hips. "And I don't much like your attitude."

"I don't give a good goddamn what you don't like." He strode over to Fred's desk and with one arm swept everything off it. "You tell him to keep his goddamned big mouth shut. You tell him he is a lying sack of shit. You tell him if I see him I will create a whole new face for him, one without teeth. You hear me?"

"I hear you. Now if you don't get out of here right this minute, I'll call security."

"Go ahead. I know what's going on in this office. Gambling, and, Sugar, you're playing with fire." He walked out, not bothering to close the door behind him.

Sugar heard his footsteps retreat down the hall, the green, black, and white squares of the linoleum floors so highly polished they appeared wet.

Breathing shallowly, she put her finger on the pushbutton phone. She was going to dial security but thought perhaps this was too big for the security in the county office buildings, housed in old Lane High School. Instead she called the Sheriff's Department.

Deputy Cooper, just finishing writing up a fender bender at the main library only a few blocks away, arrived within fifteen minutes. Sugar told her everything as accurately as she could. She injected no personal feeling into her report.

"Did you know that Fred called a press conference to question the plans for the sports complex?"

The surprise on Sugar's face proved she didn't know. "What?"

"Look, I don't know whether Tazio's plans are good or not. They're beautiful, that's what I know, and I know that Matthew Crickenberger has built large structures and done a good job. So he won the bid. Up to this point I don't recall there being a public denouncement of anything Crickenberger has done—not from your department. From the public, yes. Any kind of development is seen as bad by some people, but, Sugar, do you have any idea, any idea at all, what is going on?"

"No."

"Did Fred come down especially hard on H.H.?"

"No." Her eyebrows shot upward. "Why do you ask that?"

"H.H. was in the running to build the complex and now he's dead and so is Mychelle."

"They had the funeral over in Louisa County. Her people are from Louisa."

"I know," Cooper said.

"I went. Fred went. Maybe he's stirred up. You know how some people get. They have to take out their emotions on someone."

"Yes. You don't appear too upset over Mychelle's death." Cooper hit her with a zinger.

Sugar's nostrils flared, a blush of color rose to her already rouged cheeks. "I didn't like her, Deputy. No point in pretending, I really couldn't stand her. She thought she was better than me. Thought she could give orders. I think she just loved giving orders to a white girl but that doesn't mean I wished her dead. I just wished she'd get another job or that I would."

Cooper folded her arms across her chest. "I believe you."

"I don't care whether you believe me or not," Sugar sassed. "I am sick of all this. Fred's been a real shit. He's never been Mr. Wonderful to begin with but lately he's been—nothing's right. I don't take his phone messages right. I don't reach him on the road fast enough. I don't— well, you get the idea. And then Mychelle. I tell you what, she played him like a harp. Oh, out in public, on the site, she deferred to him. Mr. Forrest this and Mr. Forrest that and he ate it up, ate it up. She could get anything out of him she wanted. This place has been no fun. Not Fun Central. I'm looking for another job. Not in government. No pay anyway. I can do better."

Cooper chose not to be offended by her tone. "I hear you."

Sugar, realizing that Cooper was also paid by the county, softened. "I'm sorry, Coop. I didn't mean to, well, you know. I'm sick and tired of it and it's just like Fred to do something like this and not warn me. He's not sitting here when Crickenberger comes on in here, his face as red as a turkey wattle. I read in the paper about people losing it and just blowing people away. At the post office and stuff, going postal."

"Fred should have told you."

"Creep." Sugar lowered her voice although no one was with them.

"You can go to court and ask for a restraining order against Matthew if you're afraid he'll come back."

"Hey, I'm out of here. Anyway, he wants Fred not me. I'm not going to court. I've seen enough around here to know I'm never going to court if I can help it."

"Amen."

"And you know what really fried me? He's standing there right in front of my desk screaming at me. Screaming that I know what's going on, that I'm gambling, that I'm playing with fire. I don't know what the hell he's talking about. I play bingo. I go with Mom Friday nights to the firehouse and play bingo. He's crazy."

What Cooper knew and no one else did except for Rick Shaw was that Mychelle Burns had withdrawn most of her savings account, $5,000. For someone in Mychelle's position, that was a lot of money. For Cooper that was a lot of money.

"Did he accuse you of gambling?"

"Sort of." She glanced at her computer then back at Coop.

"M-m-m, office pools?"

"Oh yeah, but I don't play. I don't care about football and

basketball. Bores me to tears. I don't know what's going on and I don't understand how they do it."

"What do you mean?"

"If you just pick a winner, I understand that, but for the office pool you have to pick the scores. For the World Series you have to select the winning game, you know, like the sixth game. I'm not doing that. It's too complicated."

"Is there ever an office pool for UVA sports?"

She thought about this. "Five bucks a head."

"Point spread?"

"I don't understand point spreads."

Cooper smiled. "Doesn't matter." She sat on the edge of Sugar's desk as her feet hurt. "What about basketball?"

She shook her head. "Fred would kill anyone who bet against the girls' basketball team. He loves those girls. No bets against UVA girls."

"Did he and Mychelle ever talk about the games?"

"Yeah, sometimes. I tuned them out. I don't like basketball."

"Well, do you ever remember them talking about point spread?"

"No. Neither one talked much, really. They usually stuck to business, but if they didn't it was basketball."

"Did you ever hear them make a bet with each other, you know, something like, oh, Jenny Ingersoll will make fourteen points tonight?"

Sugar's brow wrinkled. "Oh, I don't know. It would have gone in one ear and out the other."

"Ever see or hear either of them pick up the phone and place a bet?"

"No." She waited a beat, though. "Could have done it on their cell phones."

"We've investigated the calls from all their phones. Nothing out of line. Fred doesn't even call home."

Sugar leaned forward. "Are you suspicious about Fred? Like he killed Mychelle?"

"No."

She exhaled audibly. "Good. I really don't want to be here if that's what you're working on."

"Do you think he could have killed Mychelle?"

"Nah."

"Why?"

"Just don't. He really liked Mychelle. Her death has hit him hard."

"Most murders are committed by someone who knows the victim, often quite well."

"I know. I read the papers. I watch TV, but Fred, nah."

"Sugar, how long have you worked here?"

"Two years. I graduated and got a job."

"Charlottesville High?"

"Murray." Sugar mentioned a high school specializing in gifted young people who often had trouble flourishing in the big high schools—Charlottesville, Albemarle, Western Albemarle.

"Ah. Didn't want to go on?"

"No. School bores me. I'm lucky I graduated." She twirled a pencil. "I was kind of rebellious, you know."

"That comes as a big surprise to me."

Sugar laughed. "Yeah, well, what can I say?"

"A couple more questions. Did you ever notice Mychelle making large expensive purchases, like a leather coat or just something that caught your eye?"

"No."

"Fred?"

"Um, no. Fred always goes someplace good on his vacation. That's about it."

"Well, thanks. Now you can say anything you want to Fred, but if you tell him how upset Matthew really was when he charged in here I expect I'll be getting a call." Cooper pointed to the mess on the floor. "You going to leave that there?"

"Do you want me to?"

Cooper considered this. "Up to you but it will fan the flames."

"Fred would take a picture. He's just the type." Sugar sniggered. "For future use."

"We're thinking along the same lines."

As Cooper reached the door Sugar asked quietly, "Am I in danger?"

"I don't think so. But if anyone frightens you or you think something is weird, you call me, I don't care if it's three in the morning, you call me." She gave her her card with her personal number and her cell number.

"I will." Sugar paused, then slipped the card in her skirt pocket. "Is Matthew right? Is some kind of gambling going on?"

"I don't know," Cooper honestly replied. "I wish I did, but that's my job. I'll find out. You can bet on that."

# 31

The St. Luke's Parish Guild gathered as usual in the welcoming meeting room. Cherry logs crackled in the fireplace. The old rugs, worn through to the backing in some places, remained on the floor. The carpet men absolutely, positively, without fail would be there Friday morning to start work. By this point no one was holding their breath.

Matthew Crickenberger, composed, chaired the meeting. Herb added information as needed. Herb believed the chair should rotate and so it did. He thought this fostered leadership. If one didn't wish to be a leader, then it taught appreciation for those who were.

Mrs. Murphy, Pewter, Tucker, Brinkley, Cazenovia, and Elocution considered raiding the communion wafers again. Given that their initial depredations had not been discovered, they all voted to leave well enough alone. And since this upcoming Sunday was a communion Sunday their misdeed would most likely be discovered. Instead they settled into Herb's office, all sitting on the large chesterfield sofa. Herb, like Susan Tucker, liked chesterfield sofas. The one in his living quarters was dark green, this one was a rich maroon.

They could hear Tazio and BoomBoom in the next room discussing fund-raising ideas.

"*How come St. Luke's has so many poor parishioners?*" Brinkley wondered.

"*Doesn't. All the churches cooperate to help with the food drive,*" Cazenovia, the senior kitty, replied.

"*Humans eat strange stuff. Asparagus,*" Tucker said.

"*I like asparagus,*" Elocution demurred.

"*You do?*" Tucker was aghast.

"*I like greens every now and then,*" Elocution replied, "*especially with my communion wafers.*"

"*What does Tazio feed you?*" Tucker loved hearing about food.

"*Puppy chow mixed with canned food. Sometimes she gives me the fat off meat, too.*"

"*Oh, that sounds delicious.*" Tucker licked her chops.

"*Tuna.*" Pewter closed her eyes, purring.

"*Chicken.*" Mrs. Murphy smiled.

"*Mouse tartare,*" Cazenovia declared.

"*A giant knucklebone, jammed with marrow.*" Tucker wagged her nonexistent tail.

"*Gee*"—Brinkley's soft eyes were puzzled—"*how do you get your human to give you such treats?*"

"*Since you can't go into the market with them, it's hard,*" Tucker advised. "*Seize the day. If you walk by a restaurant with big picture windows, wag your tail if someone is eating steak or a hamburger. Point with your right paw. Gets them every time and they really figure it out. You can train them with food.*"

"*Don't expect miracles,*" Cazenovia added.

"*Well, you need to practice being cute.*" Mrs. Murphy rolled over showing her beige tummy with the stripes lighter than on her back. "*Like this.*"

"*Do I do that in front of a restaurant?*" Brinkley innocently asked.

"*No, no. Your human will pitch a fit because you've rolled in dirt or whatever is on the sidewalk. Just point.*" Tucker demonstrated a point. "*Trust me, they get the point.*"

"*Very funny,*" Pewter dryly said.

"*How long does it take to train a human?*"

"*Brinkley, all your life. Now some lessons they retain such as your feeding time because it's tied to their feeding time.*" Mrs. Murphy liked the yellow Lab. "*Going to sleep, waking up at the same time, they learn that pretty quickly, too. Truth is, we're usually on similar schedules so it's not too taxing for them. But other things, getting them to notice something out of the ordinary or warning them that another human isn't right, oh, that's hit-and-miss.*"

"*Really?*" He nudged the tiger cat who patted his nose.

"*Now our human is very smart.*" Pewter puffed up.

"*Our human? I thought you didn't claim any human,*" Mrs. Murphy teased her.

"*I changed my mind.*" Pewter tossed her head. "*And she is smart.*"

"*Highly trainable.*" Tucker nodded in agreement.

"*She's a country person so she's not so far away from her real self,*" Pewter added.

"*Real self?*" The growing fellow was curious.

"*You know, the animal in them.*" Mrs. Murphy thought this would be self-evident.

"*They don't know they're animals?*" Brinkley was astounded.

*"No, they really don't."* Pewter turned up her nose.

*"And the more they live away from other animals, the worse it gets."* Elocution, a lively girl, held the tip of her tail in her paw but forgot why she had picked it up in the first place.

*"What about your human? Is he smart?"* Brinkley asked.

*"Depends,"* Cazenovia, who had lived with Herb the longest, answered. *"He's smart about fly-fishing. He pays attention to the signs in the runs and branches when he's fishing but he can walk right through a meadow and miss fox poop. Or worse, bear poop."*

*"Can't he smell it?"*

Cazenovia hopped onto the back of the sofa to be at eye level with the Lab, who was sitting upright. He was already so big he couldn't stretch out on the sofa. There wouldn't be room for the others.

*"They can't smell."* Cazenovia delivered the shocking news.

*"Can't smell?"* Brinkley felt terrible. This was his sharpest sense.

*"Now that's not true."* Mrs. Murphy countered the longhaired calico. *"They can smell a wee bit. If they don't smoke they can smell better. But for instance, if you put out a piece of bread, say, fifty yards from them, they wouldn't smell it even if it was fresh. A smell has to be very strong or right under their noses to affect them."*

*"Those poor creatures."* Brinkley's ears drooped for a moment.

*"Eyes. They rely on their eyes."* Elocution kept staring at her tail tip. *"'Course their eyes aren't nearly as good as a cat's but they aren't bad. They're better than your eyes."*

*"Really?"*

*"Oh yes."* Pewter smiled up at the big dog. *"You can't see*

*nearly as well as they do, but you can hear and smell way, way beyond them.*"

"*Harry's got good ears.*" Mrs. Murphy loved Harry.

"*Actually, she does. She quite surprises me.*" Tucker thought Harry exceptional for a human.

"*Well, they could all hear better if they'd yank those stupid phones out of their ears, turn off the computers, TVs, and radios. They can't hear because they're surrounded by noise.*" Elocution finally dropped her tail.

"*No animal would willingly shut out information about what's around them,*" Brinkley sensibly said. "*Why do they keep noises?*"

"*Oh, they think it's information. They will sit in front of the TV and watch something that happened in New Zealand but they won't know what's happening in Crozet. Or they sit and watch things that don't happen.*" Cazenovia giggled.

"*How can you watch what doesn't happen?*" The Lab thought this was insane.

"*Made-up stories, films. Or books. They'll sit down and read fiction. It's stuff that never happened!*" Cazenovia watched the yellow handsome fellow just get bowled over with the information.

"*How can they tell the truth from what they make up?*"

"*Brinkley, they can't!*" Cazenovia laughed so hard she fell onto the Lab's back, then rolled under his tummy. She quickly righted herself but remained under his tummy.

"*Now wait a minute, Cazzie. You aren't exactly fair.*" Mrs. Murphy swept her whiskers forward, all attention. "*Brinkley, humans are afraid. They're not fast, you see. They can't outrun danger and they aren't strong or quick. They are much more afraid than we are because of this. So these stories that are made up are made up to let them learn about other humans' lives. See, it gives them courage. They don't feel so alone.*

*They're herd animals. Always remember that they fear being alone and they fear the dark. Their eyes are good in daylight but pretty bad at night. I would have to say that the made-up stories serve a purpose and I think most humans do know the difference between those stories and what's happening around them."*

*"Oh, Mrs. Murphy, you're too kind."* Cazzie shook her head. *"I've seen Herb weep over a story."*

*"Daddy's sensitive."* Elocution nodded in agreement.

*"They have a great range of feeling if they choose to use it,"* Mrs. Murphy said.

*"Mostly they blunt their nerve endings, listen to the noise, and wonder why they feel out of step."* Cazzie moved to sit alongside Brinkley. *"They're too caught up in words."*

*"We can talk. We have words,"* Brinkley said.

*"Yes, but we don't confuse the word with the deed. They do,"* Mrs. Murphy told him.

*"Better yet, they substitute the word for the deed and do nothing."* Pewter laughed uproariously, the others laughing with her.

*"I had no idea humans were so complicated."* Brinkley liked Cazzie rubbing along his side.

*"They are and they aren't. They need to go back to their senses, live where they live instead of worrying about something thousands of miles away. Too much planning."* Elocution liked humans nonetheless.

*"Hey, if you live in a temperate climate, you have to plan. Winter changes how humans think. Humans who live in the tropics or subtropics don't have to plan."* Mrs. Murphy read along with Harry who had been reading about these things. *"But any animal that lives with winter has to figure things out. Even squirrels bury nuts. Humans, too."*

*"I haven't seen Tazio bury nuts."*

*"Her bank accounts. That's where the nuts are,"* Pewter sagely noted.

*"You mean that's what she does when she goes to the bank?"*

*"Oh yes. They store things. Lock them right up, they do."* Cazenovia nodded in agreement. *"That's why we have, I mean had, those boxes of communion wafers."*

With this all the animals screamed with laughter.

"What's going on in there?" Harry called from the next room using her "mother" voice.

*"Wouldn't you like to know?"* Pewter sassed.

# 32

Harry drove from the meeting to the Clam. She'd missed the first half of the game because the meeting went on and on. The animals curled up in the blankets and she hurried into the building.

Matthew, BoomBoom, and Tazio also rushed to get to the game. The rest of the gang was already there.

Fred flipped a bird at Matthew when he looked over his shoulder at him. Harry saw it and couldn't believe Fred was that childish.

Anne Donaldson had given her seats to friends. Harry, Fair, and BoomBoom introduced themselves.

Tracy and Josef officiated a tough game, a dirty game, too. The opponents stuck out elbows under the basket, tripped players if no one was looking. Tempers frayed. Despite their efforts to throw the UVA team off stride it didn't work. UVA easily won by twelve points, which was a boost after their last game.

Miranda joined Harry, BoomBoom, Susan, Brooks, and Fair for a bite to eat down at Ruby Tuesday's, which wasn't that far from the Clam.

Tracy said he'd join them after he showered. He pulled on his clothes, picked up his gym bag and was all ready to go out the side door. Josef, in a hurry, had already left. The players' locker rooms were on the other side of the officials' locker room.

Tracy walked into the hall. He marveled at how quiet a large building could become after a game. The silence created a pensive mood; one could almost hear the echoes from the dispersed crowd.

He passed a closed door, the lacrosse coach's name on it. No one worked late on this January night. He passed by the equipment room and stopped. He thought he heard sounds coming from inside even though no light spilled from under the door. Given that Mychelle had been killed at the Clam he was extra alert. He pulled out his cell phone, hit the On button. He was so intent on punching in the numbers that he didn't hear someone tiptoeing behind him. The last thing he heard was a crack and he sank like a stone.

# 33

When Tracy awoke he was flat on the cold floor and it was dark. He touched his head, and a knot the size of a golf ball with a thin crust of dried blood greeted his fingers. He sat upright. He felt pain but he wasn't dizzy or nauseated.

Good, he thought to himself, I don't have a concussion. Where am I? Tuesday night. Game. Twenty-six referee signals. He stopped. That was irrelevant. Perhaps he wasn't as clearheaded as he thought. He breathed deeply. He reached into his pants pocket, retrieving a plastic lighter. Tracy always carried a lighter and a small Leatherman all-purpose tool. He flicked it on, discovering he was inside someone's office. He carefully stood up and switched on the light. The lacrosse coach's office. He sat down at the desk, picked up the receiver of the phone, and punched nine for an outside line. Where was his phone? He'd worry about that later.

"Miranda—"

"Honey, where are you? I've been calling and calling and

I get that infernal recording, 'The cellular customer you have dialed is not available at this time or has left the reception zone. Try again later.'" Her voice accurately mimicked the inflection of the recording.

"Well." He didn't want her to worry. "A little delay here after the game. I'll explain when I swing by." He checked his watch. "Maybe I'd better wait until morning. It's eleven-thirty. Forgot about the time."

"You come right over here. I don't care if it's three in the morning. Tracy, are you all right?"

"Yes." He felt in his right pants pocket for his car keys. Still there. "I won't be any longer than an hour."

"Are you sure you're all right?"

"A little headache. Be right along. Okay?"

"Okay. Love you."

"Love you, too. 'Bye." He hung up the phone, stood up and scrutinized the office. It seemed orderly enough. No skid marks on the floor from his shoe soles meant whoever dragged him, if one person, dragged him by the feet. Two people would have picked up both ends and dumped him but he didn't feel as if he'd been dumped. No other bruises or aches and pains. Just his head, which throbbed the more he moved about.

He opened the door. The hallway was dark. The building seemed deserted. He checked the shelves in the office to see if there was a flashlight. None. He checked the desk drawers. The lacrosse coach, Jason Xavier, didn't keep so much as a penknife in his drawers. Nothing but paper, rubber bands, a playbook, pencils in various states of sharpness, and one leaky ballpoint pen. Tracy shut the drawers. He walked out into the hall, carefully closing the door behind him.

He felt along the circular walls intermittently using his

small lighter for guidance. Finally he could see the stairs sign, lit, down the hall. He didn't want to turn on lights.

He hadn't thought of it before. He reached into his left pants pocket. His money was still there. He made the full circle of the building, returning to the equipment room.

He listened outside. Silence. He tried the door. Locked. He continued walking along the corridor, stopping at each door, listening. This bottom level of the Clam was deserted.

The white rectangular light with Stairs written in green beckoned him. He opened the door, listened, then climbed to the next level, the main level. Carefully he walked all the way around. The silence was eerie. He looked up to find himself standing outside the broom closet where Mychelle was found. He listened. Nothing.

Because of the glass doors the lights from the parking lot cast a glow into the front of the main level. He moved to the double interior doors of the basketball court. These were unlocked. The long stainless steel bar across the door clicked as he pressed it down, and opened into the cavernous pitch-black space enlivened only by the small red exit lights. He bent down, wedging a handkerchief between the two doors so the one he opened didn't completely close. If anyone was outside, he hoped he'd hear them. He stood just inside the door and listened. Not even a mouse scuttled along the seats. He strained to hear anything at all. A creak, not a human sound, finally rewarded him. The building breathed, or so it seemed, and that was all.

After ten motionless minutes, he retrieved his handkerchief, carefully closed the door behind him, and left through the main doors which would lock when they closed behind him. The doors had been designed so a person couldn't get locked in the building but once you left they would lock you out.

The cold air, in the low twenties, stung his face. His black Explorer started right up. No one had tampered with it. He drove to Miranda's. His gym bag and cell phone were missing.

When he walked into Miranda's she hugged him so hard she nearly squeezed the breath out of him.

"I've been worried sick."

"Well, I had a little encounter." Tracy proceeded to tell her what he remembered.

She checked the left side of his head. "Oh honey, I need to clean this right up." She hurried into the bathroom, brought out a washcloth and hand towel, then carefully washed the wound with warm water as he sat on a chair by the kitchen sink.

"It's not so bad."

"It's not so good." She gingerly dabbed. "It's not bleeding anymore which is good because you know how head wounds can be."

"Yep." He'd seen enough of that in Korea and later in Vietnam.

"You could have been killed." Tears welled up in her eyes.

"Now, sweetheart, don't worry. There's no reason to kill me. I'm not that bad of a referee." He laughed.

"Oh Tracy, it's not funny. Something awful is going on at that place."

"Yes," he quietly agreed. "I heard something or someone in the equipment room and then—lights out. How's it look up there? Do I need to shave my head?"

"Don't be silly." She wrung out the washcloth, dipping it again in warm water. "And I will never understand why young men shave their heads bald. If that isn't the ugliest thing I've ever seen."

"When they forget Michael Jordan, they won't do it

anymore. Takes about five years. Next group of kids, he'll be ancient history. People used to shave their heads to get rid of the lice. You shave a head wound if it's bad to keep hair out of it. If young people knew history, they might not want to look like cue balls."

She peered at the cleansed wound. "I'm going to put some ice cubes in this washcloth. Let me wash it out first. Actually, let me fetch a fresh one. You don't need to hold a wet washcloth. Maybe we can get some of the swelling down." She bustled into the bathroom, returning with another washcloth which she filled with curved ice cubes.

They repaired to the living room where both sat on the sofa. The fire in the fireplace crackled.

"I'll call Rick in the morning. No point getting him out of bed. And I guess whoever is in charge of the equipment room better run an inventory."

"You'd better call Rick now. What if this is related to Mychelle's murder or H.H.'s?"

"You're right, honey. I guess I'm not as clearheaded as I thought." He stood up, still holding the washcloth to his head, called Rick. He told him everything he could remember, then hung up and rejoined Miranda.

"He's going down now to see if he can get prints."

They watched the fire for a little bit.

"Honey."

"Hmm," he answered.

"You won't go down there by yourself? If you have a game to ref, you and Josef should stick together afterward."

"You're right. I don't think anyone should be alone there until these cases are solved."

"You could have been killed." Her eyes filled up again.

He put his arm around her. "But I wasn't. What does that tell you?"

"That your Guardian Angel works overtime." She dabbed at her tears.

"No. Well, yes. But it means I'm not important. If whoever hit me had wanted to kill me, it would have been easy enough. Right?"

"Yes." She nodded.

"But they didn't. However, H.H. and Mychelle were killed, and H.H. was killed in front of everyone."

"But we all thought it was a heart attack at the time."

"Sugar, there's a meaning to this, a reason. I'm not part of the reason."

"But you got in the way."

"That I did and whoever hit me was intelligent enough not to kill if he didn't have to kill. So whatever is going on will tie those people together in some way or tie them into whatever is going on at that building."

"Isn't it odd that all this is happening in one spot?"

"I don't know. If I just had even one idea, I'd feel better. The only thing I can think of is someone is pilfering equipment and selling it. But that doesn't seem worth two murders."

"And you're sure that no one else was in the building when you came to your senses?"

"I'm pretty sure it was abandoned. Not a creature was stirring, not even a mouse." He squeezed her shoulder.

# 34

The next morning, Deputy Cooper and Sheriff Shaw met Tracy Raz at the Clam. Tim Berryhill, in charge of all the buildings and grounds at the university, including the Clam, also met them at the front doors. He was one of the Berryhill clan originating in Crozet although he lived in North Garden outside of Charlottesville. He held an electrical engineering degree from Penn State and had gone to Darden Business School at UVA.

Late last night, Rick and his team had found Tracy's gym bag, cell phone inside, tossed in the Dumpster. It was being checked for prints.

Tim said that given all that had happened he personally wanted to be in charge. He would closely examine the building from an engineering standpoint and he would personally check inventory.

Rick and Tracy left Tim and Cooper at ten-thirty A.M.

Tracy walked with the sheriff over to his squad car. "Rick, if there's any way you can use me, do."

"Thanks. I appreciate it."

"No reason for anyone to know about last night." Tracy shrugged. "Could have been a stupid mugger."

"Really stupid. He didn't take your money."

Tracy grinned. "Hell, he might even have knocked some sense into my head. Or she. Don't want to leave the ladies out of this."

"Crime has become an equal opportunity employer."

As the two men drove off in different directions, Rick replayed his two interviews with Anne Donaldson in his head. The first time he spoke to her she was completely distraught and all he could get out of her was that she couldn't imagine why anyone would kill H.H. He called on her again, after the memorial service. This time he had to ask the unpleasant question, "Did you know with whom your husband was having the affair?"

She pleaded ignorance but he didn't believe her. Not that he challenged her. He just chipped away. Little questions like, How many nights a week did he stay out or stay late at work? The answer: None. Were there strange expenses on his credit cards? No. It didn't matter how he approached it, he ran into a wall.

She knew, all right. She knew and she wasn't telling.

Perhaps it was the sin of pride.

# 35

The storm's first lazy snowflake twirled to the frozen ground. Tombstones from the early eighteenth century looked particularly forlorn as heavy gray clouds roiled ever lower.

Matthew Crickenberger, slumped in one of the comfortable chairs by the fireplace, glanced out the windowpanes, the glass wavy since it was handblown.

Elocution and Cazenovia dozed on the back of the sofa, the warmth from the fire making them even more sleepy than they usually were at four in the afternoon. Nap time for cats, tea time for people.

Charlotte, still snuffling from her cold, brought the two men hot tea, a crystal decanter of port, and another of sherry, should either need stronger spirits.

"Oh, thank you, Charlotte."

She placed the tray on the coffee table then put her hands on her hips. "Would you look at that."

The snow began to fall steadily.

"Isn't that a beautiful sight?" Herb smiled.

"Yes, as long as you don't have to drive in it," was Charlotte's somewhat tart reply.

"There is that. Odd, though. We've had a dry fall. Bone dry." Herb minded the weather; outdoor thermometers were placed by his workroom window and his bedroom window. "No sooner did we ring in the New Year, and the snow started falling with nary a stop."

"That's about right."

"Anything else? I've got some cookies."

Herb held up his hand. "No. I really have to exercise some self-control."

"Oh la." She smiled, then winked at Matthew. "Self-control for you, too? I hope not."

"I could use a little, Charlotte. I'll pass on the cookies, but if you have a can of self-control back there in the pantry, bring it on out."

She nodded and left them.

Herb sipped his tea. "Never drank tea as a young man. Not even when I was in the army as a chaplain stationed in England. That's a lovely, lovely country. You've been there?"

"Once. This summer, though, Sandy and the kids and I are going to spend August in Scotland. We'll start in Edinburgh and work our way up to the Highlands."

"Stop at any distilleries?"

"Every one."

"They say the fly-fishing is good in Scotland. Ireland, too. I'd go back across the ocean for that. Or to Wyoming or Montana or you-name-it." He offered Matthew a wee spot of port which the younger man did not refuse.

"Port chased by hot tea with lemon. A taste sensation." He felt the robust flavor of port on his tongue. Matthew always thought of port as a man's drink and sherry as a woman's.

"I know you are beset with many and sundry things, but I'm glad you dropped by." Herb crossed one leg over the other. "I am having a terrible time getting these carpet people to come on out here. Might you give them a push? You're a big fish. I'm a minnow."

"I'll make it my mission. I'll personally talk to Sergeant." Matthew named the owner of the carpet company. "I've been letting my secretary call his secretary. Enough of that. Anyway, what if the Parish Guild changes its mind?"

Herb held up his hands in mock horror. "Don't breathe a word. No. No. No."

Matthew laughed. "Consensus really means you just wear everyone out. In my lifetime I haven't seen too many people change their mind nor have I seen too many people learn."

"Perhaps it's the business you're in. I'd have to say that my experience is just the reverse." Herb eyed the ruby port glowing in Matthew's glass. What a beautiful color. He thought of it as the color of contentment.

"I never thought of that." He shifted his weight. Matthew, a large man, wasn't fat but he wasn't thin anymore, either.

"We all see life through the prism of our own work, our own needs, I guess. I think of stories in the Bible, Scripture." He paused. "Although that Miranda can out-quote me any day of the week. I see the spiritual struggle perhaps more than the material struggle."

"Your work to feed the poor contradicts that."

Herb looked out the window; the bare tree branches were turning white, the large lovely blue spruce at the other end of the quad appeared covered in fancy white lace and the black walnut close by the window appeared more majestic than ever. "I am my brother's keeper. Those simple lessons. Not so simple to enact, are they? And I am so glad you've stopped by because I did want to talk to you about more than carpet, Matthew." He leaned forward, pouring himself more port. "Just what is going on with you and Fred? Can I be of any service?"

"You could cover his mouth with duct tape for starters," Matthew ruefully replied. "Herb, Fred and I have been crossways with one another since we were teenagers. I guess it's a personality thing. He looks for problems. A born complainer. I look to build, I look for what's positive. He looks for the negative. He's even worse than Hank Brevard, God rest his soul." He mentioned a man who had gone to his reward in the last two years, another nitpicker.

"M-m-m, Fred does look on the bleak side of life."

"And why does Lorraine stay with him? She's one of the nicest people."

"To make up for him, no doubt." Herb laughed as did Matthew. "But I would have to say that in the last few months, since Thanksgiving, I've observed Fred being more combative, looking for fights. Unpleasant even in passing. I haven't been able to discover the reason. At first I thought, well, maybe Lorraine is tired of him. But no. Then I thought perhaps there's a health problem. Seems fine. Not that Dr. Hayden McIntyre would betray a confidence, but you know, he basically indicated that Fred is fit as a fiddle."

"Pity." Matthew knocked back his port, then drank his tea. "Hateful of me, I know. In fact, downright un-Christian of me. And in front of you."

Herb poured him another cup of tea as Matthew helped himself to the port. "I'm the one person to whom you can tell the truth."

Matthew slumped back in the chair, gazed into the fire for a moment. "I hate him. I do my job and I do it well. I cooperate with him on that level. But he's out to get me and I don't know why."

"Every time he sees you he's got to be reminded that he had as much chance as you did to succeed. He passed it by."

"His choice." Matthew threw up his hands.

"He's jealous."

"Why now?"

"He's in his fifties. Money becomes more important as one gets older. Actually it becomes both more important and less important if you know what I mean." Matthew nodded and Herb continued. "Maybe it's finally getting to him that he'll never really make much money. He's got nowhere to go. There is no higher level if he stays with the county. He's topped out."

"Everyone makes their choices."

"For the most part, yes, but you know, it takes you a good decade to figure out the choices you made in the previous one." He laughed low.

"*Whiteout.*" Elocution opened one eye.

Cazzie opened both eyes. "*Bet the mice will snuggle into the woodpile.*"

"*I'm not going outside to get them.*"

Cazzie thought about the animal door in the back. "*Me, neither.*" She giggled, then closed her beautiful eyes again as the humans talked on.

"Herb, I'm thinking about hiring Ned Tucker. Fred hasn't exactly slandered me or libeled me but I think his behavior is pretty damned close to harassment."

"Ned would know."

Both men sat quietly for a moment, all outside sounds muffled in the falling snow.

"Dropped by Anne's on the way over. She's holding up. Cameron cries, she said. She's realizing Daddy isn't coming home from a business trip. It takes a while to sink in and I guess it hits pretty hard when you're a sixth-grader."

"Anne's been through a lot," Herb simply said.

"She's well off. He took care of that. That's some comfort or at least it will be down the road." Matthew folded his hands together. "I've been wrestling with my conscience. I bet you hear that a lot."

"In one form or another."

"You see, Herb, I'm pretty sure I know who H.H. was sleeping with and I can't prove it, but, well, I'm pretty sure. I usually knew who he was sleeping with on the side. He wasn't always as discreet as he might have been. He's damned lucky his wife always looked the other way."

"I see. That would certainly put a new shading on events."

"I suppose I should go to Sheriff Shaw but I don't have definitive proof and I feel, well, not quite right if I don't have it cold. Hearsay."

"He's accustomed to unsubstantiated leads."

"Yes, I guess he is." Matthew downed his second glass of port. "I hate this."

"The snow?"

"The way I feel."

"Ah."

"Aren't you going to ask me?"

"No."

Matthew unfolded his hands then folded them again. "I see I can't abdicate my responsibility for a minute. You aren't going to worm the name out of me so I can feel relieved."

"Right."

Matthew stood up, walked over and tossed another log in

the fire. He turned. "Mychelle Burns. For the longest time I thought it was Tazio Chappars. She's elegant, very attractive, very bright. I could understand leaving your wife for Tazio." Matthew shook his head. "If I'd stop off at the Riverside Cafe for lunch and he'd be there, if a pretty girl walked in, H.H. had to send her a beer. He was just that kind of guy. And like I said, he didn't brag, he didn't complain about Anne, but he, well, the way I started to realize it was serious and it was Mychelle was that he pointedly did not pay any attention to her. I'll tell you I was shocked because she wasn't what I expected. If H.H. was going to jeopardize his marriage I always thought it would be for some real babe. Mychelle was attractive, don't get me wrong, but she wasn't a trophy."

"Yes, but they spoke the same language. She understood his work. Anne may have appreciated it, but Mychelle lived and breathed construction. More to it than sex when men get serious."

"His one-day separation must have put both women through hell."

"Put him through it, too."

"I guess. He'd worked hard. He would lose a big chunk of change in a divorce. Then there's the social fallout. Doesn't seem worth it."

"The price of success seems to be that you become somebody else. Maybe he didn't like himself." Herb watched the sparks from the fresh log spiral up the chimney.

Matthew returned to his chair, sitting on the arm now. "Maybe that's why I'm looking forward to Scotland this summer. I need to remember who I am. I promised Sandy we'd go for our fifteenth wedding anniversary. How was I to know I'd get the contract for the sports complex? I almost canceled the vacation. Obviously, there's a lot of money at stake, and then I thought, no, I'll take my computer. I'll stay in touch with Tazio and my foreman, who is both literate and computer literate. As you know, most of my workmen aren't proficient that way. I'm not letting my wife and kids down. And you know, if there's some huge crisis I'll get on a plane, fly home, then fly back. There are options."

"Glad to hear you say that, Matthew." Herb dabbed his mouth with one of the small linen napkins Charlotte had placed on the tray. "You haven't asked for my advice. Do you want it?"

"I do."

"Go to Rick. Tell him just what you told me. He isn't going to think you're a gossip. Two people are dead. If their murders are related, he needs whatever information he can get."

"I know that. I know that." Matthew's voice rose. "But if H.II. and Mychelle . . ." He leaned forward. "Motive. Who has the motive to kill them both? Anne."

"I understand that, but you still have an obligation to talk to the sheriff."

They heard the door open and Charlotte's voice. Then footsteps back to the room.

"Herb, Harry's here. She says she can see you some other time if you're busy."

Herb looked at Matthew.

"I'm done."

"Bring her back." Herb looked back to Matthew. "I'm glad you came."

Harry bounded into the room as both men stood up to greet her. "Hey, Big Mim says we can sled down her hill. There's enough light. Come on."

"Be dark soon." Herb looked at the clouds turning from gray to dark blue.

"Yeah, but she's going to line the hill with torches. Oh, come on. We all need to be a little spontaneous."

"Harry, you're right. Think Mim would mind if I came along? I'll call Sandy. Hey, we'll bring fried chicken. She can stop on her way out of town."

*"Go on, Daddy,"* Cazenovia encouraged Herb.

Harry threw her arm around Herb. "Come on, Rev."

"Well—who am I to refuse a lady?"

"All right!" Harry clapped her hands.

Within half an hour they were screaming as they tobogganed down the hill. Little Mim, Blair, Fair, BoomBoom, Miranda, Tracy, Herb, Jim, Ned, Susan, Brooks, Matthew, Sandy, their children, Ted and Matt, Jr., were all there along with the redoubtable Aunt Tally who had more fun than the rest of them put together.

Mrs. Murphy, Pewter, and Tucker stayed in Mim's big house as they visited with her Brittany spaniel. All the animals watched the humans, their noses leaving smeary imprints on the glass.

*"If we made them slide down hills in the cold and the snow, they'd say we were cruel."* Pewter laughed.

As they watched, Tazio drove up, parked, and she and Brinkley got out, joining the others.

*"No fair,"* Tucker barked.

*"What, that Brinkley gets to play in the snow and you don't?"* the Brittany asked.

*"Yeah."*

*"You'd whine to be taken on the toboggan. Then you'd wiggle. They'd crash into a tree. Aunt Tally would break a leg and it would be all your fault."* Pewter helpfully created a dismal scenario.

*"Would not,"* the corgi pouted.

*"Get over yourself,"* Pewter admonished her.

*"Do you think BoomBoom wears a support bra?"* Mrs. Murphy wondered.

*"Well, of course she does,"* Pewter replied seriously.

Mrs. Murphy giggled, the Brittany guffawed, and Tucker's mood improved.

*"I'd never wear a bra,"* the corgi declared.

*"Four in a row. How awful."* Pewter rolled on her back to display her tiny pink bosoms.

*"Four bras. How expensive."* Mrs. Murphy flopped over onto the gray kitty, she was laughing so hard.

*"Tit for tat,"* the Brittany said, tongue in cheek.

*"No, for cat,"* Mrs. Murphy replied and they all howled with laughter.

# 36

The pure silence of the snow had a calming effect on Harry, who usually couldn't sit still. "Idle hands do the Devil's work." If she heard it once in her childhood she heard it a thousand times. But occasionally one needed to be idle, to sit still and allow energy to flow back into the soul.

Chores done, Harry took a hot shower and stirred up the fire in the lovely old fireplace in the living room. Her robe, worn at the elbows, the shawl collar frayed, no longer provided as much warmth as it should. She plopped on the sofa, draped her mother's cream-colored alpaca afghan over her legs, plumped up a needlepoint pillow, opened *The Masks of God* by Joseph Campbell. She plucked this off a pile which contained David Chandler's *The Campaigns of Napoleon*, Jane Jacobs's *Cities and the Wealth of Nations* and G. J. Whyte-Melville's *Riding Recollections*. Harry's tastes encompassed just about everything except for medicine and math, although she'd soldier through the math to solve an engineering or building problem. Her mind was completely open to any and all ideas, which isn't the same as saying her ethics were. But she was willing to entertain different concepts whether they be Muslim, Buddhist, or the difference between Boswell and Gladstone. She wanted to know whatever could be known, which might explain why she couldn't bear a mystery.

*"You take the feet, I'll take the chest."* Mrs. Murphy settled on Harry's chest.

*"I'm reading up here."* Pewter delicately curled herself on top of the pillow, her tail resting on Harry's head.

Tucker leapt onto the sofa to Harry's feet.

*"If the sofa were an inch higher, you'd never make it,"* Pewter teased.

*"Anyone ever tell you, you have a fat tail?"* Tucker considered rolling over on her back but decided if Harry moved her feet she might land on the floor.

*"At least I have one,"* the gray cat shot back.

"Lot of talk around here." Harry peeped over the top of the book.

*"Why don't you read aloud something we can all enjoy? You know, like* Black Beauty," Tucker suggested.

*"Oh, that's such a sad story."* Mrs. Murphy's whiskers drooped for a moment. *"I want a happy story."*

*"There are no happy stories,"* Pewter grumbled. *"In the end everyone dies."*

*"That's life, not fiction. In fiction there are happy endings.* Lassie Come Home *has a happy ending."* Tucker liked novels with dogs as central characters.

*"Maybe dying's not so bad. There is such a thing as a good death,"* Mrs. Murphy thoughtfully said.

*"You mean a brave death?"* Pewter asked.

"*That's one way. To die before the walls of Troy or at Borodino. Fighting. Or to die at home surrounded by those who love you, like George Washington. Better than getting run over by a car.*"

"*If you ask me, not enough humans get run over by cars. Too many of them.*" Pewter dropped her tail over Harry's eyes with malicious glee.

Harry pushed the gray tail back.

"*I was thinking about us, not them,*" Mrs. Murphy replied.

"*Oh. Well, there can never be too many cats.*" Pewter dropped her tail again.

"Quit it." Harry flicked the tail away again.

"*Hee hee.*" Pewter was enjoying herself.

"*There* can *be too many cats. There can be too many anything if we overrun the food supply. Look how the deer population has ballooned because hunting laws have changed. They'll walk right into people's backyards in the suburbs and eat everything. Wouldn't dare try it here. Not with me around.*" Tucker puffed out her chest.

"*You are good at that.*" Mrs. Murphy complimented the corgi.

"*If only we could kill that hateful blue jay,*" Pewter said wistfully.

"*Arrogant.*" Tucker thought it was funny the way the blue jay tormented the cats with name-calling and ferocious dive-bombing. However, she wouldn't want her skull pecked at by the loudmouth bird.

"*He'll slip up someday. Patience,*" Mrs. Murphy counseled.

"*Think the person or persons who killed H.H. and Mychelle will slip up? Think they're arrogant?*" Pewter swished her tail over Harry's eyes this time but brought it up on her head before she could grab it.

"Pewter! I am trying to read."

"*Well, read a Dick Francis or one of those seafaring novels. Or that series about Richard Sharpe during the Napoleonic Wars. Read something that doesn't tax us too much but we get to learn,*" Pewter sassed back.

"*I don't know if the killer will slip,*" Mrs. Murphy replied to Pewter's question. "*Think about how smart you have to be to drive an object into someone's neck without the victim feeling it, it doesn't bleed, and you do this in front of an auditorium full of people. That was planned. Carefully.*"

"*Mychelle's death didn't seem well planned,*" Pewter remarked.

"*Back to our discussion. Did H.H. die a good death?*" Tucker still felt terrible about Mychelle so she changed the subject.

"*Yeah,*" Pewter said.

"*Why?*"

"*Because it was swift, maybe not too painful. Better than operation after operation. Lingering. Ugh.*" She shuddered, which made Harry reach up to steady her.

"What is your problem?"

"*Read something we want.*" Pewter batted at Harry's hand.

"*H.H. wasn't very old.*" Mrs. Murphy would have preferred more innings for the fellow.

"*There are worse things than dying young,*" Pewter said with conviction.

"*Like?*" Tucker asked.

"*Like living for eighty years and not doing a damn thing. Like being afraid of your own shadow. When the Great Cat in the Sky jerks your string, you're going home.*"

"*Dog,*" Tucker countered.

"*Cat.*" Pewter remained steadfast in her spiritual belief.

"*Harry thinks it's a human up there. Christians think there's*

*a man with a white beard who has a son with a dark beard."*
Tucker couldn't figure out where to fit in the Holy Ghost.

*"M-m-m, Harry isn't a dogmatic person. She's a Christian.
She goes to church, but she's not rigid. I bet if she ever told us
what she thinks we might be surprised."* Tucker snuggled into
the blanket. She loved the way the old alpaca throw felt.

*"I don't mind, really, that every species thinks whatever is
spiritual and powerful is a version of themselves. I really don't,
but you'd think they'd figure out that the spiritual is all-
encompassing. It's got to be more than we are, don't you think?"*
Mrs. Murphy rubbed her cheek with her paw.

*"It's too complicated for me,"* Tucker honestly replied. *"If I
think about a Big Corgi, I feel much better."*

Pewter leaned forward, reached down with her paw and
touched Harry's nose. *"Gotcha."*

Harry snuffled, then laughed. "Okay. You have made
yourself crystal clear. You don't want me to read this book."
She closed the book, reached onto the pillow, steadied
Pewter while she sat up. "Time for a squeaky toy for Tucker
and two little furry mice for you two."

*" 'Ray!"* they cheered.

The prized furry mice were kept in a cardboard box in
the kitchen cabinet. Milk-Bones, catnip, and new squeaky
toys were housed there, too, because the animals would
throw them all over the house at once. They didn't believe in
delayed gratification.

With three upturned faces at her feet, Harry opened the
cabinet door, pulled out a squeaky bone. She tossed it for
Tucker who skidded across the kitchen floor. Then she
threw a white mouse for Murphy and a gray one for Pewter.

The cats pounced, grabbed the toys by their skinny tails,
threw them over their heads, pounced again. Curiosity got

the better of Pewter who ran over to see if Murphy's mousie was better than hers.

Mrs. Murphy growled. Pewter huffed but returned to her own mouse.

Harry placed another log onto the fire, settled herself again, but this time picked up the Whyte-Melville book.

The two cats knocked their mice around like hockey pucks. They collided into the kitchen cabinets and one another.

Pewter, eyes large from excitement, slapped one paw on her gray toy. She said in a low voice, *"This mouse will die a good death. Crack."* She imitated snapping its neck.

Mrs. Murphy whispered, *"Mychelle—not a good death."*

They both glanced at Tucker, under the coffee table in the living room, merrily chewing on the bone, which squeaked with each chomp.

*"It's a good thing Harry doesn't know. Think how guilty she'd feel,"* Pewter said. *"I'm surprised she hasn't figured out that's why we were in front of the broom closet at the Clam."*

*"She has. She's not saying anything. It's one of the reasons she wants to solve this. She feels guilty."*

*"Could be,"* the gray cat mumbled, then her voice became clear. *"BoomBoom was there. She knows then, too."*

*"BoomBoom's got a lot of unnecessary stuff up there, but I expect she kind of knows."* Mrs. Murphy tapped Pewter's head.

The phone rang. Harry reluctantly rose to answer it, swearing she was going to buy a cordless phone. "Hello."

"Harry, it's Coop."

"Hey, girl, apart from a few cars sliding off the road maybe this will be a slow night."

"Actually, I'm not working tonight but on my way home

I stopped by Anne Donaldson's. You haven't happened to see her, have you?"

"No. Is this light surveillance?"

"Uh—"

"Okay, don't answer that."

"Well, she could have stopped at a friend's or her sister's and decided to stay there."

"If you're calling me you've already called them."

"Sometimes I forget just how smart you are," Cooper half-laughed. "Yes, I have called them."

"Do you think she ran off?"

"I don't know. We've sent out her license plate number. Maybe someone will see her."

"Any officer on duty tonight can't see the hand in front of his face," Harry said.

"You're just hopeful tonight, aren't you?"

"I don't mean to sound negative but it *is* a difficult night."

"Yes."

"Is Rick worried?"

"Concerned. Not worried."

"Ah."

"Next question."

"I thought you were off duty."

"I am."

"And you're smoking a cigarette, too." Harry smiled.

"I already have a mother."

"Did I tell you to stop?"

"No. Harry, how well do you know the girls on the basketball team?"

"The only one I know is Isabelle Otey because she came to our volleyball games while her knee was healing from surgery. So you know her, too."

"Tammy Girond."

"No. Just see her at the games."

"Frizz Barber."

"Uh, she came into the post office once with a friend. But no."

"Jenny Ingersoll, Sue Drumheller, the Hall sisters?"

"No, I just watch them play."

"Well, you know the coach."

"Not well, but yes. She's terrific."

"Honest?"

"You know she is."

"Yeah, I do know but I'm interested in your opinion. What about Andrew Argenbright, her assistant?"

"M-m-m, seems pretty good. Occasionally I'll see him in Charlottesville out and about but I don't know him other than to say hello. Why are you asking me about the team?"

"Well, I've been sequestered in the equipment room with Tim Berryhill. There was so much stuff we finally brought in two other officers, and, Harry, we counted every single piece of gear in that huge room. I thought I'd lose my mind. I hate stuff like that."

"And?"

"And there's no doubt equipment is being pilfered to the tune of about twenty-five thousand dollars last year. We don't know about other years."

Harry exclaimed, "What tipped you off?"

"Tracy was hit on the head two nights ago."

"He never told me."

"He wasn't supposed to tell anyone. Now that we've run the inventory it's not quite so crucial."

"I hate not knowing these things." Irritation crept into Harry's voice.

"You're getting as bad as Mim."

"Did you call her?"

"About Anne Donaldson, yes. Not about this," Coop answered.

"She won't be happy when she finds out."

"Maybe. You watch people. You notice things. Did you ever see H.H. at the Clam other than for a game?"

"No."

"Any ideas who's stealing the stuff?"

"Not right off the bat, forgive the pun. Since you've been running inventory whoever's been stealing knows you know," Harry sensibly said.

"Well, sometimes guilt or fear or both will flush the pup right out of the woods." Coop inhaled again, grateful for the nicotine.

"Do you think this has something to do with the murders?"

"I wish I knew. I'm starting to get irritated."

"Me, too." Harry watched as a gray mousie was batted by her feet. "You called Mim about Anne and Cameron, of course—"

"Yeah, I told you that."

"I know but you interrupted me."

"Sorry. Yes, and Mim, as smart as you are, knew it would be too obvious if I called around, so she is doing it. Her excuse is she heard Anne's four-wheel-drive is in the shop and she's happy to lend Anne hers."

"Then Mim knows, too."

"What?"

"That Anne is your suspect."

"That's why she's calling and not me. Except for calling you."

"Are you worried that Anne's slipped the net?"

"Not yet."

"What if she's not your killer? What if the killer wants her?"

"That thought has occurred to me."

"Damn."

# 37

The sky, clear but pitch-black the next morning, was filled with stars. Some seemed white, others bluish, one had a red tint. The first hint of dawn, a slender thread of dark blue underneath the black, gave way to a lighter blue by six-thirty. A pink haze shimmered on the horizon.

Harry had already accomplished her barn chores. She was shoveling snow, making a walkway between the house and the barn. She stopped to watch the sun's rim, deepest crimson, nudge over the horizon. The snow, blue now, turned pink and then crimson itself. The icicles, some over a foot long, exploded into hanging rainbows. The dazzle was so intense, Harry had to squint.

The mercury shivered at seven degrees Fahrenheit but as long as Harry was working, she didn't mind. A muff covered her ears but they still stung a bit. She heaved snow to the right as the crimson, pink, and gold colors with blue still in the shadows made this an exceptionally beautiful morning.

The cats, after visiting the barn to check on the horses and Simon, returned to the house. Tucker, her luxurious coat perfect for a frosty day, chased each shovelful of snow.

Although hungry, when Harry finished shoveling, she couldn't resist putting on her cross-country skis and sliding silently over to the creek that bordered her land and that of her neighbor, Blair Bainbridge.

The massive lone oak at the family cemetery stood out against the sky. Beyond that she could see a plume of white smoke curling out from Blair's kitchen chimney.

The fresh snow barely had any tracks in it. Animals snuggled in their burrows and nests. She turned right, gliding past the huge domed beaver lodge and dam. Tucker growled but kept behind her human. She didn't like the beavers. It was mutual.

Harry pushed up the ridge, the first in a series of ridges, some with narrow, perfect little valleys between them, until finally one was in the Blue Ridge Mountains. She turned right again, heading north on the low ridge, perhaps eight hundred feet above sea level. It was good apple country and quite a few orchards dotted the land in western Albemarle County and Nelson County. Nelson County, home of the famous pippin apple, looked like snow in the spring when the apple trees blossomed. The fragrance all through this part of Virginia made everyone a little giddy.

Today the only fragrance was the tangy hint of cold for no scent could rise up to Harry's nostrils off the frozen land. Even Tucker couldn't smell much and her olfactory powers far exceeded Harry's. As no animals had been about, the sturdy little dog couldn't even content herself with the aroma of a bobcat or a deer who had passed. Wild turkeys, in flocks of over seventy, gave off a distinct odor. Tucker chased a turkey hen once when she was a puppy and was quickly cured of that. That old turkey hen swirled around to chase *her*, gobbling hateful, scurrilous insults until Tucker raced into Harry's arms. Only then did the outraged bird stop. She turned and left with dignity.

But Tucker, happy to be alone with her human, knew there would always be a myriad of scents once the temperature climbed above freezing. Something it wouldn't do today. The swish of Harry's skis, the rhythm of her walking, hypnotized Tucker. It wasn't until the last moment that she heard the sharp feathers of a large hawk overhead. The bold animal swooped low then flew to a high tree limb where he gazed down on the groundlings.

*"Scared you."*

*"Did not."* Tucker bared her formidable fangs.

"Jeez, you're a big one." Harry stopped, looking up at the golden-eyed predator who stared right back at her.

*"I'm big and I'd like a tasty mole, shrew, or mouse right now,"* he complained.

Harry reached into the pocket of her down coat and a tired pack of Nabs, the cellophane crinkling, was still there. She took it out, removed her gloves and crunched the Nabs once, then opened the cellophane, dropping the orange crackers on the snow. "Tucker, leave it. I'll make you breakfast."

Tucker did as she was told, and as they pushed off, the bird swooped down to eat the crackers. Tucker called over her shoulder, *"You owe us one."*

The large fellow thought a moment while tasting peanut butter, a new delicious taste, and he cocked his head. *"You're right, little dog, I do."*

Tucker stopped, turning to face the hawk. *"If it gets really bad, Mother throws out seeds in front of the barn. She puts out a lot and sometimes bread. It's not flesh but it's better than going hungry. No one will bother you. The owl sleeps during the day."*

*"Flatface."* The hawk respected the huge owl. *"Best hunter around. She's conceited about it, too. Being domesticated, do you have to do everything that human tells you?"* The hawk thought the collar around Tucker's neck a badge of slavery.

*"You don't understand, I want to do what she wants. I love her."*

The hawk swallowed another piece of Nab. *"Incomprehensible."*

*"If you knew her, you'd love her."*

*"Never. Humans get in the way. They disturb our game, they tamper with migration patterns, they are the kiss of death."*

*"My human gave you food."*

*"Your human is the exception that proves the rule."*

*"Perhaps."* Tucker chose not to argue. *"I hope winter isn't too fierce. I hope you have plenty to eat. I won't chase you if you come to the barn. There are lots of mice in the barn and the outbuildings."*

*"Thank you. I'll see you again."* The hawk opened one wing, each feather standing out against the sparkling snow.

Tucker scampered after Harry, puffs of snow shooting out from under her paws.

"There you are. Thought about that big hawk, did you?"

*"Yes. I'm glad I'm not wild. I wouldn't get to live with you if I were."*

Harry stuck a ski pole into the snow, launching herself down a mostly cleared path back into the pastures. Tears welled up in her eyes from the cold. Tucker dashed after her, once falling into a deeper bit of snow than she had anticipated.

When they were finally cozy inside the kitchen, Tucker

gobbled her kibble, a drizzle of corn oil and a tablespoon of beef dog food on top.

The cats listened as she told them about the hawk.

"*What kind?*" Mrs. Murphy inquired.

"*A marsh hawk.*" Tucker called the northern harrier by its common name.

"*About two feet high?*" Pewter didn't think that was that big but big enough.

"*Yes, you know, plowing through the snow after talking with him I got to thinking about wild animals. They eat what they kill. Animals that aren't flesh eaters, say a squirrel, might stash some acorns but animals aren't greedy. Wild animals.*"

"*And we are?*" Pewter arched a gray eyebrow.

"*Uh, well, we can all overeat, I suppose, but I think greed, true greed, is a human characteristic. How much does one human need to live? But they'll kill one another for more.*"

"*That's true,*" Mrs. Murphy said.

"*I don't think Anne Donaldson killed H.H. My instincts are better than a human's.*" Tucker, invigorated from her exercise, was chatty. "*It's bigger than jealousy.*"

The phone rang and Harry picked it up to hear Susan's voice.

"Found Anne and Cameron." Susan had been called by Big Mim. She didn't believe the car story for a minute.

"Where were they?"

"BoomBoom's."

"Why didn't anyone call to tell me?" Harry complained.

"No one knew until"—Susan checked her wall clock— "seven-fifteen. Power went out on that side of town and it wasn't restored until early this morning. It doesn't appear to be anything sinister. Anne decided not to drive as the roads are treacherous."

"Sounds reasonable. Well, I'd better get down to the post office. I'm already late."

"No one's going out today. Stay home."

"Crozet might collapse without me."

"Pulease," Susan laughed and hung up.

Harry, usually punctual, had lost track of the time. She called Miranda. No one at home. She called the post office.

"Hello."

"Miranda, I'm late and I'm sorry."

"Don't worry about it. Nothing is moving in town this morning. You stay there. The roads aren't cleared, Tracy's with me."

"Coop told me he got clunked on the head. She also told me a lot of stuff has been walking out of the equipment room."

"Yes. I know Tracy can handle anything, but I don't think he or anyone should be in that building alone. Not until things are, well, whatever they are."

"Is Tracy sorting mail?"

"There isn't any. Rob Collier probably won't get through or, if he does, it will be late."

"Miranda, Coop said about twenty-five thousand dollars' worth of equipment had been stolen last year. She said they'll be able to determine what had been stolen from earlier years. More or less." She paused. "People kill for less than that."

"That they do," Miranda agreed.

"Nothing makes sense."

"No, it doesn't. But whether things make sense or not, there's something dangerous about. Now you stay there. If Rob makes it out and there's a lot of mail, I'll tell you, but I think the road plows will be running all day. You might as well build a snowman."

Harry hung up the phone, put her down vest and jacket back on, and went outside to do just that. The cats thought they'd play in the snow for a little bit until their paws became too cold, then they'd go back into the house. Tucker joined them. They raced around, threw snow over their heads, barked, meowed, ran in circles. Tucker chased Mrs. Murphy, who struggled because of the snow. Usually the dog was no match for the nimble cat, but although slowed by the snow, the tiger had lost none of her guile. She floundered over toward the barn, icicles gleaming from the roofline, and just as Tucker, fearsomely snapping her jaws, closed in on her, the cat arched sideways. Tucker, her momentum hard to stop, bounced into the side of the barn door. The icicles dropped, tinkling as they hit the earth. One small one fell onto Tucker's hind leg, the point so sharp it nicked the skin.

*"Ow!"*

Mrs. Murphy hurried to her friend, pulling it out with her claws. A little spot of blood stained the white fur. *"Bet that hurt."*

Pewter, at a more leisurely pace, joined them. She sniffed the tip of the icicle, the blood smell fresh and enticing.

Tucker twisted around to lick her leg just above her foot.

*"That's it."* Mrs. Murphy's eyes enlarged, her ears swept forward and back, her tail thrashed.

*"What are you talking about?"* Pewter half-closed her eyes, enjoying the blood odor.

*"Ice. H.H. was killed with ice!"*

Tucker stopped licking, and Pewter stopped smelling to stare at the excited tiger.

*"Huh?"* The dog was beginning to understand.

*"If H.H. had been hit with a dart, he'd have to pull it out. If Anne had stabbed him with some thin thing like a needle she'd*

*have to pull it out. If the weapon wasn't pulled out it'd be obvious, right? You'd think someone would notice, wouldn't you?"*

"We've heard all this." Pewter crossly said.

*"You could stab someone with ice, jab it into someone's skin. If there's a painkiller at the tip, the victim might not feel much and cold blunts feeling as well. When the ice melts, the toxin is delivered, it gets into the bloodstream but there's no weapon. It's absorbed into the body."*

*"God."* Pewter's mouth hung open, her bright pink tongue even brighter against the white snow background.

*"That's diabolical."* Tucker rubbed her head against Mrs. Murphy's.

*"If H.H. is outside the building, if he's hit with an ice dart or arrow, even though it's freezing, his body temperature will melt it. The killer can choose his or her best moment."* Mrs. Murphy grinned.

*"Like slapping him on the back to divert his attention, and with the other hand stick the little ice needle in?"* Pewter's imagination began to work.

*"Perhaps. We'll figure out how later, but I swear that's the weapon."*

Tucker stood up and shook herself. *"A person would need a tiny mold, pop it in the freezer. Of course, they'd have to be smart about toxins, wouldn't they?"*

*"Yeah, they would, but even a person with average research skills could find the right substance. There's stuff sitting on supermarket shelves that can kill you if you know what you're doing. You could mix up a lethal cocktail and not spend more than five dollars."* Pewter even forgot the cold in her enthusiasm.

*"Did we see anyone slap H.H. on the back in the parking lot?"* Tucker tried to remember that night.

*"No,"* Mrs. Murphy said.

"*Well, someone had to.*" Pewter became quite suspicious. Tucker thoughtfully replied, "*Maybe not.*"

"*If only we knew why.*" Mrs. Murphy headed back toward the house. The others followed. "*But we've got the weapon.*"

"*Is there any way we can get Harry to understand?*" Tucker looked up at the icicles hanging on the roofline of the house.

"*No. We could slam into every bush, tree, building. They could all drop. She wouldn't get it. If she does understand, it will be by other means. But we know. So let's go in the kitchen where it's warm and try to remember every single thing, every person, we saw in the parking lot. Before the game and after.*" Mrs. Murphy pushed open the animal door.

"*This human is incredibly smart.*" Pewter fluffed her fur for a moment once in the kitchen.

"*Yes,*" Mrs. Murphy simply said.

"*I find that terrifying.*" Tucker's brow furrowed.

## 38

Schools closed, sporting contests were postponed. The airport was closed. The trains continued chugging along with stops in the mountains as snowdrifts spilled over the tracks. Then crews with shovels would disembark to clear the snow. Central Virginians concentrated on digging out. The only vehicles on the roads were the huge yellow snowplows and the smaller yellow snowblowers as they methodically cleared the major arteries first. By the afternoon, the temperature had risen only to the mid-twenties but the road crews managed to begin clearing the secondary roads such as Route 240 into Crozet from Charlottesville.

Fortunately, no more snow was in the forecast so by Friday business should return to normal, people would be back in their offices, their snow boots lined up outside the doors, their heavy coats neatly arranged on coatracks.

The Reverend Jones mournfully looked at the tattered carpets. One more day without new ones. True, Job suffered greater tests in life but this certainly qualified as a scabrous irritation. He kept his temper, concentrated on positive projects and hoped the Good Lord noted his maturity and restraint.

Elocution and Cazenovia certainly did.


Big Mim had exploded in a flurry of closet organizing. As her closets were already organized with a neat square of paper hanging on each dress and on each pair of shoes noting when and where she had worn the ensemble, this really was taking coals to Newcastle.

Jim Sanburne, as mayor, hitchhiked a lift with a road crew to check his town. Satisfied that all was being done that could be done, he allowed them to drop him back home where he got underfoot. Frustrated, his wife gave him the chore of sharpening all the cutlery while she repaired to her closet followed by her dog.


Susan Tucker browbeat Brooks into getting all her homework through next week done.

"You'll be amazed at how happy you are to be ahead of the power curve instead of behind it." She smiled as Brooks bent over her books.


Miranda and Tracy sat in the deserted post office but used the time to go over plans for the bank building. He'd even brought over color swatches along with his rough drawings. This pleased Miranda enormously, and she would reach over and squeeze his hand from time to time. Miranda realized she was in love and she had thought that would never happen to her again. That he was her high school beau made it all the sweeter.

Those who didn't know the good woman well might have thought she'd resist the emotion but Miranda had lived long enough to know that it was far better to surrender to joy.

Tracy, too, gave himself up to the tide of happiness.

BoomBoom, bored beyond belief, sat on the phone calling everyone she knew, including a semi-current boyfriend in San Francisco. She preferred her beaus at a distance. After her husband died and she was left a widow at thirty-two, BoomBoom had gotten used to coming and going as she pleased, answering to no one but herself.

Harry might not express it in those same terms but the truth was she'd come to value her own company, as well. Like BoomBoom, although it would have killed her to admit it, she didn't feel like walking out the door declaring where she was headed and when she'd return. Nor did she have any desire to submit to the horror of cooking supper every night or food shopping for two.

Anne Donaldson and Cameron spent time in the stable after watering plants and checking on the thermostat in the greenhouse. Both mother and daughter enjoyed riding and H.H. had built Anne the stable of her dreams, complete with automatic, heated waterers, automatic fly spray which of course clogged, interlocking rubber bricks in the center aisle so no horse would slip, handsome Lucas Equine stall facings and dividers made expressly to her dimensions from Cynthiana, Kentucky. Each of the six stalls bore a brass nameplate shined to mirror gloss. Each stall door had a heavy, handmade brass bar upon which to hang a winter blanket; a brass bridle rack on the side of the sliding door gleamed. They'd been bolted into the steel of the doors and all of the Lucas equipage had been painted a rich maroon since Anne's stable colors were maroon and gold. Every stall had a skylight, covered with snow today.

Cameron cleaned her tack. Her mother was strict in that. No pleading or trying to get out of work. If Cameron didn't do the ground work she didn't ride.

Anne opened the small refrigerator in the tack room, removing a needle with a thin point. She needed to tranquilize Cameron's pony. The fancy little guy hated having his ears clipped, his nose whiskers trimmed. Without the chemical help, he could demolish the barn as well as Anne and Cameron.

She walked into his stall and slipped the needle upward into his neck as he munched apple bits. He flinched for a second but she had removed the needle before he really knew what stung him.

Sheriff Shaw closely cruised the opened highways. Thanks to accurate weather reports no stranded motorists needed pulling out or carrying home. For once people had the sense to stay home.

Deputy Cooper manned headquarters with the dispatcher. The quiet was refreshing. She took the opportunity to go over Mychelle Burns's bank accounts. In her neat hand, sloping forward, she'd written every deposit and withdrawal. Apart from the five-thousand-dollar withdrawal from her savings account, which she'd gotten up to seven thousand two hundred and nineteen dollars, her accounts were pretty much like everyone else's: electric bill, oil bill, gas bill, the occasional restaurant bill.

Mychelle's sense impressed Cooper. She kept only one credit card and she used it sparingly even at Christmas when most of us throw caution to the winds, overcome by seasonal cheer as well as guilt. She maintained no gas credit cards, no debit cards. She owned no cell phone, and according to Sugar McCarry, the secretary at the county office, Mychelle did not abuse the business cell phone.

When Cooper questioned Mychelle's mother, the sorrowing woman said although she didn't know about the money she thought her daughter might be saving for the down payment on a house. Mychelle had wanted to move into downtown Charlottesville, hopefully around the Lyons Court area. If she couldn't swing that then she'd look around Woolen Mills, which was lovely except for the sewage treatment plant. When the wind shifted you knew it.

As Cooper read the neat notations she had a sense of a life lost. Mychelle may not have been the most personable woman, but she was tidy, efficient, hardworking, and to all appearances, she kept her nose clean.

Was she having an affair with H.H.? Cooper could find no sign of it in these white checkbook and savings book pages.

So the call from Mrs. Burns startled her.

"Are you keeping warm out there, ma'am?" Cooper tried to put the nervous, grieving woman at ease.

"Wood-burning stove. Works a treat," Mrs. Burns replied in her working-class accent, which was noticeably different from the speech of Harry, Big Mim, and the others.

"What can I do for you, Mrs. Burns? I know this is a painful time."

A little intake of breath, a moment, then the wiry lady said, "You take what God gives you."

"I'm trying to learn that, ma'am, but it's hard."

"Yes, 'tis. Yes, 'tis. Sittin' here. Can't get to work. Mind's turnin' over." She paused, longer this time. "I lied to you."

"I'm sure you had a good reason." Cooper, like all law enforcement officers, was accustomed to people lying to her. In fact, they lied more than they told the truth. She was fighting not to have it pervert her sense of life.

"Wanted to protect my little girl—but can't. She's gone to the light of the Lord." Another pause. "She was seeing a married man. I read her scripture and verse." Mrs. Burns used an expression meaning they'd had a knock-down-drag-out argument. "Uh-huh. She said I was old, forgot what it was to be in love. You know, she was right about that. Don't really want to remember, I guess." Cooper held her breath and Mrs. Burns finally got to the point. "Was H. H. Donaldson."

"Ah."

"Never met him. Might have been a nice man, but he was married, had a child. Didn't want to meet him. Didn't want her being no backstreet woman, no colored girl waiting around for her vanilla lover."

"Mrs. Burns, he must have loved her very much. He left his wife for her."

"Mychelle swore he would. Didn't believe her. They all lie like that."

"But he did leave. Did she tell you?"

"No." Mrs. Burns stifled a sob. "I said some mean things. Oh Lordy, I wish I could take 'em back. And I didn't talk to my baby for three days before she was taken from me."

"She knows you love her, ma'am. I promise you she knows what you told her was right."

Mrs. Burns composed herself. "But he left his wife and child?"

"He did. For a little while."

"Mychelle was afraid of his wife." Mrs. Burns carefully spoke. "She knew. Said she'd kill him if he left her."

Cooper didn't jump on this right off. She tacked toward shore instead of sailing in a straight line. "I guess it's so humiliating for a wife. It's easier to be angry at the other woman than at your husband."

"Doesn't work. Put up with it or throw him out. I threw mine out fifteen years ago. Mychelle knew better, Officer Cooper, she did. That's what got me crossways with her."

"I can certainly understand that. Do you think Mychelle was afraid that Mrs. Donaldson would become violent? Take out her revenge?"

"Feared for him. And maybe for herself, too. Said he could be blind sometimes. Like most men."

"Did you . . . fear for your daughter?"

"My fear was about a different kind of hurt. I didn't imagine this. When I got the call"— she breathed heavily again—"I didn't think about nothin'. Had some time to order my mind, kind of like arranging furniture. You find stuff behind the sofa cushions. And I remember that Mychelle said she found something. She didn't say what it was, but she said she told H. H. Said he'd put a stop to it."

"Maybe someone was gossiping, getting close to the affair?"

"I don't know."

"Do you know why she withdrew the five thousand dollars? Do you think they were going to run away together?"

"No. Know that for a fact. I didn't know she had withdrawn the money. I told you the truth about that. Like I said, we hadn't spoken for three days. She said H.H. was going to help her with a house."

"Did she say he was going to live with her?"

"No." Mrs. Burns considered this. "Even though she was in love with the man, she would have waited. You know, it's oh so easy to move them in and oh so hard to move them out."

"Yes, ma'am. When Mychelle talked to you about finding something, did she sound frightened?"

"More surprised. She said, 'Momma, people do the damnedest things.' That was all she said 'cept H.H. would take care of it. And I was so mad at her I didn't care 'bout that. I wanted her to stay away from that man. And I believe she's dead because of him."

"You think his wife killed her?"

"She had the reason."

"Did Mychelle ever talk to Mrs. Donaldson?"

"No."

"Mrs. Donaldson never tried to contact your daughter, to scare her off or shame her off?" Cooper gently prodded.

"Mychelle would have told me."

"Do you think she told anyone else? A best friend?"

"She had her running gang but Mychelle didn't ever get close to people. She would tell me things but I don't think she talked to her girlfriends. When she did get close, it was with H.H. He was her world. When he died in the parking lot, she died, too, I think. Part of her, but I tell you, she never let on. Iron will, my girl."

"I see." Coop kept writing as she talked. "Apart from Mrs. Donaldson, can you think of anyone who bore your daughter a grudge?"

"Oh, sometimes contractors would fuss at her. She was strict." A note of pride filled Mrs. Burns's voice when she said, "They couldn't get 'round my girl no way. But none of them said they'd kill her. Be crazy to kill someone over a roof shingle."

"The world's full of crazy people."

"You got that right." Mrs. Burns sighed. "But I tell myself whoever done this, Mrs. Donaldson, whoever, they et up with guilt, just et up, and sooner or later it will all come out like a poison."

She was wrong.

The murder didn't bother the killer one tiny bit.

# 39

Although their Friday game had been canceled, the storm moved off more quickly than the weatherman predicted. Coach Debbie Ryan saw no reason to waste the evening so she had the girls come in for practice. Those with dates were disappointed. Others, like the Hall sisters, ate, slept, and breathed basketball.

Tim Berryhill had told coaches that he had to oversee an extensive inventory because of purchasing errors. He apologized to all. Most of the coaches, under pressure to perform, would work around the inconvenience. Those few coaches without tunnel vision might wonder, to themselves at least, why such an exalted person as Tim Berryhill was performing the actual work, but they wouldn't dwell on it. Coaches had far too much to do and too little time in which to do it.

The only person or persons who would worry were the ones pilfering the equipment.

Since Irena Fotopappas was new to the force, Sheriff

Shaw had her dress as a student and assigned her to Coach Ryan. Debbie Ryan, wanting to assist Rick in any way, explained Irena was a graduate student in sports psychology. Coach's words to the team were, "Ignore her."

Irena watched, fascinated, as the girls drilled. Repetition was the best thing in the world in any sport. Master the basics, the fancy stuff will take care of itself. Games were won and lost on the basics. Maybe a trick play would win a football game in the last second or a full court desperation shot, but ninety-nine percent of the time, basics.

Andrew Argenbright, the assistant coach, kept feeding the girls balls as they ran downcourt in a passing drill. Tammy Girond grabbed the basketball and flipped a crisp pass to where she thought Isabelle Otey would be. However, Isabelle tripped and was a step slow.

"The best pass is a caught pass," was all Coach Ryan had to say.

Tammy, red-faced because she hadn't kept her eye on her teammate, wouldn't make that mistake in a game.

Basketball, a fluid game, calls for constant adjustment. Even soccer, a game similar to basketball, has a goalie socked into the goal, or midfielders assigned to a portion of the field. A player can defend turf because there is so much of it, but in basketball, the dimensions are small, fifty feet by ninety-four feet. You keep moving or you lose.

As the two women crossed under the basket to turn back up the court, Jenny Ingersoll brushed by Tammy. The other woman ignored her, but the tension between them crackled.

Ego is a part of sport, a part of any endeavor where a human being wants to excel. Basketball is a team sport. A player needs to keep that ego in check, in the service of the team. Many a coach has spent a sleepless night trying to figure out how to make a team player out of a talented self-ish egoist.

One other thing Irena, a good observer, picked up: Tammy and Andrew spoke to one another only when necessary. As hot as the friction was between Jenny and Tammy, the space between the assistant coach and Tammy was frigid.

After practice, after the girls showered, Irena visited the equipment room, then patiently walked through the two levels of the building. She also went back to the basketball court to familiarize herself with the setup.

As she was walking around the aisle behind the topmost row of seats she heard snow slide on the roof. She noticed, as had Pewter, that a little trickle of water, just a small bit, wiggled down the back wall.

# 40

Saturday, cold and clear, exhilarated the Reverend Herb Jones not because of the weather but because the carpet men actually showed up. The white van doors slid open with a quiet metallic noise. The two men shouldered the heavy rolls of carpet and floor protector, the cushy rubber pad placed under the carpet. They returned for a five-gallon drum of powerful glue as well as a few carpet tacks for those difficult corners.

In a fit on Friday night, the Reverend Jones had torn up all the old carpets. He had had to vent his anger on something. The carpet men, JoJo and Carl Gentry, brothers, happily carted out the old and since the Reverend Jones tipped them they wedged it into the back of the van to haul to the dump later. Otherwise the good pastor would have had to haul it himself or pay someone else to do it. This was easier and JoJo and Carl always liked pocket money.

*"Inbred."* Cazenovia sat on the stairway above the communion wafer closet.

*"Oh, Cazzie, you're mean. Just because JoJo and Carl don't have chins doesn't mean they're inbred."* Elocution had heard enough Cazzie theories on bloodlines to last forever. The point was always the same: cats are better genetic specimens than humans.

Saturdays, sermon day, made the Rev, as Harry called him, tense. He'd find a myriad of things to do to delay writing the sermon, then he'd finally sigh, surrender, and sit down at his desk. Once he was in the middle of his task he enjoyed it. It was getting there that was so hard.

The bare floor felt odd under his shoes as he squeezed into his desk chair. JoJo decided they'd do Herb's office last.

The color, a rich forest green, was quite attractive and Matthew surprised Herb by paying extra, out of his own pocket, for a simple mustard yellow border inset four inches from the edge. Once down it would be very handsome.

The carpet, precut at the factory, proved easy to install. The men made a few adjustments but technology had invaded their craft, too.

The vestibule, finished in an hour and a half, looked splendid. The two cats tested it.

Cazenovia kneaded the carpet, smelling of dye and glue underneath. *"M-m-m, what fun."*

*"Don't get any in your claws or he'll pitch a fit. For a preacher, he can swear when he has to."* Elocution smiled as she, too, worked the carpet.

*"It's bad manners to give orders to your elders."* Cazenovia pulled up a thread of carpet, dangling it in front of the slender cat. *"I'll drop this in front of you."* Her eyes glittered.

Elocution ignored her as she listened to JoJo and Carl carry the padding down the hall to the closet containing the communion wafers. They propped up the rolled padding on the foot of the wide stairway behind the closet. As they slopped down glue, the brothers laughed, talked about friends, turkey season, the new pro-football league which both thought would bomb.

"Hey, it's twelve o'clock. No wonder I'm hungry." Carl checked his square Casio watch.

"Let's go to Jarman's Gap." JoJo cited a local eatery.

"JoJo, you're on." Carl laid his brush, full of rubber cement, across the top of the five-gallon drum which he closed first, gently tapping the lid so it wouldn't be on too tight.

"Brush will be useless." Carl pointed to the dripping bristles.

"I'll get another one out of the truck. I'm too hungry to care." He wiped his hands on his overalls. "I'll pay for it."

"Yeah. Yeah." Carl closed the box of carpet tacks, placing his small hammer next to the box and five-gallon drum.

Hunger must have clouded their minds because they grabbed their coats without realizing they'd left a section of floor exposed, full of glue, in front of the communion closet. Perhaps they forgot, or perhaps they figured they could sand it off if it hardened by the time they returned.

Cazenovia and Elocution watched them leave.

*"Bet the skinny one could eat you out of house and home,"* Cazenovia remarked of JoJo.

*"Yeah. It's quiet in Poppy's office. Think he's having a brainstorm?"* Elocution loved Herb.

*"Let's see."*

He looked up as the two cats walked into his office. "Hello, girls."

*"Hello. The carpet looks good as far as it goes,"* Cazenovia replied.

"Epistle, Romans chapter thirteen, verses eight through

ten and Gospel Matthew chapter eight, verses twenty-three through twenty-seven. I'm torn. Do I take my sermon from Romans, 'Thou shalt love thy neighbor as thyself,' or do I take it from Matthew? That's such a great story about Christ calming the seas. 'Why are ye fearful, O ye of little faith?' They're both so complex, so many levels of meaning." He looked down at his cats, now at his feet. " 'Course, I never know what people will hear. Some hear nothing. Others hear a rebuke. Someone else finds comfort. But each parishioner usually believes I am talking only to them. Well, I am." He smiled, warming to his subject. "You know, I wouldn't be surprised if Jesus practiced His sermons with cats. Our Lord loved all creatures but surely He must have loved cats best."

*"I should hope to holler."* Elocution blinked and smiled.

"You know, I'd better check the closet. Tomorrow is communion and Charlotte didn't get in to work Friday. She usually checks the supply." He stood up.

*"I'm outta here."* Elocution burnt the wind scrambling out of the office.

*"Dope!"* Cazenovia called after her. *"You look guilty as sin."*

Elocution ignored her, gracefully leaping up and over the exposed rubber cement part of the hall and clutching onto the side of the stairwell. Deep claw marks attested to the fact that she had done this before. She pulled herself up, squeezing through the banisters, hopping over the rolled padding, then raced up the stairs. She'd hide up there until the tempest blew over.

Cazenovia meowed prettily as Herb stepped into the hall. *"Look at the vestibule."* She took a few steps toward the vestibule then returned to her human.

He paused then walked out to the vestibule. "Hey, this looks good. You think so, too."

*"I love it when you understand."* Cazenovia rubbed against his pants leg while she purred.

"That border—such a nice finishing touch. I'll have to be sure to write Matthew a thank-you." He folded his arms across his chest, smiled then turned to go back down the hall, his rubber-soled shoes quiet on the new carpet.

He stepped over the large roll of carpet at the edge of the vestibule. This would be used in the hall. He didn't look down as he walked to the closet and he stepped right into the rubber cement before he realized it. The other foot slopped into it, too.

Cazenovia prudently remained where the vestibule connected to the hall. She saw him wobble a minute and then he tumbled over. Now his hands were in it. He pulled up one hand, the goo stringing out like a fat spiderweb off his fingers. He tried to reach a banister but couldn't. With all his might he yanked the other hand out of the ooze, which was affixing itself to his rubber soles.

Leaning forward he grasped for the closet door handle but he couldn't quite make it. He tried to pick one foot up but it wasn't budging.

"Dammit to hell!"

*"I'm not coming down the stairs,"* Elocution called out.

*"You're missing a good one."* Cazenovia laughed out loud.

*"He's opened the closet?"*

*"No, he's stuck in the glue and he's got it all over his hands, too. He can't even untie his shoes and step out of them until he cleans off his hands. Oh, it's not a pretty sight."*

Elocution, curiosity raging, crept to the top of the stairs. *"If he falls backwards he'll knock over the drum and the carpet tacks."*

*"He's in a pickle,"* Cazenovia guffawed.

*"If he has any sense he'll stay where he is until JoJo and Carl*

*come back."* Elocution tried not to laugh at Herb's predica-
ment, but it was funny.

"What are you looking at?" Herb roared as he beheld the
cat peering down at him through the banisters.

*"You. I came down for a closer look."* She slipped halfway
through the white banisters.

"Elo. Don't you dare. Stay where you are." Herb had visions of Elocution getting stuck in the glue with him.

A knock on the front door startled them.

*"I'll see who it is."* Cazenovia turned, her long hair
swirling out from the speed.

"I'm in here!" Herb bellowed.

The door opened and Harry gingerly stepped through,
accompanied by Mrs. Murphy, Pewter, and Tucker.
Cazenovia quickly filled them in—except for Harry, of
course.

The animals rushed forward to see. Harry didn't lag behind.

"Rev."

"This goddamned carpet has been nothing but a trial!"
He lurched to and fro.

"Uh, well, let me go find cardboard or something so you
can step onto it."

"I can't pick my feet up."

"No, but you can untie your shoes."

He held up his fingers. "The laces are too thin."

"Can't you pull that stuff off your hands?"

"What do you think I've been trying to do!" he crossly
said. "It just transfers from one hand to the other and then
my fingers get stuck."

"Okay, okay. I'll find something I can kneel on and I'll
untie your shoes. Then you can step out."

*"Does he know?"* Mrs. Murphy asked the church cats.

*"Not yet,"* Elocution answered in a singsong voice.

*"Boy, will you all be in trouble."* Tucker affected an innocent air.

*"You lying sack of you-know-what! You ate as much as we did."* Pewter boxed her ears.

*"Prove it."* Tucker loved tormenting the cats.

*"I have ways to get even."* The gray cat flattened her ears. Quite a scary sight.

Harry, who had dashed to the little kitchen, came back with Coke cartons she'd flattened. She carefully put them on the rubber cement then stepped onto them. She only had two and she put them side by side so she could kneel down on one knee. She slipped a little, her arms flailing, but righted herself.

"'That's all we need, two of us stuck. I will wring their necks! I will bless them in every language I know,"

"Right." Harry put one knee down, holding her foot over the goo. It wasn't that easy. She quickly untied both shoes, secretly thankful that he hadn't been able to bend over and try it himself because he would have smeared the powerful glue over the laces and then she would have had to cut him out. She stretched out the laces so he could step out, then she slowly stood up on one foot while bringing the other foot over and down onto the red Coke cardboard carton.

Nimbly she stepped back onto the safe part of the hall holding out her hand for a grateful but angry Herb.

"Thank you."

"It was an adventure."

"I will kill them." He stomped to the kitchen to try and peel off the cement.

The animals stayed behind to gossip.

Harry walked into the kitchen. "Can I help get that stuff

off? If you have rubber gloves maybe I can pull it off more easily."

"No. It's worse with rubber. I think that's why I got stuck in the LaBrea Tar Pits. Rubber-soled shoes." His sense of humor was returning. "Of all the damned, dumb things. To walk off and leave that shit on the floor. Sorry." He apologized for swearing in front of a lady.

"I'd say worse."

"Is there worse?" He used a paring knife to peel off the blackish stuff.

"Oh sure," she cheerfully replied.

"Where do you hear such stuff? Your mother would have been horrified."

"All you have to do is tune into rap music. Every other word is the F-word and it's filled with romantic notions of rape, pillage, and revenge. It's probably what the Norsemen would have sung in the seventh century A.D. if they'd known how to rap."

"I see. A true cultural advance." He'd cleaned one hand, holding it under the cold tap because it burned a little.

"Hey, we can't take all the credit. The English went to an art museum to see a dead sheep."

"I thought they got over that. The dead sheep. I remember reading about that."

"Maybe they have but as I said Americans can't take all the credit for these cultural improvements."

"You're right. My patriotism got the better of me." He'd held the other hand under the water now even though little round bits adhered between his fingers. "This stuff is nasty."

"I'll say. Got any hand cream?"

"Charlotte has some on her desk."

Harry walked outside to Charlotte's office, nabbed a blue

THE TAIL OF THE TIP-OFF          279

jar of Nivea off her desk, and came back to Herb. He rubbed the soothing cream onto his hands.

The door opened, and JoJo and Carl, full and happy, clomped down the hall. Herb emerged from his kitchen, keeping his temper in check. He described his ordeal.

Blushing, they apologized, said not another word and immediately returned to their task. The first thing they had to do was liberate Herb's shoes, ruined.

All four cats watched from the stairway. Tucker, who couldn't leap over the glue, watched from behind the brothers.

*"Can't even give those to the Salvation Army,"* Pewter remarked.

*"Since when have you given anything to the Salvation Army?"* Mrs. Murphy said.

*"I haven't. Humans can take care of themselves. These guys are sure working fast, aren't they?"*

*"Fear and guilt will do that to you."* Elocution wanted to bat JoJo's ponytail.

*"Look who's talking."* Cazenovia then informed the others about Elocution racing up the stairs when Herb headed for the closet.

Back in the kitchen, Herb made Harry a cup of tea, one for himself, too. They sat down to go over the calendar. Since Harry was on the Parish Guild, the calendar wasn't her responsibility but Herb wanted feedback so she dutifully listened.

"—tricky."

"April is. Why don't you have the church picnic the first weekend in May? It shouldn't be too hot and the only real worry you'll have is rain. If it rains we'll have it here."

"I like to get the jump on spring but—you're right. On a day like today you have to have faith to believe in spring. 'O ye of little faith,' " he mused. "Uh, tomorrow's Gospel reading." He had told her of his two choices.

"Jesus and the disciples in the boat and the waves crash over. They wake Him up and He calms the wind and the waves. My vote." Harry smiled.

"I guess I suffered my own tempest," he sheepishly admitted.

She whispered, "They were dumb. I mean I like the Gentrys but they can't chew gum and walk at the same time."

He laughed. "Let's see how far they've gotten."

They both walked into the hall. The brothers had gotten the padding down to the foot of the stairs. Next would come the carpet.

"It's going to make such a difference."

The four cats watched with apprehension as the two humans approached the closet. Tucker, on the stairs with the cats, lowered her head.

The Gentry brothers were now at the vestibule end of the hall. On their knees, they were unrolling the lovely carpet.

"You know, I started down the hall to check on communion wafers. I can't remember if Charlotte reordered some or not. I've got enough to get through tomorrow but I'd better check. That's how I got stuck."

Harry followed him back. He didn't notice that Cazenovia and Elocution disappeared. Mrs. Murphy, determined to stand her ground, watched her tail swishing. Why would he think she had eaten the wafers? Pewter leaned on Murphy, but she wasn't so certain they wouldn't come in for a blast. Tucker headed up the stairs in the church cats' footsteps.

Harry, knowing her children well, sensed they were guilty of something.

Herb opened the door. "Here we go." He reached in. No box on the shelf. He looked down. Shredded cellophane. Torn boxes. Communion wafer bits scattered like Hansel and Gretel's crumbs.

"Elo! Cazzie!" His face turned beet red.

*The dog did it,"* Elo called from her hiding place.

Harry stared at the desecration, then threw back her head and laughed. She laughed until tears rolled down her cheeks.

Herb sputtered. He fumed. He kicked the tattered boxes out of the closet. He sighed. Finally he laughed, too. "Give me a sign, Lord."

"He has." Harry wiped her eyes, laughing even harder. "He's sent you two very holy cats." She wondered if her animals had participated in this. After all, they attended the Parish Guild meetings. She knew Mrs. Murphy, Pewter, and Tucker were capable of it. She thought it wise not to point the finger.

Mrs. Murphy and Pewter watched, their eyes large, their tails twitching too much.

Tucker, flat on her belly, was just around the corner at the top of the stairs. *"Elo, I'll kill you for that,"* the dog threatened.

Harry knelt down to pick up the wafer bits.

"Wonder if Father O'Mallory has any to spare?" Herb's brow furrowed as he held a box, cellophane tatters spilling over his reddened fingers which still stung. More evidence covered the floor.

"If he doesn't, I'll go to the market and buy crackers, you know, little cocktail crackers. If you bless them why aren't they as good as communion wafers?"

"Well, they might be but if they're salty everyone will be sitting in their pews thirsty."

"Give them more wine." Harry smiled devilishly.

"Harry, you've got a point there. Wait, don't go until I know." He hurried into his office, handing her one of the fang-marked boxes. She tagged after him.

"Thanks, Dalton." Herb hung up the phone. "He's got them. Oh dear Jesus, thank you for Father Dalton O'Mallory. Well, I'd better go pick them up." He stopped. "Harry, you know I forgot to ask why you dropped by." He slapped his hand against his thigh. "I'm sorry."

"You had a lot on your mind and, uh, don't you need shoes?"

"Uh—yes." He walked to the closet in his office, pulling out a pair of galoshes and a heavy loden coat.

"I dropped by to tell you Tracy Raz closed on the old bank building yesterday and I thought if we all chipped in twenty dollars each we could afford to have a sign painted for him, whatever he wants, 'Raz Enterprises' or something."

"Why, sure." He slipped his foot into the rubber boot. "More rubber. I'll watch where I put my foot down." He stared at the old wooden floor for a minute. "When I come back, hopefully this will be covered up. Good thing Fred Forrest isn't here. He'd find something wrong with the floor. You don't notice the tilt when it's covered up."

"It's a couple of centuries old. He can get over himself. Anyway, all he can do is make trouble on new construction."

Herb shook his head. "No. If he wants to be a butthead he can march right in here and declare this floor unsafe."

"No way."

"He can. If Fred has it in for you, watch out. I'm not just worried about Matthew's taking on the sports complex. I wouldn't put it past Fred to worry him over buildings already up, and let me tell you, that gets really, really expensive."

"He wouldn't. There's enough upset in his office."

"He would. Something's wrong with Fred."

Yes, there was.

# 41

Later that day Harry shopped with Susan at Foods of All Nations. As she owned two trucks, no car, a big market shopping tested her ingenuity—especially where to put the stuff when rain or snow poured into the bed of the truck.

Usually she borrowed Susan's wagon or they both shopped together, which was the case today. Also in "Foods" as it was known was BoomBoom.

The three women emerged, heading to their vehicles in the cramped parking lot.

Harry closed the back wagon door and noticed out of the corner of her eye two cars side by side, noses in opposite directions. BoomBoom observed it, too, as she filled up her Explorer. Matthew Crickenberger was in one. Fred Forrest was in another.

Harry couldn't hear what they were saying but she noticed that Fred rolled up his window, driving off without looking to the right or the left. Matthew's electric window glided up as he shook his head in anger, his face red.

"See that?" Harry asked Susan who had been moving stuff in the wagon's backseat.

Susan, sliding behind the wheel, answered, "What?"

"Matthew and Fred. Appeared they had another, uh, moment."

"Missed it."

BoomBoom walked over. "Well, I didn't. Fred said, 'Cover your ass.' Wish I'd caught the rest of it."

"*Been a day of moments,*" Mrs. Murphy observed.

"*Yeah and it's only one-thirty.*" Tucker wanted to stick her nose in the grocery bags.

"*Saturday's Harry's day off. And we're spending it shopping. I want to do something fun.*" Pewter slid over the gearshift onto the front seat and Susan's lap. Harry bid BoomBoom goodbye and got into the passenger seat as Susan started the engine.

"*The Reverend Jones provided excitement,*" Mrs. Murphy tittered, recalling the scene.

"*And you were such a chicken,*" Pewter called back at Tucker.

"*I was not. Elocution and Cazenovia were the chickens.*"

"*Well, I want excitement. The day is young.*" Pewter stood on her hind legs, her paws on Harry's left shoulder as she looked back at the others.

"*Excitement comes in both good and bad varieties,*" the corgi sagely noted.

# 42

Each time he thought of Fred, Matthew gripped his steering wheel until his knuckles turned white. He'd catch himself, then stop. He pulled his dark green Range Rover onto Garth Road and headed west.

As late as the 1960s, these rolling hills sported few houses. Horse farms, hay farms, and down at White Hall, apple orchards dotted the road.

Berta Jones, former Master of the Farmington Hunt Club, kept three retired Kentucky Derby winners at her farm, Ingleside. She hunted those fast Thoroughbreds, too.

But the redoubtable Berta had been long gone. Her daughter, Port Haffner, another bold rider, kept to the old Virginia ways, but surrounding the beautiful farm were expensive houses on anywhere from two to twenty acres.

The homes, red brick with white porticos, security systems, sprinkler systems, and big-ass family rooms, were built for the "come heres" to impress one another. Natives wondered why anyone would pour their money into a house instead of the land.

But the new people gave Matthew his start in building. He soon realized the money was in commercial construction and by the mid-1970s, quick to master new technologies and materials, Matthew pulled ahead of larger, more established firms. Now he was the large established firm.

He got along with most people, newcomers or old families. He often wondered why the newcomers didn't learn the ways of the place—"When in Rome"—but so often these people whipped out their checkbooks expecting that to supplant simple good manners. They'd write a check for a charity but would keep their maid on starvation wages. The Virginian would not write a check for charity but would properly take care of the maid.

The law of Virginia was, "Take care of your own."

The problem was the new people didn't know who "their own" were. Maybe they wrote the checks to cover their bases.

Well, Anne knew the rules. Matthew pulled into the crushed-stone drive on the north side of Garth Road, a little winding road tucked away, and soon he was at the door of a charming 1720-inspired frame house, simple, well built, and of pleasing proportions. Charleston-green shutters framed the sash windows, the white of the house blending in with the snow.

He used the brass knocker in the form of a pineapple.

Anne opened the door. "Matthew, do come in."

"Forgive me for not calling. I was on my way home and thought I'd stop by to see if you need anything."

"Please come in. I'll make us both a drink. It would be lovely to have some company."

Upstairs the squeals of two girls captured his attention as he entered the house. "Party?"

"Georgina Weems. I'm trying to keep Cameron's routine as normal as I can. Children mourn differently than we do. She needs her friends. I need mine." She looked into his eyes with her hazel green eyes. "Scotch? Vodka martini? Isn't that your drink?"

"A little too early for me. I'll take a cup of your famous coffee."

"You're in luck because I was just going to make espresso. H.H. bought me that huge brass Italian thing with the eagle on the top. Restaurants don't have espresso makers this huge." She led him into the kitchen.

He folded his coat over the back of a kitchen chair. "A major machine."

She showed him the steps for making espresso, then brewed him a perfect cup, cutting a small orange rind to accompany it. She poured herself one, too, in the delicate white porcelain cup with the gold edge that H.H. also gave her for Christmas.

"Let's go in the living room. What's wrong with me? I should have taken your coat."

"Everything happens in the kitchen anyway, and I don't care about my coat. Sandy sends her love, by the way."

Anne sat down at the kitchen table. "You two have been wonderful throughout this ordeal. It's bad enough I've lost my husband"—she put her cup on the saucer—"but to have people think I killed him is a deep dose of cruelty. I know what is being said behind my back."

"Now, only the sheriff is going to take that route. He has to investigate all possibilities." He tried to soothe her.

"Rick was here yesterday. Cooper, too. You know my little greenhouse? They went through it with me and asked me questions about belladonna. They were quite obvious so I pointed out that even an azalea if ingested in large quantities can induce a coma. Buttercups can shred your digestive system. The berries on mistletoe can be fatal." She paused. "I must look like a husband killer." She dropped her head slightly, then raised it.

"Not to me you don't."

"Thank you."

"This espresso is better than anything I've ever had in a restaurant." He sipped appreciatively. "Need any shopping done?"

"Thank you, no. The weather has kept me in more than anything. Let them stare. I'll stare right back."

"That's the spirit. Most people are so damned bored anyway they're looking at you with envy in their eyes. 'If only I could be that interesting.'" He mimicked what he thought such a voice would sound like.

"Oh, Matthew, you're pulling my leg."

"Hey, I'll pull your arm, too." He drained his cup.

She refilled it. "Should I call Sandy and tell her I'm peeling you off the ceiling?"

"One of the advantages of being big is that I can ingest a lot more of everything before it affects me." He smiled. "You know, I've been thinking a lot about H.H.'s death. We both know his temper might piss off someone, excuse my French, but a deep-dyed enemy? Can't think of a one."

"What about his lover when he ditched her?" Anne was surprisingly frank, but Matthew was an old friend.

"I didn't know about that—not until everyone knew and then the next evening there he was at the basketball game with you."

"For Cameron. He was waffling. 'I'll go. I'll stay.' It really was hell and I suppose that's why I'm not mourning the way people think I should. I suppose I do look guilty." Her jaw set.

"Why didn't you tell us? Sandy and I would have talked to him. You know that."

She lightly tapped the table with the head of the small spoon. "I was furious that he would think I was so stupid, so pliable, that he could do this to me again. When I did confront him he denied it. Don't they all? But I wore him down. He said he was sorry but he also said he needed a lift. He needed too many lifts over the years." She rose, opened the refrigerator and put out cookies, then drew herself another espresso. She also poured a shot of McCallums for good measure. She held up the bottle but Matthew shook his head no. "The only thing I didn't do was take an andiron and brain him."

"Did you know the woman?"

"Eventually. Mychelle Burns."

"Ah." He chose not to say what he knew about that.

"Now she's dead, too, and it doesn't look good for me."

"There are very good lawyers in this town. Don't you worry."

"I'd be a liar if I said I wasn't worried. More worried for Cameron than for me. What if her little friends hear their parents talking? What if they tell Cameron, 'Your mother murdered your daddy'? My God, that terrifies me."

"We aren't there yet." He exhaled. "Presumably Rick will find out why Mychelle was killed but that's not really my concern. I've been thinking. Could this have had anything to do with H.H.'s business?"

"How?" She sipped the scotch, the warmth as comforting in its way as the espresso was.

He paused a moment. "Oh, money under the table. Rigged bids. That sort of thing."

"Not that I know of. It wasn't that H.H. kept his business life from me but by the time he'd come home, the food would be on the table and we'd talk to Cameron. That was her time. After supper he might mention what happened in his day. I guess most couples are like that or become like that. You move in separate worlds unless you're in the business together."

"True. Sandy and I rarely talk about business. I don't want to bring it home." He made a motion with his hands as though pushing something away. "Men and women have better things to talk about."

"From time to time he'd blow his stack over Fred Forrest."

"Fred's such a pain in the ass. Now if someone murdered him, I could understand that. What about firing someone, a guy who holds a grudge?"

She shook her head. "Given the type of business you're in, I know you have to fire people but he never brought that up. If an ex-employee bore a grudge, I knew nothing of it."

"H.H. used to make fun of me because a lot of my boys are functionally illiterate, but I'll tell you, they are loyal. They know it's hard to get hired and they know most bosses will trim down their pay if they can hardly read and write. I pay them well and I get good work, steady, good work. It's been years since I've had to fire anyone."

"Isn't it a pain, though? You can't leave written notes."

"You'd be amazed at what they remember. They don't need to have a note. Tell them and they remember. Granted, it's a problem if something comes up and Opie's down at the store getting lunch. Or you're going to leave the site and you need to leave him a note, but that doesn't happen very much. Anyway, I have a good foreman and that helps."

"I wish I could tell you something, anything."

"You may not be able to answer this—do you think you would have divorced him?"

"For Cameron's sake, I wouldn't want to."

"What about yours?" Matthew's voice was soft.

"Oh." She glanced at a spot over his head then dropped her gaze to his. "He'd become a habit. I was used to him. There were days when I loved him and days when I didn't. Lately there were more of the 'didn't.'"

"Anne, I'm sorry. Truly sorry." She shrugged, tilted her head and smiled. He continued. "If you need a good lawyer, let me know. You know you can call Sandy or me any time of night or day. If you need some time alone, we'll be glad to take Cameron. Matt and Ted adore her. They'll be big brothers."

"Thank you. Do you think I did it?"

"No. Absolutely not."

"Thank you, Matthew."

# 43

White cartons of Chinese food, tops opened like flower petals, decorated Harry's kitchen table. Cynthia Cooper brought the delicacies, a ritual she and Harry shared on those Saturday nights when neither of them had a date.

Sometimes Miranda would join them but now that her Saturdays were filled, it was the two younger women.

"I can't eat another bite." Harry flipped a shrimp to Pewter with her chopsticks.

*"I can!"* Pewter gleefully caught the shrimp.

Mrs. Murphy chewed some cashew chicken while Tucker worked on pork lo mein.

The two humans folded back the tops, putting the cartons in the refrigerator. They took their coffee to the living room.

Harry sat in the wing chair. Cooper plopped on the sofa, stretching her feet to the coffee table. She could relax with

Harry. She pulled an unfiltered Camel from her shirt pocket.

"Serious."

"It's Rick's fault." Cooper squinted as she lit up. "For the last three months he's switched brands hoping to cut back on the nicotine content. So instead of smoking one pack a day, he'd smoke three packs of the diet cigs. Then he reverted to the real deal but was still trying other brands. I don't know why. He said maybe if one of them tasted bad to him, he'd slow down. Finally, he went back to Camels. Swears they taste the best. I concur." She exhaled a blue curlicue. "I tried those different brands with him. Of course, the really expensive stuff, Dunhill, Shephard's Hotel, that's heaven but this is good. You never smoked, did you?"

"Once in a blue moon, I'll smoke my father's pipe. It's kind of soothing and it makes me think of Dad."

"I'm sorry I never met your father."

"He was a good guy. He knew a lot about the world. Very realistic but not, uh, cynical."

Harry smiled as the three animals came into the living room to clean faces, whiskers, one another.

A good grooming after a meal was essential to mental health, especially for Mrs. Murphy who had a vain streak.

"You think H.H.'s murder or Mychelle's has anything to do with drugs?" Harry switched back to the problem at hand.

"No."

"Me, neither."

"Then why'd you ask?" Cooper laughed.

"You're closer to the case than I am. You know things I don't."

"It's not drugs. The more we investigate the more it looks like lover's revenge."

"Anne?"

"Yes."

"That is so awful. I hope it's not true."

"When you get right down to it, I'm surprised that more women don't kill their husbands."

"Cynic."

Cooper swung her legs to the floor, leaned over and ground out her cigarette. "Maybe."

"Well, if it is Anne she was brilliant to kill him in front of everyone. Not so brilliant to kill Mychelle."

"No fingerprints. Not a scrap of physical evidence and no murder weapons."

*"Ice. An ice bullet,"* Mrs. Murphy meowed loudly.

"Indigestion?" Harry glanced down at her tiger cat who was looking right up at her.

*"I love you, Harry, but you can be so obtuse."* Mrs. Murphy leapt onto Harry's lap.

*"Don't waste your breath. If you get upset you* will *get indigestion,"* Pewter advised.

*"We'll all be hungry in an hour anyway."* Tucker delivered her assessment of Chinese food.

Pewter and Tucker scrambled onto the other end of the sofa, quickly settling down.

"Do you mind?"

"You ask?" Cooper laughed as she reached over to pet the two friends.

"I've been thinking."

"God, no." Cooper covered her face with her hands.

"The next girls' game is Tuesday. Wake Forest, I think. Well, it doesn't matter who the opponent is. These events, including the attack on Tracy, all happen during or after women's basketball games. Tonight's the men's game and I bet you nothing happens."

"So far nothing has happened except around the women's games, but we can't find a connection." She put her feet back up on the coffee table. "What's your idea?"

"I've ruled out gambling."

Cooper laughed. "Keep going."

"This Tuesday night why don't you and I and these guys stay in the Clam all night. The animals have much keener senses than we do."

"No way."

"You agree the site may be important."

"I don't know. I mean that. I don't know. H.H.'s murder was planned. I think Mychelle's was opportunistic."

"Yeah, well, what can it hurt to have us there overnight?"

"Tracy escaped with a knot on his head. Maybe he was lucky. I can't risk you or even me without Rick's approval. Besides, Harry, if he thought a surveillance was needed, he would assign someone to stay there at night after the game."

"Well—ask him."

"He'll blow his stack at me, not at you. By the time he reaches you he'll have cooled down enough for harsh words only."

"Chicken."

"I have to live with the man during work hours. You go talk to him first. You take the blast."

"Aha, you don't think it's a bad idea."

"I didn't say it was." Cooper knew that Irena Fotopappas, posing as a graduate student, was there during the day. No one was there all night. She'd bring it up to Rick but leave out Harry, Mrs. Murphy, Pewter, and Tucker. "But it's a dangerous idea. Most especially since we don't know what we're looking for. If we knew, say, it was a gambling ring and a player shaves points, we might be able to do it, but Harry, we don't know what's going on if it isn't Anne Donaldson. That's risky."

"I have a .38."

"You could have a bazooka. If you don't know what or who your target is, he might get you before you get him. If this isn't Anne it might be another lover. We might even know the woman. We'd be disarmed, off guard."

Harry dropped both arms over the side of the wing chair. "I still say we should stake out the place."

"I'll bring it up to the boss but don't try it—especially don't try it without me. This one scares me."

That really surprised Harry and it reflected in her voice. "Why?"

"If this is a crime of passion, then Anne Donaldson has more self-mastery than most of us as well as intelligence. If it isn't Anne, it's still someone who can dissemble with ease and who is frighteningly intelligent."

"Damn."

"Double damn." Cooper sighed.

They lapsed into silence, both staring into the fire, a blue edge surrounding the yellow flames.

"Harry, carry your .38 on Tuesday."

"Are we going to do it?"

"No, not exactly, but I'm going to call the people who sat behind H.H. to stay after the game. I have an idea. I'll ask three department people to sit in for H.H., Anne, and Cameron."

"What if she's given the tickets to friends, which I bet she has?"

"Doesn't matter. We'll do this right after the game."

"Cool." Harry beamed.

# 44

By Monday morning at eight-thirty, Tazio and Brinkley had already been at work for an hour. Tazio drove carefully to the office, too, because the roads were slick, the plowed snow on the side turning greasy gray.

Her assistant wouldn't be at work until nine on the dot. Greg Ix, always punctual, kept her in a good humor.

She didn't look up when the door opened. "How wasted did you get this weekend?"

The door closed.

Brinkley scrambled to his feet. *"May I help you?"*

"Tazio." Fred Forrest strode up to the opposite side of the drafting table.

"Hello. I thought you were my assistant. I amend that, my young and wild assistant."

"I haven't been either for a long time." Fred showed a rare smile.

"What can I do for you? Or what shall I fix?"

"Nothing. I mean, everything is in order. I'm here"—he cleared his throat—"I'm here to find out if Mychelle spoke to you. I heard she approached you at—"

Tazio interrupted, something she rarely did. "We never got to our meeting."

"I see." He looked at the drawings on the drafting table but didn't really see them. "Do you have any idea why she wanted to talk to you—in private, I mean?"

"No. I wish I did."

"Guess you told the sheriff that."

"Sure." She reached down to put her hand on Brinkley's head. The handsome young dog was filling out a bit. Once full grown and well nourished, he would be quite gorgeous.

*"Mom, he's upset."*

Tazio scratched his ears.

"Did you ever spend time with Mychelle?"

"No. Why would you think that?"

"Uh, well, you're both colored." Fred used the old polite word because he couldn't keep up with the new ones and Tazio understood that.

She smiled. "It's funny that you bring that up, Fred. Our jobs put us on opposite sides of the fence, don't you think?" He nodded and she continued. "And don't get me wrong, I'm not touchy, but just because people are the same color doesn't mean they're going to get along. People in the same family don't get along."

He blushed. "You're right. I, uh, well, Tazio, I used to know how to act in the old days. I knew my place and so did everyone else, but now I get confused. Lorraine"—he mentioned his wife—"says people are people and don't fret over these political fashions. She calls them 'fashions' but Lorraine doesn't work for the county government. She works at Keller and George"—he named the town's premier jewelry store—"and what she says isn't going to get blown out of proportion or wind up in the newspapers. You can't even say 'Boo' at Halloween without someone calling you a pagan."

"Mom, what's a pagan?"

"Sweetie, you're vocal this morning." Tazio smiled at her boy and wondered how she ever lived without a dog's perfect love. "You know, Fred, I never really thought about how it is in a government job. I guess there are people out there just trying to set you up."

"You wouldn't believe it." He put his index finger on the smooth maplewood tabletop. "I apologize for my extended bad mood. Lorraine says it's extended. Guess it is. You haven't seen my good side. I have one, actually."

"I'm sure you do." Tazio knew something was eating him. "Mychelle's awful death has been a great blow to you. She was your student. I'm sure she was grateful for all you taught her."

"I still can't quite believe she's gone. And that's why I wondered if she had said anything. I'm grasping at straws but I want to catch her killer as much as Rick and Cooper do, only if I catch him, I'll kill him. I swear I will. Taking the life of a young woman. Leaving her to bleed to death. My God, Tazio, they're more humane at the SPCA."

"Yes," she quietly replied. A silence followed, then she spoke. "Have you had breakfast? Let me take you up to the corner. Scrambled eggs?"

He held up his hand, palm outward, "No, no, thank you. Hot oatmeal with honey this morning. That will carry me to lunch. I'm sorry to come in here and bother you."

"You haven't bothered me. I wish I could be helpful. I've told Cooper all I know—which is very little."

"When Mychelle came up to you in line that day, was she frightened?"

"Agitated. I thought she was mad at me but I couldn't for the life of me figure out why."

His eyebrows knitted together. "Wasn't mad at you. No. Afraid. A bluff. Instead of showing it, she got angry. I knew her pretty good."

"Do you have any idea what she was afraid of?"

"No."

"Fred, sooner or later, the person who killed Mychelle will be caught. I really believe that and I know that Sheriff Shaw and Deputy Cooper won't rest until they catch him."

He sighed. "I hope so." Then he turned for the door. "You be careful. Make sure no one thinks you know anything."

"Well—I don't." A small ripple of fear ran through her.

"Thanks for your time. 'Bye." He left.

"I don't know anything. Why would anyone think I knew something just because they saw us in line or out in the parking lot or on-site? Or because we're African-American. Half. My other half is Italian. So what do I do, Brinkley, serve spaghetti one night and cornbread the next? I'm just me. Why is it so hard for people to let you be yourself?"

"*I don't know but I love you and I'll protect you and I'll eat anything you give me.*" He thumped his tail on the floor.

Greg opened the door, skidding inside. "Yehaw!"

"Must have been a great weekend." Tazio smiled, her spirits somewhat restored by his rosy-cheeked face and lopsided grin.

# 45

Pewter, reposing on the arm of the sofa, opened one jaundiced eye. *"She's got that bounce to her step."*

*"Scary, isn't it?"* replied Mrs. Murphy, nestled just below Pewter on the afghan thrown on the sofa cushions.

*"Think she'll take us?"* Tucker hated being left home.

*"Even if she does we'll be stuck in the parking lot. Doesn't do us any good if we can't get in the building to see what's going on."* Murphy could think of better things to do than sit in the truck.

"Now, you babies be good. No tearing up things. I am speaking to you, Miss Puss." Harry walked into the living room to directly address Mrs. Murphy.

*"How do you know it's me?"*

"You're a bad kitty and too smart for your own good."

*"Right."* Pewter opened the other eye.

"Pewter, you go right along with her. I am still furious

over those silk lampshades in the bedroom you sliced and diced."

*"That was fun."* Mrs. Murphy recalled her evening of destruction much as old college chums recalled getting blasted at a fraternity party in their youth.

*Youth is more fun in retrospect.*

*"I'll go. Leave the cats at home."* Tucker wiggled in anticipation.

*"Brownnoser."* Pewter turned her nose up.

*"Sacrilegious cat,"* Tucker called back.

*"You ate those communion wafers as much as I did."* Pewter was quick to defend herself.

*"You started it."*

*"Tucker, I'd be ashamed to lie like that."* Mrs. Murphy sat up. *"Elocution started it."*

*"Sure was funny seeing the Rev stuck. It's the unplanned, stupid things that get you. Like glue on the floor."* Pewter giggled.

*"People think life is going to be as they imagine it, not as it really is. That's why murderers are caught sooner or later. They get stuck just like Herb. Somewhere out there, there's glue."* Mrs. Murphy smiled.

*"That's why we should be there tonight,"* Tucker seriously stated.

*"She isn't going to spend the night. Cooper will be there. So will other people. She isn't going to be able to hang back or sneak in. Don't worry, Coop will take care of her. It's another night we have to worry about. The Sheriff's Department will drop its guard or get called off and Mom will fly down there to the Clam. If she thinks she can get away with it,"* Mrs. Murphy logically deduced.

*"Yeah."* Pewter backed her up.

"All right, see you later." Harry sailed out of the house, the .38 in a holster on her belt in the hollow of her back.

"*'Bye,*" the animals called back in unison.

They listened as the Ford truck coughed to life.

"*We have the whole house to ourselves. What can we do?*" Murphy gleefully asked.

"*Sleep.*" Pewter was tired. Traffic had been heavy in the post office this Tuesday.

"*U-m-m, we could open the cupboard doors and pull stuff onto the counter.*"

"*If we do that we might break china,*" Pewter replied.

"*We could pull out canned goods. We don't have to open the china doors. Or we could sit on the floor and pull open the lower cabinet. A little Comet strewn over the kitchen floor will look worse than it really is.*" Mrs. Murphy wanted to play.

"*No,*" the other two replied.

"*Party poopers.*" The tiger jumped down from the sofa and walked back to the bedroom. She pressed the On button on the television remote control. This would make Harry think she was losing her mind because she'd swear she turned off the Weather Channel before she left home.

Mrs. Murphy watched the curve of a low pressure system now in the Ohio River Valley. It was pointing Virginia's way. More bad weather was due to arrive, tomorrow night most likely.

She pressed the channel changer to the Discovery Channel. The program highlighted elephants. She settled on the bed to watch it. At least the program was about animals. The cat couldn't abide sitcoms. Not enough animals. Many didn't even have one. Heresy to her.

As Mrs. Murphy watched elephants wallowing in the mud, Harry met Cooper at the main doors to the Clam and they walked inside together.

"Anne didn't give the tickets to anyone, so Rick, myself, and Peter Gianakos will be in front." Cooper had met Peter at the New Gate shopping center when she questioned him about H.H.'s work on that project.

"Peter, he's pretty cute."

"Yeah, he is."

They entered the basketball arena, the crowd filling the seats, and the band already playing behind the goal. For all but the big games the band was a smaller version of the marching band, and they wore T-shirts of the same color. Being more relaxed made them play better, or so people thought because the band really got into it. They added a sense of heightened fun to the happenings.

Everyone was in their usual seats. Harry, Fair, Jim, Big Mim, Aunt Tally on one row. Behind Harry sat Matt and to his right were Sandy, Ted, Matt, Jr. To his left sat Susan, Ned, Brooks, and to everyone's surprise, Dr. McIntyre's new partner, Bill Langston, a very, very attractive man. Behind that row were BoomBoom, Blair, Little Mim, and Tazio, whom Little Mim had invited since the seatholder was out of town for two weeks. Four rows behind this happy crew already swapping drinks and nibbles sat a glowering Fred Forrest.

On the opposite side of the court were Tracy and Miranda. Josef P. was reffing with a very tall former college star, Moses Welford, called Mo. Tracy, off duty, wanted to enjoy the game.

From the first whistle the game took off and never slackened. The Wake Forest team played defense like ticks, they stuck close and sucked blood.

Tammy Girond and Frizz Barber, probably the two quickest players on the UVA team, rather than being rattled by the superior defense, rose to meet the foe.

All the Virginia women played well, kept their cool. Isabelle Otey put eight points on the board in the first half. Mandy Hall added four and Jenny Ingersoll, despite being double-teamed sometimes, managed six. At halftime the score was Virginia 26, Wake Forest 24.

The second half was even better. The fans screamed, pounded the seats, stomped the floor, waved pennants and pom-poms because the game was so close, so clean, and everyone in the arena knew they were watching one of the best games of the season.

Coach Ryan would bound out of her seat from time to time. She had a commanding court demeanor without losing her cool. Andrew Argenbright paced on the sidelines. Every time the fast six-foot-three-inch Wake Forest forward rose up to block a shot, his hand would smack his forehead. She was beyond impressive. She was awesome. This year Virginia didn't have one outstanding player. What they had was a team, all talented and well matched. Wake depended too much on that forward. The Virginia team could depend on everyone.

The game went into three overtimes and finally Virginia pulled it out with a three-pointer off the hot hand of Jenny Ingersoll.

Bedlam.

Who was more exhausted, the teams or the fans?

Finally, fans filtered out.

The people Cooper had called stayed behind, and she asked Tazio Chappars and Bill Langston if they would mind filling in for the people usually sitting in their seats.

Fred Forrest, although four rows behind, didn't budge and Cooper didn't ask him to leave. If he wanted to sit through it, fine with her. Maybe she'd learn something. She was suspicious of Fred.

Tracy and Miranda remained on the other side of the court, as Cooper had asked them to stay as well. Tracy, who reffed the game the night of H.H.'s murder, took off his shoes and came out onto the court in his stocking feet.

Rick sat in H.H.'s seat. Peter sat to his left, which was the side of H.H.'s neck that had been pierced. Cooper sat on Rick's right but she stood up and turned around.

"Think back. Does anyone remember seeing anything thrown at H.H.?"

People shook their heads.

Rick slapped the back of his neck.

"Does anyone remember H.H. grabbing or rubbing his neck?"

Again, negative.

Cooper stepped back a row, standing next to Harry on her right. "Harry, you're behind H.H., a little to his left, and Fair, you're right next to Harry. Surely if he had been stabbed or hit with anything, you would have seen it."

"Nothing." Harry shrugged.

"What about Anne putting her arm around him?" Cooper pressed on.

"No," Harry said.

"Our eyes were on the basketball court," Fair concurred.

"Well, yes, but sometimes we see things out of the corner of our eye. A flashing light, the buzzer, and it triggers that memory." She rolled her fingers over a bit, a gesture of thoughtfulness. "Bear it in mind. And let the pictures roll in your head." She then walked in front of Harry and Fair to stand before Jim, Big Mim, and Aunt Tally. "Anything?"

The nonagenarian pointed at Cooper, the silver hound's head of her cane gleaming in her right hand. "You think the deed was committed here, don't you?"

"Still a hunch, Aunt Tally, still a hunch."

"But I don't understand why H.H. wouldn't yell or slap his neck if he was stabbed." Jim puzzled over the obvious stumbling block.

"He didn't feel it," Big Mim replied.

"Because the game distracted him?" Jim asked.

Bill Langston, the new doctor, surprised the others when he spoke. He sat directly behind Aunt Tally. "It's possible for a victim to not feel what pierced his skin—not at first anyway. A painkiller on the tip of a dart would deaden sensation. He would feel it later, whether ten minutes later or a half hour, that would depend on the type of painkiller and the amount injected, naturally. And curiously enough, some wounds aren't as painful as others despite the damage. Cold can also blunt initial pain for seconds or even minutes. If he was attacked outside, the cold might have helped numb the puncture."

"Thank you—"

"Bill Langston." He smiled. "Hayden will get around to formally introducing me."

"We're glad you're here," Cooper smoothly said.

Now the assembled knew what she and Rick had known, there was a painkiller. She hoped this would prove useful and she knew that as she moved from row to row, person to person, Rick was observing everything. He had a tremendous feel for people.

The tall blonde deputy stepped up to the next row. She smiled at Matthew and Sandy's two sons.

"It'd be so cool if we could solve this crime," Matt, Jr., the elder, said.

"Yeah," Ted, a fifth-grader, affirmed.

"That's why we're all here." Cooper turned to Sandy and Matt. "Two rows back but close. Can you remember what you were doing those last, oh say, five minutes of the game?"

Sandy laughed. "Matthew was handing out beers when he wasn't cheering."

"That's why I had the beers. Our throats were raw." He genially put his arm around his wife's shoulder.

"Susan?"

"Oh, I remember being on my feet most of the time. I'd no sooner sit down than I'd jump up again. And noisemakers. We all had noisemakers."

"Kazoos?"

Ned answered Cooper. "Kazoos. Little tin horns. A big cowbell and, uh, you know, those things you blow at New Year's parties."

"They furl and unfurl," Brooks added.

"We make a lot of noise in this row." Matthew pulled a kazoo out of his pocket.

"Who had the cowbell?"

Matt, Jr., called out, "I did."

"Where is it tonight?"

"I forgot it," he sheepishly answered Cooper.

"Yeah," Ted said, "because we were late and Mom was on our tails."

"How big is the cowbell?"

Matt, Jr., held his two hands about ten inches apart. "Big Bessie."

"I guess." Cooper laughed, then she stepped up to the third row behind H.H.'s seat. "BoomBoom, what do you remember?"

"What a great game it was. The noise was deafening."

"Nothing unusual?"

"No."

"Blair?"

The handsome model, his eyes a warm chocolate, thought, then shook his head. "Nothing."

"Did you have a noisemaker?"

"No."

"What about a pennant or one of those foam rubber fingers that says Number One?"

"No. The less I have to carry, the better."

"Little Mim?"

"Well, I confess, I do have a noisemaker." She reached into her purse, pulling out one of the New Year's type. She handed it to Cooper.

"This seems a bit sturdier than the party variety."

"I bought it down at Mincer's." She mentioned a university institution on the corner across from the University of Virginia. "As you can see, blue and orange. Lasts about a season before it finally dies."

Cooper handed it back, glancing at Tazio.

"Like Dr. Langston, I'm just sitting in."

"Unlike Dr. Langston, you knew H.H. Can you think of any reason why anyone would want to kill him?"

"Anyone in the world or anyone in this group?" This response from Tazio made everyone sit up straight.

"Keep it small. This group."

"No."

Cooper called up to Fred. "Any ideas?"

"No," he called back.

"You can come closer, Fred."

"No, I want to sit where I sat. Where I was the night of the murder."

"All right then." Cooper stepped down the tiers back to Rick. "You all knew H.H. Would it be possible for him to be involved in a theft ring here at U-Hall, at the Clam?"

This also got their attention.

"What do you mean?" Matthew kept putting his index finger over the mouth of the kazoo.

"We are investigating a theft ring." She held up her hand as though quieting them even though they were quiet. "It hasn't been made public. Is it possible that H.H. was part of this?"

"Stealing what?" Aunt Tally sensibly asked.

"Sports equipment," Cooper answered.

"H.H. died for sports equipment?" Matthew was incredulous.

"You think he could have been part of it?" Cooper homed in.

"I didn't say that," Matthew, red-faced, instantly replied. "No. H.H. wasn't that kind of man."

"Wasn't that kind of man or believed, 'Never steal anything small'?" Tracy called out from the middle of the basketball floor.

"Not that kind of man." Matthew spoke with conviction.

"Of course, you were watching the players, Tracy, but what about after the game as people filed out? Where were you?"

"In front of the timekeeper's desk. Both Josef and I. Then we went back to our lockers."

"Did you happen to notice H.H. at all?"

"No, I didn't."

"Does anyone here think H.H. could have been part of something dishonest?"

No one said anything.

"Is there anything anyone wants to say?"

An embarrassed silence followed, at last punctured by Aunt Tally who figured at her age she could say anything she wanted to, but then she always had, even when she was twenty. "The affair."

"Yes."

"H.H. strayed off the reservation." Aunt Tally used the old expression for a wandering husband or wife.

"If he was that careful about hiding an affair, don't you think he could hide criminal activity?" Cooper persisted.

"It's not the same thing." Matthew chose his words with deliberation. After all, he was sitting next to his wife and two sons. "Many men put sex in a category. You know what I mean."

"Compartmentalize," Tazio called down to him.

"Thanks. That's the word I'm looking for. They compart-mentalize, so sexual behavior isn't a reflection of how they might behave in a business context."

"Do you believe that?"

"Believe it? I see it every day," Matthew said.

"He's right." Fair agreed since he himself had thought like that and it cost him his marriage.

"And women don't?" Cooper prodded.

"We can but usually we don't." BoomBoom's voice, a mellow alto, seemed to fill the vast space.

"So the woman or women with whom he was having the affair did not compartmentalize."

"Well, Cooper, how would we know?" Harry innocently asked.

"Would you boys like to leave?"

"No!" both Matt and Ted shouted.

Cooper looked apologetically at Matthew and Sandy. "I forgot about their ages."

"Oh hell, Coop, this stuff is on television every night." Matthew shrugged.

"Yes, but they don't know the people on television," Sandy perceptively added.

"Sandy, do you want to go outside with the boys?"

"We've gone this far. I mean, as long as we don't get into physical detail."

Cooper shook her head. "No. Would the affair be reason enough in your minds? You've all said you can't think of another reason why H.H. would be killed. You can't think of anyone with a motive."

"I'm surprised there are as many men alive as there are." Aunt Tally, as usual, scored a bull's-eye.

Another uncomfortable silence followed since no one wanted to state the connection between Anne and the possible motive.

"You all are awfully quiet."

Little Mim said what everyone was thinking. "We all adore Anne."

"I can understand," Cooper responded.

"So that girl killed here. She was the one, wasn't she?" Aunt Tally put it on the table.

"She was."

"I don't believe it." Fred finally came down to BoomBoom's row.

"Fred, we have proof. I'm afraid it's true," Cooper declared.

He sat down. Visibly upset, he put his head in his hands.

"Well, you've all been a great help to us. Thank you for your time. Rick, anything else?"

"No. Go on home, folks. We appreciate your help."

Fred stepped down another row and spoke over the boys and Sandy. "Matthew, come up here with me a minute."

The larger man slipped the kazoo into his coat pocket and reluctantly followed Fred back up over the seats. Fred led him to the hairline crack in the wall where it joined the roof near the stairs.

"See this?"

Matthew put his face close to the crack, then felt the dampness. "Uh-huh."

"You fix it."

"Fred, this building is thirty years old. Shifting is natural. Besides, I worked on it but I wasn't the general contractor back then."

"I don't give a good goddamn. You fix it."

"What's the matter with you?"

"Nothing's the matter with me. You fix it before I find more shit to throw on your plate."

"Don't talk to me like that."

"Fix it!" Fred was losing control.

"Aren't you laying it on a little thick?"

Fred, without warning, pushed Matthew hard and he fell backwards, entangled in his own feet. Like most large men, he wasn't agile. He rolled down the stairs toward the basketball floor to the horror of the others.

Little Mim, acting quickly, and closer than the others since she was the last person in the row, stepped into the stairs to break his downward progress. He was so big, though, that he knocked her down as he rolled. Blair grabbed Little Mim as Bill Langston stopped Matthew, his face banged up, cut from the hard surface.

Tracy Raz, still quick as a cat, bounded up the other side of the group, reaching the top. He put his strong hand on Fred's shoulder. Miranda, fearing a fight, stood up from her seat on the opposite side of the court.

"I'm not going anywhere, Tracy." Fred, calm now, walked down the steps, Tracy right behind him.

"Oh, honey, are you all right?" Sandy ran over to her husband, now on his feet with Bill's and Fair's help.

"The padding helped." He patted his stomach.

Cooper reached Matthew as Rick came up alongside Fred.

"Fred." Rick simply said the man's name.

"Do you want to press charges?" Cooper asked Matthew, while Sandy dabbed his face with a linen handkerchief.

"No."

"You're being noble," Fred sneered.

Matthew, face crimson, controlled himself. "Fred, you need help."

Before anyone else could explode, Cooper and Fair escorted Fred out of the basketball arena.

The others all talked at once. Bill Langston proved very helpful. Ned, smart about these things, introduced him formally to Tazio Chappars.

Fair reminded Harry and BoomBoom he owed them drinks and that they could collect at the Mountain View Grille in Crozet proper. They both agreed to meet him there but Harry warned them she'd be about ten minutes late.

Finally Rick, Cooper, Tracy, and Harry were left in the basketball arena.

"Well, Fred blew," Harry simply said.

"He did but he sits in the wrong place to have killed H.H." Rick stepped toward Harry. "You, on the other hand, had a clear shot."

"I did," Harry agreed. "But I have no motive."

"Before we go, let's go up to where Fred pushed Matthew. He kept saying, 'Fix it.'"

The four of them climbed up the stairs. At first nothing much seemed unusual, then Tracy stepped over to the wall and noticed the hairline fracture.

"Here."

The other three came over.

"That? He's screaming about that?" Harry was incredulous. "He's got it in for Matthew."

"I think it's beyond professional distaste," Tracy noted.

"Mental." Harry delivered her judgment.

Cooper put her hand to the wall, feeling the coolness, the dampness. "Harry, don't even think about coming back in here. This place is dangerous."

"It's going to fall apart because of one little crack in the wall?" Harry joked.

"I don't want anyone in this building alone at night." Rick glared at Harry then.

Rick reached for a cigarette even though the signs read, "No Smoking." He didn't flick out his plastic lighter until they were back down on the floor. "This place *is* dangerous. Tracy, whoever you ref with, leave together from now on."

"I will."

Rick inhaled gratefully, then said, "Folks, this one ain't over."

# 46

As Tazio drove west on Route 250 heading toward Crozet, she reflected on how attractive Bill Langston was. Brinkley, who snuggled in the sheepskin left for him in the truck, loved riding around with Tazio. He usually sat up, looked out the windshield as though he were driving. He noticed other dogs, of course, but also farm signs swaying in the wind, cattle, horses, Canada geese flying in a V. Being next to his human made him feel important. When they went places, people now spoke to him as well. He liked that.

She turned right onto Route 240 and within five minutes was in the middle of Crozet, a little town devoid of pretension and perhaps even charm except that its residents loved it. She counted Harry's truck, Fair's truck, BoomBoom's BMW, Herb's black Tahoe, and other cars, then said, "Party."

The Mountain View Grille, usually full, strained at the seams tonight. People had been sitting at home long enough thanks to the snow. The roads were good enough so everyone was out and about.

"Brinkley, let's join everyone. 'Cept I need to pop into the office for one skinny minute." She turned left at the intersection, swooped under the railroad overpass, and pulled into her office parking lot.

She pulled right up front, stepped out, and Brinkley hopped out with her. As he relieved himself at the corner of the building, he noticed a new Toyota Sequoia lurking at the back.

*Mommy, don't go in the office,* " the Lab warned.

She turned to her canine friend. "Brinkley, you could water every bush, pole, and garbage can in this town. Hurry up."

*Stay here.* " He hurried over to her.

She had her office keys on the same chain as her truck key. As she slipped the cold metal key into the lock, the tumbler rolled back with a click.

Brinkley gently sank his fangs into her skirt, holding her back.

"Don't." She smacked his head, not hard. She swung open the door. Before she could flip on the lights she heard a bump, then someone pushed her hard. She lost her balance, tumbling down in a heap.

Brinkley leapt onto the intruder. He bit hard, a nice fleshy calf.

"Ow!" a woman's voice cried out but she socked the dog and he let go.

She ran out the front door and around the back of the building.

Brinkley thought about pursuing her but decided Tazio was much more important. He licked her face.

"I'm okay." She stood up and lurched outside in time to

see the dark-colored car. She couldn't identify the color but she recognized the make. "Jesus, that's Anne Donaldson's car. I swear it!"

Brinkley, never having met Anne Donaldson, wouldn't know her but her perfume was a very expensive brand named Poison. Brinkley would recognize it if he smelled it again.

*"Are you okay?"* Brinkley whined while licking Tazio's hand.

"You tried to tell me. Brinkley, thank God you were with me. What would she have done if you weren't?" Finally, Tazio, shaky, stepped inside and switched on the light.

To her relief the place wasn't turned upside down but her long blueprint drawers were open. They were like the old bins used in newspaper offices, pages laid flat in thin drawers.

Nothing had been stolen, but Anne had been looking at Tazio's latest, larger projects.

Tazio thought about calling Rick but then nothing was taken, plus she couldn't prove it had been Anne Donaldson. Instead she drove down to the Grille.

She walked in. Harry, Fair, and BoomBoom motioned for her to join them. Herb, Miranda, Tracy, Bill Langston, Big Mim, Little Mim, Blair, Jim, Aunt Tally, Matthew, Sandy, Matt, Jr., Ted, Susan, Ned, and Brooks were also there, reliving the game. Herb had missed the game but he was enjoying the verbal replay.

However, no one recapped the after-game session with the sheriff and Cooper.

Herb had regaled them with his tale of the carpet glue and the devoured communion wafers.

Then Tazio, more disturbed than she realized, astounded them with what had just happened to her.

"Are you sure it was Anne?" Herb asked, his gravelly voice supportive.

"No. But I'm, um, seventy-five percent sure. Toyota Sequoia, brand-new. Brinkley warned me and I didn't listen."

"Call Rick." Tracy and the others nodded as Matthew and Sandy rose to leave. Tomorrow was a school day and it was eleven o'clock. Matt, Jr., and Ted had had enough excitement for one day.

"Nothing was taken. I can't prove anything. If it wasn't her, I've added to her troubles."

"Do you know what she wanted?" Harry's curiosity was high, per usual.

"She'd been pulling out the drawers where I keep blueprints. But I don't know what she wanted."

"Tazio, change the locks on your doors." Matthew bent down and kissed her on the cheek, then waved goodbye to the others.

After the Crickenbergers left, the conversation continued.

"How did she get in?" Miranda wondered.

"Well—I don't know. Maybe I'm a little more shook up than I think." Tazio exhaled. "Probably the back door. I forget to lock it sometimes, but even when I remember it's the kind, you know, the kind you can open with a credit card."

"Tazio!" BoomBoom said, eyebrows raised.

"Nobody steals anything," she replied.

"You've got computers in there." BoomBoom couldn't believe Tazio sometimes didn't lock up.

"If they want to get in, they'll get in," Aunt Tally forcefully said.

"True, but why make it easy for them?" her niece, Big Mim, said. "Now listen, this talk has gone on long enough.

I'm calling Rick on my cell phone and we're all going to sit here until he arrives."

"Oh, Brinkley's in the truck and he's been there most of the night. Can't I bring him in?"

Lynn Carle, who owned the restaurant along with her husband, said, "Sure. It's almost closing time anyway. I was going to lock the doors so if he's in here, hey, who's going to notice?"

Tazio ran back out, returning with the dog. Everyone fussed over him since he tried to protect his human. He loved it, of course.

Rick and Cooper arrived in a half hour's time. Tazio told them everything as she remembered it.

"Why'd you wait so long to call me!" Rick angrily said after hearing her report.

Taken aback, Tazio said, "I'm fine. It's not late."

"It may be too late for Anne."

He and Cooper flew out of the Mountain View Grille, jumped into the squad car, hit the siren and skidded out of there.

47

Although the distance from the restaurant to the Donaldson house was only eight miles, the slick roads demanded careful driving.

Twenty minutes later Rick and Cooper reached Anne's front door.

Relief flooded their features when Anne opened it.

"Are you alone?" Rick removed his hat.

"The baby-sitter's here. Come in, Sheriff. Come in, Deputy."

"Thank you." They both stepped into the front hall.

"Has anyone called on you this evening?"

Anne looked at Rick. "You mean at the door?"

"Yes."

"No. Margaret, the baby-sitter, well, her mother dropped her off. I had a few errands to run and didn't want to leave Cameron alone. This was also a way to ensure she gets her homework done. Sixth grade, and they pile the homework on these kids. Uh, won't you sit down? Come on into the living room."

They followed her in, sitting down in chairs facing the sofa where Anne took a seat.

"Mrs. Donaldson, has anyone phoned? E-mailed?"

"No. Since H.H.'s death the phone's been silent most of the time and my messages on the computer are either advertisements or from my sister." She smiled without happiness. "When people think you've murdered your husband you fall off the 'A list,' if you know what I mean."

"I can imagine," Cooper replied.

Rick shifted in his chair, leaning forward. "Mrs. Donaldson, I have reason to believe you were in Tazio Chappars's office tonight. Why?"

A long, long pause followed. "Are you charging me with, well, whatever one charges in those cases?"

"Not yet," Rick replied. "Were you in her office?"

"No." Anne folded her hands in her lap.

"Tazio has made a positive ID," he fibbed while Cooper took notes as unobtrusively as possible.

"Let her make it in court." Anne was quite calm.

"All right then. You weren't in Tazio's office tonight but if you were what would you look for?" He smiled.

"Nothing. Our relations have been cordial even when people hinted she and my husband were having an affair."

"Were they?"

"No. But any attractive single woman is suspect by those who feed off that kind of thing." A note of bitterness crept into her voice.

"H.H. worked with her on—" he turned to Cooper, "how many expensive homes?"

"Last one on Beaverdam Road, six hundred fifty thousand dollars. Delay in completion due to H.H.'s demise and weather. New move-in date, March first."

"Yes, the crews have resumed working." Anne brought her hand to her face, resting her chin for a moment on her thumb. "I'm running the business now."

"You worked with your husband prior to his death?"

"No. I know very little, but I do know the Lindsays need to get into their house. The crew keeps working, the foreman is good, and I'm studying as much as I can as fast as I can, but I expect like most else in this life you learn by doing it. I don't want to put all these men out of work. My husband built up a fine company. I've got to keep it going until I feel I can make better decisions. I don't trust myself right now."

"Do you think you can work with Tazio?"

"Of course. She's a gifted architect but now that she's gotten a taste for grand design I don't know if she'll piddle and paddle with residential design."

"Do you suspect her of wrongdoing?"

"No."

Rick leaned back in the chair, then leaned forward again. "You must suspect something."

"No."

"Did H.H. say anything to you before his death that made you question her? Or question the business?"

A very long pause followed this. "Once when I challenged him about the affair, not with Tazio, as I said, but his latest"—she shrugged—"the argument escalated, and at one point he said, 'You have no idea what goes on in my business. None. You just take the money I make and spend it. I'm under a lot of pressure. Competition, Anne. You know nothing of competition. So what if I indulge myself? Blow off steam. It's better than booze or drugs.' I thought it was another attempt at justification. Oh, the human mind is so subtle in the service of rationalization! But now, now that I've had time to think, I wonder. I'm still shell-shocked. I know that. I don't trust my emotions right now but I trust my mind. Sex, love, and lust are motives to kill. Well, I didn't kill him but there must be some women out there with those motives."

"We have questioned, uh, other women. They have alibis." Rick patted his breast pocket. The crinkle of the cellophane on his Camel pack offered some succor. He knew better than to ask Anne if he could light up.

"I see."

"Mrs. Donaldson, did he ever use the term 'double-dipping'?" Cooper finally spoke.

"No. Charging twice for the same service or materials?"

"Yes." Cooper nodded.

"No. I think H.H. was aware that some people did it. Not many. Most of the reputable firms in Charlottesville really are reputable. There's so much competition among construction firms, if someone was double-billing sooner or later the word would get out."

"But double-dipping, if one wanted to be crooked, would be a way to bypass Fred Forrest." Rick heard the baby-sitter come to the top of the stairs and then walk back down the upstairs hall.

Anne heard her, too. "Margaret, it's okay. Do you need anything?"

"Uh, Mrs. Donaldson, Mom expects me home."

"All right, dear. I'll run you home in about"—she looked at the law officers—"ten minutes."

"Thanks, Mrs. Donaldson."

"Actually, I'll take Margaret home." Rick spoke firmly. "You stay put and Deputy Cooper is staying with you."

Indignant, Anne sharply said, "Am I under house arrest?"

"Far from it. We happen to think you may be in danger and I don't want you left alone until we wrap this up."

"You're close? You're close to arresting H.H.'s killer?" Dread and excitement filled her voice.

"I think we are."

"Were you in Tazio's office to find a second set of books? Did you think she was in on it?" Rick stood up.

Anne stood up, too, and slapped her hips with her hands. "Well, if an architect were in on it, it would spread the risk, wouldn't it? It would be easier to jack up the costs, too, if, say, an architect and a construction firm were in collusion. That's not double-dipping. That's padding the bill. It could be quite elegantly done, you know." Anne betrayed a greater knowledge of the business than she had previously admitted to.

"Why Tazio?"

"Young, ambitious, very smart, rising in this world."

"Maybe you thought she was vulnerable because she's African-American. Less principled? More eager for money." Rick knew just when to slip the knife in.

"Actually, Sheriff, that thought never crossed my mind. Aren't we beyond those petty prejudices?"

"No," Rick simply said.

"Ah, well, I am." She paused. "Sheriff, I shall assume that you no longer believe I murdered my husband."

"Let's just say you're slipping down the list of suspects." He smiled.

"Then may I ask why I may be in danger?"

"Two reasons. The first is the killer's fear that—for whatever reason—you'll put two and two together. The second is that the story about being in Tazio's office will make the rounds. Why would you be there unless you were looking for something that had to do with business?"

"I never said I was there."

"You don't have to. Others will say it for you."

"One more question, Sheriff, before you leave me in the capable hands of Deputy Cooper. The toxicology report?"

Rick said, "The minute the substance is identified I'll call you. It can't be too much longer."

# 48

The party broke up at the Grille. Little Mim took out her noisemaker, a little worse for wear, and blew an olive pit through it at Blair. Emboldened by her accuracy, she also hit Harry, BoomBoom, and Fair.

"Really, Marilyn," Big Mim disapprovingly chided.

"Oh, Mother." The daughter, in the process of her emancipation, sailed by her and out the door.

"Good evening, ladies." Blair inclined his head, the gentleman's version of a small bow, and left with Little Mim.

"What is the matter with her!" A flicker of genuine anger flashed across Big Mim's well-preserved face.

"She's in love. Leave her alone. The question is, 'What's the matter with you?'" Aunt Tally, as usual, was painfully direct in her manner.

"You saw what happened to her first husband, a wastrel if ever there was one."

Miranda and Tracy slipped by, not wishing to participate

in the discussion. Big Mim and Aunt Tally blocked the door. Harry respectfully stood behind the two older women. Jim paid the bill for everyone over the protests of the men and a few of the ladies.

"Honeybunch, don't get yourself exercised," he called from the cash register counter.

"You always take her side." Big Mim grimaced.

"No I don't, but she has to live her own life. We made our mistakes. Let her make hers and you know what? This may not be a mistake. Now, honeybunch, you relax."

"Men," Mim muttered under her breath.

"Can't live with them. Can't live without them," Aunt Tally concurred, but she rather liked the living-with-them part, not that she'd married. She hadn't, but she certainly had had a string of tempestuous affairs starting back in the 1930s. As a young woman, in her late teens she blossomed into a beauty and even now, in her nineties, vestiges of that ripeness could still be glimpsed.

"I'm doing okay," Harry whispered to Aunt Tally.

"Me, too," BoomBoom agreed.

"You're both deluding yourselves." Tally did not whisper her reply.

Both women knew better than to disagree with Aunt Tally.

"Why are you all standing here looking at me?" Big Mim crossly addressed the others.

"You're blocking the door. Miranda and Tracy just squeezed out before you took up your stance." Harry couldn't help but laugh a little. She truly liked Big Mim despite her airs.

"Oh. Well, why didn't you say something?" Big Mim stepped aside.

Each bid her good evening. Fair had walked back to Jim to fuss over the bill.

"Get out of here. I have more money than is good for me. You go take care of horses," Jim good-naturedly said to the veterinarian.

The Sanburne generosity was legendary. Fair thanked Jim but made a mental note that his next barn call to Mim's stable would be gratis.

He opened the door and the chill brought color to his cheeks. Harry and BoomBoom were already in the parking lot.

"Hey, girls, wait for me."

"Oh?" Harry laughed.

BoomBoom, prudently, unlocked her BMW without comment.

"What this town needs is an after-hours bar," Fair jovially replied.

"In Crozet? Right. Get two people every Saturday night." Harry, like most residents, worked hard and rose early.

"You're right, but we might be the two." He waved as BoomBoom flashed her lights, then pulled out. "I know two kitties and one corgi who are lonesome for me."

"We like ourselves a lot tonight."

"I like you a lot every night."

The clear winter sky, the snow on the ground, the glow from a good meal, all added to Fair's potent masculine appeal. Plenty of women's eyes widened when they first met the tall blond. His warm manner, his slow-burn sense of humor, he just had a way about him.

"You are too kind." She fluttered her eyelashes, mocking what Northerners thought Southern belles did to ensnare men. Harry's experience was that men wanted to ensnare her a lot more than she wanted to ensnare them, but tonight Fair did look good.

"What about a nightcap?"

"Uh, okay."

They reached the farm in fifteen minutes. The cats and dog joyously greeted them.

Harry poured a scotch for Fair and made herself a cup of Plantation Mint tea.

They sat side by side on the sofa.

"Big Mim's being a snot about Blair."

Fair felt the warmth of the scotch reach his stomach. "He'll win her over—if that's what he wants to do. I still can't make up my mind about that guy."

"What do you mean?"

"He seems like a real guy but I don't know, modeling is, well, it's not a guy thing."

"Fair, that's not fair."

"Terrible to have Fair for a name. Am I prejudiced? To a degree."

"Well, at least you're honest." Harry decided not to get into an argument about male sexuality.

*"Pewter and I ought to be models for Purina or IAMS or one of those cat food brands. We could sell ice to the Eskimos,"* Mrs. Murphy purred.

*"Bet I could, too."* Tucker put her paws on the sofa.

*"You'd be irresistible, Tucker,"* Pewter complimented her. *"Those expressive brown eyes, that big corgi smile."*

*"Thank you."* Tucker, with effort, got up on the sofa.

"I don't know if I've ever seen Little Mim be silly. She wasn't even silly when we were children," Harry mused. "Nailing us with olive pits."

The tall man got up from the sofa.

*"Where's he going?"* Mrs. Murphy rubbed her paw behind her ear.

"Where are you going?" Harry echoed her.

"More ice."

He walked into the kitchen. Harry's refrigerator did not have an icemaker. He removed an ice tray, held it over the sink, twisted the plastic tray and the cubes popped out into the sink, onto the counter. Some broke, leaving little shards like glass glistening in the light.

Harry heard him curse. She joined him in the kitchen. The animals came in, too.

"I'll clean it up." Harry grabbed a dish towel.

"I made the mess. I'll clean it up. Damn, Harry, I'll buy you a new refrigerator with an icemaker!" He began picking up the fractured ice cubes. "Ouch!" A spot of blood bubbled on the tip of his forefinger.

*"That's it!"* the animals shouted.

Fair sucked his wound.

Harry tore a little strip of clean, soft napkin and held it to his forefinger.

The animals continued making a racket.

"Will you all shut up?"

*"Pay attention! You want to be a detective. Detect."* Mrs. Murphy thrashed her tail.

Harry shushed them.

Fair laughed. "It's not that bad." He put his hand over Harry's. He pulled her hand away. She still had a grasp on the napkin. The dot of blood, cherry red on the white, almost sparkled.

Both humans stared at it for an instant, then at one another.

"Fair?"

"I'm thinking the same thing." His eyebrows shot upward.

"Good God. It's diabolical." Harry sagged against the kitchen counter for a moment.

*"Yes! Ice!"* all three animals bellowed.

"But it makes sense." Fair swept the ice fragments into the sink. "Bill Langston mentioned cold's ability to numb. I should have thought of that." He frowned.

"None of the rest of us did. It's, well, it's so imaginative." Harry took his hand, leading him back to the living room.

They sat down. The cats jumped on the sofa as did Tucker with more effort.

*"We're finally getting somewhere,"* Pewter said.

"You forgot your ice cube." Harry rose.

Fair pulled her down. "Forget it. Ice. An ice dart. The dart melts. No weapon. The poison is on the tip of the dart. The person wouldn't risk ingesting it. Perfect."

"Right. And the poison, I mean toxin—BoomBoom did some research on that—is delivered as the ice melts. But Fair, what in the world could work that fast?"

"I don't know." He sipped his scotch. "But our tiny weapon could have been delivered in a number of ways. Think about it. Fred could have stuck him in the parking lot. Or someone could have thrown it at him as he walked to his car. But how do you throw a piece, a little piece, mind you, of ice?"

"You don't. You'd have to stab." Harry listened to the logs crackle in the fireplace. "Unless you blow it. Like Little Mim blowing the olive pits."

"Yes—yes." He folded his hands together. "Some kind of blowgun. With that it would be pretty easy to hit H.H. as he walked through the parking lot. Or even the hallway." He thought a moment. "Too crowded. The parking lot."

"That gets Fred off the hook."

"Yes."

"A noisemaker. That could hide a blowgun. Fair, this could have been done at the end of the game while we were in our seats. H.H.'s body melts the ice sliver and the toxin hits him in the parking lot." She paused a long time. "Behind me. The killer sits behind me."

"But what does Mychelle have to do with this?" He felt confused. "Maybe her death isn't connected."

"It's connected. It's connected and the killer is Matthew Crickenberger."

Fair's eyes widened. "But why? That makes no sense. Anne makes sense. And, Harry, much as we like her, she has the motive."

"So how did she kill him?"

"Puts her arm around him or touches his neck."

"And the warmth of her fingers won't melt the ice? This has to be a thin, sharp dart delivered with force."

"Blowgun." He nodded in agreement.

"But why?"

"I don't know. Harry, other people sat behind you."

"I know, but the Sanburnes, BoomBoom, Hayden McIntyre—no motive. Matthew was connected by business."

"Or Mychelle?" Fair said.

"He'd won out over H.H. He has a boatload of money. Why?"

Fair took a deep breath. "Well, this is all conjecture. We don't really know that it's Matthew."

"Maybe he hit Tracy over the head. He was removing evidence." She clapped her hands together, startling the animals. "After a while, your head spins."

# 49

The first thing Harry did the next morning, Wednesday, was call Rick, also an early riser. She was just thrilled with herself.

He seemed less thrilled. "Thank you, Harry, that's very interesting."

"Interesting?"

"Harry, the investigation is moving along. I thank you for your effort. Go to work. Goodbye."

Harry hung up the phone. "Damn him!"

She bundled her animals into the truck and drove to work. Fair had already left at five-thirty in the morning as he had early farm calls. January meant breeding for the Thoroughbred people who wanted foals born as close to the next January as possible. Too late and the horse would be at a disadvantage racing. All Thoroughbreds have the birthday of 1 January in the year they were born for racing purposes. Of course, if they were born 2 February, that was noted in the foal's records. Since a mare carried for eleven months, people were getting their mares prepared for breeding. It was a lot of work for the owners and vets.

Harry dreamed of a small broodmare operation someday but on this frosty morning she was too angry to bask in her dreams. She pulled in behind the post office, unlocked the back door, clicked on the lights. It was seven in the morning. By the time the teakettle was singing, Miranda, wearing red fuzzy earmuffs, walked in.

"Good morning." She hung up her quilted coat, stamped her feet, unwound the cashmere scarf and hung it with the coat. She put the poppyseed muffins on the table.

"Miranda, I am so mad I could eat a bug!"

"Oh dear." Miranda thought she'd had a fight with Fair or Susan.

She told Miranda everything, including the call to Rick. "He didn't pay the least bit of attention to me."

"Now you know he did. He probably can't say what he's up to—you know, he might be close to an arrest."

"Sure." A dejected Harry reached for a moist poppyseed muffin. A few savory bites restored her spirits, somewhat. "I'll call Cooper."

"That's a good idea," Miranda appeased her.

Although Cooper received Harry's thoughts with more enthusiasm, she, too, remained noncommittal.

Frustrated, Harry attacked the duffel bags filled with mail when Rob Collier dropped them off.

*"She's going to put that case of the mean reds somewhere."* Pewter laughed as she ate up poppyseed crumbs.

*"God only knows what she'll do next,"* said Mrs. Murphy.

*"You're such a pessimist."* Pewter rubbed the side of her paw along her whiskers.

Harry's mood sank again although when Little Mim

came in for her mail she asked if she could borrow her noise-maker. Little Mim laughed but agreed, going out to her car, returning to give it to Harry.

Miranda tidied up the package shelves. "Harry, sugar, don't fret. It's a slow day anyway. Oh, Vonda called you from the Barracks Road post office."

"Did she say what she wanted?"

"Yes. She said she heard it from the postmaster at Seminole Trail. We are getting a new, modern post office."

Seminole Trail was the location of the county's main post office.

"No way." Harry grabbed the phone. Within minutes Vonda was giving her the blow-by-blow. When Harry hung up, she said quietly, "I guess we are. We don't really need one, Miranda. This one works just fine. And Vonda's moving back to Charleston, West Virginia. I can't stand it. Barracks Road P.O. won't be the same without her. Bet the gang down there isn't thrilled, either." Harry considered her compatriots at the Barracks branch an overworked bunch.

"Growth projections." Miranda quoted what she had heard when she spoke to Vonda. "And I'm sorry she's leaving, too."

"It's a waste of money. A new P.O. A big waste!"

"You haven't learned that government exists to squander your tax dollars? If we can put in our two cents maybe we can make it functionally, m-m-m, useful."

"I don't want a new post office." Harry stubbornly sat down.

"To tell you the truth, I don't, either." Miranda sat opposite her. She looked out the front window. "It's like a ghost town today."

"Yeah."

"You aren't going to do something foolish, are you?" Miranda tilted her head.

"No. Why would you think that?"

"Your jaw has that set to it."

"Oh."

Miranda quoted Psalm 141, verse 3: "'Set a guard over my mouth, O Lord, keep watch over the door of my lips!'"

Harry said nothing.

# 50

Rick and Cooper labored at their desks. The sheriff had taken the precaution of assigning an officer to stay with Anne Donaldson.

"Sheriff, pick up the phone!" Lisa Teican, at the switchboard, hollered as Rick had been ignoring the blinking light on his phone.

"Sheriff Shaw."

"Joe Mulcahy. You wanted me to call you—" The head of toxicology in Richmond was interrupted.

"Thank you. What was it?"

"Batrachotoxin."

"Never heard of it."

"There's no reason you would. I've never seen this stuff before in my life, either. Never once has it shown up."

"Well, what is it?"

"It's an acutely lethal substance, so lethal, Sheriff, that

nanograms cause instantaneous death to an organism. A microgram could wipe out a platoon."

"Jesus! Is this something some nut can cook up in a lab?" Rick, like other sheriffs throughout the United States, had undergone training to combat bioterrorism.

"That's highly unlikely. I mean, it can't be cooked up in a lab and it's unlikely some nutcase could acquire enough of the batrachotoxin to pose a large-scale problem."

"So, how did the killer get it?"

"From the skin of poisonous frogs, little tiny, actually, like two to five centimeters, tiny frogs. Bright colors with stripes and spots. Beautiful little things, really." Joe opened a book then continued. "Once we isolated the toxin I became fascinated. These little buggers live in the rain forests of South America and the natives would catch them and stress them out. Now they wouldn't necessarily kill them but they'd worry them and the frogs would secrete liquid from the bumps on their back. The natives would collect that, carefully, obviously, and let it dry. Then they'd smear it on darts, arrows, whatever."

"And you said it works quickly?"

"Amazingly fast. It blocks the transmission of nerve impulses and the heart just stops. Dead."

"Jesus."

"He can't help the victim." Joe couldn't resist a joke.

"Guess not. In your research did you find out just where someone could procure these frogs?"

"Well, that's not my department but there's an underground for exotic creatures. Smuggling in contraband animals is a big business and Dulles Airport is a big, big airport. Be pretty easy, I'd think. And hey, all you need is two, a male and a female. You're in business."

"But you'd need to create a specialized environment."

"Sheriff, they're tiny. A small aquarium with the correct humidity and lots of bugs would keep Mr. and Mrs. Frog very happy. And water. Lots of water. Pretty fascinating."

"Mr. Mulcahy, thank you."

"I'll send the full report out FedEx Ground."

"I'll read every word but this phone call is what I've been waiting for."

"Glad I could be helpful." Joe hung up.

Rick motioned for Cooper to come to his desk. She did and he told her what he'd just heard.

"Damn, how can we trap him?" Cooper, like most everyone in town, knew about Matthew's rain forest. It wasn't a stretch to figure out he could provide a wonderful place for poisonous frogs. Who would know?

"Could be someone in the biology department at UVA. Don't forget, Anne is a botanist."

"It could be her but it isn't. It's Matthew."

Rick held up his hands, palms outward, a gesture of supplication and in this case a bit of frustration. "Yes, I think he's our man. It's not Anne. I just don't yet know how to prove it."

"Gut feeling—Mychelle?"

Rick knew what she meant. He nodded. "Yes, I think he killed her, too. Different MO but somehow she got in the way."

"Maybe he was having an affair with her or had in the past?"

"Possible." He tapped the side of his cheek with a pencil. "Something cold about these murders. If it were sex or love, it'd be different. I just think it would be different."

"He's close to Anne."

"That worries me. In fact, it all worries me. We've got our killer. All my instincts tell me that and the donkey work is leading us right to him, as well. But why? Why?" He threw up his hands.

# 51

Friday night the girls played North Carolina State. Harry, Little Mim's noisemaker tucked into her blazer pocket, sat next to Fair.

In front of her, Cooper sat between Greg Ix and Peter Gianakos in H.H.'s seat. Irena Fotopappas, back in uniform, was home with Anne and Cameron. Rick had given the young officer strict orders not to allow Matthew or his wife, just in case, into the house.

Harry had a handful of dried peas in her pocket along with the noisemaker that she had altered by running a small peashooter inside the paper.

Everyone else sat in their usual spots with Bill Langston taking Dr. Hayden McIntyre's seat. Little Mim had once again invited Tazio. Bill leaned back quite a bit to talk with Tazio. BoomBoom on Little Mim's right side noticed. Blair sat on Little Mim's left next to Tazio. Usually he sat where BoomBoom now sat and she was one seat away from Little

Mim but both women had cooked up the idea that Blair should be next to Tazio. It would make the new man in town pay more attention to her, even if he'd heard that Blair and Little Mim were an item. BoomBoom and Little Mim, great believers in testosterone, figured Bill would have to be more attentive, more clever, simply because there was another very handsome man there.

Aunt Tally from time to time would look backward and observe. She kept a keen interest in anything that might involve sex.

Big Mim, on the other hand, focused on romance.

Tally told her she should know better.

Harry kept her noisemaker in her pocket. Matthew, jovial as ever, handed out drinks, blew his noisemaker. The boys struck the cowbell.

Susan Tucker sat next to Matthew. Harry told her what she thought about Matthew, and Susan believed her. As for sitting next to the man her best friend decided was a killer, Susan shrugged. Why would he kill her? She didn't think she had anything he would want if in fact Harry was right.

Fred Forrest scowled behind them all.

The game, tight, turned into a nail-biter.

At one point, Harry looked up at the scoreboard and wondered if she shouldn't have used it. Maybe put a message on it to scare Matthew, but then she'd probably scare everyone else, too.

In the last two minutes of the game, Mandy Hall, Virginia's center, blocked a shot under the basket and Isabelle Utey stole the ball right out of the North Carolina State forward's hands. Isabelle streaked down the center of the court to soar up for an easy layup. That was the game.

Harry turned around just as Isabelle scored and she hit Matthew with a pea. His hand slapped his cheek but he didn't see that Harry was the perpetrator so she fired off another. He saw her this time. She smiled.

He smiled back.

After the game the fans piled out. Fred Forrest hurried down the steps to the court where he upbraided Tracy for a call he felt was wrong.

Harry, full of herself, blasted Fred with a pea. He turned around and she shot another one which bounced off his head.

"You stop that, Harry."

"Fred, you're a crab." She pocketed her noisemaker.

While Fred's attention was on Harry, Tracy adroitly slipped away and was halfway to the locker room before Fred had turned back to lambaste him.

Harry walked out to the parking lot, waving to everyone. She retrieved her pets and returned to the Clam, making certain Matthew saw her.

She returned to the basketball arena as the last stragglers filed out. She sat in her seat firing peas at H.H.'s seat.

Pewter couldn't resist leaping up to bat away the peas.

Mrs. Murphy, vigilant, watched the doors as did Tucker, who kept sniffing, overwhelmed by fresh odors. There were still too many people around and too much noise.

Sure enough, as the tail end of the fans walked out BoomBoom walked back in.

"BoomBoom, what are you doing here?"

"Lost my gloves." BoomBoom bounded up to her seat and found her trampled black gloves. She joined Harry.

Harry explained her theory.

Tucker barked, *"Someone's here."*

Fred Forrest, lurking in the top shadows, came down from the upper levels. "Explain that to me, Harry."

Both BoomBoom and Harry regarded Fred with suspicion, but Harry willingly explained her theory and demonstrated.

"And who have you told this theory to, Harry?" His voice was shaky.

"Anyone who would listen."

*"I'm behind him,"* Tucker told the girls.

*"We'll stay in front. Do you think he has a gun?"* Mrs. Murphy asked her canine friend.

*"I don't know."*

"You really think Matthew killed H.H.?" Fred's eyebrows darted upward.

"Do you?" BoomBoom flippantly asked.

"If I did, I wouldn't tell you or anybody. How do I know he wouldn't kill me?"

The doors swung open on the court level and Matthew sauntered back in.

"Ask him." Harry reached in her blazer pocket, filling her hand with peas. She did not withdraw her hand.

"What are you all doing here?" Matthew, wreathed in smiles, walked over.

*"Damn,"* Mrs. Murphy hissed. *"Mother did this without telling Rick or Cooper."*

*"I'll watch Matthew."* Pewter moved toward the large man.

"We were talking about you," Harry brazenly said. "Fred won't tell us why you killed H.H."

"Fred, what's the matter with you?" Matthew didn't change his expression.

"I don't give a damn about H.H.," Fred snarled, "Whatever happened to him, he deserved, but Mychelle—that's another matter. I'd like to hear your answer, Matthew."

"What's good for the goose is good for the gander." Matthew moved closer but not within striking range.

Harry wondered if she could knock him over. His heavy

coat might slow him down. If he was armed it wouldn't matter.

BoomBoom played dumb. "Where's Sandy and the kids?"

"On their way to Duner's for a late supper."

"Are you on foot?" Harry noted the exit doors.

"We're a two-car family." He smiled, then turned his focus back on Fred. "What kind of bullshit are you peddling today?"

"Nothing. Harry has a very interesting theory about how you killed H.H. I wondered myself how he could be murdered in front of everyone but her idea makes a lot of sense."

"No murder weapon." Matthew clapped his hands together as though rounding up his children.

*"Ice."* Mrs. Murphy spoke.

"An ice dart," Harry said as though mimicking the cat.

"What are you doing here?" BoomBoom asked.

"I could ask you the same thing." Matthew became less upbeat. "I'm here to inspect that hairline crack up there. I'll send a man over Monday morning."

"They're on to you, Matthew." Fred smiled maliciously.

"Ah, but are they on to you?" Matthew shrugged as though this were of no crucial concern to him.

"Shut your mouth." Fred took a step down the stairs.

Harry elbowed BoomBoom and threw the peas hard in Matthew's face. The two women hopped over the seats, streaked across the basketball court, and slammed open the doors onto the circular hall.

The cats and dog followed, scooting out behind the humans.

"You take BoomBoom, I'll take Harry," Matthew ordered Fred as the men ran after them, slipping on the dried peas.

"*Stairwell!*" Tucker barked.

Harry turned when Tucker barked, "*BoomBoom, here!*"

The women and animals hurried down the stairwell just as Matthew and Fred entered the circular hall.

Matthew hesitated for a moment, then ran to the stairwell door, opening it just as the door on the lower level closed with a click and thud. "Here."

He and Fred clumped down the stairwell.

Both men knew the Clam inside and out. They knew that Harry and BoomBoom, while not as familiar with the structure, knew it well enough to know where the doors to the outside were located. They had to cut off those doors.

Once on the bottom level, Matthew motioned for Fred to move left. He would move right.

"Try every door," Fred barked.

Harry and BoomBoom ran for the outside door but heard Fred's running footsteps.

"Shit! He's closer than we are," Harry said.

"*Hide. We'll attack them.*" Mrs. Murphy nosed at office doors.

Now they plainly heard running footsteps from both directions.

BoomBoom tried the handle on the equipment room door. Luckily, it was open. They slipped in. The lights were off.

Harry flattened against the wall to one side of the door.

BoomBoom did the same against the other side so that when the door opened into the dark room, they'd have a chance to be undetected. If Matthew or Fred stepped inside, the women could slip by him or knock him down.

The cats could see much better.

"*On the shelf!*" Mrs. Murphy lost no time in leaping up,

then climbing to where the light switch was located. She crouched just behind the switch.

*"Tucker, do your duty,"* Pewter, now next to Murphy although her climb was less graceful, exclaimed.

All five creatures held their collective breath. The footsteps drew closer.

Murphy whispered to Pewter, *"We're not alone in here."* She stretched out her paw toward the back of the cavernous room.

*"You're right,"* the gray cat whispered back. A human figure could be seen, barely, in the back but stealthily moving closer.

*"We can't warn Tucker. We'll make too much noise,"* Murphy whispered.

But the corgi's keen hearing and even keener nose picked up the sound and the scent. She prayed she could handle whatever happened next, and she prayed that Harry's quick wits and courage would spring from this fix. The dog had confidence in her human and knew Harry had confidence in her.

The footsteps outside stopped next door. The lacrosse room door opened then closed as did the door on the other side of the equipment room. Matthew and Fred had met in front of the equipment room.

Matthew made no attempt to be quiet. No reason, he wasn't the hunted. "They're in here."

"Guess we'll find them with the soccer balls," Fred replied.

The door opened, a shaft of light falling across the floor.

Matthew reached for the light switch, which was located where the shelves were but the space was left clear, naturally.

Mrs. Murphy bit down hard.

"Jesus Christ!" Matthew yelled as those sharp fangs sank all the way into the fleshy part of his palm.

Fred instinctively took a step back and whoever was in the room hurtled past the two shocked women, blocking Matthew so hard the heavy man was picked up off his feet. He hit the floor hard.

Tucker followed after and savaged Fred's ankle.

The unidentified blocker swept past Fred, knocking him flat, then raced down the hall toward the stairwell door. Tucker glimpsed him from the rear, a man, but Tucker had bigger fish to fry. She jumped on Fred's chest and while Tucker was not a big dog Fred was unprepared for this new assault. The corgi bared her fangs, lunging straight for his throat.

He threw his forearm up, instinctively, to protect his jugular.

"*Die!*" Tucker savagely growled.

Harry, the shaft of light sliding by her face from the opened door, yelled to BoomBoom, "It's now or never!"

Without replying, BoomBoom sprinted beside Harry out of the equipment room and into the hall. The cats bit into Matthew extra hard for good measure, then tore after the two women.

"*We should have taken out his eyes!*" Mrs. Murphy fretted as they ran for the stairwell door, which seemed so very far away.

"*Not enough time,*" Pewter replied.

Matthew, blood dripping from his right hand, reached into his jacket, pulling out a handgun. He stepped over Fred who had rolled on his side struggling to get up.

Tucker, hurrying after her friends, glanced over her shoulder. "*Gun!*"

"*Run!*" Murphy flew down the corridor with its curving

smooth walls, no right angles giving them a place to hide. Their only hope was to run for their lives and pray Matthew was a bad shot, pray Murphy's bite had hurt his gun hand.

He took a few steps, aimed at BoomBoom, the taller of the two women, and fired. The bullet whizzed past her right shoulder.

"Drop and roll if you have to!" Harry called over to her as BoomBoom matched Harry stride for stride.

Instead of dropping, BoomBoom swerved toward the wall where there was a fire alarm box. She paused, smashing the glass on the fire alarm. When Matthew fired at her, she dropped. The bullet smashed into the wall above the alarm, then she stood up and grabbed the tiny hammer again, blasting the alarm to life for all she was worth. Then she dropped and rolled as another bullet smashed near her, concrete powder spraying over her and the floor.

Harry reached the stairwell door. The clanging as she pushed on the long bar echoed down the hall. She held it open for BoomBoom and her animals.

They raced up the stairs to the main level, the door closing behind them. The alarm seemed even louder there.

"Boom, good move!"

*"Brave move."* Tucker heard footsteps, then the door opened to the stairway below them. Matthew and Fred would be up the stairs in seconds.

Harry flattened herself against the wall on the side of the door she knew would open. If she and BoomBoom tried to hold the door closed, Matthew would fire through it. Harry also knew they couldn't reach the exterior door in time to save themselves. Even if they did, they'd be easy targets in the vast parking lot. They'd have to fight.

BoomBoom flattened herself against the wall on the hinge side of the door.

*"Turn back!"* Murphy shouted to Pewter, who, being far faster than any human, skidded toward the exterior door. As Pewter skidded, her hind end sliding behind her, the stairwell door opened with tremendous force and Matthew, never dreaming the women would fight, stepped through, his arm outstretched, hand bleeding, gun ready to fire.

BoomBoom, no fool, knew what Harry intended. As Harry, hands folded together, brought down her arms onto Matthew's forearm with all her might, the gun clattered across the floor. Drops of blood splattered, too, for the deep cat bite had done damage.

Tucker swiftly picked up the warm gun in her mouth.

BoomBoom stepped up behind Matthew, wrapping his neck in a painful hammerlock. He was a large, strong man but she was a tall, surprisingly strong woman. He choked, twisting and turning. His windpipe aching, he couldn't shake her.

Harry heard Fred, moving more slowly than Matthew, trot up the steps. She brushed behind Matthew and BoomBoom, launching herself at Fred from the top step. She hit him so hard he fell over backwards, cracking his skull loudly against the wall. A thin smear of blood stained the wall. He was out cold.

Harry kicked him once to see if he was a danger. She realized he was probably concussed.

The cats joined BoomBoom in subduing Matthew, who bent over in an attempt to toss her over his head.

Pewter sank her fangs into his left calf while Murphy attacked his right one. He bellowed in pain and frustration.

Tucker, gun in her mouth, flew past the struggling pair down the first flight of stairs to Harry.

Harry turned to run back up the stairs to help BoomBoom when Tucker reached her.

"Thank God!" She bent over to take the gun from the intrepid dog.

Then she bounded up, two steps at a time.

The fire alarm seemed inside her head but her mind remained clear.

"Matthew, stop." She hurried in front of him now, about three paces away. "Or I'll give you the third eye of prophecy."

BoomBoom did not relax her grip until he stopped struggling.

"Harry, you've got it all wrong. It was Fred. I just kind of got roped in," Matthew choked out.

*"He's a liar, Mom, be careful."* Murphy stopped biting his calf.

*"Yeah."* Pewter did likewise as Tucker circled around in front of Matthew in case he did something stupid.

"You girls know me. We work together on the St. Luke's Parish Guild. You know I'd never kill anyone." He took a step toward Harry.

"Matthew, don't move."

"Ah, come on, Harry."

BoomBoom, breathing hard, stepped up behind him ready to grab his arm.

"Boom, move away," Harry told her.

The tall blonde stepped to the side.

"You're not a violent person, Harry. I know you." He smiled.

The three animals never took their eyes off Matthew.

"I am as violent as I have to be, Matthew." Harry prayed the fire department, the sheriff, *anybody* would answer the alarm. As if in reply, she heard two sirens in the distance.

Matthew heard them, too. "You know me. You know I'd never hurt anybody. It's all Fred. He ran away. Isn't that proof enough?"

"He didn't run away. He's out cold on the stairs." Harry spoke firmly.

BoomBoom remained ready to fight, her fists clenched.

The sirens drew closer. Matthew assumed, as did many men, that a woman wouldn't really hurt him. He had to get out of there. If he could reach his car, he had a chance to escape.

He lowered his voice, a false warmth infusing his words. "It looks bad for me. I know. But I'm innocent. I need to call my lawyer. If you'll just let me go, I'll—" He took another step toward Harry.

"Matthew, stop." She didn't budge.

Then he leapt toward her.

She fired once. He dropped like a stone.

Blood spurted from his knee for she'd blown out his kneecap. Writhing, screaming, he slithered on the floor like a fish out of water.

*"Should I tear out his throat?"* Tucker bared her fangs.

*"No. He's out of commission,"* Mrs. Murphy advised.

*"I'd kind of like to."* Tucker's eyes sparkled.

*"You could lick up all that fresh blood."* Pewter giggled, which sounded like *"kickle, kickle."*

*"Gross out the humans. You know how they are."* Murphy would have gladly killed Matthew herself.

Harry kept the gun trained on Matthew. His screams of agony pleased her. He or Fred or both had snuffed out the lives of two people, tried to pin the blame on an innocent widow, and would have killed Harry and BoomBoom to boot.

Let him scream his head off, Harry thought to herself. He's lucky I took out his knee and not his heart, if he has one.

"Harry." BoomBoom didn't get a response so she raised her voice. "Harry!"

"Huh? Are you all right?"

"Yes. I was about to ask the same thing of you." She shouted over Matthew's howls and the fire alarm.

The sirens sounded as though they were right outside. Within seconds Sheriff Shaw, Deputy Cooper, and the fire chief, Dodson Hawley, burst through the doors followed by firemen.

The clanging stopped as Hawley cut off the alarm.

"Here!" BoomBoom hollered above Matthew's screams.

Cooper ran toward them.

"There's no fire." Harry handed Cooper the gun when she reached her. "Fred Forrest is on the landing and needs attention. He's in on this." She pointed to the stairwell. "And this sorry son of a bitch is lucky to be alive. I hope he's tried and fried."

"*Yeah!*" the three animals concurred.

As Rick came up, Cooper said, "Fred's on the stairwell."

Rick's footsteps could be heard descending the stairwell.

BoomBoom, suddenly exhausted, leaned against the wall.

Harry knelt down to pet her animals. She, too, felt as though someone had pulled the drain plug. Her energy was ebbing away.

"Boom?" Cooper's eyebrows shot upward.

"I'm okay."

"Boom, I was wrong about you." Harry stood up. "Forgive me."

BoomBoom smiled, too tired or too overwhelmed to respond. She held up her left hand, palm outward, a sign of acceptance.

"Can you two give a statement now? How about if I have

someone fetch you a coffee or a Coke?" Cooper asked, ignoring the commotion around them.

*"Tuna!"* Pewter resolutely requested.

Harry glanced down at her gray cat. "These guys fought as hard as we did."

"I'll order a ham sandwich for each of them." Cooper smiled.

The ambulance crew arrived.

Harry, oblivious to the chaos around her, followed Cooper back to the main entrance, a little bit away from the gurneys being rolled in. BoomBoom, Mrs. Murphy, Pewter, and Tucker followed also.

"We can tell you what happened," BoomBoom said, "but we don't know why it happened. Harry, what on earth were you thinking, going back to the Clam, knowing Matthew was going to follow you?"

"I don't know. I had to get to the bottom of it. I was pretty stupid to be unarmed. *Really* stupid." Harry inhaled, then touched Cooper's arm. "Do you know what's going on?"

"Think I do," Cooper tersely replied above Matthew's screams of pain and innocence.

$$52$$

The ham sandwiches and coffee appeared within fifteen minutes. Cooper used up all her quarters in the vending machines to purchase the indifferent fare.

"I promise better food tomorrow." She smiled as she slid the blister-wrapped sandwiches across the table to the humans and animals.

She'd shepherded them into an office. With the door closed, it was almost quiet.

*"If you don't want your ham, I'll eat it,"* Tucker helpfully offered.

*"Why wouldn't I want the ham?"* Pewter tilted her head sideways, staring at the dog.

*"You said you wanted tuna."*

*"Nice try."* Murphy laughed as she bit into the ham, which tasted better than Matthew's hand or leg.

As Harry and BoomBoom began to breathe normally, Cooper took out her notebook, flipped open the top cover.

"Okay, let's go."

She listened carefully, jotting down notes. When the two had completed their statements and she'd asked a few questions, she flipped the book closed.

Harry, somewhat restored by the sandwich and coffee, pleaded, "Can you tell us what's going on? Now that we've made our statements?"

"I can try." Cooper slipped the notebook back in her chest pocket. "Matthew Crickenberger knew we were closing in. Anne was under our protection. She was a suspect initially but once we realized she was in danger, we kept someone with her. Matthew knew that. But Harry, you were the one—you pushed him over the edge."

"When I pelted him with the pea! The noisemaker!" Harry tapped the table with her forefinger.

BoomBoom's eyes widened. "I still don't get it."

Cooper sipped her coffee for a moment. "H.H. was furious at continually being in Matthew's jet stream, so to speak, and figured out their scam. I'll tell you about that later. He put in months of patient research, visiting old and new projects Matthew had built. H.H. was determined to find something, and he found more than he bargained for. We think he confided in Mychelle—and clearly Matthew thought that as well—but we don't know that for a fact. I would think Mychelle would have come directly to us after H.H.'s death and tell us H.H. was blackmailing Matthew. I don't know, but"—Cooper shrugged—"people are often afraid of us. Of course H.H.'s death looked like a heart attack. When Rick gave a statement to the press that H.H.'s death was suspicious, Mychelle must have known why H.H. was killed. If she had any doubts about his demise she should have seen the handwriting on the wall. We don't know if she contacted Matthew. After all, it could have been worth money. We still don't know why Mychelle withdrew five thousand dollars from her bank account. Was she going to run away? But Matthew either had hard evidence that Mychelle knew what he was doing or he didn't want to risk that she knew. Her hesitation cost Mychelle her life and could well have cost Tazio hers once word got around that Mychelle wanted to see Tazio that Monday. I think Tazio would have been the next victim if you hadn't triggered Matthew. He was losing his composure. The manner in which he killed Mychelle suggests that."

"But what's Fred got to do with all this?" Harry was exasperated.

"You think he killed Mychelle?" BoomBoom asked Harry.

"No. That's what set him off," Harry replied. "Am I right?" she asked Cooper.

"Terrified. He was absolutely terrified." Cooper reached for her cigarette pack in her other pocket. "We don't know if he approved the murder of H.H. or not. He's in intensive care and it might be days before the brain swelling subsides. Fred is in a medical coma, if that's the term. Fred didn't want to go to jail any more than Matthew but when Mychelle was stabbed to death, dying alone the way she did, Fred realized that Matthew would stop at nothing. Matthew lured her to the Clam. How, we don't know. Fred must have believed he could neutralize Mychelle without hurting her. Matthew was taking no chances. Killing Mychelle really did set off Fred. He truly liked her. And he knew if he faltered, Matthew would kill him. As I said, Matthew was losing his composure."

"But wait a minute, what's with Fred and Matthew? I'm missing something here. What was the scam?" Harry stroked Murphy, now in her lap.

"A clever, clever deal. I've got to hand it to them. Fred passed substandard materials and construction that was under code. Matthew's crews were illiterate. Not only could they not read, they didn't know what the building codes were. They didn't have to know, that was Matthew's job. Fred would even pick up a few empty cartons of high-grade materials that had been tossed at other building sites, dumping them at Matthew's sites when no one was around. Or he thought no one was around. Matthew would purchase some good stuff to put out where everyone could see it. You know, a few rolls of R-20 for insulation, stuff like that. Matthew's foreman, handsomely paid off, was also in on it. He's in custody right now. We took him in for questioning yesterday. That and your little escapade during the basketball game did it."

"I can't believe it. I thought Fred and Matthew hated one another." BoomBoom was flabbergasted.

"Carefully orchestrated. And remember, Fred was a prick to every other construction firm in the county, so Matthew's wails of mistreatment fell on eager ears. Over the years those two bilked millions out of clients."

"Good Lord," Harry exclaimed. "I figured out Matthew was H.H.'s killer but I didn't have any idea of the scope of this."

"It has been going on since they worked on the Barracks Road shopping center as young men. Fred left construction, supposedly in a huff. What's also interesting is that Fred had the discipline to hide his money. He kept an account in the Bahamas."

"Well, who was in the equipment room?" BoomBoom wondered.

"Andrew Argenbright," Cooper replied. "The decision there was to act as though the inventory were completed.

No public statements were made as to the results. The university police set up a trap. Well, he came back to steal some more. Small cameras with capabilities of getting a photo in little light had been set up inside the equipment room."

"Lucky for us he was there," BoomBoom said. "Even if he did run like a thief at least he knocked down Matthew."

"What if this were the reverse, Coop?" Harry's mind whirred along. "What if it were Mychelle who figured it out and she told H.H? After all, she worked with Fred."

"Possible. We're hoping Fred will tell us when he's able in exchange for a lesser sentence. Obviously Matthew's going to put up a front, tell nothing, and have a battalion of lawyers. Fred was smart, though. He always inspected Matthew's work. This wasn't given over to a subordinate. His reason was that Matthew's projects were large, the inspection had to be entrusted to the senior official, which, in fact, isn't out of the ordinary. Those two had an airtight cover. H.H. was so damned mad at losing the bid for the sports complex he wanted to bring down Matthew despite his seeming acceptance of things."

"But surely over the years subordinates did look at Matthew's work," Harry said.

"The subordinate, and the last couple of years that's been Mychelle, would go with Fred to inspect that part of the work which was up to code or better. It's not like everything Matthew did was substandard. They were experts, remember, this was their trade and Matthew and Fred picked those things that would be easiest to hide or replace. You know, put in an expensive brand of pipe where it will show, while using cheaper materials where it won't show. I don't have all the details, but I hope we can squeeze them out of Fred. With any luck those two will turn on one another."

"And if you think about it, the last thirty years have been one long construction boom in Albemarle County. There's so much work, who could come after Fred to double-check?" BoomBoom thought out loud.

"Well, that's the thing. Fred was so ferocious, such a stickler at every construction site, no one dreamed he'd be in collusion with Matthew. If Fred signed off on a building it must be okay." Cooper folded her hands together. "I'm telling you, it was a well-thought-out, well-executed scam and they almost got away with it. No one would have ever known if H.H. hadn't decided to bring down Matthew any way he could."

"H-m-m." BoomBoom folded up the clear wrap that had covered the ham sandwich. "This is one basketball season no one will ever forget."

"The strange thing or maybe I should say the brilliant thing is the toxin, the secretions from those little frogs in Matthew's rain forest at his office, that's what killed H.H. He used a blowgun hidden in his noisemaker." Cooper tapped her notebook.

"Like this?" Harry reached in her pocket retrieving Little Mim's altered noisemaker.

"Damn, Harry. Why didn't you tell me?"

"Well, I wasn't a hundred percent sure. I wanted to test-drive it."

"Your test-drive nearly got you, BoomBoom, Mrs. Murphy, Pewter, and Tucker killed."

"Yes, well, I wasn't as smart as I thought I was. I mean, I never figured on Fred."

Cooper made an imaginary slap at Harry's face. "Don't you ever do that again."

"I'm lucky BoomBoom came back. If she hadn't fought

them off and set off the fire alarm, I'd be dead." Harry bit her bottom lip. "I really have been stupid."

"As long as you recognize that. The one thing still puzzling us is the weapon. No trace."

*"Ice,"* Mrs. Murphy, Pewter, Tucker, and Harry said in unison.

# 53

Later as Harry watched the fire, Mrs. Murphy, Pewter, and Tucker snuggled up against her on the sofa, she thought about what had happened.

What kept nibbling at her was how she accepted Matthew at face value for so long. But then how else can you live in a community? She couldn't very well spend all her time being suspicious of everyone, trying to ferret out their secrets. He had fooled her for a long, long time.

She felt stupid but not totally stupid.

She felt totally stupid about her attitude toward BoomBoom. True, they were very different kinds of personalities but BoomBoom had held out the palm many times and Harry had refused it. For whatever reason, Harry was getting something out of being angry, out of not letting go.

Time to let go.

Time to grow up.

Time to accept Fair's genuine apology, to cherish him for the man he had become.

Mrs. Murphy put her paw on Harry's forearm. *"Close call."*

*"Yes,"* Tucker agreed.

*"Think Matthew will get the death penalty?"* Pewter wondered.

*"No. Rich people don't get the death penalty, their lawyers see to that, but he'll spend some time in jail. I just hope it's a lifetime,"* Mrs. Murphy sagely predicted.

*"BoomBoom has guts,"* Pewter purred as she snuggled even closer to Harry.

*"Mom, too. I'm proud of her. She finally apologized to Boom,"* Murphy said.

*"Why are things so hard for humans?"* Tucker sighed.

*"They walk on two legs. Beginning of all their troubles,"* Pewter saucily replied and they all three laughed.

Dear Reader,

A certain party has taken to demanding tuna packed in water.

She plops her striped derriere in the best seat in the house.

A photo of her oh-so-adorable self without me (have you noticed?) graces the back of this volume.

Alas, she's gotten the big head. Where will it end?

Yours truly,

P. S. She lies!

P.O. Box 696
Crozet, Virginia 22932
www.ritamaebrown.com

Don't miss the new mystery from

**RITA MAE BROWN**
and
**SNEAKY PIE BROWN**

# Whisker of Evil

Now available in hardcover
from Bantam Books

*Please read on for a preview...*

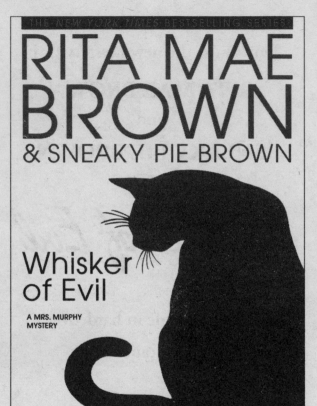

# RITA MAE BROWN

## & SNEAKY PIE BROWN

## Whisker of Evil

A MRS. MURPHY
MYSTERY

It Takes a Cat to Write the *Purr*-fect Mystery

# Whisker of Evil

## on sale now

Barry Monteith was still breathing when Harry found him. His throat had been ripped out.

Tee Tucker, a corgi, racing ahead of Mary Minor Haristeen as well as the two cats, Mrs. Murphy and Pewter, found him first.

Barry was on his back, eyes open, gasping and gurgling, life ebbing with each spasm. He did not recognize Tucker nor Harry when they reached him.

"Barry, Barry." Harry tried to comfort him, hoping he could hear her. "It will be all right," she said, knowing perfectly well he was dying.

The tiger cat, Mrs. Murphy, watched the blood jet upward.

*"Jugular,"* fat, gray Pewter succinctly commented.

Gently, Harry took the young man's hand and prayed, "Dear Lord, receive into thy bosom the soul of Barry Monteith, a good man." Tears welled in her eyes.

Barry jerked, then his suffering ended.

Death, often so shocking to city dwellers, was part of life here in the country. A hawk would swoop down to carry away the chick while the biddy screamed useless defiance. A bull would break his hip and need to be put down. And one day an old farmer would slowly walk to his tractor only to discover he couldn't climb into the seat. The Angel of Death placed his hand on the stooping shoulder.

It appeared the Angel had offered little peaceful deliverance to Barry Monteith, thirty-four, fit, handsome with brown curly hair, and fun-loving. Barry had started his own business, breeding thoroughbreds, a year ago, with a business partner, Sugar Thierry.

"Sweet Jesus." Harry wiped away the tears.

That Saturday morning, crisp, clear, and beautiful, had held the alluring promise of a perfect May 29. The promise had just curdled.

Harry had finished her early-morning chores and, despite a list of projects, decided to take a walk for an hour. She followed Potlicker Creek to see if the beavers had built any new dams. Barry was sprawled at the creek's edge on a dirt road two miles from her farm that wound up over the mountains into adjoining Augusta County. It edged the vast land holdings of Tally Urquhart, who, well into her nineties and spry, loathed traffic. Three cars constituted traffic in her mind. The only time the road saw much use was during deer-hunting season in the fall.

"Tucker, Mrs. Murphy, and Pewter, stay. I'm going to run to Tally's and phone the sheriff."

If Harry hit a steady lope, crossed the fields and one set of woods, she figured she could reach the phone in Tally's stable within fifteen minutes, though the pitch and roll of the land including one steep ravine would cost time.

As she left her animals, they inspected Barry.

"*What could rip his throat like that? A bear swipe?*" Pewter's pupils widened.

"*Perhaps.*" Mrs. Murphy, noncommittal, sniffed the gaping wound, as did Tucker.

The cat curled her upper lip to waft more scent into her nostrils. The dog, whose nose was much longer and nostrils larger, simply inhaled.

"*I don't smell bear,*" Tucker declared. "*That's an over-powering scent, and on a morning like this it would stick.*"

Pewter, who cherished luxury and beauty, found that Barry's corpse disturbed her equilibrium. "*Let's be grateful we found him today and not three days from now.*"

"*Stop jabbering, Pewter, and look around, will you? Look for tracks.*"

Grumbling, the gray cat daintily stepped down the dirt road. "*You mean like car tracks?*"

"*Yes, or animal tracks,*" Mrs. Murphy directed, then returned her attention to Tucker. "*Even though coyote scent isn't as strong as bear, we'd still smell a whiff. Bobcat? I don't smell anything like that. Or dog. There are wild dogs and wild pigs back in the mountains. The humans don't even realize they're there.*"

Tucker cocked her perfectly shaped head. "*No dirt around the wound. No saliva, either.*"

"*I don't see anything. Not even a birdie foot,*" Pewter, irritated, called out from a hundred yards down the road.

"*Well, go across the creek then and look over there.*" Mrs. Murphy's patience wore thin.

"*And get my paws wet?*" Pewter's voice rose.

"*It's a ford. Hop from rock to rock. Go on, Pewt, stop being a chicken.*"

Angrily, Pewter puffed up, tearing past them to launch

herself over the ford. She almost made it, but a splash indicated she'd gotten her hind paws wet.

If circumstances had been different, Mrs. Murphy and Tucker would have laughed. Instead, they returned to Barry.

"*I can't identify the animal that tore him up.*" The tiger shook her head.

"*Well, the wound is jagged but clean. Like I said, no dirt.*" Tucker studied the folds of flesh laid back.

"*He was killed lying down,*" the cat sagely noted. "*If he was standing up, don't you think blood would be everywhere?*"

"*Not necessarily,*" the dog replied, thinking how strong heartbeats sent blood straight out from the jugular. Tucker was puzzled by the odd calmness of the scene.

"*Pewter, have you found anything on that side?*"

"*Deer tracks. Big deer tracks.*"

"*Keep looking,*" Mrs. Murphy requested.

"*I hate it when you're bossy.*" Nonetheless, Pewter moved down the dirt road heading west.

"*Barry was such a nice man.*" Tucker mournfully looked at the square-jawed face, wide-open eyes staring at heaven.

Mrs. Murphy circled the body. "*Tucker, I'm climbing up that sycamore. If I look down maybe I'll see something.*"

Her claws, razor sharp, dug into the thin surface of the tree, strips of darker outer bark peeling, exposing the whitish underbark. The odor of fresh water, of the tufted titmouse above her, all informed her. She scanned around for broken limbs, bent bushes, anything indicating Barry—or other humans or large animals—had traveled to this spot avoiding the dirt road.

"*Pewter?*"

"*Big fat nothing.*" The gray kitty noted that her hind paws were wet. She was getting little clods of dirt stuck between her toes. This bothered her more than Barry did. After all, he was dead. Nothing she could do for him. But the hardening brown earth between her toes, that was discomfiting.

"*Well, come on back. We'll wait for Mom.*" Mrs. Murphy dropped her hind legs over the limb where she was sitting. Her hind paws reached for the trunk, the claws dug in, and she released her grip, swinging her front paws to the trunk. She backed down.

Tucker touched noses with Pewter, who had recrossed the creek more successfully this time.

Mrs. Murphy came up and sat beside them.

"*Hope his face doesn't change colors while we're waiting for the humans. I hate that. They get all mottled.*" Pewter wrinkled her nose.

"*I wouldn't worry.*" Tucker sighed.

In the distance they heard sirens.

"*Bet they won't know what to make of this, either,*" Tucker said.

"*It's peculiar.*" Mrs. Murphy turned her head in the direction of the sirens.

"*Weird and creepy.*" Pewter pronounced judgment as she picked at her hind toes, and she was right.

Welcome to the charming world of

# *MRS. MURPHY*

Don't miss these earlier mysteries . . .

## THE TAIL OF THE TIP-OFF

When winter hits Crozet, Virginia, it hits hard. That's nothing new to postmistress Mary Minor "Harry" Haristeen and her friends, who keep warm with hard work, hot toddies, and rabid rooting for the University of Virginia's women's basketball team. But post-game high spirits are laid low when contractor H.H. Donaldson drops dead in the parking lot. And soon word spreads that it wasn't a heart attack that did him in. It just doesn't sit right with Harry that one of her fellow fans is a murderer. And as tiger cat Mrs. Murphy knows, things that don't sit right with Harry lead her to poke her not-very-sensitive human nose into dangerous places. To make sure their intrepid mom lands on her feet, the feisty feline and her furry cohorts Pewter and corgi Tee Tucker are about to have their paws full helping Harry uncover a killer with no sense of fair play. . . .

## CATCH AS CAT CAN

Spring fever comes to the small town of Crozet, Virginia. As the annual Dogwood Festival approaches, postmistress Mary Minor "Harry" Haristeen feels her own mating instincts stir. As for tiger cat Mrs. Murphy, feline intuition tells her there's more in the air than just pheromones. It begins with a case of stolen hubcaps and proceeds to the mysterious death of a dissolute young mechanic over a sobering cup of coffee. Then another death and a shooting lead to the discovery of a half-million crisp, clean dollar bills that look to be very dirty. Now Harry is on the trail of a cold-blooded murderer. Mrs. Murphy already knows who it is—and who's next in line. She also knows that Harry, curious as a cat, does not have nine lives. And the one she does have is hanging by the thinnest of threads.

## CLAWS AND EFFECT

Winter puts tiny Crozet, Virginia, in a deep freeze and everyone seems to be suffering from the winter blahs, including postmistress Mary Minor "Harry" Haristeen. So all are ripe for the juicy gossip coming out of Crozet Hospital—until the main source of that gossip turns up dead. It's not like Harry to resist a mystery, and she soon finds the hospital a hotbed of ego, jealousy, and illicit love. But it's tiger cat Mrs. Murphy, roaming the netherworld of Crozet Hospital, who sniffs out a secret that dates back to the Underground Railroad. Then Harry is attacked and a doctor is executed in cold blood. Soon only a quick-witted cat and her animal pals feline Pewter and corgi Tee Tucker stand between Harry and a coldly calculating killer with a prescription for murder.

"Reading a Mrs. Murphy mystery is like
eating a potato chip. You always go back for more....
Whimsical and enchanting...the latest expert tale
from a deserving bestselling series."
—*The Midwest Book Review*

## PAWING THROUGH THE PAST

"You'll never get old." Each member of the class of 1980 has received the letter. Mary Minor "Harry" Haristeen, who is on the organizing committee for Crozet High's twentieth reunion, decides to take it as a compliment. Others think it's a joke. But Mrs. Murphy senses trouble. And the sly tiger cat is soon proven right...when the class womanizer turns up dead with a bullet between his eyes. Then another note followed by another murder makes it clear that someone has waited twenty years to take revenge. While Harry tries to piece together the puzzle, it's up to Mrs. Murphy and her animal pals to sniff out the truth.

And there isn't much time. Mrs. Murphy is the first to realize that Harry has been chosen Most Likely to Die, and if she doesn't hurry, Crozet High's twentieth reunion could be Harry's last.

"This is a cat-lover's dream of a mystery.... 'Harry' is simply irresistible.... [Rita Mae] Brown once again proves herself 'Queen of Cat Crimes.'... Don't miss out on this lively series, for it's one of the best around."
—*Old Book Barn Gazette*


# CAT ON THE SCENT

Things have been pretty exciting lately in Crozet, Virginia—a little *too* exciting if you ask resident feline investigator Mrs. Murphy. Just as the town starts to buzz over its Civil War reenactment, a popular local man disappears. No one's seen Tommy Van Allen's single-engine plane, either—except for Mrs. Murphy, who spotted it during a foggy evening's mousing. Even Mrs. Murphy's favorite human, postmistress Mary Minor "Harry" Haristeen, can sense that something is amiss. But things really take an ugly turn when the town reenacts the battle of Oak Ridge—and a participant ends up with three very real bullets in his back. While the clever tiger cat and her friends sift through clues that just don't fit together, more than a few locals fear that the scandal will force well-hidden town secrets into the harsh light of day. And when Mrs. Murphy's relentless tracking places loved ones in danger, it takes more than a canny kitty and her team of animal sleuths to set things right again....

"Told with spunk and plenty of whimsy, this is another delightful entry in a very popular series."
—*Publishers Weekly*

## MURDER ON THE PROWL

When a phony obituary appears in the local paper, the good people of Crozet, Virginia, are understandably upset. Who would stoop to such a tasteless act? Is it a sick joke—or a sinister warning? Only Mrs. Murphy, the canny tiger cat, senses true malice at work. And her instincts prove correct when a second fake obit appears, followed by a fiendish murder...and then another. People are dropping like flies in Crozet, and no one knows why. Yet even if Mrs. Murphy untangles the knot of passion and deceit that has sent someone into a killing frenzy, it won't be enough. Somehow the shrewd puss must guide her favorite human, postmistress "Harry" Haristeen, down a perilous trail to a deadly killer...and a killer of a climax. Or the next obit may be Harry's own.

"Leave it to a cat to grasp the essence of the cozy mystery: murder among friends."
—*The New York Times Book Review*

## MURDER, SHE MEOWED

The annual steeplechase races are the high point in the social calendar of the horse-mad Virginians of cozy Crozet. But when one of the jockeys is found murdered in the main barn, Mary Minor "Harry" Haristeen finds herself in a desperate race of her own—to trap the killer. Luckily for her, she has an experienced ally: her sage tiger cat, Mrs. Murphy. Utilizing her feline genius to plumb the depths of human depravity, Mrs. Murphy finds herself on a trail that leads to the shocking truth behind the murder. But will her human companion catch on in time to beat the killer to the gruesome finish line?

"The intriguing characters in this much-loved series continue to entertain." —*The Nashville Banner*

## PAY DIRT

The residents of tiny Crozet, Virginia, thrive on gossip, especially in the post office, where Mary Minor "Harry" Haristeen presides with her tiger cat, Mrs. Murphy. So when a belligerent Hell's Angel crashes Crozet, demanding to see his girlfriend, the leather-clad interloper quickly becomes the chief topic of conversation. Then the biker is found murdered, and everyone is baffled. Well, almost everyone... Mrs. Murphy and her friends Welsh corgi Tee Tucker and overweight feline Pewter haven't been slinking through alleys for nothing. But can they dig up the truth in time to save their human from a ruthless killer?

"If you must work with a collaborator, you want it to be someone with intelligence, wit, and an infinite capacity for subtlety—someone, in fact, very much like a cat.... It's always a pleasure to visit this cozy world.... There's no resisting Harry's droll sense of humor... or Mrs. Murphy's tart commentary." —*The New York Times Book Review*

# MURDER AT MONTICELLO

The most popular citizen of Virginia has been dead for nearly 170 years. That hasn't stopped the good people of tiny Crozet, Virginia, from taking pride in every aspect of Thomas Jefferson's life. But when an archaeological dig of the slave quarters at Jefferson's home, Monticello, uncovers a shocking secret, emotions in Crozet run high—dangerously high. The stunning discovery at Monticello hints at hidden passions and age-old scandals. As postmistress Mary Minor "Harry" Haristeen and some of Crozet's Very Best People try to learn the identity of a centuries-old skeleton—and the reason behind the murder—Harry's tiger cat, Mrs. Murphy, and her canine and feline friends attempt to sniff out a modern-day killer. Mrs. Murphy and corgi Tee Tucker will stick their paws into the darker mysteries of human nature to solve murders old and new—before curiosity can kill the cat . . . and Harry Haristeen.

"You don't have to be a cat lover to love *Murder at Monticello*." —*The Indianapolis Star*

# REST IN PIECES

Small towns don't take kindly to strangers—unless the stranger happens to be a drop-dead gorgeous and seemingly unattached male. When Blair Bainbridge comes to Crozet, Virginia, the local matchmakers lose no time in declaring him perfect for their newly divorced postmistress, Mary Minor "Harry" Haristeen. Even Harry's tiger cat, Mrs. Murphy, and her Welsh corgi, Tee Tucker, believe he smells

A-okay. Could his one little imperfection be that he's a killer? Blair becomes the most likely suspect when the pieces of a dismembered corpse begin turning up around Crozet. No one knows who the dead man is, but when a grisly clue makes a spectacular appearance in the middle of the fall festivities, more than an early winter snow begins chilling the blood of Crozet's Very Best People. That's when Mrs. Murphy, her friend Tucker, and her human companion Harry begin to sort through the clues...only to find themselves a whisker away from becoming the killer's next victims.

"Skillfully plotted, properly gruesome...and wise as well as wickedly funny." —*Booklist*

And don't miss the very first

## MRS. MURPHY

mystery . . .

### WISH YOU WERE HERE

Small towns are like families. Everyone lives very close together . . . and everyone keeps secrets. Crozet, Virginia, is a typical small town—until its secrets explode into murder. Crozet's thirty-something postmistress, Mary Minor "Harry" Haristeen, has a tiger cat (Mrs. Murphy) and a Welsh corgi (Tee Tucker), a pending divorce, and a bad habit of reading postcards not addressed to her. When Crozet's citizens start turning up murdered, Harry remembers that each received a card with a tombstone on the front and the message "wish you were here" on the back. Intent on protecting their human friends, Mrs. Murphy and Tucker begin to scent out clues. Meanwhile, Harry is conducting her own investigation, unaware that her pets are one step ahead of her. If only Mrs. Murphy could alert her somehow, Harry could uncover the culprit before another murder occurs—and before Harry finds herself on the killer's mailing list.

"Charming . . . Ms. Brown writes with wise, disarming wit." —*The New York Times Book Review*

# RITA MAE BROWN

| | | |
|---|---|---|
| ___56497-8 | **VENUS ENVY** | $7.50/$10.99 in Canada |
| ___38040-0 | **BINGO** | $19.00/$28.00 |
| ___27888-6 | **HIGH HEARTS** | $6.99/$9.99 |
| ___27573-9 | **IN HER DAY** | $6.99/$9.99 |
| ___27886-X | **RUBYFRUIT JUNGLE** | $7.50/$10.99 |
| ___27446-5 | **SOUTHERN DISCOMFORT** | $6.99/$9.99 |
| ___26930-5 | **SUDDEN DEATH** | $6.99/$9.99 |
| ___38037-0 | **SIX OF ONE** | $12.95/$19.95 |
| ___57224-5 | **RIDING SHOTGUN** | $6.99/$9.99 |
| ___56949-X | **DOLLEY:** <br> A NOVEL OF DOLLEY MADISON IN LOVE AND WAR | $6.50/$8.99 |
| ___34630-X | **STARTING FROM SCRATCH:** <br> A DIFFERENT KIND OF WRITER'S MANUAL | $19.00/$28.00 |
| ___37826-0 | **RITA WILL:** <br> AN AUTOBIOGRAPHY | $14.95/$22.95 |

Please enclose check or money order only, no cash or CODs. Shipping & handling costs:
$5.50 U.S. mail, $7.50 UPS. New York and Tennessee residents must remit applicable
sales tax. Canadian residents must remit applicable GST and provincial taxes. Please
allow 4 – 6 weeks for delivery. All orders are subject to availability. This offer subject to
change without notice. Please call 1-800-726-0600 for further information.

| | |
|---|---|
| Bantam Dell Publishing Group, Inc. | TOTAL AMT $_____ |
| Attn: Customer Service | SHIPPING & HANDLING $_____ |
| 400 Hahn Road | SALES TAX (NY, TN) $_____ |
| Westminster, MD 21157 | TOTAL ENCLOSED $_____ |

Name _____

Address _____

City/State/Zip _____

Daytime Phone (_____) _____